FEDERATION COWBOY

JOYCE REYNOLDS-WARD

A TRANSLATION OF TIME MEASUREMENT

Translation of Time Measurement in the Galactic Federation of Solid Peoples to Earth Measurement:

Cycle = year (ten spans in a cycle)
    Span = month (four ten-turns in a span)
    Ten-turn = week (ten turns in a ten-turn)
    Turn = day (sixteen nodes in a turn)
    Node = hour (100 clicks in a node)
    Click = minute (100 taps in a click)
    Tap = second

Common meal times:
    First Meal: 4th Node.
    Second Meal: 8th Node.
    Third Meal: 12th Node.

Schedules in the Galactic Federation Congress:

Most work schedules run from 5th Node to 11th Node.

Spans and turns are identified by number in the Federation to avoid bias, not a given name since so many span and turn names are tied to planetary identifications which are either religious, seasonal, or cultural.

Congressional Schedules: Two cycles in a Session.

Sessions run for nine spans, then take the Long Break of one span before resuming the second cycle of the Session.

Congressional business runs for seven turns, with a three-turn break. Each break is labeled by number, up to the Long Break. Planetary Representatives use the mid-Session Long Break to return home and connect with constituents. The three-turn breaks are not sufficient for most Representatives to travel back to their planets.

1

A QUESTION OF RELLA

"Geraint, is this for real?" Caroline Starshine frowned at the file projected in front of her before looking over at her crocodilian boss. "We're recruiting a—a *rodeo duelist* to run as the Federalist candidate for Planetary Representative on Cartain?"

She sniffed. The antiseptic scent permeating their private cabin in the runabout hauling passengers to the planetary surface of Cartain from the interstellar transport *No Skies, No Limits* irritated her nostrils. This one carried a faint floral scent that Caroline recognized as proprietary to Hart Mercantile Services.

Lilac Number Nine. Lilac Nine could be cloying if too much was used. The light hint of scent was just about perfect—a testimony to the skill of the housekeeping staff on *No Skies, No Limits.* At least in the VIP cabins. Too bad she had developed a minor reaction to Lilac Nine—too many useless years spent in her childhood training to discern the application levels. And now such knowledge was just a sideline to Caroline's *real* work.

"S-s-s." Her boss, Geraint Ssprin, raised his long head from his secured heating pad and platform set at about Caroline's waist level. Crocodilians needed more heat than mammals. "Mr. Tophand is a very *good* candidate for Cartain, Caroline."

As always, Geraint managed to manipulate his translator implant so that it *almost* sounded like it was a real voice, and not full of hisses and static. By now, Caroline was used to it.

"Well, yes, I can see that he would appeal to a certain group of Cartainians. But what about his policy positions?"

Caroline studied the portrait. Jeff Tophand was a lanky, dark-skinned man. He wore a tan broad-brimmed hat, long-sleeved dark blue shirt with sponsor decals woven into the fabric, a tan vest with fringes, and dark blue pants—*jeans*, Caroline had heard them called—with some sort of fringed tan leggings over the jeans in a shade that matched hat and vest.

Exotic clothing that she had never seen before, even on Earth. Just like the whole concept of rodeo duelists. Caroline had thought that rodeo was a dead sport. It certainly was no longer popular on Earth—but other species adopted the concept, expanding it to sentient mounts battling non-sentient riders, sentient mounts and riders herding non-sentient species in particular patterns, and the ultimate rodeo duelist competition—sentient riders versus sentient mounts.

It still didn't seem right.

Geraint smacked his jaws together before answering, pushing himself up on all four legs.

"His policies are close enough to the Federalist platform to make recruiting him worthwhile. Cartain's agriculturalists —the largest segment of the voting population on the planet —look favorably on duelists, whether they're human, bovine, avian, reptilian or equine. That is why Rifanel of the Councilists has brought Hrwhinir's new Planetary Representative, Fenarmin, to recruit a candidate amongst Cartain's Converted population. Fenarmin is a tertiary leader in Hrwhinir's Court of Stallions, but is already rising as a voice in the Congress's Converted caucus. And he's another former duelist."

"Fenarmin's a horse, correct?" Caroline twisted a strand of curly brown hair around her forefinger. That cast a different light on the situation. The Councilists were the other dominant party in the Galactic Congress. If they were recruiting amongst Converted species using a rodeo duelist, then it made sense for the Federalists to do so as well.

Need to look at the species dominating Cartain's agriculture production to be sure. Though Geraint had probably already done so.

Geraint took his time before responding, his tongue flicking along his great teeth as he clacked his jaws further. "Yes, Fenarmin is a horse, like Rifanel. And the species they are recruiting amongst for the Councilists on Cartain are not the usual rodeo dueling partners, though they will respect Fenarmin for his success. Fenarmin and Rifanel are focusing on finding a candidate amongst Converted species." He showed more teeth. "My reports suggest that they are struggling, because Cartain biases toward human representatives. So far they've yet to find an appealing candidate. If we can recruit Tophand...."

Caroline nodded. Converted species, like the crocodilians that Geraint belonged to, had been created by the old Plasmoid scientists who had managed to develop an unpredictable formula for creating sentience. Not every member of a Converted species possessed sentience, but all of the Converted species had a secretive method to bring their non-sentient members to sentience—if they were eligible. Those standards varied from planet to planet, in some cases requiring younglings to qualify at an early age before being granted sentience. Modern Plasmoids disdained their ancestors' actions. However, they didn't go so far in their disdain as to create counteractive measures to remove sentience.

She bit her lip. Mars University didn't teach anything

about Converted species. Everything Caroline knew about them came from her nine spans interning with Geraint in the Galactic Congress. And she didn't know enough about Converted—or the Plasmoids, for that matter. The Plasmoids locked themselves into bubbles to protect their amorphous, blob-like forms from Solids. Odd to realize they were the oldest of sentient species in the Galaxy.

Oh well. Thinking about Converteds didn't help her with Cartain. Caroline pulled up the planetary analysis generated by Federalist party researchers. Only a very limited portion of Cartain's main continent, Blass, was agriculture-friendly. Cartain's native sentient species had been avian, and originally welcomed settlement from populations of Converted as well as smaller numbers of natural sentients.

The planet managed to feed itself even with the addition of other species, and produced some export items. Besides horses, reptilians, and cattle, Cartain had a large number of smaller sentient species that had been created by the old Plasmoid scientists—rabbits and birds, primarily. She frowned.

"I see. The Councilists are gambling that the Converted species on Cartain aren't human-friendly. But while a horse might appeal to those Converted species on Cartain because horses are prey, not predators—still, why should we run another duelist against the Councilist candidate, if they have one?"

"Excellent point, my dear." Geraint eased himself back down with another, approving clack of his jaws, looking like he was grinning big—or at least as big as any crocodilian species could smile. He curled his tail round his body—nearly as long as Caroline's torso—and crossed his forelegs in preparation for a lecture, looking down his snout thoughtfully, just like some of Caroline's human professors would when gathering their thoughts before speaking.

Caroline settled in to wait. When Geraint took this position, it meant he was taking his time to think about what he was going to say. Something she had learned was typical amongst Converted reptilian species. A behavior that was highly regarded in political circles.

You will learn a lot from interning with Geraint, Dr. Knowledgechaser, her Mars University advisor, had said when assigning Caroline this cycle-long position with Geraint, the current head of the Federalist Party in the Congress of the Galactic Federation of Sentient Worlds. *And you might even earn yourself a working position with the Congress.*

She *was* learning a lot about Converts while working with Geraint. Mars U didn't cater to species beyond the humanoids. But Caroline—who had taken her name upon her majority, as part of her *Get-Away-From-Parochial-Earth* plan— had told Dr. Knowledgechaser that she wanted an internship with as diverse an exposure to other sentient species as possible. Spending time on Galactic Central as well as in the Congress provided lots of diversity.

Beyond that, if any of the Congressional parties were friendly to multiple species, it was Geraint and the Federalists. But she still didn't understand the appeal of the Galactic Rodeo to nonhuman worlds, much less why the duelists would want to strive toward the ultimate battle—a duel between sentient competitors. Those sentient duels usually ended in the death of one or both of the participants.

Caroline shivered. She had seen recordings of those duels.

"Cartain is a world that has struggled for some time," Geraint said finally, after ten clicks of silence. "Unstable solar system. Two moons. The native sentient birds developed sensitivities to a strain of a respiratory virus that had previously been a minor concern. You humans managed to correct for the system instability and develop weather management protocols, but in the process, the members of your species who have shown up on Cartain have not been particularly friendly to other sentients. Including less-fortunate humanoids."

Caroline winced. *Not surprising, considering human history of exploitation and dominance over other species as well as our own kind on Earth.*

"And recruiting this Jeff Tophand will somehow overcome this issue?"

"Jeff Tophand was born on Cartain, a descendant of the original human settlers, albeit one of the less fortunate groups. Before he became a duelist, he was a low-level agricultural worker who had good relationships with other species, including the non-sentients he dueled before his accident. If anything, he is a unifying factor on Cartain. Consistently high polling numbers." Geraint clacked his jaws. "And it is our job to persuade him to take that final step and run for Planetary Representative. Or, rather, *your* job, Caroline. He has shown interest in becoming political. You need to ensure that he chooses the Federalists."

"What? Me? But—but—I've never done this before."

Geraint flicked his tail to indicate agreement and emphasis. "You are most definitely ready to do this, Caroline. You have done well in simulations, and you are my best intern this cycle, with one more span in your internship. It is time —" his jaws parted in a *most* crocodilian smile—"for you to, as it were, fly. I have all confidence in you."

"But our majority in the Congress depends on this election."

"Yesss. And you will be able to do this, my dear."

Caroline swallowed hard and returned to scanning the file on Jeff Tophand.

Dr. Knowledgechaser never told me that I might be responsible for the balance of power in the Galactic Congress.

But if she could pull this off—

Well, then she might just land a position working in the Congress, straight out of Mars U. Perhaps even as an assistant to a Planetary Representative instead of laboring as one of the Congress's nameless secondary support staff. Even so, she would take a position as a lowly page over returning to Earth. All that training she had undergone, both as a malleable scion tied to Hart Mercantile, plus what Caroline considered to be more valuable—her university study and her internship— should qualify her for being a page, at least. If not bill or archives management staff.

However, any position higher than that of a page would be a most exquisite *see what I'm capable of? More than you thought!* show-not-tell to her family.

That said, her family probably wouldn't pay attention, except to mourn that Caroline had left Earth. That she couldn't be exploited as unpaid labor for Hart Mercantile Services, until her mother finally found someone with suffi- cient influence and lack of interest in a spouse's physical attractiveness to marry her.

Not that Caroline would be attractive to a traditional Earth man these days, after attending university and working in the Galactic Congress. *Good Earth girls* were supposed to pop out babies until they reached the number of offspring prescribed in their reproductive marital contracts. Then, and only then, with limits, could they do something other than have babies and throw elaborate parties.

None of which appealed to Caroline—well, except perhaps planning the parties and working them for informa- tion. A skill useful in the Congress. Otherwise, she had stopped being a *good Earth girl*, at least in her thoughts, some time ago.

She gulped and nodded. "So how do you advise me to start this process, Geraint?"

"Well—" Geraint's pleased expression, jaws wide and showing his full range of teeth, told Caroline that she had asked the correct question.

Caroline and Geraint were the last to disembark from the runabout at Jeff Tophand's ranch, the Interstellar Roundup. Caroline disconnected Geraint's heated platform from its restraint, placing it on the floor. Geraint used his forefeet to activate the controls that powered his platform. It rose to the height of Caroline's waist before slowly proceeding past the runabout's attendant and down the corridor to the open doorway. He displayed their electronic credentials to the ground crew, two women who wore outfits very similar to Jeff Tophand's in that file portrait.

"Mr. Ssprin. Ms. Starshine. Welcome to the Interstellar Roundup Ranch," the paler woman said.

Both bowed first to Geraint, then Caroline. Geraint raised himself up on his hind legs to nod his head politely, putting him at head-height for Caroline and the women. Caroline matched the greeters in depth of bow.

"Come this way, please," the golden-skinned woman said. "Are you two planning to spend the night? We have room."

Remember, Cartain prizes hospitality. You need to be extremely polite in declining.

"Most likely not," Caroline said. "We are just here for the celebration. We are honored, however. If possible, I would like to express my thanks directly to Mr. Tophand, both for the invite to the celebration and for his generous offer to spend the night."

"Understood," the paler woman said. She glanced at Geraint. "We are definitely honored to have so many leaders from the Galactic Congress. No one from the Statists, of course—"

Not only were the Earth-centric Statists heavily involved with the Plasmoids—who did not have a good reputation on Cartain—but Logan Easystar, the duelist responsible for ending Tophand's career, was a failed Earth Statist candidate for Planetary Representative. Easystar now worked for the successful candidate, Lara Wordtrust.

"Of course," Caroline said calmly. "It wouldn't be appropriate for Statists to show up at Mr. Tophand's celebration for winning his lawsuit against Easystar now, would it?"

Both women laughed.

"Ms. Wordtrust and Mr. Easystar have been explicitly denied access to the ranch's transport station," the paler woman said. "Come. We will introduce you to Jeff."

Informal, not formal address from his workers when they're talking about him.

That was a promising sign.

Geraint waved Caroline ahead of him. She followed the two women, very conscious of the fact that the future of the Federalist majority in the Galactic Congress might very well depend on what she said and did today.

A test not only of the skills she had acquired working in the Congress over the last nine spans and while studying at Mars U for three cycles, but all those cycles spent observing her mother while serving as an assistant.

Caroline swallowed hard.

I can do this. I don't need to be married or to be a part of Hart Mercantile Services. I am Caroline Starshine, and I am going to soar. Openly. In politics, as myself, and not under the guise of working for someone like Uncle Royce, as Mother does.

A mantra she had been repeating to herself ever since that first turn in the shabby Mars U dorms.

THE TWO WOMEN passed them over quickly to a Converted rabbit at the edge of the landing field. The black rabbit sat on a platform similar to Geraint's. He did not have a built-in translator like Geraint—some species, such as rabbits, did not do well with the neural implants. Instead, a human interpreter stood next to his platform, a small dark-skinned boy who appeared to be in his early teens. The boy bowed to

Caroline and then Geraint, glancing quickly at the black rabbit on his platform. The rabbit twitched its nose, flicking one ear. The interpreter nodded, then turned to Geraint and Caroline.

"Honorable Representative Geraint Ssprin. Assistant Caroline Starshine. I am Moonshadow, Jeff's ranch manager." A faint grin spread across the interpreter's face as he pointed to his chest. "And I'm Trace Ford, Jeff Tophand's nephew and Moonshadow's interpreter. Do either of you need an explanation of my role?"

"No, no," Geraint said.

"Neither do I," Caroline said quickly.

She had learned very early while working for Geraint that predominantly nonvocal species such as rabbits frequently engaged the services of interpreters to interpret and explain their body language—and, rumor had it, the highest level of interpreters also engaged in mindspeech with their partners. While the Federation's mechanical translators worked well with vocals, they were lamentably horrible at reading body language—cycles of history documented those failures.

"Good," Trace said. "Come with us."

Moonshadow's platform took the lead, followed by Trace and then Caroline, next to Geraint's platform. They walked through double gates secured open into a fenced area; the entrance marked by a huge, inflatable arch emblazoned with A VICTORY FOR JEFF IS A VICTORY FOR CARTAIN.

Caroline assessed the party layout. Beyond the arch, a mix of species spread out in small gatherings around assorted food stands in a large fenced meadow with purplish-green grasses. Lavender-tipped conifer trees shaded a large stage set up at one end of the field. Multiple canopies scattered about the rolling field to provide more shelter, with chairs and benches of varying heights and widths set both under the canopies and in the open.

Well done. Good conversational flow. Plenty of diversity in food and drink. Lots of places for people to hang out without feeling crowded. Man knows how to set up a party—or has hired someone with that knowledge. Maybe it won't be so hard to recruit him to run for Planetary Representative. Looks like he's thinking about some sort of political activity.

Caroline turned her attention to the attendees. The mix of species at this party was amazing for a world like Cartain, with two tiny continents and no ocean-bound sentients. Crested birds as tall as Caroline. Rabbits whose backs were as high as her waist. They didn't need to use platforms to move around because they didn't fear being crushed. Horses. Cattle. Reptilians like Geraint, some of the smaller ones on platforms. Larger reptilians with shorter forelegs similar to humanoid arms who walked on their hind legs. Two large snakes slithered through the crowd. One was bright yellow and white, nearly as wide around as Caroline's upper thigh and quite long. The other one was brown and green, shorter and about as thick as her wrist.

About half the attendees wore Cartain flag badges—green and blue background with a human, cow, rabbit, the upright reptilians, and those crested birds, standing within a white circle.

Cartain's major sentient species.

Those flag badges—indicators of local political involvement? Probably.

Outside of the meadow, in neighboring fields, assorted plants grew tall. Caroline recalled them from her planetary study en route. Cartain's major export was bioengineered plant-based drugs, cultivated in fields like these. She recognized one field as producing ixtnatal, a popular antibiotic that worked on most mammalian species, and another that produced rella, a reptilian and avian antibiotic. She knew rella well—Tsfalnel, Geraint's homeworld, was a major rella consumer and frequently encountered shortages.

Another reason to cultivate ties on Cartain.

What Jeff Tophand's Interstellar Roundup Ranch did *not* produce was painkiller drugs, unlike some other ranches on Cartain. The Interstellar Roundup produced generally useful antibiotics. Not a big money-earner, but necessary.

A clue to how Tophand thinks about society and politics? Or a reflection of the additional security expense involved in growing painkiller medications? Won't hurt to try an altruistic approach on Tophand.

A loud nicker to her left caught Caroline's attention. She recognized Rifanel, head of the Councilist Party in the Congress, the outgoing Planetary Representative for Hrwhinir. The mare's dark brown, dappled body with striking cream mane and tail made the powerful horse stand out amongst other equines. Next to her stood a big, bulky chestnut stallion who glowered at a lop-eared black rabbit lounging on a platform. This rabbit was attended by a slender dark-haired woman. Caroline recognized them from their testimony before Congressional committees, though she had never been introduced to either person.

Blackburn and his interpreter, Laura Richardson.

Caroline raised her brows. Blackburn was *famous*. The Galactic Congress often assigned him and Richardson to manage difficult negotiations with new prospective members. Blackburn had tamed the difficult Bit-five *Blattidae* insectoids that tended to throw food and make major messes as part of their negotiations. Until Blackburn, the Bit-fives had been rowdy and uncontrolled, a danger to all sentient Solid species.

As a result of Blackburn's negotiations, while the Bit-fives still were problematic, their scheming now centered on their own kind, not predating on more vulnerable species and designing plans to disrupt the more powerful ones.

So why were Blackburn and Richardson here? Caroline didn't see any Bit-fives around.

Geraint moved alongside her. "Once we have been introduced to Mr. Tophand, I intend to speak to Blackburn. There appear to be concerns arising about sentient planets," he said, using French, one of the ancient languages from Old Earth. Caroline had been raised with French as her first language, which was uncommon. Geraint had studied it during his youth, and made it clear to Caroline that her ease with French was one reason he had chosen her to be his head intern.

"I understand." Giving her the opportunity to be persuasive with Tophand on her own.

Gotta start somewhere.

She had to wonder why sentient planet concerns would involve Geraint. They hadn't been discussed during the recently concluded Congressional session—unless such discussion was part of a confidential briefing she wasn't cleared to cover. That level of security would make it need-to-know—which wouldn't fit Geraint's casual mention of the topic, even in French. And Geraint wasn't on any of the committees who might be discussing such concerns.

Oh well, sooner or later she would find out. She had an assignment to fulfill.

To Caroline's surprise, when they finally approached Tophand, who was standing near the big stage, those surrounding him were more Converts than humanoids. She spotted some of the crested birds, several rabbits on platforms, cattle, and a couple of horses with a handful of humans in the mix. As they drew nearer, she realized that one of the crested birds was complaining about the monopoly held on the distribution of plant-based drugs by the Ribonit Cartel, the major pharmaceutical distributor to this quadrant of the galaxy.

And the bird knew quite a bit about pharma distribution—Hart Mercantile was a minor competitor to the Ribonits, and Caroline had listened to many rants from both her mother and her uncle about them over the years.

Tophand listened to the bird with his arms folded,

nodding between the squawks of the crested bird, who was apparently one of his neighbors. The bird's translator buzzed and popped, clearly having issues with the squawks from the speaker.

"That's why I grow rella and ixtnatal and nothing else, Zzink," Tophand said finally. "Sure, I understand that the psychotropic meds get you the highest prices in the market. But antibiotics are reliable sellers, unlike psychotropics or analgesics that go in and out of fashion."

"SQUAWK. But if too many of us grow antibiotics, SQUAWK, then the price ends up declining even further!" Zzink protested. Their green and cream-colored topknot flared high, then settled again. "I owe too much on my loans, SQUAWK, to grow antibiotics! SQUAWK. Yes, it's a steady income—" once again, the topknot rose and fell, "—but, SQUAWK, it is just short of what I need."

"Something has to be done about the Ribonits," Tophand agreed. "Excuse me, please, Zzink, it appears that Moonshadow wants to introduce me to someone." He bowed politely to Zzink, then moved out of the circle as one of the cattle began to speak, apparently talking further about the low price of plant-based drugs as opposed to the costs of cultivating them.

Aha. A potential campaign issue. And it confirmed Caroline's hypothesis that *altruism* might be the correct approach to Tophand.

As he walked toward Caroline, Geraint, Moonshadow, and Trace, Tophand put on a forced, weary smile that suddenly made Caroline go watery inside.

"Howdy there," he said. "Welcome to the Interstellar Roundup Ranch and my victory party over Old Earth interests—" and then he stopped, frowning at Caroline. "Excuse me. You're from Old Earth, aren't you."

"Yes."

How did he know? Is it how I'm dressed?

She *was* trying to move beyond the prudish habits of her youth.

"I'm sorry if I've offended you, ma'am."

She smiled back at him. "Not at all."

His grin in response was more real, less forced. "Fantastic. Moonshadow?"

Trace spoke. "I have the pleasure of introducing you to the Honorable Geraint Ssprin, Planetary Representative for Tsfalnel and Federalist Party Leader in the Congress of the Galactic Federation of Solid Peoples. Honorable Ssprin, I introduce you to Jeff Tophand, owner of the Interstellar Roundup Ranch."

Tophand bowed to Geraint. "Very pleased to meet you, Honorable Ssprin. Please call me Jeff. I definitely want to speak to you at some point today."

"It is a pleasure for me as well, Jeff. Thank you for the invitation and your generous offer of overnight hospitality, even though we will probably not take advantage of it. Please call me Geraint." Geraint rose to his hind legs, carefully balancing himself using his tail as he inclined his head respectfully toward Tophand. Tophand still stood about half a head taller than Geraint. "I would like to introduce you to my very capable head intern, Caroline Starshine, of Mars University. I will be happy to speak to you at some point, but please also feel free to share your concerns with her. Caroline has my focus and knows my opinions on most major issues. I trust her implicitly."

Wow. Just wow. For Geraint to say *I trust her implicitly*—that was significant.

"Ms. Starshine." Tophand's smile grew even wider and more friendly as he turned to her. "I am pleased to make your acquaintance."

"Please call me Caroline—and thank you for the invitation and the offer of overnight hospitality."

"Call me Jeff."

"I have an urgent matter I need to discuss with Blackburn, but I am certain that Caroline will be happy to hear your concerns if I do not get back to you soon." Geraint inclined his head again, then lowered himself back to all fours. "If that is acceptable—I hope?"

"Always acceptable to speak to a pretty lady."

Caroline flushed. It wasn't often that someone called her *pretty*. *Handsome*, perhaps, as a means to acknowledge her regular albeit plain features, but she was far from the slender, large-busted, big-hipped ideal frequently exported from Earth as the epitome of human femininity.

"Thank you, Jeff."

"Bonne chance, Caroline." Geraint switched back to Galactic Standard. "Then please excuse me, but the sooner I can speak to Blackburn, the better. The Bit-fives are being problematic again." He spun his platform and left.

Bit-fives? I thought he said he wanted to talk to Blackburn about sentient planets—or are the Bit-fives a cover story?

"Do you need our services further?" Trace asked.

Jeff waved at them. "Not really. We should have more notables arriving for you to greet. By the First Seed, I swear I didn't expect half the Galaxy to show up at this party!" He offered his arm. "So, Ms. Caroline Starshine, who is clearly from Old Earth but is not offended by critiques of it, shall we walk and talk?"

Caroline hesitated, then linked her arm in his. *Old-fashioned manners.* That was probably all this was, nothing more intense or suggestive. And it could be a good thing—or bad. After all, even her most obnoxious brother, Albert, could be capable of such mannerly behavior, when he wanted to show it.

"Aren't you worried that they will be offended if you leave?" She nodded toward the group clustered around the stage.

Jeff grinned conspiratorially. "You and I are the same

species. Most of 'em will think it's just a form of courtship. Let's just say I have a few old mare friends who act as grandma matchmakers, along with Zzink and their buddies. All of 'em get involved with potential mates a lot faster than us humanoids tend to do."

Oh. Her cheeks burned as he guided her away from the others. Had she done the wrong thing by accepting his arm?

"I hope I'm not giving you or them the wrong impression. And how did you know I was from Old Earth?"

"Well, paler skin to begin with—most of us born off Earth end up with darker skin."

Caroline nodded. She had noticed that. "But there's enough of us paler sorts at Galactic Congress who aren't from Earth—Cartain's outgoing Planetary Representative for one."

"Eh, that's true about Robbie-boy. But there's more. You and Geraint talking in French." Jeff grinned broadly. "My great-grandma was from Old Earth, and she spoke a Cajun dialect."

Hmm. Need to tell Geraint that French may not be as secure as we thought. At least it's not my clothing. Maybe I am getting better at this.

"I was raised in Quebec," she admitted.

"Starfaring family?"

"No." She flattened her voice, hoping to discourage further questions. "So were you born on this ranch?"

"As a matter of fact, I was. Not as Owner, however. The Roundup used to grow hemp and cotton, back before the then-Boss of Cartain discovered that growing plant-based drugs was much more profitable." His voice dropped. "I became a duelist to get away from being nothing more than another field worker. Hoped to make enough to provide for my family. Which I have." His voice lightened. "Let me show you around the place. How much do you know about agriculture on Cartain?"

"Cartain's primary agricultural export is plant-based

drugs—you have a monopoly on certain items, such as rella. And from what I overheard, it sounds to me like you may be having problems with the Ribonit Cartel and their price structures."

"Do we ever." Jeff stopped by the fence. "Now this is what a field of rella looks like."

Caroline nodded. Rella's primary use was as a broad-spectrum reptilian antibiotic that helped cure a lot of infections. "That's always in demand, isn't it?" She eyed the dark purple and gold grassy plants, frowning at the size of the field. So little! "The yield on this field after rella is processed must be pretty small."

"Under normal circumstances this field alone produces enough rella to keep Tsfalnel stocked for a year."

"That doesn't sound right." Caroline bit her lip. Rella supply shortages were an ongoing issue that Geraint's constituents kept bringing up. "Tsfalnel has a shortage of rella."

"Because Ribonit quality control procedures reject about half the crop." Jeff's voice turned bitter. "The slightest cosmetic imperfection causes them to reject an entire field at the end of the growing seasons, and we can't sell it to anyone but the Ribonits. Cosmetic damage doesn't affect the quality of the final product because it goes through processing, but —" he shrugged. "One bad leaf is enough to condemn the whole field. And the Ribonits aggressively monitor our fields."

Interesting.

"That's not right. The price of rella is skyrocketing on Tsfalnel. Geraint's office keeps getting requests for financial assistance for those who need it." Caroline shook her head. "Some of them...the stories are just heart-wrenching."

"There should be plenty of rella, to provide not just for Tsfalnel but other reptilian worlds. Twitl—another neighbor who grows rella—suspects that even with the Ribonits' claim of a strict chain of custody, a lot of the rejected raw crop ends up being diverted to Plasmoid worlds instead of being destroyed, like it's supposed to be. He claims to have evidence to bring to the Congress."

"*Really*. The Federation doesn't have a trading contract with the Ethereal Confederation for rella."

Rella had a recreational psychoactive effect on some species, which was why the Ribonits had a lock on distribution off-planet. A means of managing the substance as dictated by the Galactic Controlled Substances Act; an exclusive contract granted by the Boss of Cartain and confirmed by the Congress. All procedures that Caroline knew too well— but she didn't know anything about how the Ethereals managed controlled substances.

"Geraint needs to know about this right away," she continued.

"Which is why I want to talk to him."

Caroline turned away from the fence to look for Geraint and Blackburn. She couldn't spot either one of them. "Geraint is talking to Blackburn. I wonder where they are?"

"Oh, I have an idea. Someplace private. I suggested to Blackburn that he have a talk with Twitl. Let's just say that the agencies Blackburn works for are *very* interested in what Twitl has to say." Jeff also scanned the gathering. "I don't see Twitl. And since they're one of the Crested Flyers, they should stand out. Even with this many attendees." He offered his arm to Caroline again. "Geraint and Blackburn are most likely talking to Twitl in private. I have a good idea where that will be. Let's continue the tour and end there."

She liked that idea. It might give them time to discuss the Planetary Representative race. It would definitely give her time to learn more about this potential candidate.

"So what do you raise besides rella?"

"Mostly rella. It's easy to grow and maintain, and since I was gone a lot rodeoing, I didn't have the time to get into the more complex crops." Jeff sighed. "But now that I'm out of rodeo, maybe I'll look at growing more ixtnatal, especially since I've been able to employ more of my family on the Ranch, thanks to winning that lawsuit. The Ribonits aren't quite as weird about controlling ixtnatal, and with all the avian species that need a good antibiotic for respiratory illnesses, it might be worth the effort it takes to grow that fussy a crop. Since I'm going to be on Cartain for the foreseeable future."

"About that." Caroline paused, considering her approach. *Oh by the First Galaxy, just go for it!* "Have you considered running for Planetary Representative?"

Jeff snorted. "Planetary Rep? Me? Come on. You know the reputation that rodeo duelists have." His voice took on that weary note again. "Showboats. Exploiters of non-sentient creatures. Boors. Drunks."

"Someone concerned about the production of rella and how it affects his neighbors of different species doesn't strike me as a boor or exploiter," Caroline said.

"That's not what Logan Easystar thinks." Jeff's voice was low.

"Logan Easystar is a Statist, and he just lost the Planetary Representative election on Earth. He's not here. Besides, you won your lawsuit against him."

"On a technicality, unfortunately."

"Technicality or not, you won." Caroline stopped, turning to face Jeff. "Listen. If you really want to help your neighbors and get to the bottom of this rella situation, what better way to do it than to become the Planetary Representative? Easystar now works for Lara Wordtrust of the Statists. The Statists are really close with the Ethereal Congress and the Plasmoids. If something shady is happening with the Ribonits and the Plasmoids, then, as Planetary Representative, you'd be in a position to do something about it."

Jeff scratched his chin. "The thought is tempting." He

paused. "Twitl might be a better candidate than me, however. They are older with much more experience, and they aren't humanoid."

"Possibly. However, you're experienced with media because of your duelist experience. How well does Twitl handle media?"

"They are not particularly comfortable being the center of attention." Jeff glanced at Caroline. "But. Why me? I'm sure there are other Federalists who are more established on Cartain."

"And many of them already fill important roles working for the Boss, or else they don't have your positives. It's not just about Cartain." Caroline began to tick off talking points on her fingers. "One. You won your lawsuit against Logan Easystar. That suit was a factor in Easystar's loss in his Planetary Representative race on Earth. Two. You're experienced in rella production—no other representative from Cartain has had that knowledge, and from what you've already said to me, that's more know-how than most Planetary Representatives possess."

Jeff arched a brow. "Really. I'm surprised by that."

"Absolutely. Very few representatives have the background to discuss the Ribonit cartel's contracts and treaties. It's not just about rella. You can speak to other plant-based drugs that the Ribonits handle. Three. You have a good reputation even as a duelist, someone who has been friendly with your non-sentient dueling partners. You treat them as if they are sentient, with respect and kindness. Shall I continue?"

Jeff laughed. "All right, all right. I'll file for the election. With one request."

"As long as it's within reason."

He grinned at her. "I want you to be my assistant. That is, if Geraint and Mars University can spare you."

"Why me and not someone more experienced?"

"From the questions you've asked you clearly know a little bit about the pharma business."

"Family ties to Hart Mercantile."

Jeff nodded. "That's one point. Second, you're new, finishing off an internship, so you're eager and have something to prove about your ability. Third, Geraint speaks highly of you. Why *should* I go through an interview process when I clearly have a good candidate right here?"

Warmth flooded her cheeks. Would she *ever* get over flushing at the slightest complement? "Thank you. I'm flattered, and I'm sure something can be arranged. I have one more span to serve as Geraint's head intern for this cycle, and once I'm done—I graduate from Mars U."

"Even better. Let's go find Geraint and get this process in gear."

Wow. Just—wow. I'm going to be working in the Galactic Congress for certain now!

Jeff would win. Caroline was sure of that.

She would have to send a special thank-you to Dr. Knowledgechaser. Should she bother to brag to her family?

Probably not—unless she wanted to be besieged by Royce Hart and her mother about providing more opportunities for Hart Mercantile.

2

———

A NEW POLITICAL WORLD

"LET'S GO BEHIND THE BARN," Jeff said. "I'm willing to bet that's where Geraint and Blackburn are. Blackburn knows that I have a private hangout space there."

"Private hangout space?" They walked along the wooden fence toward the barn. "What would you need that for?"

"Sometimes it's a really good idea to be able to get away from these big parties. Business discussions that you don't want to have others overhear. Or sensory overload. Ever seen how rodeo duelists party—humanoid and others?"

"Can't say as I have."

Jeff laughed. "Let's just say it can get pretty wild. We compete hard and play hard. Sometimes you want to get away from the crowd and talk quietly."

"*Really.*" Caroline side-eyed Jeff. Was this a proposition? While she wanted to get away from Earth's prudish attitudes, wasn't this a little fast—especially given their future employer-employee relationship?

He laughed again. "Not what you're thinking! Not at all sexual. People bring their kids to my parties. The area behind the barn is fenced so that children, kits, chicks, colts, and calves can safely play without any need to worry about intoxicated adults causing problems. Anyone wanting to—get friendly—well, humans take it to the house. My house manager ensures that they have a private room. There are other spaces for horses and cattle. The rabbits—even the Converted ones don't care who sees them. And who knows about Crested Flyers? They're very private about mating."

"So it's just a quiet talking space."

"Absolutely. There's been more than a few deals cut behind this barn. Not all of them are about rodeo." He grinned. "The Rella Producers Association meets here frequently. And I've held a few Federalist party organizational meetings for the Boss's Conference."

"Oh? Sounds like you've been thinking about running for office already."

Good.

"Eh, until I won my lawsuit, I didn't have the time to consider political office. I've been interested, but—" he shrugged. "Just no time. Or money. The Conference is a bigger deal on Cartain than the Congress. Until recently, we've been nothing more than a second-tier participant in the Federation. Even with the discovery of rella."

But you've already been active in planetary politics. Good to know.

"That sounds like you have a good foundation for your campaign, based on that past organizational work."

"True." He grinned. "I also know that the Councilists are scrambling to replace Robbie Windsor."

"You're up on political gossip, then."

Jeff laughed. "I'm good at listening and learning, then not repeating things said in confidence. It pays off, especially with the Flyers." His voice turned solemn. "The Flyers won't run for office themselves, but they are *significant* in funding and running the government here. It's only been in the past few cycles that their focus has started to turn toward the Congress. The Boss's Conference has taken a priority."

"Good to know."

They walked through the center alleyway of the barn. Several horses stood in the stalls, coming to the doors and sticking their heads through the U-shaped openings in the protective grills. Jeff slowed, fumbling in his pocket. Caroline noticed how shiny the horses were, coats glistening with a sheen, as if they had been polished.

Jeff turned to her. "Want to give them a treat?"

"It's safe?"

"Oh yes." Jeff handed her a small cookie. "We'll start here because he'll kick up a fuss if he isn't the first one to get treats and attention. This is Red." He pointed to the horse who was, indeed, bright red except for the wide white stripe running down the length of his face. "He likes duels where he and I go one-on-one with a sentient cow—that doesn't count as a sentient duel. I can't put him in a field with non-sentient cattle because he'll herd them constantly. He knows better than to take on a sentient cow without me."

"Is he sentient?" Caroline tentatively held out her hand, fingers curled around the cookie.

"Don't feed him a treat like that," Jeff said. "Keep your hand flat. He can't see your fingers, and he might bite them accidentally otherwise."

"So he's not sentient." Caroline flattened her hand and held the cookie out to Red. He picked it up with his lips, brushing her hand softly.

"Not—officially. Rifanel is not able to talk to him using Standard, like she can with Converted horses. General equine body language, yes." Jeff reached up and scratched the wide white spot at the top of the white stripe on Red's face. "But he and I communicate very well, either with me on the ground or in the saddle. It's mostly body language. How I move and carry myself on the ground, then how I shift my weight and use my legs in the saddle. Sometimes I use voice, but that's for specific directions or else using a tone that he responds to. I don't need to use a bridle with Red anymore. It's a different form of sentience."

Red blew a long snort. Jeff laughed again.

"Did he just say something?" From the sideways glance the big horse gave Caroline, she would have expected a snarky comment to follow, if he had an implant.

At least that was what that look and snort would mean from Rifanel.

"Oh, he's annoyed that he can't be part of the party. Same for the other horses. We have too many species at this party who aren't familiar with the behavior of non-Converted beings. It's different when it's just us duelists. Then everyone knows how to read what's going on, sentients and non-sentients alike. There are several stock contractors who will bring their non-sentient cattle and horse performance strings here to relax when I throw a party, because they can play with the rest of us."

"It's safe to have a gathering with non-Converted species?" Caroline frowned. That didn't make sense. Mixing Converted and non-Converted species in a party setting *just wasn't done*, at least not at the Congress. Even when the species were similar.

"Oh yes. But us duelists know each other so well that it doesn't really matter when it comes to party time. We *have* to cooperate with each other in order to perform safely. And most of us are almost—well, family."

Except when it comes to sentient duels. But she suspected sentient duels were a touchy subject, given that Logan Easystar's sabotage derailed Jeff's dueling career before he could rise to that level. Best not to bring them up.

Caroline moved to the next stall. This horse was black

with brown undertones, its nose a light brown, a big diamond-shaped patch of white on its forehead.

Jeff joined her. "This is Star—her color is called dark bay, not black. Many people confuse the two. She likes going on trail rides. Very smooth-gaited. I use her to ride the fields rather than drive a floater. We both have fun that way. She tells me when she sees something wrong."

"How does she do that if she's not sentient?"

"She's very observant. If she sees something different or out of place, she will look at it for a long time. Or she'll insist that we go in that direction. She's less expensive than a robot, and her responses are faster. And—we just have fun riding out."

"Wow."

They continued down the alleyway, Jeff telling Caroline a little bit about each horse.

As they left the barn, Caroline spotted Geraint, Blackburn, Richardson—and Rifanel, without Fenarmin. Another Crested Flyer—*must be Twitl*—was speaking, though they were too far away for Caroline to hear much more than the higher-pitched tones of their voice. Twitl's voice was steadier than Zzink's, without the loud, irritating SQUAWK that Zzink's translator issued.

The Crested Flyer noticed their approach first. "Jeff!" it called. "What perfect timing! I have been telling them—" it gestured with one of its rudimentary, cream-and-red-shaded wings— "about the rella situation."

"I've been talking about it with Caroline."

They joined the others gathered around a picnic table set under the shade of a deciduous tree with red-edged green leaves. The leaf shape looked like an Earth maple, but Caroline had never seen a maple with red-edged, lavender-shaded leaves—and with purple veins, she noticed as they came closer.

"The situation is quite concerning," Geraint said.

Blackburn flicked his ears, focusing on Richardson, and fluffed.

"There needs to be an audit of Cartain's rella production," Richardson said.

Blackburn added an authoritative *thump!* that echoed from his platform. Rabbit and human focused on each other. Caroline couldn't *see* what the two were saying to each other, and wondered if indeed this was all nonverbal communication, or if Blackburn and Richardson were amongst the rare beings capable of mindspeech. It was entirely possible, considering Blackburn's prominence.

"There is a problem with unilaterally calling for an audit." Jeff guided Caroline to one of the benches by the picnic table. He leaned against the table, facing the others. "The Boss's people won't do it."

"Are you saying that the Boss may—" Geraint clacked his teeth, "have problems with corruption?"

"No, no, no." Jeff raised his hands. "More a matter that the Boss needs to have a significant reason to ask for an audit. We producers aren't enough. But if the Congress asks for it...."

Twitl let loose with a deafening SCREECH that made Caroline cringe. "Jeff, you are not *seriously* suggesting that Robbie-boy is going to have the feathers to bring up the notion to the Federation Congress? He is afraid of the lightest zephyrs! He treats the slightest bit of controversy as if it were a hurricane that will blow him away."

Hmm. Twitl exhibits a similar degree of control as Geraint over the nuances of his translator implant, for the most part. Perhaps he's not candidate material, but he can certainly testify at a hearing.

Something she would need to consider.

"Rumor says that Robbie isn't running for re-election," Jeff said flatly. "He would happily bow out if the right person runs."

"*I* am not running." Twitl flapped his wings for emphasis. "Sorry, Rifanel. To begin with, I do not entirely agree with the

Councilist agenda. Secondly, I cannot handle staying at Galactic Center for very long. The air there is—" he shuddered and flapped his wings again. "Too heavy. Too thick. It would shorten my life. Furthermore, I am not of the temperament to handle the negotiations it would take for me to properly represent Cartain in the Federation Congress. There are other, more reasonable candidates."

"If you are suggesting Bloohowt, I do not consider him as a possibility for the Congress," Rifanel said. Her translator conveyed a husky tone. "He is more concerned about how his herd will profit, and his angry explosions make Fenarmin's meltdowns look like a weanling's temper tantrum when their dam refuses to let them nurse. I do not like the way that he dominates his cows and calves. I doubt that the Federalists would care for that aspect of Bloohowt either."

"There is someone else," Jeff said quietly. The steady, firm tone in his voice resonated deep inside of Caroline.

He is going to make a superb orator. Just needs a little coaching from Geraint.

"Who?" Twitl's crest fanned high, showing traces of red and green amongst the dominant cream color.

"Me."

Silence fell for two clicks.

Then Rifanel blew a long, rolling snort. "Which party would you align with? The Councilists, like Robbie?"

"The Federalists," Jeff said firmly. "I agree with Twitl. With all due respect, Rifanel, there are parts of the Councilist agenda that I can't support. Cartain is a small world. We can't solve our problems ourselves, in spite of the plant-based drug trade—this issue with the Ribonit cartel and rella makes this very clear. The Councilist emphasis on each world managing their own interstellar trade resources without Federation support does not work for us."

Rifanel switched her tail and tossed her head. "We do allow for exceptions."

"Understood. But—overall, I support a greater flexibility toward change than I suspect your Councilists would tolerate." A faint smile spread across his lips. "And what experience I have with Fenarmin suggests to me that having the two of us trying to cooperate within the same Party caucus would not be the best of ideas."

"And you would definitely not fit within the Statists," Richardson said, as Rifanel snorted again. "Given your history with Logan Easystar—"

"Sss. Exactly." Geraint raised himself up on all fours.

"I have *one* requirement for me to run as a Federalist candidate," Jeff said.

"And that is?" The tip of Geraint's tail twitched.

"I formally petition that Caroline Starshine be released from her obligation to you so that she may serve as my assistant."

"It will take negotiations with Mars University," Geraint said. "She still has thirty turns left in her internship with me."

"I'm very willing to negotiate a transfer of her internship, even pay for any expenses that might be connected. I know it's doable. We've had interns working for rodeo contractors."

Geraint nodded. "I will send you the necessary information. We should have an answer by the time Caroline and I return to Galactic Central. She needs to close out some tasks for me before I can release her."

"How long will that take?"

"We can have her back on Cartain within a ten-turn."

"Which gives me two ten-turns working for a candidate before I graduate." Caroline bit back her smile.

"Not that there will be much competition," Jeff said. "I'm sure Robbie would happily bow out, even if I do go Federalist. Do the Councilists have a backup candidate?"

Rifanel snorted and shook her head. "One reason I am here is that Robbie has told my caucus that he does not desire to run for re-election. We had hoped to recruit Twitl for the Councilists, but—" she switched her tail. "It appears that your recruitment efforts have been more successful, Geraint."

"Oh, I do not think it was *my* efforts." Geraint showed his teeth. "I give all the credit to my soon-to-be-former intern, the *quite* capable Caroline Starshine."

"And this situation with rella," Caroline said. "It's clear that something needs to be done at the Federation level."

Blackburn thumped. Richardson glanced at him.

"Blackburn agrees," Richardson said. "There are—*many* concerns about rella. It will be quite helpful for the Congress to have the expertise of someone like Jeff Tophand, who knows about the production of rella."

Twitl bobbed his head. "You have my support, Jeff. I will speak to the Flyer community."

"Thank you, Twitl."

Rifanel blew hard. "I need to talk to Fenarmin. He will not be thrilled to learn this news, but—unless he has encountered a better candidate while we have been meeting, the Councilists do not have anyone to run against you, Jeff." Her ears flicked back, then forward again. "Would you mind coming with me to speak to him?"

Jeff tensed slightly before answering. "Of course, Rifanel. Caroline, would you join me?"

She glanced quickly at Geraint. He nodded. "Yes."

"Then we should do it now." Rifanel whirled neatly on her hind legs. She picked up a trot as she headed to the gate. "Open," she commanded.

Jeff and Caroline followed.

"So that's how you keep the non-Converted species confined in this space—verbal gate commands?" Caroline asked.

"Yes." Jeff exhaled, whistling through his teeth. "Not looking forward to this discussion with Fenarmin. He had a reputation on the rodeo circuit for being quick to anger during duels. It's telling that he's not very dominant in Hrwhinir's Court of Stallions."

"If that's the case, then why did Fenarmin get elected as Hrwhinir's Planetary Representative?"

Jeff knows political gossip, even about his fellow duelists. Yeah. He's definitely ready to move into politics.

"From what I heard, the Court of Stallions endorsed him, along with Rifanel. She's committed to becoming his assistant in Congress since she reached the term limits that Hrwhinir sets for their Planetary Representatives. Plus, Fenarmin is the herd stallion in her band—as his lead mare, she has the final say in a lot of things." Jeff shrugged. "Temper's the main issue with Fenarmin. He does have some decent policy ideas, and I think we—*you*, anyway, could persuade him to take action against the Ribonits."

"Getting angry easily could cause him issues in Congress."

During her eleven spans of working for Geraint, Caroline had seen what happened to quick-tempered new Representatives—either they learned how to manage the anger appropriately, or else they lost influence. Temper flares were more common amongst Statist Representatives, who often behaved as if it were the only means by which they could gain attention.

"I'm confident that Rifanel can manage him as far as dealing with Congress in general. No. The big issue is between me and Fenarmin. If the two of us hadn't gotten hurt, we probably would have met in a sentient duel. That could make the situation difficult between us. You and Rifanel should probably talk."

"Understood."

So that would be one of her first tasks as Jeff's assistant. As they followed Rifanel, Caroline added a "to-do" note to her planner.

The first of many that she would be creating in her new role, she was certain.

CAROLINE FLINCHED at the loud bellow coming from the party, as she and Jeff rounded the corner of the barn.

"Damn it, Rifanel's already told him. I thought she was going to wait for me!" Jeff broke into a run.

Caroline hobbled along behind him, held back by her lightweight sandals. They were pretty, but woefully impractical for Cartain, especially if she was going to be spending a lot of time going through pastures—which seemed to be quite likely.

One thing I'm doing when I get back to Galactic Central is getting sensible shoes! Bet I'll need to be traipsing through all sorts of natural settings.

"STOP TEARING UP MY TURF, FENARMIN!" Jeff yelled.

That suddenly hushed the loud chatter of the party.

Caroline excused herself as she blundered through a group of Crested Flyers. Their attention was on Jeff, hands on his hips, facing Fenarmin, who screeched again and shook his head, rearing high before landing to paw furiously at the ground.

Rifanel squealed—no translation from her device—and whirled to kick Fenarmin in the side with both hinds. He arched his neck as he faced her, snorting. She turned toward him, her ears pinned and teeth bared.

Jeff looked around, spreading his arms wide. "Back off, everyone," he said, voice low. "I suggest you clear the area."

Caroline took that as her cue to gently encourage the crowd back. It took some persuasion. One big, red, white-faced bull stood his ground, snorting, lowering his head at her and shaking it. He pawed at the turf without touching it, the tips of his cloven hoof barely hovering above the grass.

"I. Will. Not. Move!" he roared.

Deep down inside, Caroline felt like she *should* run.

No. She couldn't afford to do that, not given her new role working for Jeff. She *had* to learn to manage and work with Cartain Converteds. This bull was from Cartain, she was sure of that.

"Oh no you don't, Bloohowt," Jeff said, coming up on her other side. "Back off and listen to her. Caroline works for me."

So this is the infamous Bloohowt that Rifanel didn't want running for Representative. Good to know.

"I hear you're running for Planetary Representative!" The bull's translator device projected a growling monotone. "What about me?"

"If you want to run, so be it. May the best being win."

Rifanel snorted. "You are not running as a Councilist, Bloohowt!"

"*I* was recruiting him!" Fenarmin's translator was deep-voiced, a lower monotone than Bloohowt's.

"And *I* am still Party Leader, Fenarmin!" Rifanel added an untranslatable squeal as she flattened her ears even more, snapping at Fenarmin. "As your lead mare, I tell you this is so! Bloohowt has—issues." More quietly, she continued. "This is not the place to discuss them. I support Jeff Tophand as Cartain's Planetary Representative. Bloohowt, I suggest you meet with Jeff—*later*—to discuss your role in Cartain's politics. The Councilists will have use for you, but not as Planetary Representative!"

The bull growled, then turned away, grumbling low in his throat.

"So." Fenarmin snorted. "*You.*"

Jeff faced him. "Yes. *Me.*"

"Fenarmin." Rifanel tossed her head, switching her tail back and forth. "May I remind you—"

The chestnut stallion squealed, ears back. He arched his neck, and raised a foreleg.

"No more pawing!" Jeff snapped. "Fenarmin, this is my unConverted horses' pasture when I'm not using it for mixed parties. Please respect their graze."

Fenarmin blew a long, rolling snort through his nostrils. "All right, then. For their sake. But Tophand—when you come to Galactic Central, watch your step!" He spun and marched off in a slow, collected trot, tail held high.

Rifanel heaved a heavy sigh. "My apologies, Jeff. Fenarmin is still—well, he will learn at Galactic Central."

"Yes," Caroline said. "He will."

Rifanel turned her head to gaze straight on at Caroline, flicking her ears forward. "You and Geraint are returning to Central tonight?"

"Yes. I'll be back here in a ten-turn, to help Jeff with his campaign."

"We need to make time to talk before you return to Cartain."

"Agreed."

"Then it will be so." Rifanel picked up a less showy trot and followed Fenarmin.

Jeff exhaled. "Well. That went better than I thought it would. And now, Ms. Caroline Starshine. I think it's time you got to know some of my friends here on Cartain." He offered his arm again. "Shall we?"

"Yes."

What am I getting myself into?

Well, what was done was done.

And she had a position working for a future Planetary Representative. Caroline had the feeling that working for Jeff Tophand was not going to be boring.

BY THE TIME they left the Interstellar Roundup Ranch that evening, Caroline had collected enough notes from her intro-

ductions that she needed to spend time sorting and organizing them.

Good thing the trip to Central will take a turn. She would
need every click—no, every *tap* of her waking period to create
contact files and organize their data. She had met nearly
every significant agricultural landowner on Cartain's major
continent, Blass, and a few from its secondary continent,
Wansa. Jeff had given her a list of other contacts who had not
been able to attend the party, both on and off of Cartain. She
needed to send them a message introducing herself as his
assistant.

I'll tell them about my candidacy myself, he had said. *Then
you can follow up. Most of them will take a hint that they should be
dealing with you. I've starred the ones who most likely won't.*

And she had to lobby the Boss's executive assistant about
placing Bloohowt in a leadership role on Cartain's treaty
negotiation team with the Ribonits. She and Jeff had finally
convinced the big bull that he needed to serve in that role—
and that is where Bloohowt's strengths truly lie, Jeff told her after
they had finished. *He's a great negotiator. Just—won't be able to
make the compromises he needs to agree to in order to be a decent
Planetary Rep. But as a treaty negotiator? I want him on my side
when we deal with the next Ribonit treaty. Bloohowt focuses on the
tiny details and when he goes into a negotiation, he already knows
what he will and won't concede.*

Rifanel had sent Caroline a list of possible times for their
meeting.

And she hadn't been able to talk to Geraint about what
she needed to do to wrap up her duties yet, either.

But first, they needed to transfer from the runabout to *No
Skies, No Limits.* Then the transport needed to exit the Cartain
system, and move to the Gate.

Only then could she and Geraint talk with appropriate
security—and it was already getting late. Caroline checked
the time.

Fourteenth Node. It would take almost sixty clicks—14:60—before *No Skies* would get through the Gate. Geraint would want to get to bed no later than the Fifteenth Node.

Caroline sighed. Would forty clicks be enough time to talk? Perhaps she should just let Geraint go to bed, and speak after First Meal. He had already turned up the heat on his platform, switched on the misting device that substituted for his usual resting water tank, and was nestled into the padding, like he was tired and wanted to sleep.

Geraint cracked one eye open and raised his head slightly, as if she had spoken out loud. "There will be time enough to talk about wrapping up your responsibilities after First Meal."

"Did I disturb you? I'm sorry."

"No. I heard you sigh, but I had been considering what you need to do and what can be done by Shshrit. She is nearly ready to step into your position anyway."

"True." Shshrit, Caroline's assistant, was another reptilian, also from Geraint's world. She and Caroline had already developed a transition plan, in anticipation of Caroline moving on to another position, hopefully in the Congress.

"I'll let Dr. Knowledgechaser know about my new position, unless it's something you have to do as part of my release."

"I have already contacted Dr. Knowledgechaser to file my release. The rest of it can wait until tomorrow." Geraint nestled back into his padding.

"Thank you." Caroline frowned at her screen projection.

Now she just needed to tell her family that she would not be returning to Earth anytime soon. Then she could get started with organizing her notes.

Get it over with.

She wrote a brief note before sending it to her parents, Gran-Gran, and the rest of her extended family.

At least she might have a few nodes of peace before she got the reactions from Earth.

It was much more pleasant to draft a memo to Dr. Knowledgechaser letting him know that she would not be attending her graduation in person, thanks to her new responsibilities as the assistant to the future Planetary Representative from Cartain.

TRANSFERRING TO *No Skies, No Limits* was reasonably uneventful. Geraint happily settled into his water tank. Caroline went to bed shortly after.

She woke shortly after 3rd Node, wincing at the bright red glow of the MESSAGES RECEIVED button when she opened her comm again.

Deal with what was likely to be a lot of family drama before First Meal or after? At least one was a video which— no, she was NOT going to watch, especially since it came from Aunt Katrina.

Get it over with, she chided herself.

Her mother's angry reaction was sufficient to set the tone for the others.

—I never thought I would have to deal with such an ungrateful daughter. What are you doing exposing yourself to all those dirty nonhumans? The Federation Congress is corrupt—

Caroline didn't read any further. She skimmed the other messages from her family. More of the same, although two of her brothers didn't respond.

She decided to write one final message, and sent it to all of them.

—Like it or not, my future is off of Earth. I am sorry that all of you feel this way. May you have a good life. I plan to do so. Farewell. You'll know where to find me.

Dr. Knowledgechaser's response was appropriately

congratulatory, and included instructions for what she needed to do for graduating remotely.

Caroline exhaled.

Well, that's done.

She doubted she would hear anything further from her family.

3

HITTING THE GROUND RUNNING

First Meal was private—Geraint had told Caroline at the beginning of her internship that his meals needed to be private, unless he was dining with other reptilians. *We crocodilians tend to be messy eaters,* he had said. He usually only ate First Meal, so he could attend Second and Third Meal meetings with other species without worry. Caroline ate in her room, then went to the main area of their shared cabin and continued sorting through her notes.

The hum of Geraint's platform didn't interrupt Caroline's focus as he settled on his usual restraint across from her. He had to clack his jaws several times before she startled up.

"Oh! Sorry, Geraint." She jumped up to secure his platform to the restraint. "These details—especially from the Rella Producers Association—Jeff threw a lot at me yesterday and I'm still figuring it out. Cartain has a complex grouping of associations for such a small planetary surface."

"The number of associations reflects the diversity of Cartain's sentient species," Geraint said. "For all that Cartain is considered to be a minor planet, it has more sentient diversity than, say Earth, Tsfalnel, or Hrwhinir." He flicked the tip of his tail. "I am very glad that you are Jeff's assistant, Caroline. You have the breadth and depth of detail focus that he needs for support. Cartain *should* be playing a stronger role in the Congress than it does."

"Because of rella and other drugs it produces?"

"That, plus the sheer diversity of Cartain. We have not investigated the oceans to determine what sentient species, if any, live there."

"If there are any native sentients in the oceans, then they haven't managed to develop comms yet. I'll need to look into that, I suppose." Caroline pursed her lips thoughtfully. "So why hasn't Cartain played a greater role in the Congress?"

Geraint took several clicks to adjust his padding before taking up his lecture pose. "The Bosses of Cartain have not placed a priority upon participation in the Congress."

"Rather like Old Earth, then."

"Almost exactly like Earth, except the Bosses of Cartain hew more to the Councilist position than the Statist. They prefer clear hierarchies and going their own way."

Caroline frowned. "That doesn't seem to be in Cartain's best interest."

"There are reasons why Cartain has a single planetary government headed by a Boss, rather than a coalition of different nations." Geraint paused, clacking his jaws before continuing. "The original Earth settlers on Cartain were very hierarchical, many coming from nations with a tradition of hereditary autocrats. That was reflected in how they managed other sentients, and has continued so to this day. The current Planetary Representative from Cartain, Robbie Windsor, spends more of his time ensuring that certain large landowners on Cartain benefit from Congressional decisions than on what choices are best for the planet. Therefore, the multiplicity of those associations that you are now studying. Those who are not amongst the Boss's cronies need to lobby not just the Conference on Cartain, but the Galactic Congress."

"That makes sense. From little things that were said yesterday, I'd almost think there was a structure of—" Caroline hesitated, searching for a means to carefully say what she was thinking. "I don't want to say slavery, Geraint, because obviously someone like Jeff found his way out of that level of forced obligation. Indenture, perhaps?"

"Closer to slavery than indenture, only class and income-based rather than any arbitrary cultural or appearance-based divisions within the species. No ownership of individuals, just their work contracts. But the results are much the same." Geraint's words came short and sharp. "Oppression of those less fortunate. Jeff took one of the few pathways out, by becoming a rodeo duelist, and was good enough at it to earn sufficient money to set himself up the way he has. In the meantime, the shift from cotton and other fabric production to plant-based drugs as Cartain's major export has eliminated the need for such—" he sharply clacked his jaws— "oppressive structures. Furthermore, the current Boss, Terrianna Abbott, strongly opposes it."

"Will Jeff's past history have an impact on his Congressional role?"

"Quite likely." Geraint bobbed his head. "Which leads to another issue. Appearances. Being an intern and being an assistant in Congress are two very different situations."

"One is short-term, and the other indefinite?"

"Exactly. But there is more to consider. Rodeo duelists have a certain—reputation, shall we say, that is not the best."

"I've heard some of that already," Caroline said ruefully. "They're considered to be frivolous. Somewhat reckless. Into partying and behaviors that might not be acceptable to polite society. I encountered some of those attitudes yesterday."

She didn't mention the barely concealed sneers and implications that she was already sharing Jeff's bed from the Cartainian humans she had met at the party. Asserting that she and Geraint were returning promptly to Galactic Central had silenced *some* of those insinuations at the party. But dealing with *that* impression was already on Caroline's list as something to manage when she and Jeff saw each other again. She *needed* to have clearly observed separate quarters, or else a marriage contract.

Geraint's lips spread in a wide grin, revealing all of his teeth. "Oh Caroline. Once again, I am so glad you are working with Jeff. Not every intern would pick up that nuance. Yes. The public perception of rodeo duelists is one issue that Jeff will be facing in the Congress." He paused for several taps. "Fenarmin was not a part of Rifanel's herd before he became a candidate for Planetary Representative. Becoming part of her herd was a necessary component for the Court of Stallions to endorse his candidacy."

"I—see. I didn't think that Hrwhinir was as moralistic as Earth—or as Cartain appears to be."

The roundabout way that Geraint approached this discussion marked it as significant—so she needed to pay close attention. She had noticed that as a crocodilian characteristic behavior.

"Mmm, it is not just that. This is part of a speech that I give to nearly all of my interns who obtain positions as an assistant to a Planetary Representative. However, the degree of moralism on Cartain adds to the necessity of this sort of arrangement."

Not as bad as Earth, however, from what I experienced.

Caroline nodded. "A marital contract of some sort?"

Geraint exhaled. "Exactly. I tell all future assistants that negotiating a basic marriage contract with their Planetary Representative is always a good idea. It can be anything from a formal association arrangement for a set period of time to an indefinite contract which includes reproductive access."

"The last is what marriage means on Earth these turns. I've not seen a reference to these arrangements in anything I've studied about the Congress. What's the reason for it?"

Her coursework had included a brief review of the standard marital contract forms common in places other than Earth, but there hadn't been any mention of it being somewhat mandatory for assistants to Planetary Representatives.

"This is—one of those unspoken traditions. A marital arrangement reduces the likelihood of scandal and simplifies security and information management, amongst other issues."

"But for no one to record it?" That circumstance puzzled her.

"It is a tradition that comes and goes. Right now, marital arrangements are more commonplace." Geraint paused. "It is unusual for me to take a human intern like you, Caroline, especially one who rises to the level of head intern. Generally, I am assessing potential new assistants from amongst my interns. Dr. Knowledgechaser was quite persuasive in convincing me to take you as an intern, based on your family connections and your determination to work in the Congress."

"I didn't know that." She *had* known that Geraint was married to several people; just not the details of their contracts. His assistant Rutan was one spouse; Ssgaldir back on Tsfalnel was another. She had children with Geraint. Rutan had been standoffish ever since Caroline had been promoted to head intern and she had wondered why he was suddenly unfriendly. Now she had some idea—a potential threat to his position as Geraint's assistant? Even though Rutan was a reptilian, just not from Tsfalnel?

Geraint bobbed his head. "Yes. Rutan and I have a formal association contract. It simplifies not just security issues but also communications, travel, and social arrangements, as well as providing better benefits for Rutan as my assistant. We have reproductive contracts with others on our own planets. The formal contract gives assistants more privileges than assistants who don't have one, no matter if it's a formal contract or if it extends to all domains, including reproduction." He clicked up a file and sent it to her. "Here is something that I wrote about the advantages and disadvantages of different types of marital contracts while serving in Congress. Please feel free to share it with Jeff."

"I will. But I'm a little confused. I can see where marital contracts reduce office scandals. But how can formal association contracts play a role in security?"

"Because the terms of the contract specify the confidentiality responsibilities each party has to the other. The existence of a marital contract between Representative and assistant is an indicator that the Planetary Representative has the utmost trust in their assistant. It also holds the Planetary Representative responsible for any breach of security that can be traced back to their assistant."

"Wow. I—had no idea."

"It also protects the assistant from any breaches that their Planetary Representative commits. So—if the assistant of a Planetary Representative does not have a marital contract of some sort with their Representative—" Geraint paused, back in professorial mode, waiting for her to answer.

"Then that indicates a potential lack of trust either from the Representative or from their assistant. After all, if the assistant is uncertain about their Representative, then they wouldn't enter into a marital contract with them, correct?"

Geraint showed all of his teeth in a big grin. "Exactly, Caroline. As always, you have discerned the deeper issue."

AFTER THEY SPOKE FURTHER about what was needed to prepare Shshrit for her new position, both Geraint and Caroline returned to reviewing files and writing reports. Caroline sent Geraint's file to Jeff, then continued categorizing her notes.

About half a node before Second Meal, Geraint disappeared into his room to take a comm.

Her comm pinged. A message from Jeff. Caroline opened it.

—*Geraint makes a persuasive case for a formal association contract at the very least. A formal marital association contract will make appearances much easier on Cartain.*

—*I agree,* she responded. —*Do you have a particular preference as to type of contract?*

—*Perhaps we start with a formal association contract that has an option for deeper involvement—that is, if you don't have any other connections? One never knows. I am free from any relationship constraints.*

—*Agree,* she answered. —*That provides us with many potential options. I have no relationships at the moment, so I am free to contract with no conflicts.*

—*Then the first thing we shall do upon your return is sign our contract formally, in front of the Boss and the Conference, if that sounds good to you?*

—*That sounds very good to me. It will provide you with excellent publicity.*

—*May I announce our intentions?*

—*Yes.*

His next message relayed a list of potential contacts both on Cartain and in the Congress that would be appropriate for her to announce their impending marital contract. Caroline reviewed the list.

She debated about adding her family, then decided against doing that. Caroline returned the list after adding Dr. Knowledgechaser and others from Mars University who would be interested in hearing the news.

SHE WORKED through Second Meal and almost until Third Meal, finally wrapping up what she could do while traveling by 11:50 Node, just in time for early dinner before needing to prepare to transfer to the runabout to take them to Galactic Central. Caroline and Geraint were scheduled to board the runabout at 13:10. Just enough time to eat and pack up.

Rutan and Shshrit met them at the spaceport. While Shshrit was crocodilian, like Geraint, Rutan looked more like a human-sized version of Earth's *T. Rex.* But he bobbed his head at Caroline with a more pleasant expression than he had possessed during her entire tenure as Geraint's head intern.

"My congratulations-ss to you on achieving as-s-sis-stant s-s-status-s-s-s, Caroline." Rutan's translator projected more sibilants than Geraint's did—a characteristic of reptilians from his home planet.

"Thank you, Rutan. It's going to be a whole new world, sounds like."

"Oh yes-s. If you would like any advice, pleas-se as-sk."

"I am sure I will need it. Thank you."

So Rutan was worried about me as potential competition after all. Interesting to know.

And, perhaps, more than a little bit flattering about his perception of her ability.

CAROLINE'S SCHEDULE was packed for the six turns before she needed to return to Cartain. The Federalist Party of Cartain certified Jeff as their candidate. The Boss was unwilling to add her certification until after the election—*annoying but she's correct about it diverging from tradition*—was Jeff's reaction. But even as a candidate's assistant, Caroline had a considerable array of tasks facing her.

Security certifications.

Filing statements with the Congressional Record Office

from her and from Jeff that they were considering a formal marital association contract, the signing to occur soon.

Express shipping Jeff's secure Planetary Representative comm to Cartain, so they could message each other with greater security.

Learning the codes that would transfer their status from candidate to elected, and the process by which she needed to manage that transition. Most of the responsibilities would fall to Caroline, not Jeff.

Meeting her opposite numbers amongst the Federalist Representative assistants, to develop relationships. Rutan was Caroline's guide for those meetings, his advice crucial as she explored the possibilities for future political alignments.

Interviews on Jeff's behalf.

And more.

More finally included a meeting with Rifanel. Caroline went to the quarters that Rifanel and Fenarmin shared. She wasn't certain what to expect—whether those quarters would be a stable, what accommodations were available for humans, what sort of climate control there would be, if any. Her role as intern had meant that she went to different species' offices, not their private quarters.

But Rifanel's invitation was to her private residence. Specifically.

Unlike the tiny shared apartment that Caroline was moving out of (another adjustment to organize, including sharing a suite with Jeff and any staffers he would want to bring from Cartain), Rifanel's quarters were on the terraformed and climatized surface of the planetoid that was home to Galactic Central. Caroline chartered a small autoskimmer to travel the short distance from Main Central to Equine Sector, dressing for the temperate but humid outside climate.

She marveled at the landscape's beauty as the autoskimmer drove to the coordinates Caroline had entered. Equine Sector was primarily large pastures set in a hilly part of Galactic Central, with copses of deciduous trees located near ponds. It reminded Caroline of pictures that she had seen of what Earth had once been.

Small houses—stables?—scattered irregularly through the rolling countryside, willy-nilly, as if they had been tossed into place by a giant. A few pastures containing what looked to be younger equines were fenced, but most of the fields were unfenced. Assorted adult equines grazed the grassy areas, some raising their heads to watch as the autoskimmer scooted along, following a dirt track that apparently marked boundaries. In some fields, equine groups of mixed ages were exercising or training, the larger equines watching while the youngers traversed courses. Some courses contained obstacles, others didn't.

At last, the autoskimmer turned off of the dirt track. It slowed, still hovering just above the ground, but seemed to follow a trail that Caroline couldn't see. After winding past a copse where several equines stood by a pond, and along a low area between rolling hillsides, the autoskimmer approached a low, blue building and stopped.

Guess I'm here. Caroline got out. She looked around. There were two doors. The larger, partially-open door led to an alleyway like the one she had seen in Jeff's barn back on Cartain.

The other door was smaller, human-sized. Caroline's watch chimed and she checked the message.

—Welcome, Caroline. Go through the smaller door. Rifanel.

Rifanel must have surveillance outside—to be expected for someone of her status. Caroline walked to the smaller door. To her surprise, it opened on a cozy parlor, one side with a faded green and pink paisley rug, chairs and human-sized tables; the other with a manger, taller tables, and a horse-sized drinking fountain. A white marble counter lined one wall, with big sinks and assorted equipment clearly designed for equine use. A dark green velvet curtain hung in a space between chairs.

"You will find a cup and saucer in the cabinet above the table." Rifanel flicked an ear toward the appropriate cabinet as she used her teeth to delicately pick up a teapot with a horse-sized handle on it from the counter and place it on one of the tables by Caroline. "I took the liberty of assuming that you would like mint tea."

"Oh, I do. Thank you, Rifanel."

The mare chuckled a deep-toned, throaty whicker. "You are welcome." She picked up a second, larger teapot and put it on a taller table on the horse side. "I did not think you would care for clover tea, which is my preference for afternoon gatherings like this."

"You know, I've never had clover tea." Caroline hesitated. "Would it be an imposition if I asked to try it?"

Another of those deep chesty chuckle whickers from Rifanel. "Not at all."

Caroline got a second cup and set it on the table next to Rifanel's deep bowl. "I'll be happy to try a small amount, along with the mint."

Rifanel deftly lifted the teapot handle with lips and teeth. She poured some tea into Caroline's cup, then filled her bowl.

"Thank you." Caroline returned to one of the overstuffed chairs. "I appreciate your hospitality, Rifanel." She sipped the clover tea. "This tea has an interesting flavor. I would be willing to share it with you in the future."

Rifanel snorted. "You are an unusual human. But this matches what I have heard from my investigations into your time as an intern with Geraint. No wonder he set you up with Jeff Tophand. Only fools will underestimate the combination of you two." She shook her head. "As I am repeatedly telling Fenarmin."

"Fenarmin. Jeff. So there are issues between those two."

Rifanel blew another long snort. "That is an understatement." She paused.

Caroline waited, because it was clear the brown mare was gathering her thoughts and considering what to say—just like Geraint would do. Fairly common amongst nonhuman sentients.

"Not every duelist is capable of rising to the level of sentient dueling," Rifanel finally said. "Many duelists are content to remain at the non-sentient species dueling level. It can be difficult for many duelists to take that next step, especially for those who have been doing really well with the lower-level non-sentients."

Caroline finished the clover tea and picked up her mint tea. "I admit that I don't know much about dueling. Especially when the sentient duelists are horses or cattle."

"There are species of great apes that can be trained to ride bucking sentient animals. Those are frequently used in early competition. Higher-level non-sentients include our traditional predators, such as the large felines. Some avians and bipedal reptiles. Once an equine duelist such as Fenarmin manages to defeat the large felines without injury to themselves, they are eligible to qualify for sentient duels."

"Fascinating."

Caroline set her cup down as a young horse, brown with a cream mane and tail like Rifanel, pushed through the curtain that separated the parlor from the connected stable. Rifanel snorted at the young horse. They exchanged ear flicks and head tosses. Then Rifanel flipped her ears back, switched her tail, and tossed her head. The young horse whirled to go back out, but it paused in front of Caroline, bobbing its head at her.

She stood up and mirrored the head bob. The young horse flicked its ears forward and carefully extended its nose toward Caroline. She reached out, holding the back of her hand for it to smell, like she had learned to do from Jeff. The horse blew softly on her hand and nudged it. Caroline scratched under its jaw. The young horse's eyes softened, eyelids drooping, a blissful expression on its face.

Then Rifanel snorted, hard.

The young horse startled, nuzzled Caroline's hand, then trotted out.

"I am sorry for the interruption," Rifanel said as Caroline sat back down. "She is young and has not qualified for the translation implant yet, much less earned her name." She blew softly. "Daughter of my sister. We have high hopes for her future—she is an experiment, the daughter of a sentient mare and a non-sentient stallion. If she does not qualify after undergoing sentient testing, then perhaps her foals may, if she mates with a sentient stallion, possibly Fenarmin."

"I did not know such matings happened." Caroline pressed her lips together to hide her immediate reaction. She could *not* imagine mating with a great ape. The very thought turned her stomach. But—primarily Converted species might not feel that way about their non-sentient relatives.

Just because there's no evidence that humans underwent Conversion doesn't mean it didn't happen that way back in Earth's early days, she reminded herself. And Plasmoids had been known to visit Earth long before humans achieved spaceflight.

"These matings are more popular amongst those of us connected to the rodeo world who are not humanoid. Such crosses, while frequently engaged as the non-sentient in a duel, often become the most challenging duelists." Rifanel flicked her ears. "When humans can defeat a horse or bull that is the product of such a cross, they are deemed ready for a full sentient duel."

"I clearly need to learn more about rodeo."

Rifanel bobbed her head. "It will help you understand the

situation between Jeff Tophand and Fenarmin. Tophand had worked his way up to successfully riding second-generation sentient equine and bovine crosses, which is usually the requirement for humans qualifying for a sentient duel. Fenarmin was successfully defeating feline and reptilian first generation crosses, which is the requirement for sentient bulls and horses to qualify for a sentient duel."

"So they were both ready to go." Caroline swallowed hard. "Isn't it hard to see your mate go for one of those duels? To the death or severe maiming?"

"Oh, I had not completed a marital contract with Fenarmin at that time. Rodeo duelists do not sign marital contracts until they retire. I was Planetary Representative. But I was a fan of Fenarmin, not just because of his prowess at dueling. I saw him as my potential successor as Planetary Representative. If he survived a sentient duel."

"What happened?"

"Tophand and Fenarmin were scheduled to duel against each other. Then the training incidents happened. Fenarmin cracked a cannon bone when a non-sentient stallion—Rostar —crashed into him during conditioning gallops. Traces of a rella-based substance were found in both Fenarmin and the other stallion—testing happens after all such incidents. The injury resulted in disqualifying Fenarmin from sentient dueling."

"Just one injury would do that?"

And rella was involved. That's—interesting. I'd like to learn more about that!

"Have you ever watched a sentient duel?"

Caroline shivered. "Not in person, just videos."

"Both participants must be in top condition, because sentient duels are so grueling. Fenarmin wanted to continue with scheduling their duel. Tophand did not, citing the likelihood that Fenarmin would not be able to participate at his full strength, and that enraged Fenarmin. Then Logan

Easystar got into that fistfight with Tophand, concussing him as well as breaking *his* leg. Well. Tophand was no longer eligible to participate in a sentient duel. But that was too late. Those two have exchanged heated words connected to that canceled duel, multiple times."

"It seems—silly." Caroline picked up her cup again, staring into it. "After all, if they're unable to compete due to injury, that seems to be fairly straightforward. They can't compete."

Rifanel snorted and shook her head. "Males! We are reasonable females. I would like to see Tophand and Fenarmin move beyond their past. Yes, we are Councilists and you are Federalists. I must keep the best interests of my caucus in mind while being concerned about what is best for Hrwhinir and the Federation as a whole. There are—issues more important than a sentient duel that did not happen."

"The Ribonits and their lock on plant-based drug distribution," Caroline guessed. "That's one reason why you and Fenarmin were on Cartain looking for candidates, right?"

Would Rifanel bring up sentient planets? Geraint hadn't said one word about them since they had left Cartain, which made Caroline wonder about that brief mention about discussing them with Blackburn. It wasn't like Geraint to talk about his meetings, unless they were significant somehow.

"Exactly." Rifanel flicked her ears back. "Rella has uses on Hrwhinir. It is part of a combination of medications to manage equine digestive issues. But it was also used in a different formulation to drug Fenarmin and his attacker—a use we were not aware of until then. Fenarmin suspects that Tophand might have played a role in that incident. Even though the evidence does not point to Tophand." She stomped a forefoot again. "Males! So stupid sometimes. Fenarmin is biased against humans."

"I see." Caroline pressed her lips together. "And Jeff

apparently has no love lost for Fenarmin, either. Though he did praise Fenarmin as having decent policy ideas."

Rifanel flicked her ears forward. "That is promising. However, I suspect that it will take the two of us working together to get Tophand—*Jeff*—and Fenarmin to cooperate. Which is why I wanted to meet with you."

"I absolutely agree. From everything I have heard already, the Ribonits need to be audited."

"This is bigger than the Ribonits." Rifanel scratched her nose on a foreleg. "The Plasmoids and the Ethereal Confederation have a role to play as well. And as one who owes her sentience to the random acts of the elder Plasmoid scientists—I have many concerns. After all, they gave us sentience." She wrinkled her nose. "Hiding in their bubbles. Who knows what is really inside? Our old traditions say they were shapeshifters, even though they look like shapeless blobs. We do not know enough about the Plasmoids. Who is to say that their descendants might not also have a means to reduce sentience? Even though they claim it is not possible."

Caroline shivered. "What makes you think that they can reduce sentience?"

Rifanel turned her head to gaze directly into Caroline's eyes. "The fight between Tophand and Easystar did not feel right, just like the incident with Fenarmin and Rostar. Tophand was in better condition, and Easystar is not as good at fighting with his fists as Tophand. Tophand should not have been injured as badly as he was. As for Fenarmin and Rostar—Fenarmin should have been able to evade Rostar—he is much more agile, and Rostar is not normally that awkward."

"Hmm." Caroline tapped her chin with a forefinger. "I wonder if there was any substance testing done on Jeff and Logan Easystar?"

"None that I know of, alas. The formulation used on Fenarmin and Rostar caused a minor regression which should not have happened—Fenarmin is fifth-generation Converted, so allegedly nothing can reverse his Conversion status. But that substance did."

"That's not good." Caroline shivered.

"I have reason to believe that humans may be at as much risk as the Converted."

"If a substance can cause regressions in fifth-generation Converted—" Caroline's voice trailed off as she considered the implications.

This was a bigger problem than anything involving sentient planets.

"Exactly. So you understand why we need to find a means to move Fenarmin and Tophand past this feud. We have a more serious issue to consider."

"Absolutely."

ANOTHER THING TO consider after this discussion with Rifanel.

Look into the details of that fight between Logan Easystar and Jeff.

Caroline added it to her to-do list as the autoskimmer took her back to Main Central from Equine Sector. That, plus researching Rifanel's disclosure about rodeo species participating in sentient/non-sentient crosses. How common were these matings, and—were humans participating as well? What did that mean when it came to the division of Federation species between what was considered innately sentient and those who had been Converted?

I need to learn more about the details of Conversion and how it applies to the definition of "innately sentient" as opposed to "Converted sentient."

This investigation was something Caroline could do while traveling to Cartain, along with further research into the possible influence by Plasmoids in human prehistory.

Then again, humans were *particularly* good at finding substances that could temporarily reduce their level of sentience, alcohol being amongst one of the biggest offenders over the span of human history.

No matter what, this latest information wasn't something that she could consult with Dr. Knowledgechaser or Mars University about. The potential uproar that would be caused if the possibility of Plasmoids being able to remove sentience became known was not something that Caroline wanted to encourage. At least not until she knew more.

CAROLINE SETTLED into her cabin on *No Skies, No Limits*. She had a much smaller solo cabin for returning to Cartain. But it was still roomy, and quite different from her experiences when she first traveled from Mars University to Galactic Central, as just another lowly intern. Now she not only had a separate workspace from her bedroom, but full connectivity, with no restrictions, and a fully stocked kitchen. Nothing at all like being crammed into a four-block with cafeteria meals for a ten-turn, and only a few nodes of access time available, at a price that discouraged doing anything more than check messages.

Is this what my life is going to look like from now on, since I'm on the Congressional payroll?

Well, she could handle that. Caroline stretched, considering her schedule. No need to step outside of her cabin until time to disembark for the runabout. A couple of nodes spent working, then bed. Up again at 3:50 Node, work until sometime around 13th Node, and then—

Jeff had already sent her a schedule for her arrival. She was booked into a hotel in Cartain's capitol, Shrum, on Cartain's primary continent, Blass. The formal signing of their marital contract would happen at 6th Node next turn. The

Boss and her Conference would throw a celebration for Caroline and Jeff, and then...8th Node meant back to work, taking a flyer to meet with Crested Flyers and Upright reptiles on Wansa, the secondary continent.

A message chimed from her father, using her oldname, Agatha McKinnon. Caroline pressed her lips tightly together. While her father usually was more reasonable than her mother, *still—*

All the same, best to open it now. Get it over with, then forget about her family for a while. She had a candidate and future spouse to manage.

With a sinking sensation in her gut that had nothing to do with transiting through gatespace, Caroline opened the message.

—Dear Agatha,

Please forgive this final use of your oldname. As your father, I feel the need to at least say the name of my beloved daughter, one last time. After all, it was my own mother's usename, and, well....

Congratulations on your new role as assistant to the future Planetary Representative of Cartain. Unlike your mother and many of our family, I am well aware of Jeff Tophand and his duelist career. It quietly pleases me to know that you have at least that slight connection with duelists. Had things happened differently, I might have pursued a future in rodeo—but your mother caught my attention instead. And I am even more pleased that you are working for a Federalist, not a Statist. It makes me happy to know that I am not the only Federalist in our family.

There have been an unusual number of Plasmoid visitations to Earth of late. I don't know if this has any relevance to what you are doing for Tophand, but they seem to be spending quite a bit of time with Lara Wordtrust and Logan Easystar.

Ah, that probably means nothing and is just the rambling of an old man far too prone to see connections where they don't exist! All the same, considering your new role, I thought this was something you might want to bring to the awareness of the Federalist leader-

ship in the Congress. These appearances do not match Wordtrust's rhetoric as she runs for re-election.

I hold out hope that we might see each other again someday. But if not—soar, my beloved daughter, who is now Caroline Starshine.

Best,

Papa.

Caroline frowned at the message, rereading it.

After a few moments, she decided, and began drafting a carefully worded message to send to Rifanel and Geraint.

It might not hurt for the leadership of the Federalist and Councilist parties to know what their Statist counterpart was doing back on her home planet.

4

———

LEARNING THE NEW ROLE

C‍AROLINE'S FIRST-CLASS treatment continued onto the runabout carrying her to the Cartain capitol city, Shrum. While her cabin still had that antiseptic stink to it—*no getting around it, that's part of biosecurity protocols, especially when landing on a planet that is so dependent upon agricultural exports*—and was so small that she could almost touch the adjoining walls with her arms outstretched, her plush seat comfortably conformed to her body shape. She had access to the fastest comm tier. A well-supplied drink cabinet, though she would only have enough time for a cup of tea.

It was like everything she had experienced on a larger scale when traveling with Geraint, only in a solo humanoid cabin instead of dual-species-first-class.

Shrum's Central Station was the first stop for the runabout, unlike when Caroline and Geraint were traveling to Jeff's Interstellar Roundup Ranch just a few turns ago. When Caroline exited the departure lounge, a Crested Flyer wearing a loose-fitting navy-blue vest with the Best Planetary Accommodations logo stood next to the floater laden with her luggage, holding a printed sign with her name.

Caroline sighed with relief as she saw the yellow-handled

bright red floater holding her luggage next to the Crested Flyer. It looked to be the same floater that she had rented—not many were that intense red—and the neon green straps holding the bags had not been moved from when she secured them back on Galactic Central. Either that, or if any officials *had* decided to inspect her bags, they had put everything back the way it was. And at least on the same floater.

This was her first time making her own travel arrangements. Rutan had always made special *arrangements* for Geraint to have escorts and greeters when they traveled. Caroline hadn't been certain how well the process would work when traveling by herself. It had been Rutan's suggestion for her to buy brightly colored and patterned bags and rent as unique a personal floater with built-in luggage straps that she could find, so that there were no excuses for "accidental" baggage mix-ups. Or inspections.

Rutan's advice worked. A good thing to know. Not that it mattered, because once she and Jeff executed that formal marital association contract, then she would be able to travel with Planetary Representative spouse credentials, which were one step higher than simple Planetary Representative assistant credentials.

Just another one of those subtle differences between plain assistant and assistant with a marital association contract.

So many class gradations in the Federation.

Before working in the Congress, Caroline had thought that Earth was the only place clinging to hierarchical class structures, but this seemed to be a Federation-wide preference, especially in places where Statists—like on Earth, or Councilists—like on Cartain—dominated. Though Jeff's being a Federalist suggested the possibilities for change on Cartain. That had been one eye-opener during her internship.

She bowed to the Crested Flyer—*Zwold*, according to the name tag on their vest. "Hello. I am Caroline Starshine. Thank you for meeting me."

Zwold emitted a soft, pleased *scree*, much quieter than the Crested Flyers Caroline had met at Jeff's party. Their temperament, or the difference between party vocalizations and professional? That was something that she would need to learn, *fast*.

"Very glad to honor you, Ms. Starshine. I believe all of your luggage is on this floater. Would you care to check?" Its crest flared. "There are quite a few pieces."

Caroline had needed to bring everything she owned with her. There was no place to store her things on Galactic Central right now, with the transitions affected by Representative elections. She and Jeff wouldn't be assigned their final quarters until after his election was confirmed—and the terms of their marital contract would definitely affect these assignments as well.

Caroline glanced at the pile. Ten bags. She brought up the picture she had taken of the floater and its load before turning it over to the *No Skies, No Limits* staff, and compared it.

The original pale green four-piece she had taken to Galactic Central from Mars University was there. Check. Then the newer, six-piece bright pink floral set she had purchased in order to hold everything she had acquired or bought during this last ten-turn to reflect the difference between intern and assistant, still where she had placed them on the floater. Check.

Everything was there—at least the bags. The contents? Probably. Caroline had twisted a couple of straps into an innocuous-looking double wrap, per Rutan's advice, and those were unchanged.

After this, I'll be entitled to share a shipping container with Jeff. Higher security would then be required for both of them, so no more open floaters. But for this one trip—

"That looks to be right," she said. "Everything was placed on that floater except for my carryon. Thank you."

"Come this way." Zwold hooked the floater's loop handle

around the tip of its vestigial wing. It led Caroline to a waiting autoskimmer. The reptilian driver—another upright-walking person who reminded Caroline of a *T. Rex*, only smaller—deftly attached the floater to the hitch on the autoskimmer. Zwold tapped the back door open, bowing to Caroline.

She nodded her head in acknowledgement and climbed in, feeling awkward and slightly guilty because she had the big, luxurious space all to herself. Zwold joined the driver in the cramped front—she had not caught the name on the driver's vest.

Need to improve noticing staff names. Don't want Jeff to get the reputation of having a standoffish partner. Another thing Caroline had noticed in both Rutan and Ssgaldir. Both were gracious to any waitbeing, making a point of remembering their names. *Our behavior reflects upon Geraint* was one of Rutan's regular lectures to all the interns. She needed to remember that the same was true for the assistant and spouse of a Planetary Representative.

The driver activated the protective clear dividers around the passenger compartment as the autoskimmer pulled away from Central Station. Caroline shivered. It was one thing to see those barriers go up when she was with Geraint.

Another to have them go up around her when she was alone. She hadn't rated this level of security on her own as an intern, even head intern. Family security on Earth was completely different from this.

This is your life, now, Caroline, she reminded herself. *You are not just the assistant to a candidate for Planetary Representative, but tomorrow you become his spouse. A different life.*

A thought struck Caroline and she quickly checked her supply of credits. Tipping was expected on Cartain, unlike Galactic Central. Once she had reassured herself that yes, she had an adequate supply of Cartain credits to tip both Zwold and the driver, she gazed out the window. She had been doing a lot of reading about Cartain and its history, but now that she was on-planet, it was time to pay attention to her surroundings and actually *see* the place for herself.

If she had thought that Cartain was a mix of species just based on Jeff's party, Shrum hammered that point even further home. The variety of peoples on the street—and in the commercial district near the Council building and where the Best Planetary Accommodations was located—testified to the diversity of the planet. Rabbits, the smaller ones on platforms, more of those big waist-high rabbits here than had been at Jeff's party. Differing species of reptilians. Crested Flyers. Cattle. Horses. Other avian species that wore clothing— mostly just vests. And humanoids, with darker skins prevailing than on Earth.

Formal dress appeared to be the norm as they neared the Council district. High-collared, dark-shaded, fitted and fastened vests with bow ties on Crested Flyers, unlike the loose-fitting one on Zwold. Neck ribbons signifying profes- sions on other avians, horses, cattle, and reptiles. Only the rabbits lacked any signifiers, but well, that was how rabbits did things. One had to look at the insignia their interpreters wore to discern the roles of individual rabbits.

Unless they wore the solid black of Blackburn's inter- preter, marking his status as a high-level negotiator and— rumor had it—spy.

So glad I made the effort to get some nice formal outfits.

Another piece of advice from Rutan.

Places like Cartain with its class structure have some very rigid attitudes about dress. They may seem prudish compared to Galactic Central, but that is one of the things you need to know as a Repre- sentative Assistant, he had said. *Learn the codes.*

Well, she knew what prudish was all about from growing up on Earth, one of the most notoriously prudish places in the Federation. All the same, she was lucky to have access to someone with Rutan's experience. He had also offered to continue providing advice, both to her and to Jeff, as needed.

A glimpse of a peach-shaded Plasmoid's tell-tale protective bubble drifting into one building interrupted Caroline's thoughts. She leaned forward to rap on the divider between her, Zwold, and the driver.

"What building was that?" She gestured toward the entrance where she had just seen the Plasmoid.

"Headquarters of the Rella Protective Association," Zwold answered.

"Thank you." Caroline sank back into her seat.

Not the Rella *Producers* Association, but the Rella *Protective* Association. So what was the difference between the two? This was the first time Caroline had seen the name of the Rella *Protective* Association. None of her briefings had mentioned it. Perhaps Zwold had the name wrong?

No matter whether it's Protective or Producers, why would a Plasmoid be going into that building? The Plasmoids are supposed to be dealing with the Ribonits for rella! Not directly contacting rella growers on Cartain.

They turned a corner. Caroline inhaled sharply as she saw the Ribonit embassy, gaudy with curlicues and flourishes outlining every window in headache-inducing, neon-bright primary colors.

As near as she could figure, the Rella Protective Association's building backed up against the Ribonit headquarters.

Definitely something to ask Jeff about.

And when she quickly queried her comm, the Rella Protective Association came up as a valid lobbying organization, located at that street address. But—a crosscheck with the Rella Producers Association did not show any principals in common between the two organizations.

Hmm. Something to investigate, or is there a simple explanation? Jeff would know.

They pulled up in front of the Best Planetary Accommodations. Caroline raised her brows as she surveyed the building. Plain but simple and elegant lines, typical for a Best Planetary facility. Lots of white stone, chrome, and windows. Zwold opened the door for Caroline. She gathered her carryon, and stepped out. The driver unhooked her floater and handed its leash to Zwold. Caroline glanced at the driver's vest.

Balni. Not a personal name but a role—*driver.* Oh well. She supposed she was required to call him that.

Another thing to find out.

"Your suite is ready," Zwold said. "I will take you directly to it."

"No check in needed?"

"Not when a Best Planetary employee meets you at Central Station," Zwold said.

Caroline took a moment to tip Balni and thank him before nodding to Zwold. Given the size of her floater, she expected to be taken to a freight elevator. Instead, Zwold whistled up a privacy screen and took her through the main lobby, where— she groaned to herself as she spotted mediacams hovering inside. Zwold's screen was enough to keep the cams from approaching too close. But they could take her picture, shout out her name, and tag along. She definitely didn't want them following to her suite!

"What do you wish to do about the media?" Zwold asked. "They *would* like to interview you at some point."

Part of the job, Caroline. But—not this moment. Eh, give them a morsel. You can always blame space lag for not wanting to spend more time talking to them.

"I'll go ahead and say something brief."

Zwold bobbed its head and whistled the screen down. The cams approached.

"Ms. Starshine, what are your plans for Mr. Tophand's campaign?"

"Ms. Starshine, do you intend to pursue a marital association with Mr. Tophand?"

"What do you have to say about the latest rella thefts?"

She *wanted* to interrogate that particular cam, because she hadn't heard about *those*. But not the time nor the place. She could ask Jeff later.

Caroline held up her hand. "I'm glad to see all of you as well. But we—Jeff and I—will have a formal press conference tomorrow, after we sign our marital association contract." She flashed a quick smile, that faint but definitely promising one she had practiced for months in front of a mirror at Mars University, when her media relations instructor said that her expressions varied between too stern and unapproachable to far too vulnerable for someone with her political career ambitions. "For now, however, I'd prefer quiet. It's been a full turn traveling from Galactic Central, and I'm a wee bit space-lagged. I will be sending out a release soon confirming the time and location of our press conference."

She bowed and turned away from the cams. Zwold whistled the screen back up. To her surprise, the cams bobbed away.

That was *not* the way mediacams behaved back on Galactic Central. Or Earth, for that matter.

Could it be that Cartain media was simply more polite?

A BOUQUET OF GREEN, magenta-edged roses waited for Caroline in her suite. After tipping Zwold and having them leave the floater just inside the door—after all, she expected to only be in this room for one night—she turned to the flowers. First order was to scan them quickly.

No poisons, radioactives, or electronic devices. Good.

Caroline inspected the flowers more closely now. She had never seen green roses like this—a Cartain specialty? An old-fashioned card envelope leaned against the vase. Caroline picked it up. Good heavyweight quality cream-colored paper, with the IRR brand in embossed silver on the front. The note card inside was of the same weight, the IRR brand centered on the top, a thin silver line around the borders.

I HOPE your travel from Galactic Central was pleasant. Would you do me the honor of meeting me in the hotel restaurant at 13:50 for a slightly late Third Meal? It is just before our marital association, and perhaps we should celebrate?

—Jeff

Caroline frowned thoughtfully.

After all, they *were* going to be signing a marital contract next turn. And while signing a formal marital association contract wouldn't be the same thing as a full-blown wedding would be on Earth, it *was* worth celebrating.

She had to wonder where this relationship would go. Strictly professional, like Rutan—and possibly Rifanel—had?

Or leave things open for the possibility of more to happen between them? She had only met Jeff that one day. They barely knew each other.

And there were just as many instances of Representatives and assistants being full marital partners as there were formal associations.

Best not to close off any possibilities too soon.

She sent an acceptance to Jeff.

NEXT, of course, was puzzling over what to wear to Third Meal with Jeff. Luckily, the Best Planetary Accommodations routinely provided a guide in the projection menu titled *Best Choices for Appropriate Local Attire in Specific Situations*, no matter what planet the hotel was on.

Thankfully this guide was keyed to Cartain and not generic. Something she would expect from an accommodation of the quality of Best Planetary, but one never knew. Caroline had heard plenty of horror stories during gossip sessions with other interns. The quality of service, even for a top-of-the-line lodging franchise like Best Planetary, could vary.

Caroline chewed her lower lip as she studied her options. She hadn't expected that the hotel would have something exactly on point—after all, how many others would be in her exact circumstance? She finally settled on *Third Meal in hotel, negotiations with fiancé before contract ceremony* as the closest to her situation. None of the options displayed were for formal marital alliances as opposed to full partners, or reproductive contracts.

All the same, she skipped over to *business, negotiations over meals* to gain a further perspective. It all came down to necklines and hemlines, and—no, her black dress would not be appropriate at all for this circumstance. Cartain assigned black clothing to high formal attire and business wear. That dress would work better for the contract signing tomorrow, as she had suspected.

Green and magenta were the typical colors worn by humanoids to announce marital engagements on Cartain—*ah ha, that matches the roses.* Which made sense. It would be appropriate for her to coordinate with those colors as closely as possible.

But still, Caroline wished she had been able to access this reference when shopping on Galactic Central. Her formal green dress was too stark for a date of this type, and that neckline! Caroline shook her head. Shshrit had gone shopping with her for the additional clothing needed. She had encouraged Caroline to buy this dress, but the neckline was so much lower than Caroline preferred—and definitely lower than was acceptable on Cartain for unmarried women, even engaged to sign a marital contract. After next turn, she could wear it without criticism. But for this meal?

Probably not the best idea.

And yet—the dress was almost the same shade as the green roses. Plus, had her magenta scarf made it into one of the easily-accessible bags, or had she used it for filler and cushioning for fragile items? That would soften the dress slightly and provide a solution for the neckline.

Caroline dug through the suitcase where she had packed her accessories, and unearthed not one, but *two* magenta scarves. One was narrower and plain, while the other was floral—peonies, Earth flowers—and a mix of magenta, pink, and black.

Yes. She could wrap the floral scarf around her neck and tuck it in. That would make the neckline acceptable for this occasion. The other scarf was long enough to tie around her waist and soften the dress's severe lines. And if she tapped on the dress to adjust the shade of green—Caroline experimented, and discovered she could turn the dress into a shade that matched the green roses. She couldn't do the same with either scarf due to their Earth origins, but they were already close enough in shade to the magenta edging on her roses. Perfect.

That decided, she pulled together her outfit for the contract signing tomorrow, a second outfit to change into for their meetings after that, then sat down to catch her breath and think about what she was doing next.

To her surprise, she was nervous about meeting Jeff for Third Meal.

***

HOTEL SECURITY WAITED for Caroline as she stepped out the door. Humanoid in appearance, dark-skinned, a couple of shades lighter than Jeff, wearing a navy dress suit that shimmered with the presence of a security shield woven into the fabric. He silently held his badge up for her to check his identity and Caroline scanned it.

Confirmed.

Still without speaking, he snapped up a security bubble, this one thicker than the one that Zwold had provided for her earlier, and only enclosing her, not him.

"Come with me." His voice was a monotone.

As Caroline followed the security man, she wondered if he was human, cyborg, or android. His behavior and tone of voice suggested the last two possibilities—something she hadn't expected to see on Cartain. Androids and cyborgs that couldn't be easily discerned from full humans generally were limited to places like Earth and Galactic Central, due to expense and maintenance requirements.

Surprising that Best Planetary would spend that kind of money here. It spoke to a regular clientele that was wealthier and more sophisticated than Caroline had expected, given Cartain's lack of stature in the Galactic Federation and its reputation as a less-sophisticated world.

But the Best Planetary managers were no fools.

Come to think of it, normally neither Rifanel nor Geraint would have come here in person to recruit a candidate. They would have farmed it out to one of the secondary Party chairs. Cartain is not exactly a Galactic hotspot.

Or if it was a hotspot of some sort, the knowledge was one of the Federation's best-kept secrets.

Because of rella?

Entirely possible.

THE SECURITY STAFFER escorted her to a restaurant table separated from general seating by dark red velvet-looking curtains. He parted the curtain and, as Caroline walked through the opening, snapped away the obscuring security bubble.

Jeff smiled and rose to meet her, bowing low before kissing her hand. Caroline shivered at the brush of his lips. It sent warm tingles through her.

"You look beautiful tonight," he said.

"You're quite handsome yourself." She surveyed him. He had opted for a formal green suit, with jacket lapels lined in magenta satin, and a pale green shirt underneath. His pocket square and tie were both magenta. It looked good against his dark skin. She wondered if that was why this color was preferred for these situations—it was certainly flattering to the darker-skinned humanoids of Cartain.

Jeff laughed and sat. "You've done your research, I see. Those colors are perfect."

"The Best Planetary usually has a local clothing guide, keyed to status, profession, and species. And their proprietary guides are often more accurate than the references even on Galactic Central." Caroline gestured to her neckline. "This would be appropriate on Galactic Central given that we're engaged to sign a marital association contract, but not here, nor on Earth. Fortunately, Cartain does not have issues if you wear a scarf like I am."

"Which—what are the flowers on that scarf?" Jeff half-rose, bending over the table to peer closely at it. "I don't think I've seen ones like that."

"Peonies. From Earth."

"Ah." He raised his brows and leaned back. "Oddly enough, I've never spent time on Earth. You would think, given that rodeo originated there, that there would be at least one performance there by the Galactic Rodeo. Nope."

"That's because Earth is very restrictive about allowing Converted species on the planetary surface." Caroline frowned at that memory. "I have family who pride them-selves on never, ever, having anything to do with exploiting other species. I have heard plenty of bigoted comments about other species, Converted or not, from them. But oh, they are so proud of not being exploiters."

"That's sad." Jeff shook his head. "I suppose they're as pale as you?"

Caroline snorted. "I'm a scandal to my family because I do things like go outside and get tan. Mother used to get so mad at me for bicycling and hiking. When I started up dust skiing on Mars, she had a huge fit."

"Interesting." Jeff smiled. "Because your father—Alan McKinnon, right?"

"Right." A chill tightened her stomach. *How would he know Dad's name?*

"He's one of my biggest Earth fans. He led my fan club."

Caroline whistled. "Dad never breathed one word about it."

Jeff chuckled. "He was one of the first to congratulate me on hiring you as my assistant—but he also wanted to know what my intentions were toward you. I told him we were signing a formal association contract, but that for more information he would need to talk to you."

She exhaled. A relief, of sorts. At least her father hadn't come flying in demanding that they commit to a reproductive contract. Unlike what her mother would do. It was surprising that Alice McKinnon *hadn't* shown up yet—on the other hand, even with Hart Mercantile credentials, the trip from Earth to Galactic Central took a ten-turn.

"He didn't bring up anything about being your fan in the message he sent me. I—am not on the best of terms with most of my family, though Dad has separated from my mother. I had no idea that he was one of your fans."

"I figured as much, once I looked into your background."

"Classic stodgy Earth-bound upper middle class," Caroline said bitterly. "According to my mother, I was supposed to do nothing more than have babies and support my spouse. In the proper retiring manner. No career beyond managing a household, at least until I had popped out enough babies, according to whatever contract I signed."

Jeff rolled his eyes. "I understand. By all rights, I was supposed to do nothing more than just be grunt labor in a rella plantation processing plant. Oh, I might eventually ascend to a managerial position, but there are so many of us —" He waved a hand. "It was one of the Converted processing plant managers who talked me into trying out for the Rodeo. Joharn thought I showed riding talent. He had been a bronc for the Rodeo, and showed me a few moves. I owe a lot to him. He never made it past the higher-level non-sentients as a duelist. But he knew a few tricks that served me well, as a rider."

"Wait, you got training from a Converted horse?"

"It happens more often than anyone will tell you." Jeff paused as the autoserver ducked between the curtains. He raised his brows questioningly at her. "Would you like to order something special to drink, or do you prefer not to have alcohol? I like a nice sparkling wine—we have some good vineyards on Cartain."

"I have no problems with alcohol in moderation." Caroline skimmed the appetizer list. "Do you eat meat?"

"Only certified non-sentient."

"Good. Same here." They had a *lot* to learn about each other's personal preferences. "What would you recommend for appetizers?"

"The mushroom and cheese mini pastries are absolutely fantastic," Jeff said. "And the relish tray. I'd avoid the meat appetizers—not that good, mostly aimed at off-worlders, and not from Cartain. But for the main course, the hnaftl is local, a freshwater fish from the mountains of Blass. Anadromous, they spend several cycles in the ocean before returning to their lake homes."

Caroline nodded and tapped in her order.

The autoserver left.

"Training with a Converted horse is more common than not?" she asked.

"And vice versa. Humanoid sentient riders will work with Converted horses and bulls to train them to perform better."

"Very interesting." Caroline paused. "Are you aware that there are second-generation Converted and non-sentient crosses? Some that hope to be fully certified as new members of a Converted species?"

"Now *that* is one of those things that isn't widely known outside of rodeo circles." Jeff eyed Caroline. "How did you find out?"

"I met one of those crosses, from Rifanel's herd."

"Ah." Jeff nodded. "Yes. There's a lot more of that going on than is realized. The challenge is to have the cross breed true to one or the other parent. Otherwise, you end up with a smarter-than-usual result that gets frustrated because they can't make that final jump to full sentience. My mare Star— the one you met in the barn—is a first generation cross. First-gens struggle a lot more than second-gen crosses."

"I—see." Caroline hesitated. Was this a safe venue to ask Jeff about the Plasmoid she had seen in downtown Shrum?

No, she decided.

The sparkling wine arrived. After the autoserver opened the bottle and Jeff poured for both of them, he raised his glass.

"To us," he said. "And our future."

"To us and our future," Caroline echoed.

After sipping from his glass, Jeff leaned back. "You've agreed to our formal contract with the possibility of a further commitment. How do you want to handle our situation?"

"There are many possibilities." Caroline studied the bubbles in the magenta-shaded wine. So much of the plant life here had that coloring. "I'm—not in a hurry to form a relationship beyond a professional association. So far. But I am open to the possibility that we could become more to each other."

Jeff nodded. "Very much the same here. We barely know each other, and, well—there are many issues to consider for the future."

"Agreed. We have much to discuss once we are in a secure location." She toyed with a spoon as the server brought their appetizers. "What happens after we sign the contract? I know we're supposed to go to Wansa, but after that? I—brought everything I own with me. It's all on a floater, but I have no idea where I am supposed to stay once we've signed the contract."

"We'll be back on the ranch in time for Third Meal," Jeff said. "There's a suite set up for you. We'll be returning to the ranch after our appearances each turn." He grinned. "There are advantages to Cartain being as small as it is. Ranch staff will take your floater after the ceremony, and you can settle in once we're back from Wansa. Any other questions?"

"A couple. I noticed that my driver from Central Station didn't have a name other than *Balni.* Is that normal for staff to only have their role as their title?"

"What species?"

"He looked kind of like an Earth dinosaur, only smaller. About my height."

Jeff nodded. "Yes, that's normal for the Uprights. They work their way up to a name." He scowled. "I don't like it, myself, but that's how the Uprights do things. Very rigid. Very structured. They tend to keep to themselves on Wansa. Assorted Converted privileges are given to them by their elders as they spend the amount of time in lower-level jobs that is considered appropriate by their elders."

"I—see."

Their first course arrived. Jeff waited for the autoserver to leave before continuing.

"It is part of a spiritual quest," he said. "The Uprights

have a very detailed faith centered around the original Plasmoid scientists. They don't choose to share it with non-Uprights, no matter what species we are."

"All right." Caroline took a careful sip of her soup. A fruit-based soup with a pleasant tang. "The other question—when I arrived at the hotel, one of the mediacams asked me about rella thefts. Is that an issue?"

Jeff nodded. "Absolutely so. It's part of what we're going to be discussing with the Uprights in our meeting with them next turn. I'll brief you on our way, after the ceremony. One thing at a time."

"Thank you."

"Hey, it's important that you understand what's going on." He grimaced. "There are certain levels of—complexity that we need to consider."

"Like the Rella Protective Association?"

His eyes widened. "That's one piece of it, and best discussed in a different setting."

She took the hint, and steered the discussion to less controversial subjects.

SECURITY ACCOMPANIED Jeff and Caroline to Caroline's suite.

"This is a promising beginning." He ducked his head slightly, smiling as they stood outside her door. "I knew there was a reason for that impulsive request I had for you to serve as my assistant. Even though I didn't know much about you at the time, the things you said, plus your being Geraint's head intern spoke to the likelihood that you would be good at what you do. What I've heard about you since then just confirms my original judgment."

"Thank you. I'm flattered."

"Then I will see you next turn. Pick you up at 5:50, then

return here after the Boss's ceremony to change and collect your things before we leave for Wansa."

"I will see you then," she said.

Now what?

He bowed to her, deeper than the normal acknowledgement of a Planetary Representative's assistant.

Caroline returned his bow, with equal depth.

Jeff laughed. "I am so looking forward to our future." Another bow, and he stepped back. "I'll watch until you've run the scan and secured your door."

"Thank you." Caroline slipped inside the suite. Her scan didn't show that anyone else had been in her rooms. She secured the door, then dropped onto the couch, slipping off her shoes.

This was going to be an *interesting* position, for certain.

And Jeff?

Well, she definitely liked the man. Whether that would be enough to eventually consider a more intimate marital contract than what they were signing next turn—would remain to be seen.

5

MARITAL CONTRACT TURN

Mother would have an absolute fit about this dress.

Caroline smirked at her image in the mirror. Her knee-length and form-fitting formal black dress accentuated her curves without forcing them into a desired shape. That meant the little bulges around her waist showed. But—unlike Earth designers, the ateliers on Galactic Central weren't obsessed about wasp waists and hourglass shapes. If anything, it seemed as if they were absolutely *thrilled* to be designing for a human woman with broad shoulders and a chunky body.

Guess my shape is closer to the majority of species that wear a lot of clothing than the typical Earth woman they see.

Caroline wouldn't get started on thinking about her mother's probable reaction to her wearing *black* to her marital contract signing, with only her peony scarf from last night to add a sense of color.

And if that wouldn't be enough to irritate her mother, then there was the snug fit of the dress. *Flaunting your fat* would put Alice McKinnon in a complete tizzy and public decline that would require multiple turns and many many special gifts to overcome—if Caroline were still on Earth and needing her mother's approval.

Adding *wearing black to a marital contract signing* to *flaunting your fat* would probably mean a span of Mother being out of sorts. And even more gifts.

Well, her mother's opinion didn't matter anymore, fortunately. Frankly, black looked better on her than white. And this was just a formal marital association contract without reproductive access, though the option would be open for further amendment, should she and Jeff choose that later on.

But here she was. Signing her first marital contract, as part of a job that would gain her power and respect. Wearing black. Flaunting her curves.

You were so wrong about everything, Mother.

Her biggest problem was her heels—higher than she usually wore. Hopefully she wouldn't fall off of them and embarrass herself.

A knock on the door.

Caroline rose, her heart pounding hard in her ears.

This is it.

Even though this ceremony was just about signing a formal association contract, not a full-blown wedding, she was still nervous.

She checked the door cam. Jeff stood in the center of its viewing field, dressed in a formal black swallow-tailed morning coat with the lapels edged in magenta, black shirt, and magenta cummerbund. He held two black, magenta-edged black roses in his left hand. Four Security—all humanoid—flanked him. And there were mediacams—of course, the signing of a Planetary Representative candidate's marital contract would be a significant occasion that would be transmitted throughout the Federation of Solid Peoples. Especially since a rodeo duelist was involved.

Caroline exhaled. She clipped her ID purse to her wrist. Then she opened the door.

Jeff bowed low, offering her one of the roses. "A rose for my soon-to-be-spouse."

She took the rose and bowed low to him, recognizing the words of the Cartain marital contract ritual that she had been reviewing for the past node. "I accept this rose, and your offer of marital association."

Offering the rose was the crucial part of the formal marriage proposal on Cartain. No matter what had been said or done or agreed to beforehand, no marital contract at any level was considered valid until the proposing spouse had offered the rose. It was based on a ritual amongst the Crested Flyers that extended into antiquity, even before the first Flyer Converteds.

Jeff took Caroline's hand as they walked to the elevator. Their security raised a transparent bubble around Caroline and Jeff so that they could be seen but protected from attacks as they marched through the lobby to their transport. Caroline focused on gripping Jeff's hand for support as she wobbled on her high heels, looking straight ahead as people swarmed toward them, murmuring.

"The rose. They're carrying the rose."

"That's Jeff Tophand and his new assistant. They're carrying the rose!"

"The rose. Jeff Tophand's marrying his assistant. The rose."

Caroline kept a soft smile on her face, nodding at the assorted species that darted in close to snap pictures, then fall back, even though she wanted to flinch away from the bright flashes. From the whispers and general tone of the crowd forming around them, Jeff appeared to be well-liked.

Not surprising, especially here in Shrum, on the major continent of Blass, where most of the humans on Cartain lived. Now Wansa—well, she hoped that positive feeling would be very much the same, since that was where most of the Crested Flyers lived. She would get some idea of what *that* continent was about soon.

They processed around the main fountain so that the two

of them could be observed, before heading for their autoskimmer. Another facet of marital contracts on Cartain, especially for those in political positions. Public exposure. Witnesses to their commitment. The black rose meant formal association, open-ended. If this had been a love match, then the rose would have been magenta-edged yellow, and both Caroline and Jeff would be wearing matching shades.

Well, yellow wasn't her best color. And she had never dreamed about a happily-ever-after, unlike her sibs.

At last they reached their autoskimmer—as big as the one she had ridden in yesterday. Caroline sighed with relief. She was getting better at walking in these shoes, but all the same, she would be happier once this was *done.*

"Here we go," Jeff said softly, after they settled in. "Any second thoughts?"

Caroline shook her head. "Just a little nervous, but that's to be expected."

He grinned. "Me, too. If anything, the formal contract makes me more anxious than if this were a love match."

"Same here, because I don't know what to expect."

Jeff laughed nervously. "Yeah. I mean—for me this is completely new. Oh, I know what our contract says. No reproductive or sexual obligations. Specific privacy and financial requirements to each other because of our work responsibilities. Particular Congressional benefits available only to maritally contracted Representatives and their spouses. But what does that mean in application? In real life for the two of us?"

"Oh, I know. I have the same questions. My parents weren't a love match. They signed a formal open-ended reproductive contract—typical for Earth. Formal association contracts aren't recognized there." Caroline sighed. "Those reproductive contracts are difficult to end because of financial obligations to children. My parents never formally separated because they couldn't meet all of the divorce terms that their parents demanded as part of their contract, but my father left my mother cycles ago. They married young. My sibs fulfilled the obligations to my grandparents. I was the odd one out. The youngest and a spare, just in case my youngest brother died before he made an alliance. I would think my family would be relieved that they don't have to find a place for me in the family structures, but—" She shook her head.

Jeff tightened his grip on her hand. "I didn't realize that about Earth."

"There are reasons why I didn't want to go back to Earth, and my family is a big part of it. I've always been the outsider. My father would have tried to find me a position upon graduation, but it would always be on sufferance. A place for the misfit that they couldn't marry off because I'm fat and don't have a pretty face."

"You? Fat? No way. When I take you to meet my parents, my mother will yell at me because you're too skinny. You're fit, with curves. And your face—" He studied her for a moment. "I would call it the face of a strong woman who isn't afraid to reach for what she wants. The face of a powerful woman who is much more interesting than a pretty face."

Caroline laughed. "Oh Jeff. You're flattering me." It felt good, though. That her formal contract partner could say such lovely things about her—that was amazing.

"Earth standards are weird. I have never understood them. You couldn't have gotten a job on Earth without using your family connections?"

"No. The positions that would be available for me on Earth if my family couldn't find a slot to stick me in?" Caroline shivered. "I'd have sooner taken a job in a Galactic Central pleasure palace if I hadn't gotten a position in the Congress. That would be much better than returning. I never want to go back to Earth. It isn't my home anymore. Not that it ever really was—I always felt out of place there."

"I'm sorry." He exhaled. "I have always loved Cartain.

Even though my family's history here—well, my parents jumped the broom. They never had the money for anything formal. For me to be able to sign a marital association contract —well, I'm the first one in my family who has the prestige and the finances to do it on my own, without help. So this is really, really big for me. And my family."

She squeezed his hand. "I hear you. I'm glad to be a part of a really special occasion for you. Sounds like your family is going to be thrilled, too."

He smiled at her. "Oh, they will. I had already become successful beyond their wildest dreams when I was climbing the ranks as a duelist, especially since I was sending money home so they could buy themselves free from debt. Then I bought the Interstellar Roundup Ranch and started purchasing family contracts, then freeing them so they could work on *our* properties and buy neighboring ranches themselves, not be someone else's property and provide their profits. For me to become a Planetary Representative—and have a nice person that I'm signing a formal marital association with —that's not something they considered to be at all possible."

"Well, it appears that this relationship—and everything else—is going to be what we make of it."

"Definitely so."

The autoskimmer glided to a stop.

Caroline swallowed hard.

Here we go.

In spite of all her—no, *their*—anticipations and fears, the signing ceremony was almost anti-climactic. It took place in the Conference chambers, a smaller version of the Congressional chambers on Galactic Central, with the Boss of Cartain herself presiding. Jeff and Caroline proceeded down the main aisle while the Conference—consisting of several representatives from each of Cartain's major sentient species—and other eminences gathered around.

As they approached the dais, Caroline noticed that the support pillars in Cartain's Conference chambers were angled to support windows that let in the soft yellow light from Cartain's sun. But it wasn't as glaring as a similar construction would be at Galactic Central, probably because Central's sun was brighter and harsher, requiring more protection. Cartain's sun was closer in color spectrum to Earth's. She liked the effect, especially the glow it cast over Terrianna Abbott, the Boss of Cartain, a tall, heavy-set woman with tightly curled salt-and-pepper hair and a big smile. The Boss wore an elegantly draped magenta dress with black piping, the reverse of Jeff and Caroline's outfits.

Caroline focused on the Boss's warm brown eyes as she swore loyalty and obligation to Jeff instead of looking directly at him. A quick side-glance showed that Jeff was focusing in the same way, both when she was vowing, and when he spoke his own oaths in return, so she wasn't out of line. Earth weddings had those getting married speaking the vows to each other. Not so with the formal association contract vowing, apparently. Or if she was wrong, then they were *both* wrong to be focusing on the officiant rather than each other.

After the vows, they placed their roses in a vase, then signed the contracts.

The Boss practically *glowed* when they were done. "It is my greatest pleasure to announce the formal marital association of Jeff Tophand and Caroline Starshine." She gestured as staff opened the great double doors behind the dais to reveal a reception area with multiple feeding stations, very similar to Jeff's party except that this was inside. "I invite everyone to join us in enjoying a minor celebration in honor of Caroline and Jeff."

Jeff and Caroline led the procession into the reception area. The tone of the gathering rapidly switched from an unfamiliar formal ceremony to the sort of reception that Caroline knew from the Congress. Brief congratulations to her and Jeff, further congratulations on his nomination, then lobbying. She ended up slipping her comm out of her purse and tapping in notes. Jeff pulled his comm out of his pocket and did the same. Before long, they were separated, being lobbied by different groups. Caroline listened, took notes, but was careful not to speak for Jeff. Not until they had time to compare notes and consider what was being asked.

At last, a chime sounded from both of their comms.

"Excuse me." Jeff moved toward Caroline. "We need to leave. Appointments in Wansa."

Two women around her—Lorelei and Rhea, paler than the others—wrinkled their noses. Caroline was already annoyed with them because they kept prying about what she planned to do on her wedding night. She hadn't encountered anyone so snoopy about sexual matters since she left Earth. The degree to which they refused to acknowledge that existence of formal marriage associations didn't necessarily mean sexual access and their gossipy speculations about Jeff's possible performance—maybe such conversations were appropriate on Earth. Not so much elsewhere.

"Wansa? Why would you bother with that place? Not many humans there," Lorelei said, tossing her head so that her mane of blonde hair flew conspicuously. Caroline ignored her. Maybe such a move would gain Lorelei attention on Earth.

Not here. The behavior made Caroline suspect that the two women were also from Earth.

"Planetary Representatives need to consider the needs of all species, not just humans," Jeff said quietly.

"Huh!" Rhea snorted. "Figures from someone like *you*."

Jeff tightened his lips.

"He's right," Caroline said, choking back anger. She didn't dare lash out, didn't dare lash out, didn't dare, it wouldn't be good for Jeff's image or hers either, *don't react don't react don't react....*

Lorelei sniffed, an all-too-familiar predatory expression crossing her face, just like the bully girls Caroline had known on Earth. "I don't know why you had to marry someone like—"

Too much.

"We need to get going." Jeff grabbed Caroline's hand and not-so-gently pulled her away before she could snap back at Lorelei.

"Sorry you had to deal with those two," he said once they were safely in the autoskimmer. "Hadran and Mosky decided to go to Earth and find themselves some brides. Boy did they ever find themselves some brides."

Aha. I called it, all right. From Earth, and those two brought all the old Earth prejudices with them.

"That makes sense, then. I was wondering why they didn't understand the concept of formal association contracts." Caroline pursed her lips. Rhea and Lorelei were most likely castoffs from somebody's family. "I didn't get their last names, but they definitely struck me as—well—they were in the position I would have been in if I had needed to return to Earth." She grimaced.

"Works for bureaucrats like Hadran and Mosky, I suppose." Jeff tapped his fingers on his armrest. "So. I have a change of clothing in the flyer. Could I impose upon you—borrow your bathroom to change into something more appropriate for Wansa? I could change in the flyer if you're uncomfortable with me doing that. However, it's tight quarters. No privacy. And the air currents can bounce those flyers around so it isn't safe."

"No need to explain. Of course you can use the bathroom to change. We're contracted now!"

He shrugged. "Just wanted to check and ensure that I

wasn't crossing any boundaries. After all, this is just a formal contract."

"A contract that's supposed to make the appearances of such situations easier," she reminded him with an arched eyebrow.

"Still want to make sure that you were all right with it."

"Thanks."

There was going to be a *lot* the two of them would need to negotiate with regard to intimacy over the next few days. Not that she was in any hurry to rush this sort of connection.

Jeff's innate politeness would make their relationship *much* easier. But at some point she would need to remind him that she had been raised with brothers, after all. Men were *not* an alien species to her.

———

It was a relief to swap out heels for solid flats, and the dress for nice slacks and a tunic. Caroline wore a long-sleeved shirt with implanted sunscreen over her tunic. Once Jeff came out of the bathroom, wearing nice jeans and a lightweight long-sleeved, yoked shirt in a pale blue, she darted in to finish gathering up her toiletries and apply sunscreen to her face. A broad-brimmed hat added to her ensemble.

Next was ensuring that she had her bigger handbag loaded with her tablet, a more powerful comm than she could carry in her wrist ID bag, and other necessities to hold her through the day. MediScanner, with various antidotes loaded for poison, antivenom (keyed to common Cartain venomous animals), bandages, and other emergency health needs. A water bottle and several nutribars, plus a flask with whisky. TempClothing spray in case something happened to either her clothes or Jeff's. Hairbrush and comb.

Jeff leaned against the desk and watched her secure each

item in her handbag. "You're ready for just about everything."

Caroline added a zapper, then closed the bag. "That's what I was taught to do. Can you think of anything else to add?"

"The kitchen sink?" He smirked at that.

She burst out laughing. "It does seem that way, doesn't it?"

"It's not gonna be too heavy for you to carry, is it?" He sounded concerned.

Now it was Caroline's turn to smirk. "Mini-floater's built into the bag so it weighs almost nothing, even if I put more into it. We'll see how well it works, but—I was told this was the best security and working bag available when I bought it on Central. Rutan—Geraint's assistant—recommended it."

"Then it's probably pretty darn good."

"I would think so." Caroline slung the bag over her shoulder and picked up the floater's leash.

"Ken will take care of that once we're outside so that we're not dragging it around behind us all turn," Jeff said. "Makes it easier. He'll make sure it gets into your suite at the Ranch."

"Good." Caroline exhaled. "I wasn't sure what was going on, and based my plans on needing to haul this stuff around with us. You said something about staff taking my luggage to the ranch, but I wasn't sure of the timing."

"No, no, no. Taking the floater along wouldn't work at all," Jeff said. "We're gonna be traveling faster than those runabout shuttles or autoskimmers do, and the flyer would leave your luggage scattered all over Blass if we tried it. Ken's gonna drop us at the flyerport, then take your stuff back to the house. He manages house and family stuff, along with his wife Wilma. He's—my little brother," he added. "But he kept the family name, unlike me. Ford. So you aren't surprised when you hear it later on."

"Keeping things in the family?" A good thing to know. "Including Moonshadow's interpreter Trace?"

Jeff nodded as he opened the door. "Pretty much. Trace is Ken and Wilma's kid. He showed an early aptitude for becoming an interpreter, and paired with Moonshadow once he graduated from interpretive school. Moonshadow had finished his management training at the same time. Since I was looking for someone to manage the property, it made sense to hire the manager who had just been paired with Trace. Makes everyone happy. Moonshadow's family comes from a couple of ranches over, so that's even better. Makes it easier to coordinate harvests and equipment use, and every-one's families get to hang out together."

"All right."

When they were outside, a tall man with skin slightly darker than Jeff's met them.

"Caroline, this is my little brother Ken. Ken, this is Caroline."

Ken bowed to Caroline and she reciprocated. He took the floater leash. "All of this is yours?"

"I had to bring everything I owned from Galactic Central. No place to store it until Jeff and I return—had to move out of intern quarters. Plus I needed to bring equipment, books, everything I'd need for our time here."

"Understood." Ken grinned at her. "Would you want us to unpack for you?"

"If you could just take the luggage off of the floater and return the darn thing to RentalSave, that would be great. I can take care of unpacking myself—there's office equipment and files in there that I should be the only one to handle."

"Understood. We'll get that floater back to RentalSave right away, then—I'm betting you had to put a good-sized deposit down, coming from Central."

"Yeah."

"Then Wilma and I'll make sure it's returned quickly. Plus

we'll have a good meal ready for you two once you've returned."

"It could be late," Jeff cautioned. "Lots of issues to cover on Wansa."

"Even more reason for us to make sure you two are well-fed at the end of the day," Ken said. He attached the floater leash to the autoskimmer.

Unlike the vehicles that Caroline had ridden in yesterday and earlier today, Ken drove an unpretentious autoskimmer that clearly served as a farm vehicle, with only a front seat and cargo space behind, which was already filled with feed bags and other items. Jeff motioned for Caroline to take the middle position in the front seat. She settled in, relaxing.

For the first time since she had come to Cartain, she didn't feel like she was out of place.

This was more along the lines of what she expected from working with Jeff Tophand, not the fancy hotel, the huge vehicles, and all the luxury. And *this* was exactly what she had been hoping for when she accepted this position. Not so much formality. A chance to get completely away from the life she had grown up with.

Once they were settled in the private flyer and on their way to Wansa, Jeff eyed Caroline. "So you had some things you wanted to discuss in a secure setting?"

"Yes. I saw a Plasmoid bubble entering the Rella Protective Association office building when we drove by it yesterday. I then noticed that the Ribonit cartel headquarters are just about exactly behind the Rella Protective Association."

"Now *that* is interesting news." Jeff tapped his lips with his index fingers. "You sure about that bubble? There are other species who use them besides the Plasmoids, for privacy rather than protection."

"I've seen enough Plasmoid bubbles on Central to recognize them easily." Caroline thought further. "It was anonymized, so no clue about the status of the Plasmoid it carried."

"Hmm." Jeff frowned, staring out the window with a thoughtful expression on his face. "The Protective Association is frequently at odds with the Producers Association. None of the growers have anything to do with the Protectives; that organization is oriented more toward expanding markets for rella and eventually growing it off of Cartain. But they're not exactly what I would call a—well—trustworthy organization. They're more interested in trying to set themselves up as intermediaries between the Ribonits and the Producers. But we—the Producers—don't have much to do with them, because of past scandals. Money-related. If they're starting to work with the Plasmoids, that's even more concerning. Especially since rella theft is becoming more common. I've heard rumors but nothing that can be substantiated."

"That was another thing. One mediacam yelled a question at me last night about rella thefts."

"Hmm. That is concerning. But why would they think you would know something about it?"

"Because I'm your assistant and spouse?" Caroline shrugged.

"Possibly." Jeff stroked his chin thoughtfully. "The rella thefts have primarily been from Crested Flyer and Upright ranches on Wansa. What we hear during this trip could be interesting."

"Definitely." She paused. "I was somewhat surprised by the security from the Best Planetary that escorted me to Third Meal last turn. Everything I'm seeing, especially around Shrum, suggests that Cartain is not the backwater that some in Galactic Central seem to think it is."

Jeff raised his brows. "Tell me more."

Caroline took a deep breath. "I could not figure out if that security was human, android, or cyborg. Security staff of that level is not cheap. You're more likely to see them on Earth or Galactic Central—but they aren't common even in those places. Best Planetary Accommodations isn't a stupid corporation. They wouldn't have security like that on site unless it was necessary, and worth the expense."

"True. There aren't many businesses that run that level of security here. But—things are changing and fast. I've—had questions about it myself the last cycle or two, since I bought the Ranch. Saw a lot of things on a lot of planets when riding with the Rodeo. It's enough to make me wonder, especially with you spotting that Plasmoid."

"Exactly. Add to that having Rifanel and Geraint come here *themselves* to recruit candidates. Party leaders just don't do that. Not with the apparent status that Cartain has."

"Another thing I was wondering about. Rifanel—well, it's entirely possible that Fenarmin insisted on recruiting here himself. Which would trigger Geraint's decision to come here as well, and bring you as a possible assistant candidate."

"Which was *not* something Geraint discussed with me, by the way. I thought that recruiting you was a test of my abilities, since I had only one span left in my internship."

"I've heard plenty about Geraint Ssprin's canniness," Jeff said. "*You* might not have been aware of his intentions, but all things considered—including your father being one of my fans—I have no doubt that he hoped this would happen." He chuckled. "I did some research on old Geraint. He's placed a lot of his interns as assistants with Federalist Representatives. He's a canny old crocodile."

"I didn't think I had the opportunity, given that I'm human," she said quietly. "Geraint doesn't usually take on human interns."

"Well, he saw *something* in you, Caroline Starshine, and I think he was right."

She blushed, the heat rising in her cheeks.

Jeff laughed again. "You're cute when you blush."

"One of the drawbacks of being light-skinned, I suppose," she said.

"*I* think it's cute."

She flushed even more.

THEY MADE several stops on Wansa. The first two of their three meetings were uneventful, predominantly with Upright reptilians. As they went into the meetings, Caroline remembered what Jeff had said the night before about Uprights and their mysterious, Plasmoid-centered faith. Could they be dealing secretly with the Plasmoids?

After those two meetings, though, she dismissed Uprights colluding with the Plasmoids as a possibility. The Uprights were concerned about rella theft, even though there weren't that many incidents happening in their fields so far. And the political instincts of the Uprights, from their discussions and their questions, did not strike her as being as complex as those of Geraint's kin from Tsfalnel.

Just because they're all reptilians does not mean they think the same, Caroline! she scolded herself. After nine and a half spans on Galactic Central, she wasn't *quite* as assuming about other sentient species as she had been before leaving Earth for Mars University.

But she clearly still had prejudices to overcome.

"I had been thinking the Uprights were colluding with the Plasmoids, based on what you said about their faith last turn," she said to Jeff as they headed for the third and final meeting. She yawned and shook her head. "Sorry! It's been a busy turn."

"That it has been—and you've been traveling. I admire how well you're handling space lag."

Caroline shrugged. "Rutan told me a few tricks to handle

space lag back when I first started my internship, and they work well for me. But I'll be feeling it next turn."

"Well, our next few turns will be spent traveling on Blass," Jeff said. "You'll get a chance to catch your breath. And as for the Uprights—in spite of the Plasmoid element of their faith, they tend to be law-abiding. They are *not* my first candidates for collusion, especially since the Rella Protective Association doesn't do business with them. No," he said slowly, thoughtfully. "If anything, I think the connection is human. Not Crested Flyers, not Uprights, not cattle or horses or rabbits. Human."

"That would make more sense," Caroline said.

Humans didn't have the best historical record in the Federation.

CRESTED FLYERS MADE up the bulk of their third and last meeting, and they were *annoyed*. Which, when it came to the Flyers, was not a good thing, because Caroline could barely make out what they were saying, thanks to all the squawking of overloaded translators. She winced, anticipating what editing the videos from *this* meeting would require.

Fortunately, Jeff was able to calm them down so that Caroline could take better notes. But she was grateful for her recorder and the cams, because she would need to listen and relisten to what was said at first to figure out what they were saying, when it seemed that every one of the Flyers was screaming and squawking.

The news the Flyers had to share was troubling. Their rella fields had been targeted by thieves over the last few turns. This was an even more blatant theft than before—the rella was cooked in the fields and processed right in the open, instead of being stolen and processed elsewhere.

Suggests small-capacity transports, she thought.

Not just rella fields had been impacted. A couple of Flyer chicks had been attacked by the thieves when they were out working in the fields. Caroline rapidly realized such behavior violated everything that the Flyers stood for. While their younglings worked in the fields, the Flyers considered them to be sacrosanct from any disputes that the adults around them might be engaged in.

She and Jeff ended up visiting the injured chicks. One was expected to recover. But the other—it took every bit of will that Caroline possessed to keep from reacting to how badly burned that chick was. Its translator had been removed, so that it could only cheep feebly. The Flyers nursing it clearly understood what it was saying, and were distressed.

Caroline shivered once they were back on the flyer and headed for the Interstellar Roundup Ranch.

"What happened to that chick was awful," she said.

"Yeah. I don't think the poor thing will last the turn." Jeff scowled. "Until now, the raiders haven't killed anyone. Just bad injuries. This—" He shook his head. "The Boss is reluctant to act against the raiders and I don't know why."

"Collusion? Blackmail?"

"No to the first," Jeff said slowly. "Terrianna Abbott is as honest as the turn is long. It's why she keeps getting re-elected as the Boss. She's honest, straightforward, and has enough income in her own right not to be tempted by any bribes. If anything, I'd say Robbie-boy is more likely to be bribed into not doing anything. No," he repeated. "The Boss isn't a willing conspirator, if indeed she's at all involved in whatever's going on. I'd bet the Ranch on that. Something has frightened her. Significantly so."

And while their conversation shifted to other topics, those words kept returning to Caroline.

Whatever could frighten someone like the Boss of Cartain? Somehow she had a hard time believing that something could seriously intimidate the proud, dominant woman who had conducted their marriage ceremony.

But something had.

Caroline hadn't the faintest idea what that could be.

———

AS PROMISED, even though it was Fourteenth Node and nearly bedtime, Wilma and Ken had a warm meal waiting for Caroline and Jeff, along with a celebratory cake and a small bottle of sparkling wine. After a bit of teasing, they withdrew, leaving Caroline and Jeff alone in the dining room.

"So what did you think about your first turn on the job?" Jeff asked.

"Considering it started out with signing our marital contract, then ending with a bunch of Flyers screeching at us and—that poor chick—" Caroline's voice trailed away. A message advising them of the chick's death had come through while they were flying back to the Ranch.

"Yeah," Jeff said. He looked worried. "But overall?"

"Overall, I'm thrilled to be here. I see a lot of possibilities, and many good things we could do for Cartain," she said.

She was rewarded by one of Jeff's big grins.

He escorted Caroline to her suite, and bowed before leaving. Caroline looked around once she was inside. The hallway door opened onto a large, airy space that looked out upon the Ranch—not that she could see anything outside after dark. Her luggage was piled in this room, clearly an office, with desk, charging station, docks for her comm and tablet, two stuffed chairs and a couch, and a large round table with four chairs. Another door was midway along one wall. Caroline opened it to discover a big bathroom, with soaking tub as well as a shower.

A second door in the bathroom opened upon the

bedroom. A huge bed, with a vanity and dresser, as well as a huge walk-in closet.

Caroline grinned.

Nicer quarters than Mother has.

Oh, she was really starting to enjoy her new life.

I did the right thing by leaving Earth behind.

A light flared outside. Caroline went to the window. Something in the sky. It slowly passed over the Interstellar Roundup Ranch, then continued on.

Probably just a runabout heading for Shrum.

All the same, it seemed uncannily close to what the Crested Flyers on Wansa had been describing as happening before their fields were attacked.

I'll tell Jeff about it at First Meal.

6

———————

PERSONAL COMPLEXITIES

Caroline wasn't certain about what to expect for First Meal, probably because by the time they reached the Ranch the turn before she was tired, jangled, and hadn't thought to ask about routines. After a shower and dressing casually in tunic and loose slacks for breakfast, like she would do in Galactic Central intern housing before beginning the turn's work, she went in search of tea and food. Cartain was supposed to have an excellent tea, Green Skrilsit, and she hoped Jeff had some. Otherwise, she would need to figure out where to buy Skrilsit. Which shouldn't be too hard to find on Cartain, right?

Jeff was in the kitchen, sitting at a rough-hewn table unlike the nicer polished one they had eaten at in the dining room the night before, sipping from a green porcelain mug as he read from his tablet. He wore a snap-button shirt and jeans, like she had seen in his Rodeo pictures, except this clothing looked faded and worn. A matching teapot with another cup sat on the table in front of him.

Is that his First Meal dress before working on the ranch? I thought we had some appearances today—surely he isn't going dressed like that?

He looked up and grinned as she entered, gesturing toward the pot. "Brought out a cup for you. Green Skrilsit."

"I was *hoping* to have some Green Skrilsit." She grinned back at him.

"Good. Grown here on the ranch. Drink as much of it as you want." He stretched. "It's the only tea I have on hand right now."

"I didn't realize you were a tea producer as well."

"Only for our own consumption. Pretty common on Cartain to grow our own Skrilsit because it's easy to cultivate in a kitchen garden. Everyone does it, so there hasn't been much of a call for commercial cultivation. And everyone has their own way of processing it. I follow what the Crested Flyers do."

"That's surprising." Caroline set her tablet on the table and filled her cup, raising it to her nose, inhaling that lovely, lovely fragrance. "I would think Green Skrilsit would be a great cash crop. Everyone I've known who's tasted Skrilsit raves about it."

And she was going to be able to drink Skrilsit *regularly*? Another unknown benefit of this job—this *relationship*.

"Skrilsit doesn't do well in commercial cultivation and while it's easy to process, it's not that durable. Overprocessing makes it taste like yuck, and there's a fine line between just right and too much. Definitely doesn't travel well off-planet except for small quantities because what works for processing on a large scale for export just wrecks the flavor." Jeff shrugged. "Plus, Skrilsit doesn't earn as much as rella or the other medical plants for all the work it takes to try to sell it off-planet. Even though Skrilsit has its fans, breaking into the tea cartel is more of a challenge than it's worth. It's a limited market."

"I see." Caroline looked around, trying to figure out where to find food. "What should I do for First Meal?

"There." Jeff gestured to the counter. "Sweetener on the

counter if you want it, not sure what you want for breakfast but there's fruit, yogurt, and cheese in the chiller and pastries, several types of cereal, and bread in the preservers."

"Thank you." Caroline exhaled as she studied the chiller and preservers. She settled for granola with yogurt and flowerberries. Flowerberries were another item found only on Cartain. She had sipped flowerberry wine a few times—it was rich-flavored, sweet, tangy, and spicy all at once. To be able to actually *eat* the berries was wonderful. She had tasted them once, at a banquet she had attended at Galactic Central with Geraint.

Probably another thing that doesn't ship well unless you're willing to pay outrageous prices.

Caroline sat down and tapped up their schedule, frowning when she saw it was blank. Hadn't she filled it out last turn? Her work might not have saved.

Darn it. I need to figure out what went wrong.

"Um." Jeff coughed, sounding awkward as he continued. "I changed things around on our schedule. Sorry. I knew you worked hard on it. But you were pretty space-lagged by the end of the turn, and, well—last turn was pretty busy. I figured it might be a good idea to give you a chance to settle in on the Ranch, go on a tour of the place, and for us—to maybe get started on learning more about each other."

"But what about the campaign?"

Jeff grinned again. "Our trip to Wansa was *quite* successful, as was our contract ceremony. Check the messages. We can afford to coast for a turn or two."

Caroline switched from schedule to messages. She raised her brows at the large number. Then she started flipping through them.

Reference to her graciousness. The two of them as a lovely pair. Comments contrasting her and Jeff to Robbie-boy, favorable to them and not Robbie.

A pair to perfectly represent the confederated species of Cartain, read one comment.

Both Jeff and Caroline listen to us. So different from Robbie-boy.

No arrogance. Even though it was their marital contract turn, they took the time to come to Wansa and listen to our problems instead of taking a holiday. That comment came from one of the Upright activists, Blodd, who had expressed concerns about discrimination toward Upright females.

They may be human, but they show genuine concern about our issues. That comment came from the mother of the Flyer chick who had died. Caroline swallowed hard at that. She looked up.

"Wow," she said.

"Wow, indeed. So, as the candidate-soon-to-be-Planetary Representative himself, I proclaim this to be a Jeff and Caroline turn. I bet you want time to get yourself set up properly in your suite, and—I'm sure that Red and Star would be happy to get out of the field for a tour." His expression went solemn. "I also want Star's feedback. Ken and Moonshadow both report seeing a strange light above our fields during the dark. Nothing set off our sensors, but—"

"That's what the Crested Flyers reported before they had thefts from their rella fields," Caroline finished for him. "I saw it too, Jeff. It matched their description." She shivered. "The one from the surviving chick in particular."

"I missed it." He frowned. "Then I definitely want to ride the fields. The fact that we couldn't pick something like that up on the sensors worries me."

"Me as well."

After all, at least until they decided to terminate their marital contract—if they did—she had an interest in the Interstellar Roundup Ranch.

More than that, she didn't want to see anyone else harmed like those two Flyer chicks had been.

AFTER FURTHER CONVERSATION, and realizing that checking on the fields wasn't urgent, Caroline decided to take a couple of nodes to unpack before taking a tour of the ranch.

Jeff offered to help, but Caroline waved him off. "Take care of your work. I'm sure you have things to do. I'll call when I've reached a stopping point and am ready to go out."

"I do have ranch paperwork," Jeff admitted.

All the same, he kept popping in as she worked, mostly just asking how she was doing and to bring her more Skrilsit, enough to give her a pleasant, energetic buzz. Her personal items—clothing, toiletries, and so on—were easily organized. Then it was unpacking equipment and putting her office together. Printer. High-security comms with locked channel to the Congress. Video editing setup. Audio setup. She could record campaign events with her portable cams and process them here. Which was something she needed to do with yesterday's footage.

Every piece of tech she set up required checking and testing. Oh well, it was part of the job. The one thing she was lacking was a working desk that was *hers*—there was one which was part of the suite, but it wasn't what she wanted. Sooner or later, she would need to buy some furniture of her own. For now, what was here would do.

"Did you want some pictures or something for your walls?" Jeff asked during one of his visits.

"I really haven't had the credits to purchase the sort of art I want," Caroline admitted. "Now that I'm on Cartain, I think the things I get should be locally produced, by as much of a variety of artists as I can find."

That brought another grin. "I have a few things in storage you might like to look at before you start buying work. Some Upright vases. Flyer feather weaves. Rabbit-woven basketry. Bloohowt's lead cow Marianet specializes in painting, using the end of her tail as a brush. And human-made things, as well. My collection might give you some ideas, but meanwhile, these bare walls—" He gestured at them. "They make my eyes hurt."

"Oh?"

"Come on, I'll show you what my rooms look like."

She hesitated. "I—um—"

"I'll behave. I promise." He gave her a questioning look. "Unless you're ready to move beyond a formal contract?"

Heat rose in her cheeks. "I—I—uh. No. I'm just being silly. Let's go."

After all, she *was* curious about what Jeff liked. They *were* now formally married. The conditioning that said *don't go to a man's room alone in case you lose your virtue* didn't apply anymore. Virtue wasn't a commodity Caroline needed to guard, now that she had signed a marital contract. She could do this, even on Earth. *She was married.*

Jeff studied her for a moment, then nodded. "Come on."

She followed him.

The contrast with her suite was significant. Instead of pale walls and stark, utilitarian furnishings and décor, Jeff's suite was painted in bright golds, greens, and reds. Abstract wall hangings, some with feathers, stones, and shells, along with brightly colored paintings, covered the walls. Heavy, dark brown wood-framed chairs and a couch with black velvety upholstery sat at the edge of a zig-zag patterned black and white rug. Plants in ceramic pots rested on solid side tables, along with ceramic vases, realistic rodeo-themed bronzes featuring bucking horses with several different species of riders, intricately woven baskets in shades of green, brown and purple, and exquisite, deeply-colored glass sculptures in green and purple.

Jeff's working space was a replica of an old rolltop desk from Earth, with tablet dock and projection discs built in.

"Wow," Caroline murmured, looking around the space.

"It's lovely, Jeff. Looks very comfortable and engaging. I like it better than what I have."

He grinned. "Your suite is your space. If you want the walls to be a different color, then go ahead and plan it. If you don't like the furniture you have, well, that can go into storage and you can buy something else."

Caroline frowned. "I don't think I'd have the time to shop and decorate." She remembered what redecorating could be like—Mother changed out her décor several times a cycle and that was a process that ate up at least two ten-turns. And when Alice McKinnon went into a remodeling frenzy…oh, that could end up being almost an entire span's worth of time with workers and living out of bags, moving from room to room and then returning to layouts that were sometimes confusing.

"My sister Darla would be happy to consult with you and contract the work." He waved a hand at the room. "She did the painting and the basic design. I've just added pieces as I've seen fit. And, well, I've seen what the intern quarters look like on Galactic Central. Pictures, anyway. I didn't know if you really preferred that aesthetic or not, so when I had your furniture set up, I kept it to Earth Modern."

"Oh Jeff. I appreciate your concern. I'm not an Earth Modern person, however, but you wouldn't have known that. I would really like something more like this." Caroline looked around the room further. "Not quite these colors, but something that isn't sterile and bland."

Jeff snapped up his comm, flicking a contact out of it to her comm. "Here's Darla's number. Give her a call. You can work in here if you need to take your equipment down while your place is getting painted. I should have brought it up sooner, before you went to all that work of setting up your office. Stupid of me."

"Not a big deal. How expensive is her work?"

"You're family. Discount, plus she was asking me what I could give you for a marital contract gift."

"I couldn't ask her to just *give* me her services," Caroline demurred.

"She used my space as advertising. I'm sure she'd love to do the same with yours. Call her. She'll be disappointed if you don't."

"Then I will," Caroline said.

Besides, since it appeared that Jeff's sister was a design professional, having Darla work on Caroline's office would probably make for good promotion for them as well as her. Caroline turned around slowly. So what in particular did she like about Jeff's décor?

All of it.

Everything was unmistakably *his.* A reflection of who Jeff Tophand was.

But did she have that sort of awareness of *herself*? What Caroline Starshine was?

"Good." Jeff shifted his weight and glanced down at his feet, suddenly seeming awkward and uncertain instead of his usual confident self. "This feels—I don't know. Unusual. I— keep thinking that I should be spending more time with you, the two of us doing things together. I don't know how these formal marital associations are supposed to work. I have some idea about how full marriage with reproductive rights operates, yes, but then we would already know each other before the contract and ceremony."

"I don't know quite what to do either," she said softly. "Formal marital association without reproductive access isn't an Earth thing, and I don't know what the boundaries are. I don't know how much we're supposed to connect outside of our work selves, given that we're also filling a political role. I know how to be an assistant. I just don't know what happens beyond the professional. Between us."

"So we're both learning," Jeff said. "I looked around for

guides to how formal associations work and couldn't find any. I'm—kind of uncertain about how we do this."

"I asked Rutan, and he said it's what we make of it." Caroline swallowed hard. "I don't—I know he and Geraint share quarters at Galactic Central. But they both have other spouses, that don't come to Central except for the most formal occasions."

"Well, we will learn what works best for us. I look forward to it." Jeff exhaled. "It's almost Eighth Node and time for Second Meal. Did you want to talk to Darla before we eat, and then we can go riding?"

"Certainly."

AFTER MANY CONGRATULATIONS and much gushing, Darla assured Caroline that she would *love* to work on a design for Caroline's quarters. They agreed that she would come to Third Meal, and plan to review possible designs afterward.

After Caroline hung up, she realized that Darla already felt more like a sister than her own sibs. Telling? Certainly both of Jeff's sibs that she had met so far were much more friendly and accepting than she could imagine her own sibs being toward Jeff.

And since Darla was going to be redecorating, Caroline didn't need to get too fussy about unpacking further. She ensured that what she needed to perform her job right now was unpacked and ready to use. Then she headed to the kitchen, where Jeff was already putting the final touches on the meal that Wilma had left for them.

"You were a hit with Darla," Jeff said over Second Meal. "But she told me that she already had been talking to Ken and Wilma about their impressions of you. Sounds like half my family is going to show up here for Third Meal."

Uh-oh. Caroline tensed. "How formal an occasion will this be?"

"Formal? My family? Unlikely. What you're wearing will be fine—unless we get too messed up while riding. But the weather projection says it's going to be nice. Not too hot, not too cold, no precipitation. Shouldn't be too much of an issue."

"I'm nervous."

He grinned. "Don't be. Wilma and Darla will have already talked to Mama and filled her in on what you're like."

"Yikes."

"Oh, you've made a good impression." He stretched. "Ready to explore?"

Caroline finished her tea. "Of course. But this for riding?" She gestured at her tunic and slacks. "I thought it might be a little dressy."

"For today, it's all right." Jeff peered under the table. "Your boots will work for this round, though we need to get you some sturdier boots with a higher heel for future rides. Working boots and dress boots as well, because we'll probably have some Rodeo appearances. But what you are wearing has a heel, and they don't look too dressy, so the stirrups won't mess them up. Just put on a long-sleeved shirt like the one you had on last turn. If you don't have a casual one, I can loan you one of mine."

"Could you?" The thought of wearing *his shirt* sent a small tingle through Caroline. But her long-sleeved shirts with sunscreen were dressy, and she wasn't certain she wanted to wear them on a ride.

"Sure. Give me a tap."

Caroline bit her lip as Jeff left the kitchen. She didn't know that much about riding horses—about horses, period. However, this was going to be part of her life for at least a few cycles.

Jeff returned with a checkered snap-button shirt in blue and green. She slipped it on over her tunic and left it unbuttoned, though there was plenty of space should she have chosen to snap the buttons.

So we wear the same size.

It felt strangely intimate to be wearing his clothing!

You are part of a formal marital contract, she reminded herself. *It's allowed.*

"Have you ridden horses before?" Jeff asked as they walked to the field where the party had been held. He had put on a worn, black, broad-brimmed hat and handed her another one before they left the house. Like the shirt, it fit.

Like the shirt, it felt *so intimate* to be wearing Jeff's hat. Was that what married people did? Share clothing sometimes?

"Not really. I did lesson sims and a couple of real trail rides with Dad. Mother was always raising a fuss about me being outside too much and getting tan." That had been back in the days when Mother still had dreams of marrying Caroline off to some heir to improve the McKinnon family status.

"You're probably best with Star." Jeff leaned on the fence and whistled to the horses, who were poking around where the feeding stations had been during the party. "She's one of those first-generation sentient/non-sentient crosses."

"Is that why you like to have her check things out, like you were telling me?"

The herd began to run toward the fence—five horses of differing shades of brown, red, and black. Caroline was glad that she was on the opposite side of the fence from them.

"Yeah. She's also good with novices. She'll take care of you." Jeff moved to the gate, extracting some treats from his pocket. "Stay back. Red and Star are well-behaved, but Blaze —that's the little chestnut guy—is still just a two-year-old and doesn't always cooperate. He gets excited about treats. You need to learn more about horses before you do much around him."

"Got it."

Jeff went through the gate, handing out treats before he opened it wider, enough to let the horses through. "Red. Star. Outside."

The two horses went through the gate. The smaller red horse with the long white stripe down his face—Blaze?—tried to follow. Another red horse with black mane and tail squealed and thrust her head and neck in front of the little horse, driving it back.

"Good work, Mona," Jeff said quietly to the black-maned horse. "Keep him in line."

The horse—Mona—female?—snorted and tossed her head. Jeff laughed and fed her an extra treat while Red and Star waited. Then he came back out, securing the gate.

"Going for a ride," he said to the horses. Red snorted and half-reared, tossing his head, then took off in a run for the barn, Star trailing behind. Jeff laughed. "I think the old man's telling me we haven't been riding enough lately."

Jeff offered his arm to Caroline and she slipped her arm into his. It felt odd, but—they had done this at the meetings last turn. And at the party. So why was she fretting about it now? After all, they *were* married.

He tilted his head toward her. "Are you all right? I noticed you seemed tense about us walking like this last turn, but I thought it was just that you were nervous about doing it in public and not at a party."

"Yes. I'm all right. It's just—" she hesitated before continuing. Did she really want to share this about herself? *You're married to him. Formal contract but for real.* "I—um—I've never walked with a man like this. Except for you."

"Arm-in-arm? You feel okay with this much contact?"

"Yeah. Yeah. It's just new to me."

"You didn't even walk arm-in-arm with dates?"

She flushed. "I've never dated. Not even in college. Not at Galactic Central. You're the only man I've done this with."

"Wha-a-t?" He stopped dead, staring at her.

Caroline fumbled for words. "Mother kept pretty tight control of me when I was on Earth," she finally blurted. "And Mars was still too close to Earth for me to get too—wild and crazy without worrying about her showing up and pitching a fit. Plus I was so desperate to get away from Earth that I didn't want to risk anything that might mess up my chance to escape. So I didn't date. And at Central—I just don't know the right things to do on a date. How to act. How to stay safe—I heard plenty of stories in college. I was so afraid of making a mistake. It was safer just to avoid dating."

Silence as he kept staring. Had she said too much? Was her inexperience going to be a problem?

"No dating. At all." Jeff shook his head. "Oh, Caroline. That's just—I had no idea."

"I had to remain pure until Mother married off all my sibs, because I might be needed for a business alliance."

"And yet Earth doesn't do formal marriage alliances, just full reproductive contracts." Jeff exhaled. "That's awful. So you were expected to—not date? What about going out in groups?"

"Not allowed either. I had to stay pure."

"Dear—" Jeff shook his head again. "So you were basically chattel for your mother to trade off for alliances. What was she thinking?"

Caroline shrugged. "My mother did not meet my father until the day that they married. It's a normal situation for anyone in the same social class as my family. I couldn't consider going to Mars University until Mother made all the alliances for my sibs, and even then she threw a fit when I took the internship with Geraint at Galactic Central."

Along with discarding my family name and taking a usename that reflects my goals. That really got to Mother.

"That is—all right. That explains some things." Jeff urged her gently along, once again walking side-by-side. "Is this going too fast?"

"No. But I have a lot to learn."

"As do I, it seems."

What does he mean by that? How much experience does he have?

They arrived at the barn. The horses stood in the alleyway next to their stalls, facing toward them, Star in front. Jeff disengaged his arm from hers.

"Star. Come meet Caroline again," he said quietly.

The big black-brown—*no, Jeff said the color is dark bay*—mare approached them, head low, ears forward. She stretched out her neck and head, extending her light brown nose. Caroline remembered giving her a treat the other turn and held out her hand. Star sniffed Caroline's hand, then nudged it gently.

"She's telling you it's all right to come close." Jeff's voice was soft.

Caroline moved closer to the big mare. Star raised her head and nuzzled Caroline's shoulder, then took a big whiff of Caroline's neck.

"She's getting your scent," Jeff murmured. "She'll know you from now on. Star, take care of Caroline. She is part of my herd and is a beginner."

Star flicked her ears toward Jeff. Then she delicately backed up to where she had been standing.

She understands what he's saying. That was startling—Jeff's direction and Red's response was one thing, because Caroline expected *going for a ride* to be one of those phrases that a horse might understand. But what Jeff had said to Star just now? That required some sort of language comprehension.

Remember what you learned about Converted species. This is an animal on the verge of being eligible for the current form of Conversion, restricted though it is because she's only a first-gen cross.

"Good girl," Jeff said. He walked over to a shelf holding brushes and held one out to Caroline. It was soft, made from some sort of firm but flexible gel, and two-sided with a center opening that she could slide her hand into. Little knobs were on one side and very small teeth on the other. "Start with this one. Then go to this one—" he pointed to another row of brushes. "Those have stiff bristles. Don't use the first brush or these on her face or legs. The bottom shelf has soft brushes, which are what you want to use on face and legs."

"Thanks." Caroline slipped her hand into the first brush. Star raised her head and began to wiggle her upper lip as Caroline brushed her neck. She burst into laughter because it was clear the mare enjoyed the brushing. Jeff looked over at them and grinned.

Soon enough, it was time to saddle and bridle Star. Jeff guided Caroline through the process, showing her how to fasten the saddle's cinch without overtightening it. Star lowered her head for the bridle and opened her mouth as Caroline fumbled with the top of the bridle, holding onto the bit so she wouldn't bang it on the mare's teeth. The mare delicately took the bit from Caroline's hand. Once Caroline got the bridle over her ears, Star shook her head. Caroline stepped back, startled.

"She's just getting the headstall where she likes it," Jeff said. "Star's picky about how it sits on her head."

"Headstall?"

"The part of the bridle that isn't the bit or the reins."

"Oh."

After that, it was a matter of walking with Star to the mounting block. Star stood still while Caroline carefully eased herself on. Jeff adjusted her stirrups.

"You don't need to take too tight a hold on the reins," he said. "Cluck to her and squeeze your calves gently against her side to walk off."

Caroline swayed a little as Star walked away from the block. Jeff stood next to Red, his arm over Red's back, as he guided her through the cues to guide Star.

"Not bad," he said finally. "You have a good sense of balance in motion."

"I used to skate a lot when I was a kid. And skied on Mars."

"Skiing. That'll do it. Skiing and horseback riding are similar when it comes to balance." He swung up on Red's back without a saddle or bridle. "Let's go."

They headed for the fence separating the pasture around the barn from the cultivated fields and went through a voice activated gate. Jeff pointed out the different stages of ixtnatal, then rella growth as they rode by each field.

"The ranch is bigger than I thought," Caroline said. She would have continued speaking, but Star stopped abruptly, raising her head high and snorting. "What's wrong?"

"She senses something. Give her a looser rein. Star, show us."

The mare headed for the gate leading to the field beside them. Jeff and Red sidled up to the gate—this one wasn't voice-activated. He bent over to open it. No sooner had he and Red pushed it open wide enough for Star and Caroline than the mare trotted through it. Caroline dropped the reins and clung to the mare's mane, trying to keep from bouncing out of the saddle. Star shifted to a canter, and Caroline nearly slid off one side. She grabbed Star's neck as the mare skidded to a stop, raising her head high and snorting.

A scorched, steaming circle bigger than Jeff's house was in front of them.

"Damn!" Jeff and Red halted next to them. Jeff slid off and headed for the circle. Star lunged in front of him. "Star, damn it, I need to see this!" He started to go around her, but the mare grabbed his shirtsleeve in her teeth.

"Jeff, *don't*." Caroline couldn't keep her voice from trembling as she pointed at the circle. "It's growing! Something's crawling along the edges—no, it's cooking the plants."

Jeff froze in place. "How is it doing that without an open

flame?" He patted Star's nose. "*Good* girl. Red. To me." He swung back up on the horse. "This isn't what the Flyers and the Uprights have been talking about. It's something else." He snapped up his comm. "Moonshadow. Ken. We have a problem in the Far Reach field."

"Wha-what's that?" A blue-shaded teardrop shape, invisible until that tap, rose from the center of the circle, the pointed end touching the ground, seeming to vacuum up the steaming plants.

"That's a Plasmoid ship! Damn it, they're cooking the rella and extracting the drug—I've heard about this but never seen it before—Moonshadow, we need Planetary Defense, now!"

Stealing the crop—our crop!

No wonder the Flyer chicks had been burned. And those chicks had tried to stop the ship—there had to be a means to keep the Plasmoids from stealing any more rella!

She had to do something. But what? Star shook her head, snorting again. She pawed at the ground, muscles tightening under Caroline. A faint sickeningly sweet scent rose around them. An unfamiliar anger rose in Caroline.

Intruders. Bad intruders. Not right. Not on our land. They have to go.

Jeff and Red turned away from the field. "Caroline, we need to get out of here! If the wind shifts and we breathe more of that rella vapor, we're in trouble!"

Caroline couldn't move as she stared at the shimmering ship. Somehow they needed to stop this. *Somehow.* The chicks had managed to drive off the ship attacking their fields—she and Star were bigger than those Flyer chicks. Certainly they could manage to drive this ship away, couldn't they?

As if Star had read her mind, the mare tensed, pinning her ears flat against her head. She bellowed. Then she charged straight toward the tip of the Plasmoid ship. Caroline grabbed Star's neck to keep from falling off, disregarding Jeff's frantic yells behind her. The world dissolved in bright colors as the giant teardrop rose. Star reared, screaming, striking at the tip with both forefeet. She connected. Hot, wet leaves fell on them.

Then everything turned shadowy around Caroline. She—no, *they*—were falling, falling, into a dark well of stars.

SHE HURT ALL OVER. Caroline blinked. Where was she? Not her suite at Jeff's. The colors around her were dark reds and greens, a big wall hanging in purple and gold with shimmering feathers and shells on the wall across from the bed.

"I don't think she's taken any significant harm, Jeff," an unfamiliar voice said.

Caroline blinked again, looking around. It was hard to focus, and everything seemed to shimmer.

"What happened to Star?" she managed to croak.

"Caroline. Thanks be to the first Void." Jeff's voice was shaky. "Star is all right. But by all the black holes in the Galaxy, what were you thinking?"

"Had to stop it," she mumbled. "Our rella. We couldn't let them take it."

"It's just rella," Jeff said. "If anything had happened to you…." His voice trailed off and he patted her hand. "By the stars, Caroline. Inhaling that much rella is dangerous for both humans and equines. I don't know what got into Star. She stopped me from going into it, but why did she attack the ship?"

"I had some unfamiliar thoughts about how they didn't belong. Then I remembered the Flyer chicks. They tried to stop the Plasmoids stealing their rella. I thought that Star and I were bigger than the chicks and we wouldn't be hurt as bad as they had been. After that, we charged at the ship."

Motion caught Caroline's attention and she turned her

head. An older woman with short, tightly curled gray hair and features similar to Jeff's studied a scanner.

"She's had enough of a rella exposure to cause a potential mind linkage with Star," the older woman said. "That might have been enough to make Star disregard her natural caution and go after the ship, especially if she was already agitated by the Plasmoid's presence. Which fits, especially given Caroline's description about unfamiliar thoughts. We know that Star is possessive about the land."

"I didn't know that rella exposure could cause mind linkages," Caroline whispered.

"Only in certain species—equines are one of them—and only if the horse is close to Converted status. Since Star is a first generation cross, yes, it's possible." The older woman frowned. "We may have underestimated her abilities."

"Well, we can fix that now, if Star's not too traumatized. What about Caroline? Is she all right, Mama?" Jeff asked.

"She'll be fine after a good sleep." The woman—must be Jeff's mother—smiled at Caroline. "This is not how I intended to meet your contracted spouse, Jeffrey! Caroline, I'm Darcy, Jeff's mother. You'll be a bit disoriented for the rest of the turn, I'm afraid. We put you in Jeff's bed because it's not as bright in Jeff's suite as it is in yours, and the light won't hurt your eyes. Besides, Jeff has more chairs and access for medical equipment in here. It's easier for someone to monitor your condition. You shouldn't be unobserved tonight."

"What happened to me? Is someone watching Star?" Caroline thrashed around, trying to sit up. If Star felt anything like *this*—

Jeff rested a hand on her shoulder. "Bloohowt is with her. He'll send a messenger if there's a problem. Better that she has a Convert from a similar species with her right now, and he's closer to the ranch than any equine who could understand what she's going through right now. Alami—the nearest mare who has gone through a Conversion process rather than being born Converted—will be here before First Meal next turn."

"What is Star going through?"

"A Conversion process triggered by a massive rella exposure," Jeff said. "Normally Conversion doesn't happen like this—there are easier substances that don't have the potential to cause as much trauma as the rella can. But the exposure to that much rella—the Plasmoid ship dropped its entire load on the two of you before it escaped. No impact on you other than disorientation and some wild visions, because you're already sentient. But Star—we're not sure yet just how far the Conversion process will go. That she's bonded with you may be a good thing—or it might not be. She might be too old to successfully go through the process."

"Oh Jeff. I'm sorry. She's such a nice mare." Caroline sniffled, remembering that soft touch of Star's nose on her hand, the way the mare wiggled her nose when she had brushed her—and the unfamiliar anger she had felt, which must have been Star's reaction to the invading Plasmoid.

"Don't be," he said softly. "Star was so close to that level already. Now we just have to hope that she pulls through acquiring full sentience without preparation, at her age. This is *not* the usual way that Conversion happens. It can be harder on a mature horse."

"I'm so sorry."

"You didn't know. And Star is already protective of me and the ranch. If you were thinking that it was possible to chase the ship off, then Star would act on it. Which she did." Jeff took her hand and rubbed her palm with his thumb. "Don't blame yourself, Caroline. We probably should have sent out a defensive crew instead of checking ourselves. But I didn't know." His voice caught. "This is an even different situation from what has been reported before. I'm just glad that you—*both* of you—are safe and didn't end up like those chicks...." His voice trailed away.

Caroline yawned. "Sorry," she apologized yet again. "Just tired."

"That's normal," Darcy said. "Jeff, let her rest."

"I want to stay here, Mama. With her."

"Then be quiet and let her sleep."

Jeff grumbled. But he continued to hold her hand, gently stroking her palm with his thumb.

Her eyelids were so, so heavy. Caroline exhaled. Jeff's hand in hers kept her centered, enough that she felt safe enough to slide back into sleep, without worrying about falling back into that well of stars.

HER SLEEP WAS RESTLESS, punctuated by throbbing colors and bizarre shapes that tried to attack her. Caroline roused more than once, only to be reassured by Jeff's comforting deep voice and his firm touch that allowed her to place herself when she thought the world was spinning around her.

At some point, he took her into his arms.

She slept better after that. His spicy, musky scent wafted into her dreams and banished the sickly-sweet smell that preluded the appearance of throbbing colors and bizarre shapes.

WHEN CAROLINE WOKE, she was in Jeff's arms. While she was still under the bedcovers, he lay on top of them. As she stirred, he grunted. She rolled over to face him.

His eyes opened—those lovely gold-flecked dark brown eyes that she hadn't fully appreciated until now. He gently stroked her cheek.

"How are you doing?" he asked.

"I'm not hallucinating colors that want to beat me up anymore," she said shakily.

"Good." He sighed heavily. "That's a relief."

"I kicked you out of your bed, didn't I?"

"I'm here, aren't I?"

"But you're still dressed in your work clothing." Her voice wavered.

"So are you." He brushed his hand against her forehead, leaving it there. She pressed gently against it. "No violation of the formal marital association."

"Who cares about that?" she whispered.

He laughed softly. "Caroline, we need to be careful, for your sake."

"We're married. I don't need to guard my virtue anymore." Uncertainty pricked at her. What if *he* was having second thoughts about their relationship? While that might make things easier—sadness prickled through her at the thought that perhaps he might have regrets about exploring possibilities beyond the formal contract.

"No. But unlike me, you lack relationship experience. I've dated, though nobody seriously. Nothing more than kissing and light fondling, but—it's still more experience than you have. I don't want to rush you. We barely know each other."

Caroline exhaled with relief. *He still wants—*

She didn't dare think about it further. Not now. Those feelings were still chaotic, still uncertain.

She leaned her head into Jeff's chest. At last she lifted her head. Looked deep into those solemn gold-flecked dark eyes, framed by his dark skin. Raised a trembling hand to touch his cheek. He turned his head, his full lips brushing gently against her palm.

"We have a lot of learning ahead, then," she said. "And I'm willing to do it." She paused. "I wonder how Star is doing?"

He smiled. "Well, we'd better find out, shouldn't we?"

Caroline extracted herself from Jeff's arms. She was shaky as she sat up, and he steadied her. Once she was on her feet, he slid his arm around her waist.

More intimate than yesterday.

But after last night, it—felt right.

They made their way outside, slowly. Her legs were wobbly and she had to lean on Jeff for support.

Star and a dainty gray mare grazed on the lawn. *That,* more than anything else, told Caroline what Star's new status was. Only Converted species had the freedom of the unfenced lawn.

"Star?" she called, her voice wobbling.

The dark bay mare raised her head. She whickered at Caroline, then galloped toward them, sliding to a stop. Star placed her head carefully against Caroline's torso. She leaned into the mare, delicately kissing the top of her head. The two of them stood together as the gray mare joined them.

"Star does not have a translator yet," the gray mare said. "It will take some time—probably a ten-turn—before she will be ready for the implant. But I can tell you this—Caroline?"

"Yes."

"I am Alami. Star is making the transition to Converted well, and she is grateful to you for making it possible. Being able to link with you as it started made a significant difference in how easy the transition is going."

Star carefully backed away from Caroline and turned her head toward Alami. The two horses communed—Caroline wasn't certain what was being said, but from the flicks of ears, raises of brows, flares of nostrils, and eyeblinks, there was a lot being communicated.

"Star says that she looks forward to being able to speak to you directly," Alami said finally. "She feels that she owes you a significant debt." The gray mare blew softly. "First-cross sentients are often aware that they aren't quite—there. They frequently don't feel like they are whole. Star is very grateful to be able to have you as a guide through the first steps of the process."

"I am *so* glad for you, Star," Caroline said. "So very glad. And I don't feel like there is a debt at all."

Star turned back to Caroline and blew gently on her chest. She raised her head and nuzzled Caroline's neck, then brushed her muzzle across Caroline's cheek.

Caroline reached out and rested her hand on the mare's neck.

If anyone had told her that she would be in part responsible for the member of another species to go through Conversion, she wouldn't have believed it. But now?

She was awed. Astounded. Grateful to have witnessed this experience.

All of this has changed my life. My world. And we're only getting started.

7

POLITICAL COMPLEXITIES

CAROLINE'S EUPHORIA over Star's Conversion status lasted only as long as it took to walk back to the house and into the kitchen. The walk helped clear her head and allowed her to think.

Going by what she had heard last turn—no, two turns ago—the Plasmoid attack on the Interstellar Roundup Ranch was a new development. Most of the reported rella thefts had happened on Wansa, not Blass. Was it a coincidence that *this* attempt was on the soon-to-be Planetary Representative's property?

From one perspective, the incident didn't make sense. The Plasmoids stealing rella from Jeff could cause a *lot* of problems, especially since Jeff was poised to assume a role that would give him greater visibility than just being Jeff Tophand, former rodeo duelist and ranch owner. This reeked of thumbing their noses—or whatever the blob-like Plasmoid equivalent was to noses—at Cartain and its power structures. Not to speak of the Federation.

So why *would* the Plasmoids want to upset the current balance of power between the Federation of Solid Peoples and the Ethereal Confederation? An irrational act by an individual or minor faction amongst the Ethereals? That was more logical than this being something official. Possibly even a criminal act that Plasmoid officials would condemn.

From another point of view—this could easily be a power play after all.

See, we have the ability to attack the incoming Planetary Representative's fields as well as isolated Crested Flyer and Upright farms. What are you going to do about it?

Now *that* kind of arrogance matched what Caroline had seen of the Plasmoids during her nine spans as Geraint's intern. Perhaps the Ethereals *wanted* to challenge the Federation. The power balance between the two groups had recently shifted toward the Plasmoid-dominated Ethereal Confederation. The Plasmoids might want to test the Federation's commitment to supporting even their second-tier worlds, albeit a second-tier world that was the only Federation source for a particular plant-based drug.

Which—honestly, given Cartain's monopoly on rella, should technically make it a first-tier world. That provided yet another motive—dissidents on Cartain allying with Plasmoids. Could the Plasmoids be seeking to lure Cartain into the Ethereal Confederation? Supposedly, the Ethereals supported mixed Plasmoid and Solid species worlds, unlike the Galactic Federation, which only admitted Solid species worlds.

No. That aspect wasn't very likely. There would be rumors about dissidents. She would think that Jeff would have heard about dissents allying with Plasmoids. Or—could that be the purpose of the Rella Protective Association?

So which was it? An unsanctioned, possibly criminal action? A deliberate provocation? Dissidents unhappy with Cartain's status who were willing to cut deals with the Plasmoids?

Caroline wasn't certain. While she leaned toward the first possibility, she couldn't rule out the other options.

There was still another factor.

What impact would Star's Conversion have on this situation? From what Caroline had been able to research after meeting with Rifanel, the Conversion process was strictly managed and controlled—it didn't happen like the experience Star just had. Otherwise, the filly that Caroline had met at Rifanel's would have a name, a translator, and a Conversion status.

How did the Ribonits fit into the equation? They couldn't be happy about these Plasmoid attacks on rella fields. Yet none of the ranchers she and Jeff had talked to yesterday reported any interest from the Ribonits in the thefts, even after they complained to the Ribonit cartel.

Were the Ribonits part of whatever was happening with these rella thefts?

Still another piece of the puzzle to put together. Throw in Geraint's brief mention of sentient planets—no, she couldn't see how sentient planets and rella fit together.

"You're awfully quiet," Jeff said, as they entered the house. "Are you all right?"

The clatter of dishes accompanied by the tantalizing scent of onions, potatoes, and peppers wafting from the kitchen distracted Caroline momentarily, reminding her that she was hungry. She inhaled deeply, focusing more on that marvelous smell than Jeff's question.

"Caroline?"

Her stomach rumbled and they both chuckled.

"I'm all right," she said. "Distracted by that lovely-smelling food, and—just thinking about the implications of this attack."

"I see. Tell me more."

She recounted her concerns. Jeff pursed his lips thoughtfully as they walked to the kitchen.

Darcy beamed at them as she cooked. "Everything better, Caroline? You certainly look much better than you did. Jeff told me that you weren't normally that pale. I can see it. You're much more pink than pale." She studied Caroline from head to toes. "But. Once you start toning up for ranch life, you're gonna lose weight. We need to keep you well-fed."

Caroline burst out laughing. "Darcy, I would *love* to lose some weight."

"That's *stupid*," Darcy said flatly. "You have a nice figure. You just aren't one of those skinny hourglass Earth ladies, for which I am very thankful. Those skinny women can't hold up to hard work."

"Mama, she's not going to be laboring in the fields!" Jeff protested.

"Field labor isn't the only hard work there is, son. Once I started managing Ford's Dream—that's our ranch next door, Caroline—I found that I was on my feet just as much as when I was working in the fields. Only I was doing different types of work. Traveling to Shrum regularly and dealing with regulators. Maybe not as much heavy work, but lots of walking and stair-climbing. And humans don't get platforms, not like Jeff's rabbit manager Moonshadow. No matter how heavy we are."

Hmm. She *had* been able to maintain her weight without getting too concerned about what she ate when working at Galactic Central. And that included going to banquets.

Caroline exhaled. "I see your point, Darcy."

"A smart woman." Darcy winked at her. "I'm glad my boy ended up with someone like you and not one of those frails. Even if it is just a formal marital association at the moment. Now." She scraped equal servings of the potato and vegetable combination into two bowls. "Here's your First Meal. Eat up, you two. There's Skrilsit brewing on the counter. Thought I'd cook you up a First Meal, see how Caroline is doing this turn. Since Caroline's doing better, I need to get along home. Things to do."

"You'd best check your fields, Mama."

"George did it already, son. Nothing. We put the word out to everyone nearby. It appears that you were the only one hit by that damn Plasmoid ship. The district is organizing watch patrols."

Jeff and Caroline exchanged glances.

This doesn't sound good.

"We'd better have a talk with the district manager, shouldn't we, Caroline?"

Caroline nodded. "I'll contact them after we eat and see how soon we can get an appointment with them."

Darcy sighed. "Politics."

"It's going to be my job, Mama."

"I know, I know. And that's a good thing because at least we won't have Robbie-boy selling out the rest of us for his rich friends. Don't know where you got the taste for politics because I sure don't have it and neither did your father." Darcy hugged first Jeff, then Caroline. "Join us for Third Meal, you two."

"I'll let you know, Mama. We may be busy. There are— things we need to deal with."

"Well, I want to serve you Third Meal before the two of you are off to Galactic Central!"

"No worries, Mama. We'll make it happen. If not tonight, then soon."

"You'd better." Darcy scowled at Jeff.

"I'll make sure of it," Caroline promised.

That earned her a big grin. "A woman who knows what family priorities are. I definitely want to get to know you better, Caroline!"

"Yes." Caroline couldn't say what she *wanted*, which was that Darcy already felt more like a mother should be than her own was.

Not yet, anyway.

Darcy hugged both of them, then left.

Jeff exhaled. "Well. It appears that Mama approves of you.

Not that I was worried." He pointed to a chair. "Go ahead and sit. I'll bring the Skrilsit and the food."

"Jeff, I can take care of myself—"

"I *know*. But you need to take it easy." He picked up the mugs and set one in front of her, the other at his place. The pot of Skrilsit was next, followed by silverware and the bowls. He finished by pouring tea for her first, then him, then their food.

"So we were the only target," she said finally.

"Yeah." Jeff sipped his tea. "Seems rather suspicious—that is, unless Star managed to disable the only ship doing the thefts."

"That seems unlikely."

"Probably." He took another sip of tea.

"I think we should call Rifanel and Geraint back to Cartain. Get the Federalists and the Councilists to call for a Congressional investigation. There's something going on with the Plasmoids and rella, and we better get to the bottom of it, for the Federation's sake. What *if* this is the beginning of a power play by the Plasmoids? We need to stop it before it gets worse."

"Now just hold on a click, Caroline." Jeff carefully set his mug down. "Aren't you getting a little ahead of things here? We have no idea what the motives are for these attacks yet. This could just be pirates. I'd like to hear from the Ribonits before we take too much of an action."

"Plasmoids haven't displayed a history of piracy until now, if that's what this is."

"But there's also the possibility of a first time. We don't *know* that much about the Plasmoids. I—I'd much rather be careful. Moving too quickly and being wrong could impact my credibility in the Congress."

"True," Caroline conceded. "But we need to *do* something. Star was lucky. Those Flyer chicks weren't. We *will* be representing the Flyers in the Congress, along with the other species of Cartain, and those families want answers. How you handle the Flyers will separate you from what Robbie-boy has done, in biasing his focus toward the wealthier human landowners and not listening to other species. Or less-wealthy humans. You can't just ignore them."

Jeff winced. "Yeah. I agree. At the same time, we need to be careful. There are potential security issues here, not just for Cartain but the Congress. Plus I'd much rather be speaking as the Planetary Representative for Cartain rather than a candidate. Waiting gives us more time to collect data. And we'll have the Boss behind us then. Now?" Jeff shrugged. "She could easily evade a commitment on the situation, just because I'm not the Planetary Rep yet. We have to play it carefully. Especially since we don't know the role that the Rella Protective Association plays in all of this."

"So we just don't do anything?" Caroline cringed because she couldn't keep that faint twinge of frustration out of her voice. Instead of saying anything more and causing a fight, she focused on sipping her tea. A move she had learned years ago, to keep Mother happy.

"I didn't say that." Jeff leaned back in his chair. "We move cautiously. We gather data. We press the Ribonits for answers —that's something we can do this turn."

"It just doesn't seem like it's enough." Caroline took another sip of her tea, sighing. Had she said too much?

"I know. It's frustrating, and I see from the way you're shutting down that it bothers you." Jeff set his tea down and reached over to rest his hand on hers. "Look. There are backchannel ways of receiving and relaying this information to people who should know about it. I have ways to share important news that I want to keep discreet on Cartain, and— don't you have a gossip network amongst interns and assistants at the Congress?"

"Well—yes." Caroline thought for a moment. "I would be

expected to speak to Rutan. Ask questions. Pass along information."

"Then find a means to talk to Rutan carefully about what has happened. We don't want the media getting their hands on this, either, because if this turns out to be a security issue, they could cause us further problems." Jeff scowled. "I'm worried that there might be a potential impact on Star as well. The knowledge that massive doses of rella bring about a Conversion process is not very widespread and could have a big backlash if it goes public. I don't want anyone trying to strip her new status away because she didn't go through the standard Conversion protocols."

"How does the link that Star and I formed affect things?"

The last thing I want to do is get Star into trouble!

"I have no idea. But the anomalies in Star's Conversion would also be an excellent opening for you to discuss the situation with Rifanel."

Caroline pursed her lips and nodded her head thoughtfully. "I can figure out an appropriate approach for both Rutan and Rifanel, based on what happened to Star."

Jeff beamed at her. "I thought you could." He reached for his bowl. "So. This turn. We need to keep our duties light for your recovery process."

"Our first priority is talking to the district about patrols," she said. "Then—well, I'll contact the Ribonits and see what they have to say. They might communicate with me where they might not you. Especially if they're still discussing the situation with the Plasmoids."

Jeff nodded. "Sounds like a plan to me."

"*Then* I'll start discreet channels with Rutan and Rifanel."

"Good. And—" he hesitated. "Talk to Star. Figure out if this link of yours is a temporary thing, an artifact of the Conversion process, or something more."

"Sure." That piqued her curiosity. "You think there's something more to it?"

"I don't know enough about how this type of link works." Jeff paused again, choosing his words carefully. "From what you've said, it *sounds* closer to an interpreter-Convert link such as Trace and Moonshadow have, even though it's not quite the same. I've seen a couple of those links in the past, before Moonshadow became the ranch manager and Trace his interpreter. All the same, you might want to consider the possibility of hiring Star to be one of our aides. That way, if there's any potential consequences of her Conversion process—"

"—She'll be with us at Galactic Central, and less vulnerable," Caroline finished for him.

He nodded.

Caroline also made a note to herself. While Moonshadow and Trace were the closest examples of the interpreter/Converted species link, they might not understand all of the implications of the connection between her and Star.

Perhaps it might be a good idea for her to talk to Laura Richardson, Blackburn's interpreter, instead.

THE REST of the turn flew by with lots of things for her to do, despite it being allegedly a recovery turn after her exposure. Darla came to do her design consultation after Caroline and Jeff had returned from talking to district officials about setting up regular patrols. Caroline spent a pleasant node going over design plans, colors, and décor for her suite with Darla, mixed in with learning about Jeff's family. Their mother had insisted that her daughters all have names beginning with "Dar," so there was Darla, Darlene, Darcinia, and Darya.

"But Ken? Jeff?" Caroline asked.

Darla shrugged. "Dad named the boys and Mom wasn't picky about their names. It has something to do with a family tradition. Grandmother's name was Darcinia. Darya would know more about it than I do."

"I get it." After all, Caroline's oldname had come from her paternal grandmother. Her brothers all had A-names, like her father—Alex, Albert, Abraham, Aaron. Being named *Agatha* originally just meant that she fit in with her siblings. Her mother had changed her name to Alice because all the McKinnons had A-names.

Apparently such naming traditions weren't just a feature of Earth.

After meeting with Darla and eating Second Meal with Jeff, Caroline messaged the Ribonit consul for Cartain. It took her almost another node to work her way delicately through the layers of Ribonit bureaucracy protecting them from unimportant communications. She had to cite her marital status several times before she was passed on to the next level of official. But once she reached the higher levels, there was much apologizing and prostrating by those acting as gatekeepers.

Once she reached the consul themself, their discussion ended up being an exhausting level of parry, thrust, finding out what the other did and didn't know, and feeling their ways through what could and couldn't be explicitly said. It was a grueling process. A headache afterward forced Caroline's retreat to Jeff's bedroom once again to lie down and take a rest, since hers was under construction—Darla and her crew had started work promptly.

But even though she lay down with a blindfold over her eyes to shut out the light—something recommended by Darcy —Caroline's thoughts kept racing, considering everything she had learned from talking to the nameless Ribonit consul who only went by their title.

Consul had been cagey, then concerned. Consul kept dropping hints that perhaps they couldn't do very much, that their ability to act was constrained.

Something she needed to cross-check with Rutan.

But most of all, Consul sounded *concerned.* Worried. Almost—frightened.

Why would Consul sound like that?

Was it because criminal elements were involved with these thefts?

Or did Consul fear that being too open about what they knew regarding rella thefts could light off a string of repercussions that went far beyond Cartain?

Their answers didn't give Caroline any clear indication. And Jeff had gone out to the fields with Moonshadow and Trace to document their losses for the district manager, so she couldn't talk to him about this. Not yet, anyway.

Which left her lying in his bed, puzzling over everything that was happening.

AFTER ALMOST A NODE of lying there with her speeding thoughts, Caroline got back up. Her headache had ebbed slightly, and she still had things to do. Rutan. Rifanel. Star. Laura Richardson.

Sending a message to Rutan was the easiest task to tackle. Caroline worded a careful inquiry to him, mixed in with her reports about their meetings on Wansa. All very light-toned and breezy, the sort of report that she had handled from other assistants to Federalist Representatives. Caroline had always suspected that there was more information implied between the lines than what usually appeared in those reports—and here she was, constructing one of her own, using private references that she knew only Geraint and Rutan would understand, based on incidents from her nine spans in Geraint's office.

She didn't have access to the regular Federalist cypher, at least not until Jeff was officially elected. But this, combined with Caroline's earlier message to Rutan about her father's observations about Lara Wordtrust, might gain her earlier access to the standard cypher.

That done, Caroline got up from her temporary desk, stretched, and went outside to see how Star was doing. That needed to happen before any contact with Rifanel or Laura Richardson.

As Caroline descended the stairs from the main house, Star trotted around the corner. She tossed her head at Caroline, then waited until Caroline was on solid ground before walking up to her. Star gently pressed her nose against Caroline's chest.

"Good. See. You."

Caroline startled as she *heard* the words without sound. Was the mare truly capable of mindspeech now? Why hadn't she shown this ability earlier?

"Star?"

"Yes." A pause. *"Know. Where. You are. Inside."*

"Does Alami know about this ability?"

A hesitation. *"No. Not. Typical for equine Conversion. Not sure talk you. Sense you. Sense thoughts. Talk? Not know. Until now."*

Hmm. *"Can you hear me?"* she asked Star, without speaking. How much vocabulary did the mare possess?

"Yes!"

"Can we talk like this without touching?" Was this too long a sentence for Star to grasp?

Star's response was slow, hesitant. *"Not know. This. Talk-type. Hard. Think. Will get better. Learning words. Want talk smooth. Like you."*

"It will come, Star. Humans build language bit-by-bit. You understand everything I say?"

"Almost. Pictures with words. When you think them. Helps."

"I will do my best to picture my thoughts."

"Helps. You feel me, when inside house? I feel you."

"No. At least I don't think I was feeling you." Caroline considered. *"There was a piece of not-me at the edge of my thoughts. It might have been you."* She *hoped* Star understood what she meant by the metaphor. How could she express it in a manner that a horse would understand?

"Think was there. Piece of not-me you felt at—fence line? Like edge? Not in pasture but other side of fence?"

"Yes! Exactly. Edge would be like a fence line." She thought further. *"Your metaphor—that's what humans call something like "edge of my thoughts"—fits. Not-me just on the other side of the fence, in my thoughts."*

Wordless joy flowed over Caroline. It didn't *feel* like her own sensation of happiness. This feeling was more like the thrill of galloping across a wide field, sun on her back, capering and gamboling with the herd, reveling in the joy of movement.

How Star felt elation.

The joyful sensation faded, though faint satisfaction lurked in the background, as part of the *not-me* on the other side of the fence.

"I understand you!" Star snorted and tossed her head.

Caroline smiled. This was a *very* interesting development. *"I wonder if this is closer to what interpreters and Converted—like rabbits, for example—actually do with each other."*

"Don't know. I ask Moonshadow?"

"No! Security," Caroline responded.

Star raised her head, eyes wide and startled by the intensity of Caroline's emotion.

"Shh. It's all right," Caroline soothed her. *"There is a lot going on. For your safety, we need to hide this ability until we know more. I will tell Jeff. And then Rifanel—carefully—and Blackburn. No one else."*

"No talk, then. Wait." The dark bay mare snorted again. *"Talk like this make me tired."*

Caroline nodded, acknowledging the new wave of fatigue

washing over her. *"Me too, Star. Just one more thing. Will you be my assistant?"*

"Me?" The mare added an excited squeal.

"Yes, you. Both here and on Galactic Central. You'll be safer with us."

Star half-reared, then popped up her hindquarters, excitement radiating off of her as she squealed a second time. *"Me? Going to Galactic Central? Yes! Yes!"*

Caroline laughed at the giddy happiness pulsing through her from Star. She scratched Star's head, relishing the warm sensation of *togetherness* emitting from the brown mare.

This means of communication might be yet another complication, but all the same—it gave her a small rush of joy.

She decided her next message would be to Laura Richardson.

After spending nearly a node wordlessly communing with Star—sending images back and forth seemed to be simpler than using language—Caroline broke away from Star, because she just had too much to do that didn't involve working with the dark bay mare. Star's mindspeech *was* improving, even if they just exchanged images. She learned quickly.

By the end of their visit, there was no question in Caroline's mind about the benefit of taking Star to Galactic Central. Social and class structures weren't as rigid on Cartain as they were on Earth, but all the same, given the unusual way that Star gained Conversion, the brown mare would find more acceptance at Central than on Cartain. There, Star was less likely to be unique, and might find better information and training than here.

"Look forward to help you at Galactic Central!" was the last

message Star sent before Caroline went inside. There was a faint tendril of *not-myself* in her awareness that Caroline now recognized as being Star's presence. And, if she thought about it, she knew where Star was at all times.

Interesting. Caroline had a lot of questions—and no means of getting answers, yet.

Sending the message to Richardson was straightforward— once Caroline realized that her status as Jeff's assistant and spouse allowed her to request a cypher link from Richardson. Richardson responded with the cypher immediately, so Caroline shared details about the connection between her and Star, finally asking *is this situation similar to the bonding process between interpreter and Converted?*

Composing the message to Rifanel took longer. Yes, it was assistant-to-assistant, like Caroline's message to Rutan, *but.* Rifanel's status as the head of the Councilist party placed her at a higher level of political influence than Rutan. And then there was the issue of Star and Conversion, as well as the problem of rella. Caroline wrestled with the wording for half a node before finally sending it off, feeling unsatisfied.

This might be a situation where they couldn't talk freely until everyone was safely on Galactic Central.

RICHARDSON WAS the first to respond to Caroline's messages.

The answer to your final question is a guarded yes. Blackburn and I will stop by the Interstellar Roundup in two turns, around your Second Meal. We will talk then.

Now *that* was interesting. Caroline added the meeting to Jeff's calendar.

Rifanel's response suggested that Caroline and Star might want to visit her very soon after they arrived on Galactic Central.

Rutan sent her a cypher link and a request for more details.

By the time Caroline finished her report to Rutan, it was 11:50 Node. Almost time for Third Meal—and she wasn't certain she felt up to meeting the rest of Jeff's family. She sent the message and settled back in her—no, *Jeff's*—chair. Maybe if she just took a little nap for about ten clicks, she would feel more like socializing.

GENTLE SHAKING ROUSED HER. "Hey, sleepyhead. You gonna go to bed hungry?"

"Huh? What?" Caroline opened her eyes. It was dark outside. She had clearly slept for more than ten clicks. "Oh no. I missed Third Meal! Is your mother very angry with me?" The part of *not-me* that was Star stirred. *"Alami told Jeff not bother you. I tell her to tell him."*

"Oh no, no, no." Jeff smiled. "Darla looked in when she was done for the turn and told me that you were sound asleep in my comfy chair—after Alami told me that you were asleep. I don't know how she knew that."

"Star told Alami."

Jeff raised his brows but continued. "I called Mama and told her that this turn wasn't going to work because you had already gone to sleep. I was already running late, and didn't want to wake you—you looked so peaceful that I just didn't have the heart to disturb you until now. Mama sent food over."

"Oh my. She must really think I'm fragile or something."

Jeff shook his head. "No. I'm amazed you were able to keep active as long as you did today." He crossed his arms and gazed sternly at her. "How do you know that Star told Alami?"

"Star told me. We—when I went out to check on her,

before contacting Laura Richardson, we started mindspeaking. She mindspoke to me just now."

So we don't have to be all that close to talk. That's good to know.

"Mindspeaking? Like some interpreters do with their Converted partners?"

"I don't know. That's why I reached out to Richardson—and why she and Blackburn are going to be here in two turns."

"I saw that addition to the calendar." He scowled. "Was this on an open network?"

"No. Cypher link."

He relaxed. "Should have expected that," he murmured. "But this. What did Richardson say to you, or did she just relay the appointment?"

"Let me show you the messages." Caroline brought them up.

Jeff flicked through them. "Interesting. I've never heard of a massive dose of rella causing the ability to mindspeak. But —perhaps it suggests an innate ability in you, Star, or both of you."

"Could be."

"Anyway. Come eat. Darla's finished with your bedroom, so you should be all right sleeping in there."

"She's fast. I've never heard of a room being done that quickly. My mother used to redecorate all the time, and it took ages for even the simplest of renovations—like mine—to be finished." Mother's redecoration projects *never* were finished that quickly. *Never.* It always seemed as if something kept coming up to cause problems. Or supplies couldn't be found.

"It's amazing how fast suppliers and contractors can work when the client has a marital association with an unopposed candidate for Planetary Representative." Jeff smirked. "But yes. Darla's fast. Plus she used good QuikDry paint so your room doesn't stink. I checked."

"Thank you."

"It's part of the relationship." His smile softened from that knowing smirk. "I want to make sure you're comfortable and safe. So I checked."

"Thank you."

Jeff took Caroline's hands and helped her to her feet. He pulled her close for a moment. Caroline leaned her head on him, inhaling deeply of the musky, spicy scent that was Jeff.

Then they moved apart.

Later, alone in her bed, Caroline realized that she missed the warmth of Jeff's presence. His arms around her. While she had medication that helped her sleep—she would have preferred the soothing effect of Jeff's arms.

Is this love, or is this the lust that Mother always used to condemn? she wondered.

The *not-me* part of her that was Star stirred. *"He isn't there. I am here. You are not alone."*

Reassurance and the image of a mare nuzzling her foal came to Caroline. She sent back her own sensation of comfort to Star. As Caroline drifted back into sleep, the awareness of Star made her realize that perhaps some of her dreams from the night before had bled over from Star.

Apparently, having this sort of connection might have its own problems.

We'll know more when we talk to Blackburn and Richardson.

That thought stirred a tendril of worry from Star. Now it was Caroline's turn to send wordless comforting images to her partner.

THE NEXT COUPLE of turns were, thankfully, uneventful, although they were busy. Caroline and Jeff went to campaign gatherings, collecting more information about Plasmoid appearances and rella thefts. When they weren't campaigning, Caroline learned more about ranch operations, met other nearby ranchers besides Jeff's family, and made contact with assorted Cartain governmental entities and lobbyists who wanted reassurance that she and Jeff would consider their interests and needs while at the Federation Congress.

The one organization that noticeably did not contact Caroline, or respond to her inquiries, was the Rella Protective Association. Meanwhile, the Rella *Producers* Association presented her with a unanimous resolution expressing their concern about rella thefts and the Ribonit lack of response.

Rutan sent the Federalist cypher, and requested more information. Caroline replied with a more detailed report about the rella thefts and the Plasmoid sightings.

Rifanel also sent a cypher, wanting more information about Star's Conversion. Caroline went to Star to discuss how much they should share before she answered—she felt obligated to include the dark bay mare in these discussions. They agreed on a careful recounting of the events, but left out any mention of the mindspeech bond between Star and Caroline. Neither of them felt comfortable disclosing that aspect of Star's Conversion until after they had the opportunity to talk things over with Blackburn and Richardson.

<hr>

WAITING for Blackburn and Richardson's arrival was nerve-racking, a mixture of her own worry and Star's. Caroline paced around her suite, unable to focus. She went outside to work in a chair so that Star could be close to her. At least being by Star made things a little bit better, at least for Caroline. The mare switched back and forth between mindspeech and sending confused, worried images as she nibbled at grass and paced.

"You will work yourself into a colic if you don't stop fretting!" Alami scolded Star.

That led to a protracted nonverbal discussion between the two mares.

"Don't want my status away!" Star's agitation made her language use less fluent than it had become over the past two turns.

"Don't fret, dear one. Jeff and I will not let anyone take this away from you," Caroline tried to reassure her. That seemed to ease Star's tension for a few clicks. Then she went back to pacing.

Jeff joined them a node before Second Meal and his presence seemed to soothe Star.

Soon enough, a runabout approached the farmhouse. Star halted and threw her head up, projecting wordless anxiety. Caroline and Jeff rested their arms over Star's back to soothe her as they waited.

Richardson was first to exit, followed by Blackburn's floater. Star quivered under Caroline's arm. Caroline sent comforting thoughts as Blackburn's floater accelerated past Richardson to stop in front of Star. The black, lop-eared rabbit periscoped upright, balancing on his hind legs as his dark eyes studied the dark bay mare. One ear canted forward.

"Speak to me," he ordered.

"I speak you?" Confusion radiated from Star.

"How is it that I can hear you?" Caroline asked.

Blackburn dropped to all fours and thumped one hind leg sharply against the platform. *"They both hear me. This is a legitimate bond. Don't you agree, Laura?"*

"Absolutely."

Caroline startled as Laura Richardson's voice echoed in her head. Star twitched her ears toward Richardson, equally surprised.

"But for it to come about from a massive exposure to rella, and with a mature horse is quite unusual. Even though Star is a first-generation equine cross. That just—doesn't happen." Annoyed tones colored Blackburn's mental voice.

"*We may need to reexamine the Convert qualification criteria for equines,*" Richardson said. "*That is what Rifanel has been advocating.*"

"*It seems that Rifanel may be correct.*" Blackburn sneezed, then reared back up on his hind legs to wash his face.

Jeff raised his brows at Caroline. By now she knew that was a request for more information. "Blackburn confirms that the bond between me and Star is very similar to the one he and Richardson has. Both of us can hear their mindspeech. This discovery may affect the Convert qualification criteria for equines."

"Wow—that's—wow. Congratulations, Star! I always thought that you should have been entitled to Convert status, but didn't have the power to advocate for you when you were a yearling! I'm so happy for you. And to have a bond with Caroline—I'm thrilled." A big grin spread across his face. "You deserve it."

"This *is* an unusual form of Conversion for horses," Richardson said. "They don't usually develop mindspeech. I'm not sure that Star will want to settle for a translator instead of an interpreter, like Caroline. Or she may choose both."

"How unusual is this?" Caroline asked.

"It's the only reported case of this type of Conversion for horses," Richardson said.

Blackburn dropped to all fours again. "*The two of you will need training. You need to know how to shut each other's emotions away from each other. The connection probably kept both of you sane during the initial reaction to that massive dose of rella. But that level of connection is not desirable on an everyturn basis. We also need to investigate to see if you can also use a translator as well as an interpreter, Star. That will serve you well.*"

"Where and when should we do this training?" Caroline asked out loud, for Jeff's sake.

"At Galactic Central, where we have access to experienced

equine scientists in particular, and many more with backgrounds in both translators and interpreters for the Converted," Richardson said. She bowed to Star, then Caroline. "Meanwhile. Welcome to the ranks of the partnered Converted. Blackburn and I look forward to working with you." Her face shifted from expressionless to a faint smile. "And *this* may have a surprising impact on our status with the Ethereal Confederation. I don't think anyone anticipated this turn of events."

"Definitely not," Jeff said. He smiled at Caroline. "And for it to happen to two of my favorite beings—I feel honored to witness these events."

"Let's hope that the Plasmoids don't become a problem," Richardson said softly. The faint smile faded. "There are already enough issues roiling before this next session of Congress opens. We need to keep Star and Caroline's mind-speech capabilities confidential. Proceed as if Star is going to acquire a translator, but—how soon can you relocate to Galactic Central?"

"The official vote and certification is in a ten-turn," Jeff said. "I'll do whatever it takes to keep these two safe. Both are dear to me."

"Good." Richardson turned to Blackburn. "We should probably hurry back to the ship so that we don't screw up the schedule too much more than we already have."

Blackburn flicked an ear and twitched his tail. "*Congratulations, Star and Caroline. Stay safe until we see each other again on Galactic Central. Do not dawdle on Cartain after Jeff's election has been certified. The quicker you can get to Central, the better it will be for all of you. We need to get your non-traditional Conversion certified, Star, and to do that means examination at Central.*"

"*Thank you,*" Star said.

"Thank you," Caroline said out loud. "We will head to Central promptly once the election is certified."

Blackburn bobbed his head and Richardson bowed. They

turned and headed back to the roundabout. Jeff patted Star's neck with one hand, even as he took Caroline's hand with the other.

"I think this calls for a celebration," he said.

EVEN THOUGH IT was a foregone conclusion, Caroline was thrilled once Jeff was certified as Cartain's Planetary Representative. Heeding Blackburn's warning about not dawdling on Cartain, she, Jeff, Star, and several of Jeff's cousins headed off for Galactic Central on the *No Skies, No Limits* within two nodes of Jeff's certification.

If anyone had told me that I would be in this position a cycle ago—

On the one hand, she wanted to share this status with her family.

On the other, Caroline didn't want to hear the hateful things that Alice McKinnon would say.

8

GALACTIC CENTRAL
COMPLICATIONS

Traveling on the expense account of a Planetary Representative, along with its privileges, had its benefits above and beyond accommodating Star's presence. They were already entitled to a top-of-the-line suite and priority processing onboard as well as priority in disembarking. However, because of Star, they had a larger-than-usual suite on the *No Skies, No Limits.* Alami came on board with them to explain the unusual aspects of Star's Conversion to customs officials, and to show Star the specific travel accommodations for Converted equines.

"Too bad you can't come with us," Caroline said quietly to Alami as Star investigated the sanitary facilities and the equine feeding area.

"I don't travel well," the gray mare said. "And besides—Star has you. Your bond is stronger than any same-species connection she has with me. If there are problems, you'll be better able to solve them than I will." She snorted and flicked an ear, then joined Star for one last discussion of horse-specific travel concerns.

Jeff put an arm around Caroline's shoulders.

"I remember my first flight off of Cartain. How about you?"

"When I left Earth for Mars, or when I left my solar system to go to Galactic Central?"

"I wouldn't imagine that a planetary hop in-system would be that big a deal—or was it?"

"Not really." Caroline grinned as she leaned into Jeff. "I had already made the Earth-Mars run often enough by the time I went to Mars U that it wasn't very impressive. But when I left the solar system, I ended up bribing my entire seatrow to let me stare out the porthole. It meant I was running short on funds for the trip to Central and had to eat basic rations for the two ten-turns from Earth to Central on a slow transport, but saying goodbye to the old home system before going into the Gate was well worth every credit I spent."

Jeff chuckled and pulled her even closer. Caroline nuzzled into Jeff. Over the past ten-turn she had become much more comfortable with affectionate physical contact. Allowable *touch* was such a new thing for her, and at times made her almost as giddy as Star was about going to Galactic Central. She looked forward to the casual brush of their hands, or the more deliberate contact where Jeff took her hand, or hugged her, or put his arm around her, like he was now.

Caroline was still tentative about reaching out to touch Jeff. Alice McKinnon had been strict about *no touching* for all of Caroline's youth, and contact with her brothers was strictly forbidden. That didn't seem to be the case with Jeff's family— his siblings openly hugged, smacked each other on the shoulders as part of teasing and joking, exchanged friendly back pats meant to reassure and praise, kissed cheeks—all new to her. The Fords clearly loved each other, and the contrast between them and the McKinnon family made Caroline's heart ache. What would it have been like to grow up in a family like Jeff's? A family where love dominated instead of mercantile ambition? She had missed so much.

Then again, you also grew up in privilege while Jeff and his family were indentured. Servitude can take many different forms, she reminded herself. *Some cages are just more gilded than others.*

At least Caroline had escaped the confines of Hart Mercantile Services. None of her brothers had.

Soon enough, the last bell for boarding chimed throughout the ship. Caroline settled herself in a chair near Star's restraint field, set up near the portholes so that Star could watch as they left Cartain's solar system before entering the Gate. Star's emotional projections were wordless and ecstatic as the *No Skies, No Limits* exited Cartain's solar system. Caroline absorbed Star's joy, sharing with Star her memory of the delight at watching Earth's solar system disappear when the ship launched itself into gatespace. Once they were in gatespace, Star continued to stare outside, even though there wasn't much to be seen.

Caroline joined Jeff. They reviewed orientation documents —even though she had Congressional experience as an intern, there was so much more for her to learn as Jeff's assistant and spouse.

Enough that *both* she and Jeff could be considered complete newbies to the Congress.

<hr>

THE PLEASANT EXCITEMENT of sharing Star's delight at travel evaporated almost immediately when they disembarked at the Planetary Representative portal on Galactic Central. They were met in the dingy gray reception area by their housing liaison, Kalanost, a reptilian from the same planet as Rutan.

Kalanost glanced at the documentation projected from her tablet and gnashed her teeth in annoyance.

"You don't have housing for a non-Converted equine. This one will need to go to the general non-Converted equine housing." She jabbed one claw toward Star.

"She's recently Converted and is my assistant," Caroline said.

"One has no record of her Conversion." Once again, Kalanost peered down her snout at the manifest projected in front of her. "My records show humans only, no equines. Much less a Converted Equine."

"This is a rather unconventional situation," Jeff said firmly.

"One still doesn't have space in your assigned quarters for this mare!" Kalanost insisted.

"Her appointment as one of my assistants should be in our records. I sent them three turns ago." Caroline frowned. She *thought* she had handled the paperwork appropriately— she had even asked Rutan to check it over and he had approved it. So what had happened?

"One sees nothing in your records about any equines, much less a Converted Equine." Kalanost remained firm, though she bared her teeth slightly in threat display.

Jeff bristled, throwing his shoulders back and thrusting his chest forward. "What does it take for me to convince you? I am the Planetary Representative from Cartain. This mare is part of my staff!"

"That is not what one's records say." Kalanost clacked her jaws.

This is getting us nowhere. Time to call for help.

One thing Caroline had learned about Jeff over this past ten-turn was that he reacted intensely to perceived injustices and slights aimed at those he cared about. But this wasn't Cartain, where Jeff's history earned him respect. On Central, he was just a novice Representative from a second-tier planet— and if there was one thing Caroline had also learned over this past ten-turn while gossiping with other Federalist assistants as part of networking, it was that Robbie-boy's arrogance had not left a favorable impression of Cartain on Galactic Central.

Jeff couldn't afford to develop the same reputation.

"Just a minute, Jeff." Caroline quickly pinged Rutan. He answered immediately and she explained the situation, including Blackburn's recommendation that Star come swiftly to Galactic Central for assessment and certification.

"Let me talk to Kalanost," Rutan said.

"Kalanost. Rutan from Geraint Ssprin's office would like to talk to you."

Kalanost flashed her teeth and rumbled slightly, twitching the tip of her tail. But she accepted Caroline's comm when Caroline handed it to her.

"Yes. Yes. This is most unusual." Annoyance colored Kalanost's voice and the tip of her tail twitched even faster. "One understands, but one *needs* the paperwork to agree with those residing in this unit!" A pause. "You say that you have the paperwork for this mare to be an assistant? Nothing shows up in my records. This is highly irregular! This mare doesn't even have a translator."

The argument continued.

"*I do not think she likes me,*" Star fretted. She projected worry, dread, and concern.

Caroline rubbed her neck—Star carried some of her things in a pack strapped onto her back so throwing an arm over her was not an option. "*We will get it figured out. Not to worry. Trust Rutan.*"

Kalanost switched to Drganent, the language she shared with Rutan, and blocked her translator so that only Drganent speakers could understand her. The language was full of hisses and snarls, accented by clacking of teeth and even more agitated tail twitches.

One last loud hiss. Kalanost turned to Jeff, Caroline, Star, and the others.

"One needs you to wait for several nodes while one finds you proper lodging." She thrust the comm at Caroline, so rapidly that Caroline had to dive to keep from dropping it. "One will call you when your quarters are ready."

Kalanost whirled and stomped off down one of the corridors connected to the reception portal, tail twitching even more, making the floor shake slightly under her weighted, ponderous strides.

"Rutan?" Caroline said into the comm, wondering if he had hung up.

"Caroline. We *are* sorry, sssss." Rutan hissed into the comm. "Kalanost was not supposed to be the housing coordinator to meet you and Jeff. Hrina was your designated coordinator, and she was briefed on your particular circumstances. Ssss!" Another sighing hiss. "Unfortunately, Hrina encountered some difficulties this turn, early in Fourth Node, before coming to work. The circumstances were unexpected. And Kalanost—sss, I do *not* understand why *that* one is working in this role! She *insists* on formal language and formalities. SSSS!"

From the number of hisses, Rutan was *seriously* upset.

"We have to wait for our quarters to be ready. Do you have any suggestions about where we can go?" Caroline frowned at the gray reception area. "This place is—nasty."

"The Representative reception portal is somewhat lacking, alas. Geraint offers you—*all* of you—refreshment and company while you wait for Kalanost to find what was supposed to be your original posting," Rutan said.

"And our goods?" That was another concern—who was handling their things?

"I have sent staff to secure them."

"Thank you, Rutan. We will be there shortly."

"I look forward to meeting our friends from Cartain," Rutan said, and disconnected.

Caroline exhaled. "All right, then," she announced. "We're invited to wait in Geraint's quarters. *All* of us."

Jeff smiled at her. "Thanks, Caroline. What would we do without you?"

She shrugged, a flush burning her cheeks. "It's just part of my job."

"Uh-uh. More than that. I would have pushed her much harder—we've had to do that with the Rodeo," Jeff said quietly. "There's a lot more bias against recent Converteds than most realize. Getting pushy works, but it can also backfire."

"Just doing my job," Caroline said.

"*Thank you.*" Star snorted and shook her head.

Jeff bent over and kissed Caroline's cheek—the first time he had done that. "Follow me," she said, her cheeks burning with an even bigger flush as she walked down the corridor adjoining the one that Kalanost had stomped down.

Jeff hurried to catch up with Caroline, and took her hand. She had to fight back an urge toward pulling her hand away, that ingrained response of *no public display of affection.*

Why did she feel like this on Galactic Central, when holding hands and allowing contact from Jeff had become second nature for them on Cartain? Central was less judgmental about public affection than either Earth or Cartain.

GERAINT HIMSELF GRANTED them access to his quarters. He was mounted on his platform instead of crawling on the floor, as was usual for his private quarters.

"Dear Star, there is a hoof bath over there—" he gestured to the right side. "A necessary precaution in our personal quarters for those of us who are from Tsfalnel, I am sad to admit. We are far too vulnerable to outsiders."

Star snorted and tossed her head, annoyance creeping through her emotions.

"*It's not just you*," Caroline told Star as she slipped out of her sandals and prepared to walk through the light bath. "Humans need to leave our shoes in the cubbies here," she said out loud. "Then follow me through the light bath."

"Thank you, Caroline."

"You are welcome, Geraint. If I had any suspicion that we would have encountered this sort of reception, I would have briefed everyone on personal visit protocol." Caroline gestured to both Star, then Jeff and his cousins Tyrone and Paula, who had sat down on the bench next to the shoe cubbies to unfasten their shoes. "However, I assumed that we would be going directly to our quarters first and I could do a briefing there, not needing to find a pleasant place to stay while our quarters are made ready."

Jeff rose after slipping off his boots, and bowed. "I thank you so very much for your kindness, Geraint. We all appreciate it."

"Sssss," Geraint hissed in annoyance. "You are very welcome, Jeff and Caroline. This should not have happened. Rutan is investigating exactly *why* Hrina's autoskimmer controls glitched on her way to work this turn."

"Oh no! Is she all right?" Caroline paused on the other side of the light bath. Hrina had been Geraint's head intern before her, and had been thrilled to land a prime position with Congressional Housing.

"Ssss." This time he clapped his jaws before continuing, clearly distressed. "Her autoskimmer was on the skyway when it went off track, for no apparent reason. She lives, but she has many broken bones."

"That doesn't sound right." Jeff finished walking through the light bath and put his arm around Caroline. "I've never heard of something like that happening with autoskimmers."

"It is very rare," Geraint said. "More likely to happen here than anywhere else due to the complexity of Central skyways, and—sss—not always accidental." He clacked his teeth again. "I would advise you to be very careful in your actions right now, Star. The same for you, Jeff and Caroline. Untoward things have been happening on Central over the past ten-turn, tied to discussions about rella. And—things I am not yet approved to discuss given your levels of clearance."

Sentient planets, perhaps? Hmm.

Caroline's comm buzzed—Rifanel's ID came up.

"Hello, Rifanel."

"I have just heard about your problems at the Representative reception portal," Rifanel said. "Do you have a comfortable place to stay?"

"Yes. We are at Geraint's personal quarters."

"*Good.* I will be there shortly." Rifanel disconnected.

"Rifanel is on her way over," Caroline announced. "She heard about our issues at the reception portal."

Geraint clacked his jaws. "Well. Then. This is *most* interesting. How did *she* find out about this situation?"

RIFANEL WAS the most agitated that Caroline had ever seen her when she arrived at Geraint's, eyes wide enough to show the white sclera, moving quickly and jerkily. She went to Star immediately after marching through the hoof bath, touching noses with the dark bay mare.

"*She can speak to me!*" Star exclaimed to Caroline.

Caroline couldn't overhear the conversation, but then again, perhaps this was an issue of same-species communication. If so, then why couldn't Alami do the same thing?

At last Rifanel snorted, tossed her head, and swished her tail. "I apologize for being rude and speaking to Star first. But I needed to ensure that she was all right."

"Quite understandable given the hubbub on Central during the past ten-turn," Geraint said.

Now what?

"I received a rather rude inquiry from Kalanost in Housing about the Converted status of Star-from-Cartain." Rifanel flipped her ears back briefly. "I made inquiries. Geraint, I understand that you requested Hrina to be the Housing intake representative, and that she experienced a rather unusual autoskimmer crash?"

"I did indeed. Rutan is investigating the incident for me." Geraint gnashed his teeth.

"Kalanost has Statist sympathies." Rifanel flattened her ears and showed her teeth. "I have reported the things she said to me. She does *not* belong doing Intake work if she has this sort of attitude toward the recently Converted!"

Caroline stifled a groan.

"Does that mean we will have problems finding housing?" Jeff asked, voicing Caroline's concerns. "Honorable Rifanel, before her Conversion, Star belonged to me. She is free and her own person now, of course. I am absolutely offended by the way that Kalanost treated her! I will not agree to any attempts to revert her back to pre-Conversion status, whether it is actual or a case of not recognizing her current status. Yes, she's first-gen, but she deserves to be recognized as a full Converted equine!"

"I am very pleased to hear you say these words, Representative Tophand." Rifanel swished her tail sharply. "In the worst-case scenario, I will simply offer you housing in my quarters. All of you, not just Star. Cartain may not have clout, but both Hrwhinir and Tsfalnel are first-tier planets. I let Housing know that Fenarmin will be complaining further on Star's behalf."

"I have already done the same for Tsfalnel. Especially since Star is a staffer for a new member of the Federalist Caucus. The Federalists extend our grateful thanks to the

Councilists for your support, Rifanel, and please pass on our thanks to Fenarmin." Geraint flicked his tail.

"Do you believe this is a Statist conspiracy tied to—certain events in the past ten-turn?" Rifanel blew long and hard, a rattling snort that made Star raise her head. Uneasiness clutched at Caroline.

"I would advise caution in speaking of that possibility, even here," Geraint said. "But yesssss, I consider this to be very likely. Even though this—*incident*—with Star is not connected to those events, the conversations about Converted status are—quite fraught right now."

"I have spoken to our scientists from Hrwhinir. We can begin the Converted assessments of Star next turn, starting around Fifth Node, after you have eaten First Meal."

"Are we taking into consideration that Star has a bond with Caroline, and they can communicate without speaking?" Jeff asked.

"Yes." Rifanel flicked her ears. "There are very limited cases where some equines have both a translator and an inter-preter-level contact with another species capable of speech either with or without a translator. Hrwhinir is familiar with those exceptions."

"I won't be able to be with Star," Caroline said, her uneasi-ness growing. "I'm scheduled for Assistant Orientation at Fifth Node. Jeff has his exclusive Representative orientation at the same time."

"That will be all right," Rifanel said. "There will be time to assess your communication with Star once you are finished with orientation."

"*It will be all right,*" Star said. "*Rifanel has promised to be there with me.*"

"I suppose it will be all right if you are with Star, Rifanel," Caroline said, reluctantly.

Rifanel tossed her head. "I will not allow Star to be

deprived of Convert status, Caroline, Jeff. I—have a particular interest in this situation."

Caroline remembered the filly she had seen at Rifanel's quarters, and heaved a silent sigh of relief.

Several nodes later, a different housing liaison, Debell, a horse, met them at Geraint's quarters and took them to a spacious suite on the edge of Equine Central.

"This is mixed housing for horses and humans," Debell said. "I apologize that it is smaller than most mixed housing, but considering you only have one equine in your group...." His voice trailed off and he lowered his head, flicking his ears partway back.

Caroline inhaled sharply. This might be considered *small quarters* by equine standards, but—there was a small barn with a doorway that opened onto the human quarters. No fences, but a lush pasture. And the human quarters—

They were *big*. Unlike other quarters for Planetary Representatives in Central, the house stood alone. No shared walls. No common environmental systems. They were *outside*. Granted, that meant they would be subject to weather changes, but they had a view. A real view.

The McKinnon family quarters on Earth were nowhere near as nice.

Jeff grinned as he looked around the house. "I suppose these are considered to be lower-status quarters because we aren't close to other Representatives?"

"Alas, yes." Debell swished his tail, facial muscles tightening nervously, nostrils flaring wide.

"That's fine. This is a marvelous place, and I thank you for making these quarters available to us. By the time we're done here on Central, these quarters will be considered to be prestigious. And from what I've seen of pictures of those other, *higher-status* quarters, I think we—all of us—will be much happier here." His grin widened. "Caroline, my dear. What do you think?"

"It's absolutely gorgeous," Caroline said, and meant it.

She wondered what the other options would have been like. This much space was luxurious by Central housing standards—even by *Earth* criteria.

"CAROLINE! OVER HERE!" Raina, one of her intern friends who had also been promoted to assistant, waved a blue-shaded hand at Caroline as she hesitated in the doorway opening onto the Galactic Congress's floor.

Caroline grinned and hurried to join Raina in the humanoid section of the Galactic Congressional floor. Other friends were there, all some variant of human. Some had antennae, others pointy ears, still others green or blue or brown skin. Apparently she was *not* the only one in her cohort of interns from assorted universities across the galaxy who had landed themselves a Planetary Representative's assistant position in the new Congressional session.

"Congratulations on your assistant position and your marriage! All the pix I've seen of the two of you are awfully cute."

"The same for you—what level of marriage contract do you have?" Caroline settled in next to Raina—who was working for Tarnina, the Representative from her planet, Knopfl.

"Formal for eight cycles, if Tarnina wins the next three elections. And you?" Raina waved at another of their friends who was sitting in the back, in the Statist section.

Knopfl, like Hrwhinir and some other planets, had established term limits for their Planetary Representatives. Tarnina had a spouse back on Knopfl, and while the Knopflese were flexible in their marital arrangements, Raina had higher hopes for her future than marrying Tarnina.

"Formal, indefinite, possibility open for reproductive."

"I'm fine with just having a formal association with Tarnina," Raina said. "She's promised to introduce me to several District Governors back home once we're done. A period working in the Congress, and I'll be a very attractive candidate for either business or government."

Caroline nodded. Knopfl was home to a significant portion of the Federation's military starship designers and manufacturers. A first-rank planet, unlike Cartain, Earth, or Mars. Time spent in the Galactic Congress granted many privileges once a Knopflese returned home. When Caroline had left for Cartain to assume her role as Jeff's assistant, Raina was uncertain about whether she would land the position with Tarnina—she had a lot of competition. Neither of them had the time to catch up afterward—Tarnina was a Councilist, though Raina's own preference was for the Federalists.

"So have you changed your mind about running for Planetary Governor someday? Or are you planning to try out for the military once you're done here?" Caroline asked.

Raina had sworn to Caroline during one of their late-night cram sessions in intern quarters that, if need be, she would take the military route to Knopflese success if she couldn't reach her goals any other way.

Raina sniffed. "Of course not!" Her antennae twitched in her equivalent of laughter. "That would be a step down in status. What about you? Will there be life after Cartain, or are you staying there?"

"I'm not certain. Jeff and I are open to more than a formal marital association, but we're taking our time—"

A far-too-familiar cough from someone standing next to her aisle seat cut off Caroline's answer. Ice clenched her gut in sharp talons as Caroline turned to look up at her least favorite brother, Albert. He wore a Statist Party icon on his jacket lapel.

"Albert, what are you doing here?"

He scowled. "I would have thought you would be happy to see a familiar face."

"I didn't think you would offend Mother to the degree that she would send you to the Congress," she snapped. *Albert, here, of all my family. Albert!* "Or are you no longer her favorite?"

Albert snickered, peering over at Raina. His face twisted into a sneer. "Oh no, my dear sister. I'm here on special assignment from Hart Mercantile. Let's just say that some of our *interests* coincide with those of Lara Wordtrust. Especially when it comes to sentient planets."

Albert and Hart interested in sentient planets? I'm starting to get the feel of this whole top-secret buzz no one will tell us about, and I'm not sure I like it. Jeff and I don't have access to information about the Congress considering anything regarding sentient plan-ets, so how could Albert know?

Before Caroline could say anything, Raina made a faint growling noise, the Knopfl equivalent of *ewww*. Either Albert didn't know what that meant or he disregarded Raina's reac-tion—Caroline thought it more likely that he didn't know. Albert wasn't that good an actor.

"I thought Logan Easystar was Wordtrust's assistant," Caroline fired back. "This meeting is for primary assistants. Or did you enter a marital association with Wordtrust? I didn't think Earth supported poly relationships in its leaders these days."

Albert grimaced, wrinkling his lip. "Logan can't make it to this meeting so I'm attending in his stead."

"I see. Well, the Statist seats are back there." Caroline pointed behind them with her thumb. "This is where the *major* parties sit."

"That's stupid. I thought you *might* want to catch up on

family news."

"I know enough about the family." Caroline bit off each word sharply. "And the Statist seats are *back there*."

"My, you're getting pretty uppity these days, little sister. Don't forget your place!"

"*My place* is at the side of my spouse," Caroline snarled. "And as the primary assistant to a Planetary Representative, I have the opportunity to speak as his agent. I'm not some mousy house-bound wife spitting out babies as fast as I can whelp them!"

"You heard her," Raina chimed in, eyes beginning to turn red with anger as her antennae stiffened. "*Go away*, Statist lackey."

"I'm her brother!"

"And you're working for Lara Wordtrust and Logan Easystar," Caroline growled. "Easystar *lost* the lawsuit my spouse filed against him!"

Albert flushed with rage. "At least I'm not consorting with animals and lower life forms!"

That almost brought Caroline out of her seat, fists at the ready. Luckily, Raina grabbed her just as Rifanel kicked the gavel box at the podium with her forefoot.

"Seats, everyone! That includes *you*, Mr. McKinnon." Somehow the big mare managed to project a contemptuous tone through her translator. "Please take your seat with the Statists."

Albert shook his index finger at Caroline. "Just you wait, sister mine. I'll see you in your place yet!"

"This isn't Earth!" she snapped back.

"*Mr. McKinnon*." Rifanel's tone was even icier. "Do I need to send the sergeant-at-arms to show you to your seat?"

"I'm going, I'm going," Albert snarled. Under his breath, he muttered, just loud enough for Caroline to hear. "And you will pay for your disloyalty to Earth and our family!" Then he marched back to his seat.

Caroline turned to face the front, so angry that she couldn't keep from shaking.

"That's your brother?" Raina whispered. "He's—he's—"

"An utter asshole. Yes."

Raina emitted another *eww* growl. "I can see why you left Earth."

"Unfortunately, most of my family is like him." Caroline sighed and focused on Rifanel's presentation.

But she couldn't keep from wondering just *how* and *why* Albert was here instead of back on Earth, much less serving as a secondary assistant to Lara Wordtrust.

Until now, Caroline hadn't considered that any of her siblings would have the slightest interest in doing anything off-planet. This had to be some sort of scheme involving Hart Mercantile Services.

But what? Albert had achieved a high position in the company, higher than the position he now held as a secondary Congressional assistant.

What is Mother up to, and why?

Caroline had no doubt that whatever it was, Alice McKinnon was up to no good. Her mother was too much of an Earth First chauvinist to send her favorite child off to Galactic Central for such a lowly position, even if he had done something to offend her. Mars, yes. Galactic Central? Uh-uh.

I'm definitely going to warn Jeff about this situation.

Especially given Albert's remarks about sentient planets.

Caroline didn't get the opportunity to tell Jeff about the incident until they waited in Rifanel's private quarters to hear the results of the Hrwhinir assessment of Star's Conversion. They were alone in the parlor where she had talked with

Rifanel earlier. Rifanel had gone with the nameless brown filly to bring Star back from the labs.

"Your brother is Easystar's assistant?" Jeff frowned. "That doesn't make a lot of sense. And then he just casually mentions sentient planets?"

"Yes. He's doing something for my mother. Has to be the case. He wouldn't venture away from Earth's system otherwise. Which means Hart Mercantile Services is up to something."

"Hart Mercantile Services *has* been agitating for a share of the rella distribution market over the past cycle or so," Jeff said thoughtfully. "It came up on the Rella Producers Association chat before we left Cartain. But that's a new move on their part—happened eight spans ago. They haven't said anything at all about sentient planets."

"Long before we met, so it happened shortly after I arrived at Galactic Central for my internship." Caroline reached for the cup of clover tea. Jeff had also decided he liked its flavor, so Rifanel had prepared a pot for them. "It's not a reaction to our formal marital association."

Jeff side-eyed her. "Your mother has that much influence over Royce Hart?"

Caroline snorted, trying to cover her uneasiness. She *did* have her relationships openly disclosed, but had Jeff looked closely at her disclosure statement?

"Uncle Royce is my mother's voice and puppet for the most part because, as a woman, she can't be the official face of the company. But if he thought he could get a lock on something like rella, he would. Mother wouldn't need to say much for him to jump into some wild scheme that could give him access to a new drug." She exhaled. "I renounced all ties to the Hart family trust and any income from the trust when I became an intern in the Congress. It was necessary to pass the security check. It's one reason why I haven't been spending a lot of credits. An intern's stipend isn't very much."

"I saw that." Jeff's voice was quiet. "It made me realize what you gave up to—come to Central. And from things you have said about your family, it's pretty clear they aren't the nicest people in the galaxy."

Caroline looked down at the tea cup she clutched with both hands. "Some aren't too bad. Dad. My brother Abe. But Albert—he's Mother's favorite. I thought that Royce was grooming Albert to be his successor. Albert married the right woman, after all. Brought the Carlin family into the Hart circles. The last I had heard, he was rising pretty fast in Hart Mercantile."

"That's one thing I don't understand about Earth," Jeff said. "I thought it was strictly patriarchal. And yet it seems like your mother's family dominates what you and your siblings were intended to do. Your mother appears to have a lot of power."

Caroline laughed bitterly. "The saying is *the men rule; the women control.* My mother had the required four children that allowed her to assume a role beyond wife and mother. I was —Mother had not made the necessarily alliances for a girl child's future. I was just the necessary number four that freed her, and she agreed to avoid gender selection at my father's request. But they both expected another boy. It might have been different if I was pretty—"

"Stop that. Please. You're beautiful, Caroline."

"Not in Earth terms." She gulped, blinking back unexpected tears. "I could not expect to marry into one of the High Families. The McKinnons—Dad's family sacrificed a lot to make him attractive to the Harts, to marry him to my mother. That left no resources for me. Beauty would have bought me a place, but my brothers were expected to marry and bring in resources for the Harts. I had no comparable resources to offer a prospective suitor on Earth."

Jeff sighed. "No wonder you don't want to go back."

"Exactly." She sipped her tea. "Mother's message when I

announced my new position and our marital association was —not pretty."

Hoofbeats thundered outside. Caroline raised her brows at Jeff.

"Doesn't sound like anything more than blowing off steam," he said. "Not panic—hear those snorts?"

If she had any doubts, joy suddenly washed over her.

"I am certified as a true Converted, and scheduled for a translator implant at Fifth Node next turn!" Star exulted.

"Your grin says it's good news." Jeff studied her closely.

Caroline set down her cup. "Yes."

"She's a true Converted?"

"Certified. Translator implant next turn, at Fifth Node."

Jeff yelped joyfully and jumped up. He swept Caroline into his arms and swung her around the room. "That is the best news I've heard since we got here!" He set her back on her feet, still holding Caroline close.

She looked up into his gold-flecked brown eyes. That smile of his. His scent—the way he leaned toward her—

And then his lips were on hers. Oh. *Oh.* Full, yet tender. The contact sent a buzzing warmth throughout her body.

He raised his head. "Correction. That's the second-best thing that's happened since we got here. This is the first best thing."

"Yes." Could she get enough of gazing up at this man? "My first kiss. I'll remember this forever."

Jeff exhaled shakily. "I'm glad you like it. And now—we'd better go outside to hear everything. There's some excited horses out there. One of them isn't a Converted and could be a little rowdy. Rifanel won't bring her inside for a while."

"Yes." She didn't want to stop looking into Jeff's eyes, but —they had other things to do right now.

But she intended to kiss Jeff again soon—and perhaps even more than that, in time.

9

CONGRESSIONAL BEGINNINGS

CAROLINE HADN'T EXPECTED to be *this* overwhelmed by opening ceremonies for the new Galactic Congress session. Granted, she had come into the Congress as an intern during the second half of the previous two-cycle session, and observed the closing ceremonies, so she had some idea about the degree of elaborate rituals involved.

Rifanel had showed video of the opening ceremonies during the assistant orientation session, but video wasn't the same experience as standing next to Jeff as he swore his oath. Or watching the procession of party leaders to the podium headed by Geraint, Rutan, and Ssgaldir for the Federalists, then Katrina Allsides and her spouse, plus Rifanel and Fenarmin for the Councilists, and finally Lara Wordtrust and Logan Easystar for the Statists.

Geraint's oath as Speaker sent chills through her as well, especially since the mixed species seating boxes they had as a result of Star's role as Caroline's assistant earned them a placement up front. It just seemed more *real* and weighty with only a small space separating them from the podium, instead of needing viewers to observe the main event from the highest balcony seating. Being able to read the subtle nuances of Geraint's positioning, as well as those of Ssgaldir and Rutan, standing proudly by their spouse.

Caroline found herself taking Jeff's hand as the ceremony proceeded. He squeezed it and smiled at her.

The major downside of their box location, however, was that they also ended up in the same row as the Party leaders. Which wasn't too great of a problem since Fenarmin and Rifanel were next to them—*just need to keep Jeff and Fenarmin from ad hoc arguing*—with Katrina Allsides and her staff next. But next to Allsides was the Statist box. Wordtrust and Easystar, along with other Statists, didn't linger for the first round of floor business once opening ceremonies were concluded, leaving Albert alone and far too close to them for Caroline's liking.

Not that she could—or would—do anything about it. Jeff's seat placement in the Congressional chambers was a huge honor, and Caroline was not about to interfere with his position. She could endure Albert's smirks and sneers because, after all, she held a higher status in the Congress than he did.

Besides, even if Albert had the influence of Hart Mercantile Services behind him, what could he do to her? Hart Mercantile didn't have the same clout in the Congress that it did back on Earth. *She* had connections to the leadership of the two major parties in the Congress.

All the same, Caroline didn't have to like the fact that she had to see her least favorite brother on a daily basis.

However, it did give her discreet amusement to see how Albert dodged the possibility of being introduced formally to Jeff when Congress adjourned after that first full session.

Upholding Mother's bigotry, even here.

At least she didn't care what Albert thought about her spouse and what she was doing.

Jeff's committee assignments had hearings that overlapped each other, regularly. Unescapable given the size of the Congress—well over one thousand members—and the many concerns that the Congress, as the Federation's governing body, had to cover. Caroline called a staff meeting immediately after the opening session to dole out coverage assignments.

"It makes the most sense for Jeff to focus on the Plant-Based Drug Controls committee," she said. "That's where the rella issues will be discussed, including cartel management." A prized assignment, usually limited to more experienced Representatives. Jeff's role as a rella grower had earned him the seat.

"And the Converted Concerns committee," Jeff added. "When I can do both and there's no schedule conflicts."

Caroline nodded. Converted Concerns was another big committee assignment. In both cases, Jeff's experience outweighed his lack of seniority.

She took the Converted Concerns committee as her primary responsibility, though she would assist Jeff when she could. Star also was assigned that committee, though she wouldn't be able to pick up those duties for at least two turns. After discussing the remaining assignments, and showing Tyrone and Paula the preferred notetaking process for committee coverage, Caroline sent Rutan the list of Jeff's attendance priorities and who would be covering for him in what committees, as well as proxy details for when Jeff couldn't make it to a committee vote. That meant they covered ten committees apiece.

She would brief Star later, once the dark bay mare had recovered from her translator implant surgery and had learned more about using the translator not just for speech but for the pictographs used for equine reading and note-taking.

Then they scattered to the first sessions of their assorted committees.

I don't know why we don't videoconference these committees. It would be so much easier, she thought as she sprinted to Converted Concerns.

On the other hand, videoconferencing would make it more difficult for lobbyists to buttonhole Representatives and their staffers as they moved from committee to committee. Caroline hadn't thought about that aspect before. Lobbyists didn't pay attention to interns.

But they *definitely* noticed the assistant/spouse of a Planetary Representative.

She would have been worried about being late to the committee, except that other assistants and Representatives were going through the same dance of acknowledging lobbyists. A first-turn ritual, she supposed, though Caroline remembered that Rutan had been accosted regularly by lobbyists when she had followed him from committee to committee. Just fewer of them.

Caroline scheduled quick appointments for both her and Jeff with a handful of lobbyists, focusing on those who had interests on Cartain. Others, she put off with bland assurances that she could schedule them for later—including the Hart Mercantile Services lobbyist, Geri Ahrens.

Not that the woman was unfamiliar—they had attended the same boarding school and debuted in the same social occasions. Ahrens appeared to be put off by Caroline's deferral, but—Caroline remembered the many times that Geri had mocked her when they were younger.

"Robbie Windsor always made time for me," Ahrens sniffed.

I bet he did. Geri possessed that classic fragile blond-girl Earth beauty that Robbie-boy preferred in women. *Wonder if you slept with him, or just tried to get into his bed?*

"Does Hart Mercantile have an active interest on Cartain?"

Caroline already knew the answer to that question. *She* was the closest thing to a legitimate interest on Cartain that Hart Mercantile might possess.

"No, but—"

"I'm sorry, but Jeff's appointments during this first ten-turn need to be reserved for those who have *active* interests in Cartain, Geri. Even when it comes to the Converted Concerns committee. We'll be able to get to you before the end of this span. That's the best I can do right now. Sorry." Caroline gave Geri her best fake smile and turned to the next lobbyist waiting for her—not a corporate lobbyist, but a Crested Flyer from Cartain who was working on Central and concerned about their child, who had been unfairly discharged from their position as assistant cargo transport pilot for—of all companies—Hart Mercantile.

Caroline smiled for real as she prioritized the Flyer for a Second Meal meeting, as Geri Ahrens spluttered and protested.

She split that first turn of committee sessions between Converted Concerns and Plant-Based Drug Controls. Albert stood in for Lara Wordtrust on both committees as well. Annoying. Caroline tried to stagger her presence between committees so that she wasn't present when Albert was.

For the most part, her juggling worked. Between that and running the gamut of lobbyists, evading Albert was easy enough.

Until the end of the session. The lobbyists had faded away when Caroline left the Converted Concerns committee. She had already forwarded her notes to Jeff and the others, and was hurrying toward their offices to meet Jeff so that they could return to their quarters together.

Albert stepped out of an alcove. "Agatha." He grabbed her arm.

Caroline yanked free. "That's not my name anymore, and *don't touch me!*"

He shoved her against the wall. "You are *still* Agatha McKinnon, *my sister*, and you are a disgrace to all of us!"

"You have no authority over me!" Caroline tried to push Albert away, but, as always, he managed to pin her. She tried to knee him in the crotch but he blocked her.

"You listen to me, *sister*. You're still a McKinnon, you're unmarried, and that means you have to listen to me. I order you to go back to Earth."

"That's where you're wrong. I'm married."

"Hah!" Albert snorted. "A formal association is not a *real* marriage and you *know* it! I demand that you break the contract. Go back to Earth. Mother has found a spouse for you."

She considered spitting in his face as Albert leaned in close, his face reddening in rage at her defiance.

No. She wouldn't bring herself down to his level. Once she got away from Albert, then she would talk to Jeff. Find support. Plan to not be alone at the end of the turn from now on. A pain, but…Caroline blinked back angry tears, her throat tight and locked down, rendering her unable to respond as Albert smirked at her. Oh, he still knew her *too damn well*. Next would come the prodding until he made her cry with rage.

Why can't I break this cycle, even now?

Then a loud snort came from behind Albert. He jumped as Fenarmin grabbed him by the collar of his suit jacket, yanking Albert away from Caroline.

"When a mare says *no*, you listen!" the big red stallion rumbled. "Humans need to do a better job of training their males!"

Albert clenched his fists. "What do you know of human families? You're just a stupid horse!"

Fenarmin's ears flicked back.

"I wouldn't tangle with Fenarmin if I were you, Albert McKinnon. He was sentient duel-qualified before his injury." Jeff walked around Fenarmin and took Caroline in his arms. "Are you all right, dear?"

She nodded, anger now bringing the tears to her eyes that she didn't dare show before. Jeff reached up and stroked her cheek.

"And you—you—you get your hands off of my sister!" Albert spluttered.

Jeff's expression hardened and he turned to face Albert, still holding Caroline tight. "Caroline is *my wife*, Albert. In accordance with the laws of Cartain and the Federation."

"Not in the eyes of her family!" Albert took a step toward Jeff and Caroline.

Fenarmin swung his heavy head and knocked Albert backwards. He arched his neck and pawed at the air, front hoof hovering barely above the floor so that he did not scuff it, emitting a deep, chesty growl—a horse, growling? Caroline had never thought of a horse doing *that* until now. However, the deep rumble from Fenarmin *definitely* sounded like a growl. Especially the way the chestnut stallion glared through his long red forelock at Albert.

"You assaulted me!" Albert's voice turned high and squeaky.

"You have shown intent to attack the spouse of a Planetary Representative and the Planetary Representative himself." Fenarmin tossed his head and blew a long, rolling snort through wide nostrils, the inner lining showing red. "That behavior has consequences. I suggest you *leave* this area. *Now.*" He slammed his hoof down hard, making the floor quiver. His ears flattened even more. "I have no love for Jeff Tophand, but I also have no regard for an impertinent, upstart young stallion who does not respect a mare's *no*. Regardless of what species he is. If you were on Hrwhinir, you would have learned this lesson from the Gathering of Mares! Go!" He bared his teeth and lunged at Albert, stopping just short of the human.

Albert backed away from them, raising his hands. "I'll go, but you watch your step, Agatha! You don't belong here! And *you*—" he pointed at Fenarmin. "One of these turns, you animals will be returned to your proper status—subservient to humans! Just you wait and see!"

Albert whirled and ran as Fenarmin darted at him again. Fenarmin stomped once more, blowing that long, hard, rattling snort, glaring down the corridor as Albert fled.

"Too bad humans do not believe in gelding. The Gathering of Mares would have petitioned the Court of Stallions to *do something* about that one, cycles ago!" he growled.

Caroline laughed shakily. "I completely agree with you, Fenarmin—and thank you."

"Yes," Jeff chimed in. "I appreciate the assistance, Fenarmin. It's probably better that I didn't beat him up, much as I wanted to do it."

"That one is dangerous." Fenarmin turned back to them. "His associates in Congress are dangerous. He calls you sibling, Caroline?"

"Unfortunately, yes."

"Then his disrespect toward you is even less acceptable. Siblings do not have control over a mare's mating choice!"

"And my mother just *loves* Caroline," Jeff said.

"Then that is the important part." Fenarmin snorted again, softer this time. "Your herd matriarch supports your choice of mate, Tophand, and that matters." He bobbed his head. "A good first turn, Tophand. We have much to consider."

"Agreed, Fenarmin. An excellent first turn for the opening of the Congress—and I thank you for your assistance with McKinnon."

"Your mare has the favor of my Rifanel. I could do no less, especially since McKinnon is one of those cursed Statists." Fenarmin's upper lip curled briefly. "Until the next turn, Tophand."

"Until the next turn, Fenarmin." Jeff bobbed his head at Fenarmin.

The big chestnut stallion turned neatly on his hind legs and walked away.

Jeff hugged Caroline. "You're all right?" he asked again, as they walked to the autoskimmer pool where they could check out a vehicle to take them back to their quarters.

"Yes," she said. "He just caught me by surprise."

"You're shaking a little bit."

"He just caught me by surprise," she repeated. "That's all."

"We can't have this happen again," Jeff said firmly. "I'm talking to Geraint. I would think this incident and the threat would be enough to justify assigning a Central Defender to you when you're in chambers. I'm sure I can get Fenarmin to support my request."

"Oh Jeff, I don't think that's necessary—"

"We both heard him threaten to send you back to Earth." Jeff tightened his lips. "I will not let him do that to you, Caroline! Not unless you *want* to go."

She stopped, turning Jeff to face her.

"I will never willingly return to Earth, Jeff. Never. That time is—gone."

Jeff leaned forward. Caroline pulled him close, into another of those marvelous, marvelous kisses. At last, they pulled apart. He smiled down at her.

"I'm glad to hear that," he said huskily. "Now. Let's head for home. Or at least what passes for home here on Galactic Central."

"Agreed."

The two of them continued down the corridor, arms around each other's waists.

I am so, so lucky.

When Caroline had come to Galactic Central her only thought had been to escape from the expectations placed on her by Earth society. She had not expected—this relationship.

THE NEXT FEW turns were anticlimactic compared to that first turn in Congress. It took Star four turns to recover from implant surgery and gain enough control of her translator that she could work. Once the translator implant was fully functioning, Star and Caroline did not mindspeak to each other very often, mainly because Star preferred to use her translator implant.

One of the Central Defenders followed Caroline around Congress whenever she left Jeff's offices. Albert didn't try to approach her again.

Jeff ended up spending all of his time in the Plant-Based Drug Controls committee, which meant Caroline needed to assign more work to Star, Tyrone, and Paula.

"There's a bigger problem with the rella supply than I realized," he told Caroline on their fifth turn in Congress, as they paused to have sandwiches for Second Meal as well as a short time together on a hectic day with many important meetings. "I did not realize that there are so many illicit uses of rella throughout the Galaxy. The Ribonits can't control it at all. Given the demand, their quality control demands on Cartain shouldn't be as strict as they are."

"Do you think those QC requirements reflect corruption at some level?"

"It's possible. Especially since you saw that Plasmoid going into the Rella Protective Association offices. The Plasmoids alone—" he shook his head. "It's absolutely amazing.

Ten different Plasmoid species; ten different reactions. One species uses rella as a voluntary suicide drug. Another for extreme intoxication. The most intriguing possibility, and the one that's the hardest to dig out details, is its use by the Plasmoids to instigate Convert transition. Has the Converted Concerns committee heard the presentation from the Galactic Controlled Substances Agency yet?"

"No. It's supposed to be after Second Meal."

Jeff tapped up his schedule. "I'm open, surprise, surprise. I'll join you because I want to hear it again. I'm really concerned. The examples that the GCSA cited about Plasmoid usage for Convert transition are far too close to what you and Star experienced for my liking. I have questions, and maybe we'll hear more about it in Converted Concerns."

"That makes sense. I'm sure there will be more Converted-specific questions in this committee. But. Didn't you tell me that usage of rella as a means to bring about Convert transition was known on Cartain?"

"Very quiet and limited to Uprights and Flyers, which is why Star is considered to be such an anomaly," Jeff said. "It's mostly used by the Uprights for that purpose. However, the Plasmoids have a particular rella refinement process for their Conversions. From what we're being told by the GCSA, the Plasmoid ship we saw was performing that specific rella refinement process when you and Star stopped that attack on our field. That may explain what happened with Star."

Caroline glanced around cautiously before speaking. No sign of Star—she had gone to Rifanel's for more translator speaking, reading, and writing practice. Star and the not-yet-Converted filly who was part of Rifanel's herd had become fast friends, choosing to spend much of their spare time together.

"Is there a chance that Star's Conversion could be reverted? Or that it requires further treatments?"

Jeff shook his head. "Not from what I'm hearing." His

expression became more solemn. "But there's a new application for Federation membership that's being considered by the Drugs Committee, and it worries me. That's another reason why I want to see for myself what the GCSA says to the Converted Concerns Committee."

"Why would a membership application go through the Drugs Committee? Are they producing plant-based drugs?"

The normal Federation membership hearing process meant that the representatives of the planet made presentations supporting their applications in front of all of the committees that dealt with products valuable enough to export off-planet. Some planets had a plethora of resources; others were—quite limited. If it hadn't been for its near-exclusive production of rella and ixtnatal, Cartain would have had more difficulties with their application to join the Federation as a full member.

Then there were the sentient planets—and no one was certain about *them.*

"They are," Jeff said slowly. "They claim to be able to grow rella, in greater quantities than Cartain can produce, and at a higher quality. And they made their application during the last session, not this one."

Caroline froze. "If that's the case…." Her voice trailed off.

"Yeah," Jeff said, his voice heavy. "Robbie-boy knew about this planet's application for Federation membership, and didn't report it to the Boss. Not even a whisper that rella could be grown elsewhere."

"Is their ability to grow rella confirmed?"

"Not yet." But the uncertainty in his voice sent a chill through Caroline.

"What's the planet called?" She would start networking to get more information, because this was *definitely* a threat to Cartain.

"Memaj." Jeff finished his sandwich. "And here's the other thing, Caroline."

"What's that?"

"They claim that Memaj supports both Solid and Plasmoid residents."

Caroline frowned. "Now that doesn't make sense." It was well-known that the planetary atmospheres friendly to Plasmoids required special protective suits for any Solids, and vice versa—therefore the protective bubbles, like the one she had seen in Shrum, around that Plasmoid going into the Rella Protective Association.

"No. It doesn't. But they make the claim nonetheless." Jeff paused. "And Hart Mercantile Systems is collaborating with the Memaj leadership in their presentations. They have put forth a proposal to replace the Ribonits with Hart as controllers of rella as well as other plant-based drugs."

"Hart's collaborating through Albert?" That would be a huge conflict of interest for any assistant—on the other hand, such a conflict might be a means for getting him out of Galactic Central. Too bad that it probably wasn't him.

"No. Their lobbyist, Geri Ahrens."

Caroline grimaced. "I went to school with Geri. Probably should have set up a meeting with her when she asked for it, but I didn't see a reason to prioritize her."

Jeff rested his hand on hers. "Not a friend, then."

"No. Not a friend."

"We'll see if she approaches me. So far, she's been pretty standoffish, and not been one of the lobbyists pushing to talk to me."

"She would be distant." Caroline couldn't keep the bitter tone out of her voice. "She's another supremacist, like Albert."

Jeff rolled his eyes. "I swear, however did you manage to escape being shaped into one of that ilk, Caroline?"

"Being big-bodied instead of the cute little buxom blonde Earth girl. Questioning everything. Being shoved into a corner because I wasn't as important as everyone else in the family. If I had been blonde, skinny with a big chest, and pretty, it would have been different."

Jeff picked up her hand and kissed the back of it, then turned it over and kissed her palm. "Even though what you went through caused you pain, I'm selfishly glad that it brought you here. My life is so much nicer with you in it."

Once again, Caroline's cheeks burned with a flush.

Would she ever get used to these compliments, enough to take them for granted?

She hoped not. They still sounded sweet to her.

───

CAROLINE AND JEFF walked hand-in-hand to the Converted Concerns committee meeting. Albert started toward Caroline as they entered the hearing room, then stopped, grimacing, as he spotted Jeff. She gratefully took up the assistant's seat behind Jeff and set up his review screen, making sure that she temporarily revoked her proxy voting privileges since Jeff was attending this meeting and could vote. Lara Wordtrust's seat was on the other end of the head table, so Albert wouldn't have any excuse to walk directly beside her.

Fenarmin and Rifanel took their position next to Jeff and Caroline. She glanced down the row and realized that nearly every Representative was there in person instead of sending their assistants.

This is more important than we realized.

Jeff spun his chair around. "Does your screen allow you to record the presentation? Slides as well as what's said?"

"Yes."

"Mine has been cranky and support couldn't get it working when the GCSA presented to the Drugs Committee this morning. Apparently, everyone else was having problems with glitches as well. Maybe it'll be better in a different room."

"Maybe."

There *were* other possibilities, including the likelihood that the GCSA was running an aggressive, high-security blocker. Geraint wasn't on the Plant-Based Drugs committee, and she didn't think that any of the other Representatives on that committee had assistants with the ability to break official blockers. Lara Wordtrust was the ranking member on that committee and the Statist was—well, not the savviest about such things.

Neither is Albert, for that matter.

One of the seminars that Caroline had slipped into at Mars University during her last term before her internship had focused on the management of official security methods, including how to get around blockers. Most agencies at Galactic Central used blockers during their presentations to Congressional committees, for confidentiality's sake to avoid leakage of sensitive information.

Working with Geraint ended up being an advanced version of the security seminar. Geraint's staff knew quite a bit about evading blocking devices. Caroline had learned a few tricks from Rutan and Shshrit about working around blockers that assorted Federation agencies might be running during their presentations. There were often discrepancies between the official records provided to Representatives and what was actually said in committees—Caroline had originally been shocked at the variance, though Rutan and Geraint accepted it as the norm.

As the GCSA head and their assistants started setting up, Caroline surreptitiously ran a scan using one of Shshrit's algorithms. She was grateful that Shshrit had passed on the most recent update of that algorithm. It flashed a warning at her—*ah*. Caroline ran the blocking counter, and stifled a grin as the first presentation slide came up clearly.

Highest security. Very interesting.

She spent more time during the presentation countering

the attempts of the blocker to shut out her recording than paying attention to the questioning. Jeff wheeled around several times to whisper a request for further clarification from her recording. She passed on the answers to his requests, too busy to focus on anything but the details of blocker management, certainly not listening in. This was a *very* aggressive blocker.

At last the presentation was complete. Caroline made a note to herself to review the full presentation as she had recorded it and compare her version to the officially provided recording. The committee chair called for a break before moving on to the next agenda item. Jeff immediately joined several other Federalist Representatives. Caroline stretched and decided to step into the hallway to get some fresh air.

As the GCSA presenters left the hearings room, Caroline noticed something familiar about one of their staffers—someone who hadn't been at the mic testifying, but had been standing in the back of the room. She gulped as they looked in her direction.

Her brother Abraham.

What is Abe doing here?

She started toward him, but was blocked by a couple of reptilians taller than she was. When she finally, politely and with many apologies, got past them, there was no sign of Abe.

Maybe it was just her imagination—after all, Abe was her favorite brother, and hadn't participated in the spew of family criticism aimed at Caroline when she announced her marriage to Jeff and her position as his assistant. Maybe it was just wishful thinking that Abe was here instead of Albert. She would feel comfortable inviting Abe to their quarters to meet Jeff.

But Abe also held a fairly responsible position in Hart Mercantile's accounting division, and had never shown any inclination to leave Earth.

Just my imagination, she thought.

Then the faint glow of a peach-shaded Plasmoid bubble appeared at the far end of the corridor. Caroline squinted. Was the person who resembled Abe the one standing there talking to it?

Before she could investigate further, a chime announced that committee was going back into session.

Caroline mentally filed that sighting away to consider later, and returned to her seat.

TRADITION in the Galactic Congress required a three-turn break at the end of every ten-turn, uncreatively known as First Break, Second Break, and so on throughout the Congressional session. Caroline was more than ready to have some down time so that they could do something other than running from committee hearings to floor sessions to private meetings. Somehow the schedule seemed more rigorous now than it had been when she was just an intern—but interns got more time off, and the three-turn session breaks could be spent studying or goofing off, without official duties unless one wanted to do some extra work.

Not so as the head assistant and spouse to a Representative. Caroline had a pile of to-dos to check off on her planner. Networking with Shshrit and Rutan because Jeff had the responsibility for shepherding a bill important to the Federalists through one of his lower-level committees. It was a small tax matter, except that in a government as big as the Federation, there weren't really any *small tax matters.* They needed time to strategize the best route for the bill's success. If Jeff could manage to get this bill passed, then it would add to his status, not just amongst the Federalists but the Congress as a whole.

Following committees. Meeting with lobbyists and constituents.

Entertaining.

For once, Caroline's training as a McKinnon-Hart scion and potential marriage alliance candidate turned out to be useful.

"You're really good at organizing this type of formal occasion," Paula said when they were putting together the first Third Meal party of First Break.

Caroline had settled for two Third Meal parties during the first two turns of First Break. The first party would include close allies and intimates with a focus on shepherding the tax bill through the assorted committees it needed to traverse. The second party was an open house with a buffet, a larger gathering intended for anyone and everyone to attend. Jeff had requested that they keep the third turn of the breaks unscheduled, for everyone's rest and relaxation before starting up Congressional business the next turn.

Caroline shrugged. "If I had stayed on Earth and remained who I was, overseeing events like this would have been my primary function. At least until I had borne the required number of children my husband wanted and could move into a more fulfilling management role."

Paula wrinkled her face into a scowl that looked like she had smelled something bad. "That doesn't sound like fun at all."

"Why do you think I left Earth?"

"I'd have left too," Paula agreed.

THE FIRST PARTY WENT WELL. But Caroline fretted over the second one. Having their particular lodging meant they could set up parties very similar to the ones she had attended on Cartain, which provided more eating options for different species. She just wasn't certain how well it would work, especially since it was an open invite. What if they ran out of the preferred food for one of the attending species? That wasn't a concern back on Earth because of the limited number of sentient species that would be attending a party. But here on Central....

As the time for the party approached, nerves tightened Caroline's gut. She wore her black dress from the wedding, accented by a magenta scarf wrapped around her waist. Jeff wore one of his nice snap-buttoned, yoked shirts in black and magenta, along with jeans and his best go-to-town boots.

"Might as well give them a taste of the rodeo duelist," he joked to Caroline as he watched her apply makeup, seated at the vanity in her dressing room. Their suites in Central were adjoining, with a shared bathroom. Even though each suite was actually bigger than the ones in the farmhouse on Cartain, they still felt smaller to Caroline, probably because of the shared bathroom. That allowed her and Jeff to visit without stepping outside of the suites. Somehow, this made her feel more married.

"Maybe I should get some matching clothes," she said.

He laughed. "No, that's not necessary, at least not for Congress. I *like* your style choices."

"I'm glad." For this event, she was wearing an elaborate shell and carved respin nut necklace and earring set from Cartain, made by a prominent Crested Flyer jewelry designer, that had been a wedding present from the Boss. The shells were a translucent rainbow shade, the respin nuts mostly green and brown, the magenta underlayer revealed by the complex, abstract designs carved on them, linked by magenta and green fallalt grass stems woven and twisted into elaborate patterns.

He rose and rested a hand on her shoulder. "You look gorgeous, Caroline. And so much of Cartain that it won't be long until people think you were born there."

"Now that's a compliment I'll take to heart." She stood up. They kissed—gently at first, then more intensely.

Jeff pulled back, smiling. "One of these turns...."

"Yes," she agreed. "One of these turns."

THE PARTY WENT WELL at first. Caroline had taken advantage of their location to set up well-separated feeding stations on the grass outside of their quarters. The interns arrived in waves, some flocking to Caroline to complement her on her fortunate position while others focused on food. As Caroline expected, they arrived, ate, socialized a little, then moved on.

Many of the attendees were equines and reptilians, thanks to their Federalist connections. Fenarmin and Rifanel made an appearance before moving on to another, more Councilist engagement.

"We would stay," Rifanel said quietly to Caroline. "But I need to make appearances at our new Councilist member gatherings. Next time we'll stay longer."

"Thank you for coming."

Even Blackburn and Laura Richardson made an appearance, lingering on the fringes as Blackburn talked shop with several other rabbits who seemed to have military or intelligence ties.

Caroline didn't know what instinct made her glide close to where visitors disembarked from their autoskimmers when Lara Wordtrust and Logan Easystar drifted into the party. So far, Jeff and Easystar had maintained a professional demeanor toward each other, but who knew what would happen at a party? Albert climbed out of a second autoskimmer and Caroline sighed, resigning herself to probably needing to endure Albert's presence as well as Logan Easystar's, possibly even Geri Ahrens.

And then she spotted the woman that Albert helped out of the autoskimmer.

Alice McKinnon's expression twisted into its usual sour disapproval as she looked around the party. Star, Tyrone, and Paula were greeting attendees but Alice swept by without acknowledging them.

Caroline inhaled deeply. She wanted to run away, but if she did now, it would be noticed. Jeff was on the other side of the party, chatting with Blackburn and some newer Federalist Representatives under a cone of silence. She couldn't leave, couldn't pull him away from that important discussion. Not even for *this*.

What is Mother doing here?

10

A NEW PLAYER

NOW SHE REALLY, really wanted Jeff at her side.

"What's wrong? Your emotion projections are kinda weird and nervous." Star! At least they still had their mindspeech link. Relief flooded over Caroline. She had *someone* supporting her who was close by.

"That new couple who just arrived? That's my mother with my brother Albert. What is she doing here?" she said to Star.

"Perhaps she is here to congratulate you."

"My mother doesn't operate that way, Star. She wouldn't leave Earth for such a simple thing as congratulating me, and the message I received from her when I announced becoming Jeff's assistant suggest that she wasn't happy with either my job or my marriage. Now she's here. At this party. She's gonna confront me and make a scene. I just know it. Jeff's talking to Blackburn and I don't dare distract him because it's a confidential conversation with a cone of silence."

It was much, *much* more difficult to handle her anxiety as Alice McKinnon looked around, then focused on Caroline, heading straight for her.

"I will be right there! Don't worry!" Star said something quietly to Tyrone and Paula, then whirled, trotting across the

grass to join Caroline. Paula followed, a worried expression tightening her face.

Alice McKinnon beat them. She halted in front of Caroline, sporting that sour look that Caroline knew so well. "So. Agatha. It appears that you claim to be married, and refuse to return to Earth. Despite my direct order by way of Albert."

"I *am* married." Caroline did her best to keep her voice level. "And my name is Caroline Starshine, not Agatha." *Albert didn't say he was issuing a direct order from Mother—not that I would obey it anyway.*

Alice snorted. "Changing your name doesn't change who you are."

"She is Caroline Starshine, wife to Jeff Tophand," Star said firmly as she came up beside Alice. She pivoted on her left foreleg to stand next to Caroline, pushing her shoulder against Caroline's right side.

"Ew! What are you?" Alice backed away two steps. "A horse that talks. That's not *right*. It's not *normal*."

Caroline cheered internally at Alice's reaction—that was one thing in her favor. If Star put Alice off of her stride, that was a good thing, right?

"Alice, this is Star, recently Converted, and part of our staff. And," she added, "a good friend." Caroline rested her arm across Star's back, taking comfort in the dark bay mare's presence.

"An animal is your *friend*?" Disgust colored Alice's voice.

"Galactic Central society is much more advanced than Earth society, Alice." Another satisfying moment as even more distaste tightened her mother's face. Was it the reminder of Earth's backwater status in the Federation, or her refusal to call Alice *mother*? "Star and I went through a rather traumatic experience recently," she continued. "That has created an even firmer bond between us."

Paula joined them. "Is everything all right, Caroline?"

Caroline glanced toward Jeff—the cone of silence was now down. "If you could get Jeff, that would be a big help, Paula. Oh." There was another thing she could do to annoy her mother, especially since she now displayed that long-suffering patient look she always had around those she considered to be lesser creatures. Alice McKinnon's fabled poker face was saved only for beings she *respected.* "Paula Ford, this is Alice McKinnon. Alice, Paula is one of my cousins by marriage."

It was *so* worth it to see her mother's eyes widen first in surprise, then tighten down in anger. "She is *what?*"

"Paula, get Jeff. Quickly. Please."

Paula hurried off.

Alice McKinnon's expression hardened. "Agatha. Not only are you consorting with *animals—*" She choked, face reddening.

Star snorted. Her back tensed under Caroline's arm.

"Don't react," Caroline told her. *"She's a raging bitch and I know it. We have to be careful, though. She is powerful through Hart Mercantile Services."*

"It's very tempting to double-barrel kick her."

"I wish!" Caroline laughed, which made Alice's lips tighten.

"You've married someone who is—who is—" Alice's anger made her fumble for words.

"A former rodeo duelist? Planetary Representative for Cartain?" Caroline kept her voice low, but allowed a note of sarcasm to creep in.

"He's *black,*" Alice hissed in a low voice. "You're a Hart and McKinnon. How is he worthy of you?"

"He qualified for a sentient duel."

"A sentient duel! As if that counts for anything! Your bloodline is stellar. He's hardly better than that animal next to you!"

"Mmm. Star, what do you think? Is Jeff your equal, or

better?" Caroline tried for a flippant tone even though she was raging inside.

How dare she. HOW DARE SHE!

"Aren't we all equal in the eyes of the Federation?" A faint grumbling note rather like that growl of Fenarmin's when confronting Albert colored Star's response.

"True, very true." Her voice was almost *too* flippant now, to cover her anger.

"Hello there." Jeff came up beside Caroline and slid his arm around her waist. "So who is this, Caroline?"

"Jeff, this is Alice McKinnon. Alice, this is Jeff Tophand, my husband." Caroline said the words firmly, almost defiantly, as her mother glared at him. "Jeff, Alice gave birth to me."

"Ah. I thank you for the gift of this wonderful woman to the universe, Alice McKinnon." Jeff turned his head and softly kissed Caroline's cheek. "We've only known each other for a very short time, and yet I feel like I have known Caroline forever."

"You—you—" Alice inhaled sharply, visibly forcing restraint on herself. A deep exhale and soft shake, and she was once again the Alice McKinnon of Hart Mercantile Services, a woman who had proven herself worthy by Earth standards and was no longer bound by their strictures on women. "Agatha. I have found an *appropriate* marriage for you, on Earth." She sniffed at Jeff, then Star. "You will not need to endure the presence of these *creatures* any longer, and can fulfill your true destiny. I order your return, and cancellation of any contract you may have with this—this—"

"Ah, but my true destiny is on Galactic Central and on Cartain," Caroline said. "I have a husband who loves and cares for me." She slid her arm around Jeff, comforted by both his presence and Star's.

"As part of a formal marriage alliance, which is no true marriage."

"A formal marriage alliance with an option for reproductive access that hasn't been activated yet, actually," Jeff said calmly. "Which I believe might fall within your definition of *true marriage*. Since both Caroline and I lack experience in dating and relationships, we are taking our time and getting to know each other before rushing into a deeper connection, both legally and personally."

"You'd—you'd have children with *him*?" Once again, Alice McKinnon appeared to be on the verge of losing her cool exterior.

"Yes, Alice." Caroline smirked. "Maybe. We have many things to do in the Congress. As Jeff said, there's no need to rush."

"Well. I hope you don't intend to make your children eligible for the McKinnon Family Trust! If you have any." Alice's nostrils flared wide. Star raised her head high in reaction, ears flicking halfway back.

"Since our children, if we have any, will not be living on Earth, I don't think you have anything to worry about." Caroline let her voice slide into a sharper note. "Don't worry, *Mother*." That emphasis made Alice cringe. "We won't embarrass you in front of your backwater bigoted associates. I'm surprised you bothered to venture off of Earth instead of leaving everything to *Albert-dear* to handle. Was finding out what I am up to that important to you?"

"I have *important business* to conduct at the Congress," Alice snapped. "Don't fool yourself. You aren't that significant to Hart Mercantile Services, and if you insist on this folly—well, girl, you've made your bed. I hope you can live with it!"

"Oh, I most definitely can." Caroline kept her voice light, trying and failing to resume that flippant note. She met Alice's pale blue eyes without flinching, though she tightened her arm around Jeff's waist. He gently brushed his lips against her temple.

Alice bristled even more at Jeff's display of affection, her entire body tensing before she stomped away.

Jeff whistled softly. "Whoo-ee. All right, then. That's your mother. Is she ever—"

"A bigot? Yes. A racist? Yes. Worse? Absolutely." Caroline shivered.

Jeff pulled her into his arms. "This encounter explains an awful lot. I'm sorry."

Caroline briefly leaned her forehead against his chest, drawing strength from this man she was becoming—quite fond of. Then she raised her head, exhaling heavily.

"And now I need to suck it up and not make a scene at our party," she murmured.

"You're entitled to make a scene, and I wouldn't blame you one bit if you did." Jeff gently stroked her cheek. "I'm proud of you, Caroline Starshine, and all that you have done and are doing."

He bent to kiss her, and not the sort of chaste, discreet kiss that Alice McKinnon might approve of in public. As Jeff pulled her close, Caroline stepped in even closer, pressing her body against him. His hand slid down her back, resting in the small of it. She gasped as an intoxicating heat pulsed through her, demanding more, more, *more*.

Jeff raised his head and she moaned softly, not wanting those warm lips to pull away from her. He smiled down at her, the gold flecks in his eyes more intense than ever.

"My darling. My Caroline Starshine. If only—" he exhaled.

Star's interrupting nicker held a laugh combined with a matching wordless thought projection about *silly humans in heat*. Caroline glanced around, suddenly aware that they were the center of attention.

Jeff chuckled, and kissed her again, this time quickly. Then he half-turned away, laughing joyfully. "Caroline Starshine is the best thing that ever happened to me!" he proclaimed to those watching. "And I am not afraid to show it."

"Oh, Jeff." A blush burned in her cheeks. But she smiled at him and pulled him close for another one of those quick kisses.

Alice McKinnon's disapproving sniff carried over the giggles from the crowd around them.

Caroline didn't care.

She had Jeff, and Star, and Tyrone, and Paula, and—

Much, *much* more than Alice McKinnon could offer her back on bigoted, backwater Earth.

She had the stars.

THE REST of the party passed in a pleasant blur. Jeff stuck close to Caroline, plying her with flowerberry wine. When they finally retreated to their suites, Caroline clung to Jeff, not wanting to let him go. They ended up in a tangle on her loveseat, lips and hands moving over each other's body, both moaning and gasping for breath.

Then Jeff pulled away. "We'd better start thinking about a reproductive access contract," he said shakily. "If that's what you want."

"Yes," she whispered huskily.

He shivered, and rested a hand on her cheek. "But I don't think we should do anything tonight. Much as I want to. I've had far too much flowerberry to drink and we need to talk about what we want for our future."

"Agreed. Thank you for being here." Her voice dropped lower than ever. "You're sure, Jeff? That you want to progress to a reproductive access contract? With me?"

"Who else?" He took her hand and kissed her palm. "But I want to do it all correctly and properly. Like my parents wanted to do, but couldn't. You deserve nothing less than that, Caroline." He intertwined his fingers with her and gave her one last kiss. "Good night, my darling."

"Good night, dear one."

It took Caroline a while to gather herself up and prepare for bed, and it wasn't just the flowerberry buzzing through her.

Jeff had stood up to her mother for her. Had pronounced her the best thing that had ever happened to him.

He cares for me. Maybe even loves me.

It felt strange to realize that she was—cherished and special to someone.

THIRD TURN of First Break was quiet and private. Star appeared to be unusually preoccupied, trotting off to the equine transit center to do some research she didn't describe. Tyrone and Paula headed out to explore Galactic Central. Caroline curled up on a couch with Jeff as they studied reproductive access contract variations, made further complex by agreements he had signed while working as a rodeo duelist.

"I thought the Hart-McKinnon marital contracts were complicated," Caroline said finally. "I didn't realize that the Galactic Rodeo wanted to control sentient duelist reproduction to this degree!"

"It's problematic," Jeff agreed. "I *had* thought that I didn't need to go back to the Rodeo for permission to execute a reproductive access contract." He scowled at the contract projected in front of him. "Apparently they want to control all sentient-qualified duelists, even after retirement. I didn't think it was a big deal because I didn't come from a Rodeo family. I thought all those clauses applied to them only."

She snuggled up next to him and pulled the projection closer, in order to study the clauses Jeff had highlighted. "And yet there's an exception for Planetary Representatives."

"But it's vague. I'm not certain that Cartain's status is sufficiently high enough for me to do as I damn well please. I mean—we could stipulate contraception and all. It's not like I'm the last best hope for producing the next generation for the Ford family. Having kids isn't a priority for me."

"And I'm not particularly interested in having children." Caroline sighed. "Considering pregnancy and calculating my fertility was forced on me as a consideration for the future, but I had myself sterilized my first span on Central."

"I think it's time to take advantage of that free legal advice that the Congress offers. I hadn't really wanted to mess around with it, but—it looks like something we might need to do." Jeff frowned. He tapped a few links, then quickly typed a response.

"At least we don't need to mess around with Hart-McKinnon legalese." That was the first thing Caroline had pulled up—examining all the releases renouncing her family obligations that she had needed to sign before coming to Galactic Central as an intern. Plus, she wanted to see the latest versions. It *was* remotely possible that her mother could have pulled some sort of convoluted contract finagling to force her back to Earth.

Nothing had changed. So either Alice McKinnon was lying about the potential suitor back on Earth as an excuse to force Caroline's return, or she hadn't cared enough about reasserting control over Caroline in order to attempt a sneaky runaround to make it happen.

A third option might be that said suitor was low-status, which put everything back into *didn't care enough to pull a sneaky runaround*. Whatever the case, they didn't have problems from her side of the relationship, which was a huge relief.

The Rodeo's rules weren't personal, not like whatever might come from her family.

Jeff exhaled. "I just dumped the whole thing in Legal's

lap. We meet with them turn after next, Third Turn, Ninth Node, right after Second Meal." His arm tightened around Caroline. "Their response is pretty encouraging. Sounds like Rifanel and Fenarmin had to go through the same dance, and it seems to be reasonably standard according to the legal advisor. That's a relief."

"Should we plan a second wedding ceremony?"

"We could." He grinned. "Have a big party at the Ranch for this one, since it's more personal and less political, even though we'll have to invite the Boss and everyone else in a leadership position on Cartain. I can just see Mama and Darla rubbing their hands in anticipation of planning our wedding!" He kissed her. "But I want to have the ceremony soon, if you're good with that," he murmured against her lips.

"Especially if we have to wait for the ceremony until we actually—" she felt her cheeks warm.

"Alas, yes. Contracts, my dear, contracts." He smirked, though she noticed that his cheeks darkened with a flush as well.

"We have a problem with the Solids from Memaj, based on observations I made at the party," Star announced on First Turn, at the Ninth Node staff meeting after First Meal. "Especially after I did some research."

"Oh?" Caroline flushed. By the time the Memaj contingent had arrived at their party, she had been so focused on Jeff that she hadn't been paying that much attention to what their guests had been doing—though she probably should have been.

Star tossed her head up and down, mimicking a human nod.

"Their body language didn't look right to me. It was

almost as if they were Plasmoids masquerading as Solids. I took the liberty of querying Rutan, and he sent me to Blackburn and Laura Richardson for their impressions about my observations."

Caroline raised her brows, surprised that Star had shown so much initiative this early in her Conversion.

Then again, Jeff did say that she had a protective nature.

He certainly didn't seem surprised as he sipped on his Skrilsit. "What did Blackburn say?"

"Watch and be careful, and he would pass this information on to his superiors in Federation Security." Star blew a loud snort, shaking her head and letting her ears flop around.

Jeff's brows shot up, matching Caroline's. "Well, that's the answer to *that* puzzle," he said slowly. "Federation Security is concerned about Memaj. I thought as much, given the discussion Blackburn and I had about Memaj at our party." He glanced at the clock. "And we need to be ready for Memaj's membership presentation before the Drugs Committee at Tenth Node. This is going to be very, very interesting."

Interesting is going to be the mildest description of what is going on, Caroline thought.

Blackburn ended up pulling them aside before they went into committee, thumping up an opaque cone of silence that was clearly military intelligence-level technology. His ears flattened and he crouched on all fours, tail sticking straight out behind him, the tension in his body making his platform vibrate slightly. The intensity of his body language as well as his mindspeech conveyed his agitation, because he was usually not this upset.

Laura Richardson interpreted his instructions for Jeff, Tyrone, and Paula. Caroline and Star were able to speak to the black rabbit directly.

"Star, as a horse you are more sensitive to body language than humans. You should stand at the back of the hearings room to observe the actions of the Memaj Solid contingent without being noticed yourself. Pay attention to their reactivity and the appropriateness of their responses," Blackburn directed.

Star bobbed her head and flicked one ear forward. *"What are you looking for? What should I do if I see something wrong?"*

"We're looking for mismatches in body language between what the Solids will be saying and expressing via their body language," Blackburn said. *"Take notes. You have the timer implant as well as the speech implant?"*

"Yes," Star said.

"Then note behaviors down to click and tap time measures, starting with each speaker. Caroline."

"Yes," Star repeated.

"Pay attention to facial expressions. Again, mismatches between words and actions."

"What exactly are we looking for?" Caroline repeated her question out loud for Jeff's sake.

"More so than other species, humans who come under Plasmoid interference are slow to show emotion. You should especially pay attention to Alice McKinnon. As her daughter, you know how she normally reacts."

"You think my mother is under Plasmoid influence?" Caroline couldn't quite believe *that.* If ever there was someone less likely to be influenced by the Plasmoids or any other nonhuman species, it would be Alice McKinnon. She was strong-willed enough to throw off any influence that Caroline was aware of.

"Anyone can come under Plasmoid influence if the proper substance is administered," was Blackburn's chilling response, emphasized by a loud thump of one hind leg against his platform that echoed within the cone of silence.

THE LINGERING chill from Blackburn's words put Caroline on alert, making her edgier than usual as she prepared for that turn's session. Jeff noticed, frowning, and rolled his chair back by her station.

"What's wrong, dear one?" he whispered.

"Something Blackburn said privately to me. He fears that Alice may be influenced by the Plasmoids. But if she can be influenced by them...." Caroline let her voice fade.

Jeff nodded. "He's right." His voice hardened, and he looked around carefully before snapping up a cone of silence and leaning in close to Caroline so that no one could read his lips. "And the Federation budget doesn't have much funding for research into ways to counter drug-fueled Plasmoid influence. Blackburn and I talked about this at our party. He's concerned. His superiors haven't been taking the possibility of extended Plasmoid influence upon Federation governance very seriously. He saw evidence of Plasmoid finagling with the Bit-fives, and it's only getting worse. There may be co-optation at a high level in the Federation systems. Plus the Sentient Planet suballiance is becoming restless, and Blackburn can't explain why because I don't have clearance. It's tied to Memaj—but from everything we're being told, Memaj isn't sentient."

No wonder Jeff snapped up that cone of silence. But how—why is he in Blackburn's confidence? Because he's new to the Congress? Or because he knows about rella?

"What's going on?"

"Blackburn was feeling out how I stood on the topic of Plasmoid influence, especially given you and Star, and things I've said and done in the past." Jeff exhaled. "I have—let's just say that I was approached when I was in the Rodeo about gathering information when we were touring in the Outer Worlds, and I said yes. As a result of that and—yes—you and Star, Blackburn decided to take me into his confidence."

"That's scary."

Jeff kissed her quickly. "It is. He's very high-ranking in Federation Security, and for him to tell me the things he did—darling, I'm worried."

"How does Memaj play into this scenario?"

"None of us know yet." Jeff unsnapped the cone, then surprised Caroline by kissing her. "Let everyone think we've been whispering sweet nothings while under the cone," he whispered. "Now that we have the reputation of newlywed lovebirds—"

She kissed him back, more than happy to go along with the façade.

IT WAS all Caroline could do to keep from jumping up and shouting about *interference* during Alice McKinnon's testimony in support of admitting Memaj into the Federation, based on their claimed ability to grow rella. Her mother's performance was stiff and stilted, almost robotic—and that was definitely *not* how Alice McKinnon handled any sort of public testimony. Caroline had served as her mother's assistant at government hearings in her late teens, before going to Mars University, performing the same role that Geri Ahrens now fulfilled of clicking up appropriate records, slides, stills, and videos to support what Alice was saying.

Oh, *that* part of Alice McKinnon's testimony was absolutely on point. Her visuals were as precise and well-designed as they usually were.

But part of her mother's trademark public speaking behavior was the drama she put into her words. Alice McKinnon didn't just recite a speech scrolling by on a projection in front of her. She put feeling into her words—sharp-edged sarcasm here, quavering with indignation there, that deep prayerful invocation that *of course honorable electeds, you will do the proper thing.* All accompanied by facial expressions, hand gestures, leaning forward to emphasize a point, slumping back in her chair while rolling her eyes to convey her opinion of the ridiculousness of someone else's argument, and other precisely orchestrated gestures.

That was what a prime Alice McKinnon public hearing appearance was all about. Almost-operatic high drama.

What Caroline observed was *not* the way that her mother normally performed. She considered sending Jeff a note, then decided against it. Not after what Blackburn had told him.

If higher levels of Federation Security were compromised—

It was all Caroline could do to stifle a shiver.

Watching this rote, mechanical version of her mother slammed home the reality of the danger the Plasmoids might well be presenting to the Federation.

How did they get to her? Is she willing or manipulated?

IT WAS a relief when the committee session was over for the turn and they could report to Blackburn, once again crammed into that opaque cone of silence with Jeff, Star, Richardson, and Blackburn.

"All of the beings presenting testimony favorable to Memaj's admission had unusual body language," Star said.

Blackburn thumped softly. *"All of them?"*

"All." Star snorted and tossed her head, switching her tail. *"I will send you my notes."*

"My mother did not present with her usual persona. Something has influence over her." Caroline repeated her statement out loud for Jeff's sake. He took her hand and squeezed it gently.

"How so?" Blackburn's lop ears swiveled, pointing directly at Caroline.

Caroline described her mother's typical presentation behavior, first in mindspeech, then out loud.

Blackburn sank back on his haunches, washing his face with his paws, grooming first one ear and then the other. Then he dropped to all fours.

"This is not good."

"No," Caroline agreed. *"It is not."*

"We have at least one session more of hearings to go," Jeff said. "Is there anything we can do?"

"Move to have a fact-gathering delegation visit Memaj. Cite a concern on your part to verify their rella claims. Suggest representatives from the Councilists as well."

"I will do that. Caroline, will you speak to Rifanel to see if Fenarmin can serve as co-sponsor of my motion?"

"I will handle that. Fenarmin is my next meeting," Blackburn said. *"Meanwhile, one thing I learned while I was meeting with my sources during the hearing. Alice McKinnon leads a faction of Earth corporatists who want to secede from the Federation and join the Ethereal Confederation. They are networking with the Bit-Fives and the Sentient Planet Alliance."*

"That's—hugely problematic." Caroline's voice quavered after Richardson repeated Blackburn's words for the others to hear. "That—that could eliminate Hart Mercantile Services as a supplier for a number of the Outer Worlds. Unless they persuade the Outer Worlds to join as well."

Blackburn thumped and twitched his tail. *"Exactly. Like it or not, Hart plays a major role in supplying and supporting regions that the assorted Ribonit cartels won't touch. And if Earth leaves the Federation—it may be a backwater planet, but there are many human colonies that will want to follow its lead. I am very concerned about your report regarding Alice McKinnon's behavior. Do you think she is cooperating willingly?"*

Caroline waited for Richardson to repeat Blackburn's words before she answered. "I wish I could give you a definite answer, Blackburn, but to be honest—I just don't know."

TENSION KEPT all of them silent as they traveled back to their quarters. Star, Tyrone, and Paula retreated to their separate areas, leaving Jeff and Caroline alone.

"Are you willing to go to Memaj, should the committee grant my request and send me?" Jeff asked as they prepared a simple Third Meal of salad and gomch, a yogurt-like plant protein pudding.

"Why wouldn't I? I'm your assistant as well as your spouse. Besides." Caroline paused, thinking through her next words. "If Alice is up to something, you may need my knowledge about Hart Mercantile Services."

"Just being silly, I suppose." He heaved a heavy sigh. "I'd almost leave you and Star here because of that rella exposure back on Cartain. What happens if you two get exposed again?"

Caroline took his hands in hers. "I would worry every single turn that you were gone. And if something happened to you—I'd sooner be there."

Jeff took her in his arms. They leaned against each other. Then, wordlessly, they separated and finished preparing dinner.

After dinner, they sat on the loveseat in her room. While there was some kissing, and careful fondling, they spent more time just holding each other. Caroline rested her head on Jeff's chest, listening to the steady beat of his heart that calmed her worries. He occasionally kissed the side and top of her head.

The clock chimed for Fourteenth Node.

"Time for bed," Caroline murmured, sitting up.

Jeff bent to kiss her once more. "It will be all right, Caroline. We'll be all right."

But the tension and worry in his voice echoed the icy claws that kept tightening around her gut.

Until Jeff, Caroline had managed to keep personal ties and

commitments at bay for fear of Hart Mercantile Services somehow bringing harm to them.

Now she had something to lose. And, knowing her mother, Alice McKinnon was already scheming about how to take Jeff away from Caroline.

ALICE MCKINNON APPEARED to be her usual self as she sat in the audience for the second day of hearings. Albert slipped in and out of his seat by Lara Wordtrust. Logan Easystar took Albert's place when he left the hearing for whatever it was that he was doing. The two of them kept coming and going, sometimes pausing to whisper in each other's ears.

What are they doing? I don't see Geri around.

That was troubling, when she took the time to consider it.

Fenarmin brought the motion for sending a delegation to Memaj, with Jeff as the secondary sponsor. Albert was sitting in for Logan Easystar at that point, and whispered furiously to Lara Wordtrust as the committee argued over who else to send with Jeff and Fenarmin. To Caroline's surprise, none of the senior committee members appeared to be interested in traveling to Memaj—that was, until Lara Wordtrust burst into the conversation.

"So why are Councilists and Federalists putting together a delegation from their parties only?" Wordtrust blurted, interrupting Katrina Allsides, a senior Councilist committee member from Glorion.

"You *are* the only Statist on the committee." Allsides straightened up huffily, throwing back her broad shoulders and glowering at Wordtrust. "I expected to hear from you at the beginning. Why are you only concerned about the delegation's makeup now, upon the return of your assistant who happens to be a part of Hart Mercantile Services?"

"Are you accusing me of ulterior motives?" Wordtrust

bristled back. "I needed some data about this situation before I made a commitment."

"Eh, add her to the party," Jeff said.

"Oh, I'd prefer to send my spouse," Wordtrust said quickly. "Unfortunately, unlike those of you with larger parties who have more members to go rocketing off to junkets during the session, *I* have to cover major hearings myself."

"What, you don't trust Frrinx nal Thogh?" Allsides asked slyly, referring to the Statist second-in-command.

Wordtrust blushed. "Nal Thogh is in the midst of a shed and is currently unable to travel, as is their spouse." Frrinx nal Thogh was a reptilian from Thrant, one of the Outer Worlds, and shed their skin four times a cycle.

"I—see." Allsides smiled shrewdly. "So who would you send in your place?"

"My spouse and assistant Logan Easystar and his assistant Albert McKinnon." Wordtrust glared over at Caroline and Jeff. "After all, Jeff Tophand is bringing his spouse and assistant, who is really Agatha McKinnon."

"Caroline Starshine is her name!" Jeff snapped.

Wordtrust shrugged. "Whatever she wants to call herself, she's still a McKinnon. We need more than one McKinnon representing the Congress."

Caroline bit her lip. Jeff looked back at her. "Should I object?" he asked softly.

"No," she said. "It's not worth it."

All the same, she didn't feel good about Albert's presence on this delegation. Not with what was at stake.

As THEY LEFT the hearing room, Albert popped in front of Blackburn, flicking up a document.

"I announce an official challenge to the Conversion status of the equine called Star, from Cartain, and the revocation of her official Congressional assistant status," he announced, puffing out his chest. "Here's the paperwork."

Before he could serve it on Star, Laura Richardson intercepted the snapped-up document. She scanned through it quickly, then faced Blackburn, clearly mindspeaking on a tight link so that Star and Caroline couldn't listen in.

The black rabbit thumped hard on his platform, ears flat. He emitted a rare growling vocalization and thumped a second time, eyes narrowing, rising to all fours as if he intended to leap off the platform and attack Albert.

Richardson nodded. She turned back toward Albert. A snap of her fingers, and a military-level nibblebot popped into being. The black dot munched away at the document, eliminating all traces of it from Congressional databases.

"ALL RECORDS PURGED," the black dot announced, before belching. "NO CHALLENGE EXISTS. JUDICIAL SERVICES REPRIMANDS JUDGE G8*P79 FOR OVERSTEPPING THEIR AUTHORITY." It belched again, then disappeared.

Albert's eyes widened. "How did you—that's not civilian technology—you can't do that!"

"By my authority as the interpreter for Blackburn, I not only have access to the technology but the right to use it on his behalf," Richardson said serenely. "The judge who signed this challenge does not have the authority to rule on Converted status matters. Star of Cartain has been officially certified as Converted by Federation authorities and confirmed by Hrwhinir scientists. She has met all qualifications for her role in the Galactic Congress, and this document cannot be the grounds for the removal of her status."

Blackburn emitted a deeper growl. He turned around so that his back faced Albert.

"Blackburn also strongly encourages you to *leave* and not bother Caroline Starshine or Star of Cartain further," Richardson continued. "He reminds you, Albert McKinnon, that you were only allowed to serve your current role upon sufferance, and that *your* status may be revoked at any time, due to your connections with Hart Mercantile Services."

"But—but—but…" Albert's voice trailed off as Blackburn took several steps away, flicking his hind feet contemptuously. He flushed. "Easy come of sentience, easy go! Even if you're born sentient, there's no guarantee that it will remain."

"Are you threatening Star? I would hope you have more sense than to threaten Blackburn." Richardson's pleasant tone changed to menacing.

"No—no—no—"

"Then *leave.*"

Albert spun and marched away. Richardson sighed. Blackburn turned back toward them, hopping to the center of his platform, and tapped up the cone of silence that Caroline was passionately beginning to hate because of what it meant. More problems. More unnerving disclosures and conversations. She just wanted to settle *quietly*, with *Jeff*, and have them left alone to do their jobs!

"Watch what is going on around you," Blackburn's mental voice was weighted and worried. Richardson's voice echoed his tones as she relayed his words. *"Guard Star well when you go to Memaj, and do not leave her behind on Galactic Central. She is safest with you two."*

Jeff nodded sharply after Richardson finished interpreting. "We will guard Star well."

"Guard yourselves as well." Now both Blackburn and Richardson sounded much older, and tired. *"While we do not know of anything that can actually remove sentience, Memaj is—a place of concern for Federation Security. I will ensure that you will have Security support on Memaj. Caroline, Jeff, the code phrases that will help you identify undercover Federation Security are now unlocked in your Congressional references. Guard them well."*

The black rabbit shook himself. He rose on his haunches to

groom his face once again. When he had finished, he dropped to all fours.

"Be very careful. I will brief Fenarmin and Rifanel. Your delegation—may end up determining the future of the Federation of Solid Peoples."

And once again, Blackburn's words ended up sending a chill through Caroline. She fumbled for Jeff's hand. It closed tight upon hers.

Warm. Comforting.

But she devoutly wished that they didn't need to go to Memaj.

11

MEMAJ

Caroline, Jeff, and Star left for Memaj on Fourth Turn, after making provisions with Rutan and Geraint for Tyrone and Paula to cover their committees, including official proxies. Caroline and Jeff also met with Legal to begin the process of expanding their marital contract—which was anticlimactic in comparison to that last meeting with Blackburn.

"We see no obstacles to expanding your formal marriage association to a full reproductive access contract," Senior Legal Voice—a reptilian only known by their title—said. "Representative Tophand, Spouse Starshine, your legal advisors on Cartain did a superb job in writing your contracts. We do not always see such carefully-drafted work. When will you choose to implement the provisions of this revised contract?"

"Next span, after we return from Memaj," Jeff said. "At this time, we do not know when that exact date will be."

"We will add the appropriate flexible language to the modified contract," Senior Legal said.

"That sounds very good," Caroline said. "Thank you."

She reviewed the revised contract carefully when Senior Legal sent it to them later on that turn. Everything seemed to be in order. And Jeff reported that both Darcy and Darla were thrilled about planning the wedding party. Even if he couldn't provide them with a definite date yet.

All the same, uneasiness tugged at Caroline. She was so close to achieving dreams she had never thought would be possible.

Didn't that mean they would be ripped away from her?

HEAT AND *STEAM* overwhelmed Caroline when they left the runabout at Memsij, Memaj's capitol city. Cloying humidity wrapped around her even inside the climate-controlled terminal. While she had dressed lightly in anticipation of the heat, wearing a loose shirt and a flowing skirt, what was comfortable in the transport was sticky and sweltering planetside. She wrinkled her nose at a faint stench that reminded her of rotting vegetation.

Seems like jungle climates are much the same, no matter what planet in the Galaxy you're on.

"You doing all right, Star?" she asked after they had met their guides and were headed for their quarters to rest before attending the delegation's first formal event, a garden party welcoming their arrival.

Caroline had not been able to acquire cooling sheets for Star before they left Galactic Central. But Rifanel's human assistant, Julia, had ordered extras for Rifanel and Fenarmin, loaned some to Star, and given Caroline leads on sources to purchase more, for future trips to other places with hot, humid climates.

"Getting used to wearing this thing." Star blew hard. "The sheets don't do much for the damp feeling. I'm all wet. At least I'm not sweating."

"It *is* hot." Jeff brushed his hand against Caroline's. "One of the hotter places I've been—and humid too. Whoo. Glad

I'm not dueling here. This humidity will suck strength and energy right out of you."

Caroline nodded, studying their surroundings. Memsij was on Memaj's primary continent, concentrated around the equator. But even with both of Memaj's weak suns overhead in mid-turn, the outside light appeared dim, almost yellowish, reminding Caroline of a late summer sunset on Earth.

She sighed and wiped away sweat beads forming on her brow. Clearly, her usual careful check of the Planetary Guide was nearly useless for Memaj and Memsij. The capitol city was much warmer than they had been originally told. Which meant she wouldn't be able to wear half of the clothing she had brought along. No room in their luggage allotment for an autotailor, so she would have to make do.

"Wish there were cooler sheets for humans," she murmured to Jeff.

He chuckled, gesturing to the Memajites around them. "You just have to wear lighter clothing, and less of it."

"Jeff!" Despite the scolding note in her voice, she smiled at his teasing tone. Teasing was something that had developed between them during the five-turn trip to Memaj. She *liked* it from him, and Jeff was careful about not being hurtful, unlike her brothers, especially Albert.

THE STRAPLESS YELLOW dress Caroline wore to the reception was not something she would ever have dared to appear in at a comparable event on Earth. The dress's bodice clung to her torso and flared slightly from her hips to her ankles. Two discreet side slits rose to mid-thigh, almost concealed by the flow of the skirt. A transparent magenta-shaded bolero jacket, meant more to protect exposed skin from insects and sunburn than conceal her upper chest, neck and shoulders, along with yellow sandals in her favorite style, completed her ensemble.

Jeff wore a magenta and yellow suit. As he had told her when they were choosing designs for the autotailor, they were entitled to those colors by Cartain standards, given the future change in their marital status. Besides, he liked yellow on Caroline, and the form-fitting strapless design of this dress was his suggestion. It made her uneasy, but—another Earth inhibition to overcome, because the strapless look was common for formal dress on Galactic Central. Plus, by now she had learned that Jeff's preferences looked good on her.

The garden party was held under a transparent dome, apparently to reduce their exposure to Memaj's biting insects as darkness descended—something Star was already grumbling about as they walked from parking to the party dome, switching her tail and tossing her head. Caroline eyed the foliage along the pathway, absently swatting at bugs targeting her face in spite of the protective screens the parking attendant handed them. This was her first chance to see anything of Memaj besides the brutalist, sterile design that dominated the city of Memsij.

One place where it sure seems like sentients are at war with the landscape, was her first conclusion.

Too much like the Old Earth mentality for her comfort.

Plant life colors on Memaj so far certainly appeared artificial. Yellow and silver shades dominated instead of the lush green Caroline would expect from the heat and humidity, a color that made her think of extreme drought in an arid climate rather than a jungle climate. The taller plants clustered into clumps that looked more bush-like than tree-like. While some plants had leaves all the way down their stems, mostly in shades of yellow and silver, most of the plants had leafless long stems and trunks. Again, not something Caroline would expect from a humid, jungle-like climate.

Humidity wasn't supposed to be good for rella cultivation. Did that mean Memaj's rella fields were placed in a more arid climate? Hopefully.

Be interesting to see if those rella plants are the same color as the fields on Cartain.

"Remember," she murmured to Jeff as they waited for their turn to be announced into the party. "Be careful about food and drink."

Jeff chuckled. "Darling, we're an official delegation. Memaj wouldn't dare endanger their membership application by doing something to us."

"I don't know. Something doesn't feel right." She waved a hand at the foliage. "Everything's off."

He squeezed her hand as the dome opened to admit them. They were the last of the Federation delegation to enter and be announced.

"I think it's fine, my dear."

Caroline bit her lip and didn't say anything more.

"I will be careful," Star mindspoke. *"Too much weirdness about this place."*

At least *one* of her companions was being mindful. Caroline stifled a sigh as she surrendered her protective bug screen to the attendant, then proceeded in with Jeff and Star as they were announced. Jeff kissed her and Star nuzzled Caroline before the three of them separated to circulate through the crowd. She swallowed hard, looking around. There were *so many* Plasmoids, some who weren't even bubbled. Caroline tried not to stare as she made her way over to a bar to collect a bulb of water. This was the first time she had seen an unbubbled Plasmoid, and the sight made her stomach churn slightly. They reminded her of pictures she had seen of moon jellies on Earth—except that she could see what they were digesting. Ugh. And they had worm-like tendrils that wobbled and wavered around what appeared to be their mouths, dripping something that didn't smell all that good. Some excretions sizzled slightly as they hit the gold and silver turf.

Need to remember to not let any of those drippings get on me.

Weren't Plasmoids usually bubbled for their own safety? Not just to protect their fragile exterior membranes but because they breathed a different air mixture? None of this made sense.

Oh well. At least she didn't *think* she was as visibly uncomfortable as Albert was. She wasn't sure if his reaction came from the heat or from the close proximity to so many nonhuman species.

What a change from childhood days.

Caroline allowed herself a wry chuckle as Albert flinched away from a large feline, then turned her attention to more important details. She, Jeff, and Star had been meeting with Rifanel, Fenarmin, and Rifanel's assistant Julia throughout the five turns spent traveling to Memaj to discuss what else they needed to learn about the planet. They had invited Easystar and Albert to their gatherings, but those two hadn't shown any interest, which was surprising. There was just too much missing data in the information provided by the Memaj applicants. Too little known about Memaj itself—for various reasons. Easystar and Albert *should* have been more interested —unless they were privy to knowledge which the others lacked, and had no interest in sharing.

Entirely possible.

One concern the six of them discussed during the trip was that the Memaj government, ruled by a revolving species mix of hereditary leaders including two Plasmoid species, claimed there had never been a native sentient species on the planet. That was unusual, because most Federation planets had a native sentient species of some sort in their history.

Not Memaj. It was entirely colonist-occupied. None of the information provided by the Memaj delegation said anything about a native sentient species ever existing there.

Such a situation just didn't happen, especially on a planet with Memaj's relatively benign climate (*that is, if you consider a jungle to be benign!* was Caroline's wry thought whenever they discussed it). Not unless some other sentient species descended upon the place and deliberately set about eliminating any competition. However, no matter how many databases and histories Caroline searched on their way to Memaj, she couldn't find any indication that sentience had risen independently there. Not even a whisper that the Plasmoids had planted sentience on Memaj, like the extinct precursors of current Plasmoids had done on just about every other sentient-inhabited planet in the Galaxy.

But if one of the current sentient species was involved in exterminating a pre-existing sentient species, wouldn't that information be covered up?

That thought haunted her as she drifted through the party, careful about the food and drink she was offered. Albert's presence made her cautious. Perhaps Memaj politicians wouldn't have a motive to put something into anything she consumed, but she didn't trust her brother. Not until she was protected by a full marriage contract.

If extermination is why Memaj didn't have a native sentient species, then they could be subject to sanctions. That will certainly benefit Cartain.

Or was the lack of a previous sentient species caused by the mix of Plasmoid and Solid species on this planet? Given the claimed history of mixed colonization, and the past record of how the ancient Plasmoids scattered sentience throughout the Galaxy, the lack of a native species on Memaj stood out.

Even more, as Caroline looked around the gathering. No one seemed to fit Memaj, unlike Cartain or even Earth.

Perhaps it wasn't extinction but removal of sentience from the native population.

Nothing *suggested* that was the case. True, there were no records of the extinct Plasmoid scientists removing sentience from a population. That didn't mean it hadn't happened.

No Federation scientist had ever set foot on a Plasmoid planet, much less investigated Plasmoid history. Memaj was the closest anyone from the Federation had ever come to a Plasmoid planet. And since none of the xenologists from Galactic Center had been allowed on this delegation, well—Caroline's three terms studying Xenology under Dr. Knowledgechaser was the most experience that anyone on the delegation possessed.

Caroline sighed. The invitation list for this reception included several Memaj academics. Now if she could only find them in the crowd! Her ties to Dr. Knowledgechaser would hopefully provide her with the opportunity to set up longer interviews with someone who might be able to tell her more about the likelihood that Memaj had ever possessed a sentient species—and, if it had, whether their demise had come about naturally.

Natural extinction of sentient species *did* happen, and might be an explanation for why everything about this planet seemed off-kilter. If the original sentient species had destroyed itself, then it was surprising that Memaj was even as habitable as it appeared to be.

But it was up to her to make those necessary connections and, perhaps, figure out what was really going on here.

I can do this, she told herself. *Jeff says I can do it. Geraint says I can do this.*

I will be the one who finds out why *Memaj is so different.*

She needed every bit of that confidence as she worked, moving from social group to social group.

Confidence kept Caroline from flinching when an unbubbled Plasmoid incinerated, inhaled, then exhaled a substance that smelled like burning rella as she walked by (though she did hold her breath as they exhaled, and mindspoke a warning to Star. Jeff might not be affected but Star certainly would be).

Confidence kept her poised and social even as she slapped at the few insects remaining inside the dome that targeted her face but also managed to bite through her jacket's fabric. While she was able to keep them off of her face, their stings raised huge, itchy welts on her exposed arms and shoulders that were a challenge to ignore rather than scratch.

Confidence allowed her to talk directly with a bubbled Plasmoid for her first time, even though its translator device popped and clicked, cutting out every few words. She acknowledged Blixxit's frequent apologies for their poorly performing translator, gracefully repeating what she said and gaining respect for this Plasmoid, at least, who seemed to be aware of human concerns and human needs. Blixxit was a third-tier aide to the human President of Memaj, and clearly did not want to bury her under thinly veiled assertions about Memaj's rella production, unlike several of their Solid colleagues.

But all that *confidence* flew out the window when a familiar voice hissed at her.

"Psst. Come here."

She startled. The voice came from a clump of bush-like plants with leafy trunks that sheltered one of the private alcoves within the dome.

"Are you calling me?" No. It couldn't be. *One* brother and their mother showing up on Galactic Central—no. This couldn't be yet another of her brothers, could it? If so, then the typically planet-bound McKinnons were showing a most unusual interest in interstellar travel.

"Yes, you, Caroline Starshine. It has been many years and many planets since we last met." She couldn't see the speaker behind the plants' broad yellow and silver leaves.

Caroline froze. *Many years.* The Old Earth term for *cycles*, and part of the Federation Security code phrases that Blackburn had sent them. Very few people outside of Earth connections knew those time measures.

"I did not think it had been that many days since we last met." A chill tightened around her gut as she responded with the response code phrase, *many days*.

"Our parting was one of the saddest weeks of my life."

Saddest weeks. Another passphrase.

"It was like a month for me," she responded mechanically.

It wasn't the fact that this was Federation Security reaching out *this quickly* that chilled her.

The speaker was her brother Abe.

Abe pushed back the leaves blocking her view of him. "In here, Caroline, quickly."

She ducked under the sticky, sappy leaves, noticing that they could not be seen at all from outside the alcove. "Thank you for remembering my usename—and what in all the stars are you doing here, Abe? How do you know those passphrases?"

"Shh. Wait." He held up a finger as he snapped up a cone of silence—opaque military-grade, like Blackburn's. "A lot has happened with the family since you left for Galactic Central."

"I guess! Albert as one of Lara Wordtrust's aides. Mother showing up to testify in favor of this planet's Federation membership, with Albert supporting her and all but openly stating Statist support for Memaj. And now you in Federation Security. I thought I was the only one getting away from Earth. Have the McKinnons suddenly been infected with the urge to travel? Did I start a trend?"

She eyed Abe. He looked much older than his thirty-four cycles. But it had been several cycles since she had last seen him—four cycles, specifically. Her last trip to Earth, at the end of her first full cycle at Mars University. The last time she bothered to attend a family gathering.

At that time, Abe had a secure position in accounting for Hart Mercantile Services, and his wife, Rhonda Desjardins, had brought in a respectable connection with a smaller shipping and supply business, Far Reaches Distribution, within Earth's solar system.

So why was he here? What had changed? Abe wasn't the rebel that she was.

Abe sighed. "I'm not Federation Security, though I'm cooperating with them. I work for the Galactic Controlled Substances Agency."

"What the—Abe, I thought you had a steady position with Hart! What does Rhonda think about all this?"

Another heavy sigh. "Rhonda and I are divorcing. It appears that Far Reaches was involved with illicit drug smuggling in the asteroid colonies, and Rhonda was up to her neck in it. GCSA approached me, and I started collaborating with them to break up the Far Reaches organization. When everything broke loose, right after you left for your Galactic Central internship, Mother convinced Royce to dump me from Hart. Rhonda followed with divorce papers. GCSA gave me a position as compensation. I'm working my way up the ladder, but—" he suddenly grinned. "I'm actually liking this new life away from Earth and Hart Mercantile."

"It *is* nice to get out from under Mother's thumb, isn't it?"

"Oh, absolutely. I've been hearing good things about you and your spouse—Jeff Tophand, correct?"

"Correct."

The smile faded from Abe's face. "Look. I need to warn Tophand and the rest of your delegation. We've been trying to trace the rella production on Memaj."

"That's why we're here, especially Jeff. He's a rella grower."

Abe nodded. "GCSA has reason to believe that the rella which Memaj claims to produce doesn't come from here."

"We *have* been dealing with rella thefts on Cartain." Caroline swallowed hard. "I saw one of the victims. A Crested Flyer chick, who died after we visited them. And one of

Jeff's horses, Star, and I got exposed to a massive dose of processed rella when we interrupted an attempted theft in Jeff's fields."

"GCSA knows about that. That's why I wanted to talk to you, Caroline. Warn you and Jeff. There is more going on than any of you realize. And a personal warning." Abe exhaled. "Hart Mercantile Services appears to have taken over Far Reaches' role in drug distribution. Not just that, but expanded upon Far Reaches' networks."

"Oh no."

"Oh yes."

Caroline shook her head.

Now everything is starting to make sense, in an odd way. That would explain why Albert and Mother came to Galactic Central. Sort of.

Except—why would Alice McKinnon want to get into drug smuggling? Her mother hadn't been interested even in alcohol while Caroline was growing up, much less cannabis or any other intoxicant. Drug smuggling stood to risk everything that Hart Mercantile had built over the past three hundred cycles.

She spoke her thought out loud. "I wouldn't think that Hart Mercantile would want—or need—to get into a business as risky as drug smuggling."

Abe's face went tight. "Caroline, Hart Mercantile has been bleeding money for cycles now. Even before Uncle Royce took over, but it's gotten worse since then." He looked away from her. "Mother managed to cover up her part in it, but the money from drug smuggling is one reason why she arranged for me to marry Rhonda."

"Oh Abe. I'm sorry. What about your kids?" She *had* thought Abe and Rhonda were a good match, and their three children were her favorite nephew and nieces. Abe was a dedicated father, spending more time with his children than his wife did.

A bitter note came into his voice. "The Desjardins claimed them in the divorce. Maternal family right."

"Oh Abe. I'm sorry," she repeated. That meant he had absolutely no custody.

He shrugged. "It leaves me free to do this work, and I'm very motivated to do it now." A deep sigh. "Not that it matters. I don't expect to return to Earth very soon, if ever. Between our family and the Desjardins, I'm not likely to receive much of a welcome there. I was more or less told to leave and never come back."

"You are welcome at our ranch if you want time with family," Caroline said firmly. "Jeff and I will always be happy to see you. His family is friendly, welcoming, and absolutely delightful—and they would be thrilled to meet at least one of my siblings. Especially you."

A faint smile tweaked Abe's lips before he turned solemn again. "I'll remember that. In any case, Caroline. Be very careful. This could come down to outright war between the Federation and the Ethereals. We're not sure exactly what role the Ribonits are playing in this situation, or if they even have a consistent position. One of their divisions has complained to the GCSA about rella smuggling; another claims it isn't a problem; and still another says it is a problem but that we should leave them alone to deal with it."

"Yikes. I'll tell Jeff."

"Good." Abe unsnapped the cone of silence. "Better let you go, Caroline." He smiled, bigger this time. "You look great. Happy. I am pleased to see that you've found a place for yourself. What I've seen and heard of Jeff Tophand has been all good. Just—be careful, all right, little sis?"

"I will," she promised. *Little sis.* The nickname sent a warm feeling through Caroline, because Abe had always called her that. It was one of her few positive memories of growing up.

"Go out first. And be careful!" he repeated.

"I will, big bro."

Another smile, acknowledging her nickname for him. Abe parted the leaves so that it was easy for her to leave without mussing her jacket sleeves.

She slipped out of the alcove, walking away without looking behind, head high.

Her brother Abe had also gotten free from their family.

But oh, the price he had paid—and the impact of this news.

If Hart Mercantile Services is losing money, there's a lot more wrong with the company than just drug smuggling.

She knew enough about the business to realize that.

AFTER TALKING TO ABE, it was hard to return to the mindset needed for her original task. The implications about what was happening with Hart Mercantile Services kept roiling through her thoughts—not least of which was worry about how this news could potentially impact her relationship with Jeff. Nonetheless, Caroline managed to set up several appointments with various academics attending the reception. Unfortunately, those appointments were several turns away—Memsij's major university was holding finals and turning in grades for the next ten-turn.

"I apologize," said Dr. Erith, the highest-ranking of the xenologists who responded warmly to her mention of Dr. Knowledgechaser. "But once I'm done in two turns, I would love to talk with one of Knowledgechaser's proteges. You know that he *is* bragging about being your mentor?"

"I hadn't heard." She smiled at Dr. Erith, a short, chunky humanoid woman with antennae, space-black skin, and spiky silver hair.

Erith came from one of the Outer Rim worlds, and had brushed off any mention of her planet with a calm *no one knows the place and even those of us from it can't pronounce what it wants to be called.* Under normal circumstances Caroline would be fascinated by the prospect of learning more about a sentient planet. After learning yet another reason why Hart Mercantile was interested in Memaj, however…in any case, the fact that Erith came from one of the sentient planets strongly suggested that sentience was not at issue on Memaj. Otherwise, she would have never been allowed on the planet. A minor relief.

"Oh, he's quite proud of the fact that one of his students is the primary assistant and spouse of a Planetary Representative so soon into her career."

Caroline smiled at that.

She repeated the conversation later on to Jeff over a late dinner, in their shared suite. It was much less roomy than any other accommodations they had together, with two small beds in a single bedroom and a tiny living space/kitchenette. This was the best facility that Memsij had to offer—no Best Planetary Accomodations on Memaj. Things were just too unsettled.

"That's good to hear," he said, smiling at her. "Much better than the news from your brother." Jeff rubbed his face. "One of those Plasmoids spilled a touch of their tendril drip on my face. They apologized, but it stings."

"You're all right?" Caroline welcomed the momentary distraction from her worries about Hart Mercantile's predicament. She rose to peer more closely at Jeff's face.

"Just fine." He smiled at her, pushing away her hand as she fussed over the slight burn mark on his forehead. "Fenarmin and I both got nailed when the Plasmoid we were talking to sneezed, and we had a Memaj medic check us. All fine."

"All right then." She still felt uneasy about that exposure, but if Jeff and Fenarmin had checked out as all right—in any case, she had other things to worry about. "Based on Abe's news, I need to review my releases from Hart Mercantile again." Her voice quavered. "I might end up being a liability to your position as Representative."

Jeff rested his hand on hers. "Caroline, I will *never* give you up because of something your family has done. Worst case, we retire to the Ranch and do political work on Cartain. It may not be as prestigious as working for the Congress, but —" Now his voice was the one with the uncertainty in it.

"It's no longer about the prestige of working for the Congress, Jeff," she said softly. "It's about us and what's happening with rella." She wrapped her hand around his. "There are other things that I—*we* can do if my ties to Hart Mercantile blow up on us. Two things that *will* not happen, however." Caroline took a deep breath. "I will not return to Earth and place myself under my family's control ever again. No matter what happens."

Jeff raised her hand and kissed it. "And the other?" His voice trembled.

"I will not leave should you lose the position of Planetary Representative." She said each word slowly and firmly. "I care for you, Jeff Tophand. You're an admirable man. I love you."

He inhaled sharply, then smiled. "Caroline. Oh my Caroline. If only—" he shook his head. "How did I ever get so lucky as to find you? I love you. But I don't want to get in the way of your professional advancement."

"It's my choice, Jeff. And I choose you. Whatever happens, we'll face it together."

"I honor your choice," he said. "And I hope I prove worthy of your decision."

"You already have," she said.

The delegation was booked into a turn-long tour of rella production facilities the next day.

"I think you'd better stay behind," Jeff said to Star.

The dark bay mare flicked her ears back. "Why?"

Jeff and Caroline exchanged glances. They had discussed this over breakfast.

"Because we think that the warning I received from the GCSA agent is most applicable to you," Caroline said. They had decided to conceal Abe's relationship to Caroline. The less known about that, the better.

"Besides, I'd like you to follow up on that information that Blixxit gave to me but not to Caroline," Jeff added. "That's suspicious."

Star blew, flicked her tail, and tossed her head. "All right. But I'm going to worry about both of you."

"We'll have Rifanel and Fenarmin with us," Caroline said. "That should neutralize any behavior from Easystar and Albert."

"Hopefully," Star said. But the uneasiness that Caroline spotted in Star's thoughts before she raised her barriers—something that she and Caroline had been working on during the trip to Memaj, to allow each other privacy—belied the apparent cheerfulness projected from the mare's translator.

Those concerning thoughts had something to do with that reception the previous turn—but what? And why wasn't Star talking about it? Star shut down that wall before Caroline could clearly see what bothered her—and it had something to do with a Plasmoid who wasn't Blixxit. A Plasmoid with the same peach-shaded containment bubble Caroline had seen too many times already, on Cartain and in the Congress.

But had she seen it at the party? Caroline couldn't remember.

THE RELLA FIELDS didn't look like anything on Cartain, and they were just as hot and humid as Memsij. Jeff's sampler analysis said the rella in the fields was the same plant, but with a much weaker potency. And they were that same gold and silver shade as the rest of Memaj's foliage, not the healthy green and purple Caroline associated with Cartain fields. Jeff didn't seem to be bothered by it, but Caroline wasn't certain. Then again, Jeff *was* their expert on rella. If he said it was the same plant—then it had to be the same plant.

However, Caroline was very, *very* glad that Star had remained behind. Both Jeff and Fenarmin were increasingly aggressive. Irritation at the presentations or something else? Both facilities had offered food and drink. Caroline and Rifanel turned their offerings down, but Jeff and Fenarmin seemed to enjoy the snacks.

"We need to have protective masks," Jeff muttered to Caroline after the first facility. "They're not taking enough precautions."

The second one was worse. Caroline felt slightly light-headed. Not as bad as when she and Star had been exposed but enough to make her wobble.

"This is ridiculous," Jeff grumbled, loud enough for their escorts to hear as they left the production facility. "We need masks. All of us."

Fenarmin snorted and stomped. "What's wrong? You mere humans are easily influenced? Not so for us horses." He tossed his head and screamed, a defiant primordial bellow that sent chills down Caroline's spine.

"Fenarmin!" Rifanel followed her exclamation with a snort and flicked-back ears.

Fenarmin squealed at her. She whirled, ears now pinned hard against her head, and popped up her hind end. When he charged toward her, she lashed out with both hinds, catching him on his chest.

"I'm protecting my spouse!" Jeff snapped. "Not attacking her like you are yours!"

Fenarmin whirled away from Rifanel, rearing high. "I'm not the one who is too cowardly to engage in a sentient duel!"

Jeff clenched his fists. "Your leg was broken! The veterinarians disqualified you!"

"I can still defeat you even *with* a shattered foreleg!"

"Jeff—" Caroline tugged at his shirt, uneasiness rising higher in her as Easystar and Albert turned away from their autoskimmer and ambled toward them.

This is wrong. This is very wrong.

Jeff pulled away from her. "It's *done*, Fenarmin!"

"Look at the two has-beens who couldn't make it to a sentient duel," Albert drawled. "All words and no actions."

"Who are you to speak?" Jeff snapped. "You've never qualified for a sentient duel."

"It's clear you two are just itching to tear into each other. How about a little duel right here and now, to settle things?"

No judges. No safety precautions. Caroline swallowed hard, glancing over at Rifanel, who had come alongside Fenarmin and was trying to shoulder him away.

Fenarmin bellowed and tossed his head. He pinned his ears and snapped at Rifanel, and for a moment Caroline thought the two would start fighting.

"Tophand hasn't the nerve to try it."

Caroline could barely understand Fenarmin's rough, deep words. It was almost as if he suddenly couldn't use his translator correctly.

"What do you mean by that?" Jeff bristled.

Caroline tried again to jerk him back, but he brushed her off.

"Jeff, *don't*."

He ignored her, striding forward, fists clenched, chest thrust forward, brows furrowed hard in anger. Fenarmin matched him, neck arched, ears back, stepping high, raising his tail—the very picture of an angry stallion facing a challenge.

Rifanel squealed. Fenarmin ignored her.

Horse and human stopped, Jeff standing just out of Fenarmin's striking reach, posturing at each other.

"If I had a saddle and bucking halter, I'd show you," Jeff rumbled, deep in his chest.

"Stupid humans who need equipment to ride." Fenarmin's tone matched Jeff's.

"Halter and surcingle, then. Only fair."

"Gentlemen." Albert insinuated into the faceoff. "I know where we can find a saddle and halter. As it so happens, Mr. Easystar has both in his possession."

"Bring them out." Jeff's voice was cold and hard, a tone Caroline had never heard from him before. "Let's get this settled. Now."

"*Jeff,*" Caroline groaned.

But he marched away from her, along with Logan Easystar, Fenarmin, and Albert. Caroline turned to face Rifanel.

The brown mare whickered after Fenarmin.

The chestnut stallion didn't look back.

"I'm sorry, Caroline." Rifanel blew hard, shaking her head. "I don't know why he won't listen. He's been getting more and more irritable all turn."

"The same with Jeff."

Mare and human exchanged direct glances.

"Something in the food?" Caroline said, voice low.

"Possibly. But why didn't it affect us?"

"Targeted." Foreboding tightened her gut. "Jeff and Fenarmin both ate more than any of the rest of us. And then there was that contact they had with the Plasmoid at the reception."

Rifanel snorted. "Fenarmin checked out as unaffected, or so he told me."

"The same for Jeff."

"This is so not good. Let's hope they don't take it to the death," Rifanel said.

Caroline nodded, numb.

This was what would break her dreams. *This.*

She could just hear her mother now, gloating over the prospect of dragging her daughter back to Earth.

A PLOWED field was oh-so-conveniently located nearby—*too* nearby, as far as Caroline was concerned. Once medical transport capable of handling both human and equine arrived at the field, Easystar saddled and haltered Fenarmin. Jeff strapped Easystar-provided dueling spurs onto his boots, with spiky, sharp rowels that had clearly been sharpened. Caroline shuddered at the sight. Fenarmin stood deceptively still as Jeff checked the cinch on Easystar's saddle. Then he nodded to Easystar.

"Remember, sentient duel rules hold," Easystar said to Jeff and Fenarmin. "The duel continues until Jeff is dismounted, one of you concedes, one of you can no longer proceed, or one of you is dead. Understand?"

"Yes."

"Yes."

Jeff leapt into the saddle. He was barely settled in with a firm grip on the thick white halter rope when Fenarmin launched himself high, twisting and squealing as he arched into a high kick that jerked Jeff hard. Jeff raked Fenarmin's shoulders with his spurs as he leaned back, using the rope to balance himself.

Fenarmin stopped after several plunges, each higher than the last, barely dislodging Jeff from his secure seat.

Is he going to concede?

No. Fenarmin reared high, higher, higher—

"He's trying to make Jeff concede," Rifanel said. "If he

goes over backwards, Jeff has to jump—and if he jumps, he's dismounted." She blew, shaking her head. "Not a fair fighting technique. Fenarmin used to be better than that!" A worried nicker escaped her. "He'll hurt himself if he goes over backwards. Not just Jeff." She stomped a forefoot. "This field isn't soft enough for him to do that!"

Fenarmin paused at the top of his rear, balancing, clearly waiting. Jeff didn't react other than to lean forward slightly so he wouldn't pull the big stallion over on top of him. Fenarmin bellowed and went over backwards. Jeff stuck with him.

At the last moment, Fenarmin twisted and crashed on his left side, landing hard on Jeff's previously injured leg, something *snapping* as they landed.

Caroline and Rifanel flinched. Easystar's lips tightened into a thin line. Albert leaned forward, staring eagerly.

Which one got hurt? Caroline wrapped her hands around each other, barely breathing.

Jeff took a tighter wrap on the rope. His upper leg spurred Fenarmin's shoulder. Fenarmin lurched to his feet, bellowing. He launched into a flurry of spectacular, twisting bucks. Jeff kept up a steady spurring rhythm with his right leg, but his left leg twisted oddly.

Fenarmin's right foreleg buckled as he landed from one of those big, big leaps. But somehow the stallion managed to launch himself into the air once more, even though something was *not right* with that right leg, just above the hoof.

Rifanel groaned. "The old break."

"Fenarmin's *hurt!*" Caroline screamed at Easystar. "Can't you stop this?"

Albert sneered at her instead, while Easystar stared grimly ahead, watching the duel. "More concerned about the horse than your so-called *husband*, sister?"

"He's hurt too! But a broken leg is more serious for a horse."

Albert laughed, then turned back to watch the duel.

Fenarmin's forelegs buckled on his next landing and he collapsed. Jeff remained steady and quiet on his back, waiting. Fenarmin groaned and shook his head. Using his left foreleg more than the right, he heaved back up. Jeff lurched as Fenarmin rose, and almost fell off. But he was secure once Fenarmin launched himself into the air again.

"They're tiring too fast," Rifanel said. "Both of them should be in better shape than this."

Caroline remembered Jeff's words when they first arrived on Memaj. *The heat and humidity just sucks it right out of you.*

"Jeff said it's too hot and humid to compete. Why didn't he remember that?"

"Something's affecting them," Rifanel said.

They both groaned as Fenarmin's left foreleg crumpled after landing. He crashed to the ground, rolling over Jeff, hanging up on his back.

Jeff screamed. Caroline gasped, and would have darted out to rescue him, except that Rifanel swung her head to block Caroline.

"It's not safe for either of us. Wait."

Caroline groaned as Fenarmin writhed, struggling to get off of his back. At last, Fenarmin rolled onto his belly, forelegs sprawled at an unnatural angle. He tried to rise but crumpled back onto the ground. Jeff slumped over the saddle horn and onto Fenarmin's neck. Fenarmin dropped his nose to the ground, shuddering and gasping. Blood dripped from Jeff's nose and mouth. Blood-splattered froth foamed from Fenarmin's mouth.

"And that is that," Easystar said, his voice hard. "A draw." He glowered at Albert. "Seen enough, McKinnon? That enough distraction for you? Neither one of them should have indulged in this. If word gets out—"

Caroline didn't pay attention to Albert's answer as she and Rifanel ran to Jeff and Fenarmin, only to be held back as medical staff worked over man and horse.

The medics had to sedate both Jeff and Fenarmin before they could transport. The head medic slowly strode over to Caroline and Rifanel, shaking his head.

"If I didn't know better…." His voice trailed off.

"If you didn't know better, what?" Caroline asked.

The medic rubbed his face, exhaling hard.

"I hope this is just temporary and a reflection of how severely traumatized they both are. But." He straightened up, face falling into tight lines. "Neither horse nor human behaved like a typical sentient should, even in extreme pain. If I didn't know better, I would say that they have both lost sentience."

"No," Caroline groaned. Rifanel echoed her with a despairing whinny.

"It's probably just an effect of injury and sedation," the medic said soothingly. "Or a temporary dementia. All the same, ladies—prepare yourselves. I've seen this before, here on Memaj. Just something about this place when people get hurt."

"So recovery is possible if we take them to Central?" Rifanel asked.

The medic shook his head. "One of my cases in a similar situation has gone ten cycles in a Galactic Central facility. No improvement."

Caroline gulped. She wanted to scream, but—no. Not the time nor the place.

12

———

AFTERMATH

"Are you all right?"

Star's anxious greeting almost sent Caroline into tears. She swallowed hard and shook her head, unable to mindspeak or say anything out loud for fear of losing control in front of everyone watching, including the cams.

Don't show emotion to the media was ground into her deepest self, from earliest childhood. The last thing they needed to have happen right now was a media scandal on top of everything else.

Though how it can be avoided I just don't know. Unless they get better soon —

She had possessed enough presence of mind during their trip back to Memsij to send short messages to Darcy and Geraint.

—Jeff and Fenarmin have been incapacitated and we don't know how bad it is. I will keep you advised as I know more.

Reporting to Geraint was mandatory, and as for Jeff's family—better they hear about it from her than from the media, even if she couldn't give them any further details yet.

Fenarmin bellowed and screamed as the medics started to

unload him, trying to bite and strike at those trying to help, fighting against the drugs that were supposed to keep him quiet. Rifanel whickered plaintively at Fenarmin, trying to soothe him.

Fenarmin's bellows set Jeff off into a spell of thrashing and shrieking.

"Jeff. *Jeff!*" It was all Caroline could do to keep from breaking into tears because he struggled against his restraints, not responding to anything she said, eyes wide and almost popping out of his head, his wordless cries echoing Fenarmin's.

How many times had they gone through this loop of Fenarmin blowing up, then Jeff reacting to Fenarmin, since getting onto the runabout? Caroline had lost count. She was at the ragged edge of her emotions and she didn't think Rifanel was doing any better.

Star's eyes widened and she blew hard. She hurried to Caroline's side, oozing between Caroline and Rifanel, nuzzling first one, then the other, sending wordless, soothing images to Caroline as she nickered softly. Caroline leaned heavily on Star as the three of them followed Jeff and Fenarmin into the hospital. Star's distress was a welcome distraction from her own.

Abe met them in the private waiting room set aside for Caroline and Rifanel while their spouses were in surgery. "What happened?" His tone was firm, unemotional, enough to keep Caroline from bursting into tears as she described the duel.

He closed his eyes for a couple of taps once she finished, sighing heavily.

"What a mess," he said finally. "The Rodeo will have a few things to say to Easystar, Fenarmin, and Tophand about participating in an unsanctioned sentient duel. And by all of the black holes in the Galaxy, why was Albert involved in this?"

"Ask our brother," Caroline said bitterly. She remembered Easystar's words. "I think he brought this about, somehow." She gulped, still fighting back the tears.

"That's *enough*," Star said. "My friend doesn't need any further problems!"

Abe frowned at Star. "Caroline Starshine *is* my sister."

Star pinned her ears flat. "She doesn't need any more interference from her family! Haven't you two and your mother done enough to her?" Star shifted so that she stood between Abe and Caroline, baring her teeth at him in warning.

Abe raised his hands, stepping back. "I mean no harm to Caroline." He snapped his fingers and manifested the badge of the Galactic Controlled Substances Agency. "I don't work for Hart Mercantile Services. I'm a GCSA agent, investigating allegations of rella smuggling. Caroline knows."

"*He speaks truly?*" Star asked Caroline.

"*Yes.*" For some reason Caroline was as choked up in her mindspeech as she was in her throat.

"Are you responsible for the Ethereal Confederation's demand that the Federation delegates leave Memaj?" Star demanded.

Rifanel stirred. "It does not matter what the Confederation demands. Neither Jeff nor Fenarmin are in any condition to travel. Nor will they be for several turns." She wheeled away from Caroline and Star to stand in a corner away from the others, head lowered, not even glancing over at the stack of hay that someone had piled there for her to eat while they waited.

"I had nothing to do with that," Abe said. "I'll investigate. I have my suspicions." He marched off, snapping up a cone of silence as he started talking to someone.

Star nuzzled Caroline. "*I'd better make sure she eats. We don't want Rifanel to colic due to stress.*"

Caroline nodded, unable to say or do anything more. She

sank into a chair, burying her head in her hands. Rifanel needed support more than she did—*she* wasn't likely to go into a potentially fatal colic if not encouraged to eat in the face of stress, unlike Rifanel, with that delicate equine digestive system.

What else could go wrong?

Whatever happens, I'm not going back to Earth. Not now.

She had no idea what would happen if Jeff never regained sentience. Oh, she would fill in as Planetary Representative for Jeff during the remainder of his term. The terms of their formal marriage association provided for that option.

After that?

Her only connection to Cartain was through Jeff. Caroline had no idea what long-term provisions Jeff had made for her —oh, there were clauses in their formal association contract for the ending of the contract, but would they give her enough financial support to live on? She could be facing significant problems with the Federation due to her family connection with Hart Mercantile, in spite of the releases she had signed. It was possible that she would be banned from further work in the Congress. That half-resolve about going into a Galactic pleasure palace before ever returning to Earth, if she had no other options, might well be a reality.

If prison wasn't a possibility.

I don't even remember anything in our marital contract about permanent disability or death contingencies. Contract ending clauses might not be sufficient.

They *should* have married before going to Memaj, rather than waiting to celebrate on Cartain. Then she would be protected.

That thought nearly brought tears to her eyes. Caroline shuddered. She couldn't cry now. Shouldn't cry now. The pain that struck deep inside of her wasn't just about protection or even mostly that. It was about the abrupt ending of her relationship with Jeff, without even the consolation of being his widow.

Oh Jeff, please get better. I want you in my life. Your laugh. Your smile. Your concern about others. I want to build a life with you. Not this—ending before we barely began.

Far too familiar squabbling voices broke the circle of her fretting.

"What the hell are you doing here, Abe?" Annoyance dominated Albert's voice.

"Albert. You have the *nerve* to show up at the hospital after your role in what happened?" She recognized that cold anger in Abe's voice.

"Just what are *you* doing here?" How dare Albert sound puzzled when he said that?

"If I wasn't an agent of the GCSA I'd deck you one, Albert! Curse you to the gas belt of Slopnt!"

"Oh, so *that's* who you're loyal to, Abe—not the family!" A thin thread of anger crept into Albert's voice.

Caroline raised her head. "Stop it. *Just stop it!*" she screamed.

Star blew a long, rolling snort.

Rifanel squealed. She stomped past Caroline and stood facing Caroline's squabbling brothers, ears flat against her head, tail switching hard and fast. "Albert McKinnon. You have no business intruding here."

Caroline dragged herself up, joining Rifanel. "What are you doing here, Albert? Come to gloat over what you did to Jeff and Fenarmin?"

"I had nothing to do with it!" Albert blustered.

"That's not what Logan Easystar says," Abe said, his voice low and hard. He glanced up. "Ah. There you are. About damn time."

Uniformed humanoid GCSA agents surrounded Albert.

"Albert McKinnon, you are under arrest for potential

violations of the Galactic Controlled Substances Act," the woman wearing captain's bars said.

A peach-shaded Plasmoid bubble glided toward them. "And for violations of the Ethereal Confederation Controlled Substances Act." It dipped respectfully in Abe's direction, then to Caroline and Rifanel. "That is, once the Federation is done with you."

"None of you have jurisdiction here!" Albert blustered. "Not the Federation, not the Confederation. None of you!" He sneered at Caroline. "I'll see you back on Earth, *sister*." He whirled and stomped away, followed by the GCSA agents and the Plasmoid.

Caroline shuddered and buried her head in her hands. Abe wrapped an arm around her shoulders. "Little sis. I'm sorry. I'm so sorry."

And that gentle touch familiar to her after a blowup within the family was enough to break the tight hold Caroline had over her tears. It wasn't the first time that she had allowed herself to cry around Abe.

At least they were private.

ABE WENT AWAY AFTER A WHILE, promising to return after he communicated with still more people. Nodes—no, *turns*, if not *cycles*—seemed to spin by as Caroline, Star, and Rifanel waited. Caroline fended off inquiries from Geraint and Darcy by simply saying *they're in surgery, we haven't heard anything yet*, over and over again. She drafted a short statement for Star to send out to media inquiries. Rifanel messaged with her assistant Julia, back at their quarters, to do the same.

But even dealing with all those urgent communications didn't fill up the times when the three of them just were there —waiting. The room wasn't big enough for any of them to pace. Caroline tapped her fingertips together. Star and Rifanel swished their tails, Star frequently nudging Rifanel to persuade her to take another bite of hay and settle her stomach when Rifanel started weaving from forefoot to forefoot.

Waiting. Just waiting.

At last the door opened and the head surgeon, an unbubbled, teal-shaded Plasmoid, floated into the room.

"We need to keep them sedated for the next three turns," they said wearily. "Both subjects have significant internal injuries. Normally that would not be an issue but—" they exhaled. "Both show signs of ristenal poisoning."

"What's that?" Caroline asked.

The Plasmoid flushed pale green. "One is not sure if one can speak freely—"

"Say it." Abe marched into the waiting room, glowering, the Plasmoid in the peach-shaded bubble directly behind him. "We already know, thanks to Whixit's information." He jerked his head toward the peach-shaded bubble.

"And your authority?" The surgeon's shade changed to pale pink.

Abe snapped up his GCSA credentials, and the Plasmoid —Whixit?—clicked up credentials of their own. The surgeon examined their credentials quickly, their shade returning to teal.

"This is embarrassing," they said. "How much do you know about our kind?"

"Almost nothing," Caroline said.

The surgeon bobbed in acknowledgement. "We have multiple subspecies of Plasmoids on Memaj. One is very toxic to Solids. Normally, they are required to be in a bubble whenever they are around Solids."

"Both Jeff and Fenarmin were hit by a Plasmoid's dribbles at last turn's reception," Caroline said slowly.

"The mark of the Fizzrt is noticeable," the surgeon said. "The placement is quite unfortunate."

"How is that?"

The surgeon's shade briefly flashed pink under teal.

"Forehead placement means a swift impact upon cognitive abilities. One has administered an antidote, but one does not know if it will work. The antidote should have been given immediately after the contact."

"Fenarmin said nothing about receiving an antidote." Rifanel stomped a hind hoof. "We had faith in the Memaj medic who looked at him!"

"The same for Jeff."

Another flash of pink under teal. "It is not the usual state of affairs to have a medic at any sort of reception here."

"What?" Caroline stared at the surgeon.

"Fizzrts are supposed to be bubbled at such occasions. That is the only choice for those who attend official functions. They are too dangerous to Solids otherwise."

Rifanel stomped even harder, swishing her tail as well. "Why?"

"Ristenal—that excretion from Fizzrts after they've consumed a certain amount of rella—when combined with internal injuries to Solids, can cause a permanent regression of sentience. Normally, if an antidote is administered quickly, the danger is relatively minor." This time the pink flush remained, the teal fading. "We must give the patients time to heal from their injuries before attempting to transport to Galactic Central for further treatment. After three turns, we will have some notion as to how well they will recover."

"They had better recover," Rifanel rumbled deep in her chest.

"Agreed." Caroline glared at the surgeon.

The surgeon flushed even deeper red. "Honorable Solids, please believe. One is doing one's best. It has already been made known to one that the future of Memaj lies in the survival of these two Planetary Representatives."

"One had best believe that," Whixit said, their voice

projecting threat. "Not just from the Federation, either. Ristenal is a controlled excretion within the Ethereal Confederation. Not adequately treating a Solid exposure—*two* Solid exposures—in a timely manner, added to allowing undisciplined Fizzrts to participate in a gathering is a *significant* violation under the laws of the Ethereal Confederation's Controlled Substances Act. The Ethereal Confederation Controlled Substances Agency has the authority to deny Memaj's application for membership if this lapse is not explained."

The surgeon blanched. "Your Grace Whixit, one is *trying* our best—"

"Wait a minute," Caroline said. "Memaj has a membership application with the Confederation as well as the Federation?"

Oh, this was a huge mess. And completely within the bounds of something her mother would advise.

"Yes-s-s," Whixit snapped.

"The Galactic Controlled Substances Agency does not possess the same authority as our counterpart," Abe said dryly, eying Whixit. "However, by the time we're through with all of the violations, Memaj may be fortunate enough to remain an independent world free of Federation interdiction. *Maybe.*"

Rifanel flattened her ears and popped her tail in angry swishes. "If Fenarmin does not survive, or if he loses sentience, *Memaj will pay.*" She bared her teeth and tossed her head threateningly.

"Yes," Caroline echoed. "If Jeff does not survive or if he loses sentience, then Memaj will pay." She glowered at the surgeon. "How soon before we can see our spouses?"

The Plasmoid bobbled up and down nervously. "Next turn. But there will not be much to see. They will both be sedated."

"Dr. Erith has just sent an urgent message to your official

account," Star mindspoke. *"She says that she is available to meet next turn."*

Now what? Caroline took a deep breath. "All right, then. Rifanel, Star, let's return to our quarters. Where we can speak —*privately.*"

"I'll come with you—" Abe began.

Caroline turned her glare on her brother. "No. Right now I don't trust *anyone*, including you, Abe! My spouse is in danger, and no one appears to have had an interest in preventing it except me! We will talk—*next turn.* Depending on what condition Jeff is in. Rifanel, Star, *let's go.*" She marched out of the waiting room, without looking behind to see if the mares followed.

Now, the tears she fought to contain were those of rage, not sorrow and fear.

"Well done," Rifanel said quietly, coming alongside. "Very much like a lead mare should conduct herself."

"My family. My damn family. And to have *two* brothers mixed up in this—" Caroline shook her head. If she said anything more, she would scream. Cry. Something that wouldn't do any of them any good, especially as the media cams buzzed around them.

"Let's wait until we are in quarters to speak," Rifanel said. "I suggest we go to Fenarmin's and mine."

Caroline nodded in agreement, unable to speak. Rifanel briefly touched Caroline's hand with the edge of her muzzle, blowing softly on it.

That delicate contact was sufficiently soothing to help Caroline maintain control as they left the hospital, cams hovering around them as they walked to the autoskimmer. A reminder that she wasn't the only one suffering through the disability of a spouse, even if the relationship was strictly formal—at least in Rifanel's case. She rested a hand on Rifanel's withers.

Once inside the autoskimmer, Caroline rubbed Rifanel's

neck. The mare exhaled a soft, shuddering sigh and leaned her head against Caroline's torso, Caroline resting her head on Rifanel's.

THEY TRAVELED BACK to Rifanel's quarters in silence—like Caroline and Jeff's, a smaller version of Rifanel's quarters on Galactic Central, without the pastures.

Rifanel's assistant Julia was solemn as she let them inside.

"All is clear," she said. "I've checked and double-checked our blockers, as you requested, Rifanel. Plus I have that cone of silence that Blackburn gave you."

The brown mare blew hard, ending with a deep groan. "Thank you, Julia. We have much to discuss. Activate the cone." She turned her head and flicked an ear at Star. "I suggest you brief Julia about what happened at the hospital, if you would? Caroline and I need to speak after she has contacted Dr. Erith."

"I will." Julia and Star retreated to the stable area.

Caroline snapped up her messages once the cone had spread through the quarters, feeling grateful that her status as Jeff's spouse allowed her to send and receive highly encrypted messages through the barrier—like the one from Dr. Erith that Star had told her about. Dr. Erith's message was at the top, colored bright red.

—Ms. Starshine. I have cleared my schedule after hearing of this turn's unfortunate events. May I join you this next turn at Fifth Node, after First Meal?

Caroline paused, thinking.

—Yes, she wrote. *—I look forward to our further discussions.*

—I will see you then.

"I have set up a meeting with Dr. Erith next turn, Fifth Node," she said. "It appears to be quite urgent. She referred to clearing her schedule after hearing of this turn's events."

"Very interesting," Rifanel said. "What do you think about the revelation that Memaj has also made application to the Confederation?"

"My first thought is that it is the sort of thing that I would expect of someone who has been advised by my mother," Caroline said bitterly. "Play multiple sides against each other. But that doesn't explain this whole damned mess. Those— unbubbled Fizzrts at the reception last night, in apparent violation of *Confederation* standards. Targeting Jeff and Fenarmin with *ristenal,* whatever in the Great Nebula that is."

"The ability for ristenal to remove sentience if not adequately treated in time," Rifanel said. "That this property of it is known not only to the Confederation but to medical personnel on Memaj."

"And just how does this all tie into rella and its connection with ristenal? Obviously rella's been grown here for a while if ristenal is a known side-effect of rella consumption by one subspecies of Plasmoid." Caroline shook her head. "Jeff swore that the plants here are the same as the ones on Cartain, only less potent. But that didn't make sense to me! They look so different." She frowned. "I didn't look at the results myself, and I'm not sure I would know what to look for. Could the ristenal have affected Jeff's thinking by then?"

"Entirely possible." Rifanel snorted. "What about Easystar having his rodeo equipment handy? If they just wanted to change Jeff's analysis, then why include Fenarmin and force them into a sentient duel?"

"They're both first-time Planetary Representatives," Caroline mused. "Not even from the same party. Incapacitating both of them doesn't make sense, and it wouldn't change Geraint's role in the Congress. Nor yours—if anything, that gives you more power by putting you back in as Planetary Rep for Hrwhinir because you're his spouse and assistant." She threw up her hands. "So much of this doesn't fit together. It doesn't make sense," she repeated.

"I had a very unusual conversation with Whixit at last turn's reception," Star said, as she and Julia returned. "They tried to get me to describe how I became Converted." Her ears flicked back, then forward. "I swore an oath not to disclose it except for people who used appropriate passphrases. They used a passphrase, but it was not the correct one."

"I wonder where that came from." Caroline paused. "I saw a Plasmoid on Cartain, in a bubble shaded very much like Whixit's. It was entering the Rella Protective Association offices—which back up onto the Ribonit headquarters on Cartain. The Protective Association is not representative of the growers. Jeff told me that their purpose focuses on expanding markets for rella, as well as cultivating it on planets other than Cartain." She tapped her chin thoughtfully. "Jeff also said that they were interested in becoming an intermediary between the Rella Producers Association and the Ribonits."

"They could have a role in rella appearing here." Rifanel swished her tail slowly.

"Who is the Rella Protective Association?" Julia asked. "Who's funding it?"

"I don't know. Jeff doesn't either. I haven't had time to investigate. But here's something else. I also saw that Whixit talking to my brother Abe in the Congress," Caroline said.

Rifanel flicked her ears forward and back. "Suspicious." She shook her head, blowing hard. "It seems that matters of sentience are important in this situation. Why expose Fenarmin and Jeff to ristenal? Were any others exposed during that reception? Why did that medic—if that person was truly a medic and not involved in this conspiracy—not administer the antidote to Fenarmin and Jeff?"

"Why are the Fizzrts producing a restricted excretion like ristenal—and *what is it?*" Caroline couldn't keep the frustration out of her voice. There were just so many things that they didn't know!

"Many questions," Rifanel said slowly. "We have space in these quarters for the two of you. I think it is safer that the four of us remain together right now. Not just for our protection, but so that it is easier to share any discoveries one of us might make in whatever research we can manage to do with limited planetary resources. *I* for one will be spending as much effort as I can to learn more about *ristenal, Fizzrts*, and everything I can about Plasmoids."

"The same here," Caroline said. "But I also want to prepare for my meeting with Dr. Erith tomorrow. It will be *most* interesting to learn what is so urgent that she cleared her calendar to meet with me—when she insisted at the reception that she needed at least two turns to complete her work at the University before she could speak to me."

"A difference of one turn might not be significant," Rifanel cautioned. "She may well have finished her duties more quickly than anticipated."

"Possibly," Caroline said.

However, based on her knowledge of Mars University, final grading and testing was never completed early. If anything, she would have expected Dr. Erith to have requested an extension of at least one more turn before they met.

———

Dr. Erith was very cooperative about meeting in Rifanel's quarters. Rifanel, Star, and Julia went into the stable area to give them privacy, while Caroline brought up the cone of silence in the parlor space. Even so, the woman looked around nervously before she sat down, her antennae agitated and twitching, clutching a big secured handbag in her lap. Julia had scanned the bag after their security had checked it, and pronounced it as non-threatening, full of clothing and data cubes.

"Are you certain this is a safe location?" Dr. Erith tightened her grip on the bag.

"Rifanel's assistant Julia has been constantly checking the integrity of her blockers," Caroline said. "This cone of silence comes directly from Federation Security at the highest level."

"All right then." Dr. Erith exhaled but her grip on the bag did not ease. "You wanted to know more about the history of Memaj native species."

"Yes. The official story is that there *were* no species capable of sentience when both Solid and Plasmoid species landed on Memaj, intent on colonization."

Dr. Erith nodded, her antennae jerking even more than before. "No mammalians, very low-cognitive reptiles, same for avian species."

"Supposedly no sign of a prior sentient species that could have bombed or developed itself into extinction by destroying the climate." Caroline kept her voice quiet—that had almost been Earth's fate.

"And no possibility of any potential development in the oceans." A faint sigh escaped Erith's lips. "A world perfect for colonization without the complications of dealing with native sentients, from both Solid and Plasmoid perspectives."

Caroline forced herself to relax into her chair. "So far, that's the summary of what I know about Memaj. So what is it that I *don't* know about Memaj's history?"

"It *is* the official record." Erith's voice quavered.

"And the unofficial record?"

If Caroline had thought that Erith's antennae twitched before, they now danced in an agitated blur.

"You understand that this is—if word gets out that I am the source of this information, I am in danger." Erith looked down, then back up. "I will tell you some of it. But I will need asylum—and I can only tell you part of it. Proper authorities must hear the rest of it first."

Caroline raised her right index finger. "A moment, please." A good thing that Star was within mindspeech range! She mindspoke to Star. *"Ask Rifanel if she or I have the authority to offer asylum to someone in danger."*

"Dr. Erith?"

"Yes."

A few taps, then, *"Rifanel says yes. Since your spouses are incapacitated, you have the authority to offer asylum."*

"Please tell her thank you." Caroline lowered her hand and exhaled. "Dr. Erith, I have consulted with Rifanel, and I do have the authority to offer you asylum, in my capacity as a Planetary Representative's spouse and likely temporary successor."

Erith's eyes widened. "How did you do that?"

"I have a mindlink with my assistant, Star, and she asked Rifanel. Now. Tell me." Caroline summoned up the sternest gaze she could think of, studying Erith carefully. "What is so problematic about Memaj's history that you require asylum to tell me only part of it?"

Erith swallowed hard. She looked down, then back up. "I will only tell part of this to a Federation Security officer for my own safety. I do have the documentation to back up my assertions, and will turn it over to them."

"Go ahead." *Come on, go ahead and say it!*

Not that she would actually *say* something like this to Erith, but—*I hope this is good information.*

"The early settlers on Memaj did not come willingly," Erith said slowly. "They were brought here by a corporation with ties to both the Federation and the Confederation. A corporation paid to take responsibility for undesirables and isolate them from both regimes."

Caroline inhaled sharply. Could this company be Hart Mercantile? That might explain Erith's reluctance to say anything directly to *her*. And oh dear stars, this made *so much sense*.

"Could that corporation have exterminated a pre-existing sentient species on Memaj?"

Erith winced. "I cannot safely tell you more. Not just for my own safety, but yours."

Ice clutched at Caroline's gut.

Hart Mercantile is involved.

Had to be.

She swallowed hard, then switched on a recorder. Erith's eyes widened and for a couple of taps Caroline thought she was going to flee.

"This is Caroline Starshine, spouse of Jeff Tophand, Planetary Representative for the planet Cartain, speaking with his authority. Recording of official action taken on his behalf."

Erith sank back in her chair, gaze locked on Caroline, a hopeful expression softening the tightness of fear. Her antennae still vibrated tensely but not quite as fast as before.

"I formally extend an offer of asylum within the Galactic Federation of Solid Peoples to Dr. Erith, currently of Memaj. Dr. Erith?"

"I accept," Erith husked, slumping in relief, her antennae briefly sagging before snapping upright and quivering. "And Honorable Starshine—I thank you."

Caroline inclined her head slightly as she switched off the recorder and sent a copy to Geraint. "I accept your thanks, and will find out how soon a representative of Federation Security can be here. Unless you would prefer to speak to an agent of the Galactic Controlled Substances Agency?"

"No," Erith whispered. "Definitely not them."

"Well, then," Caroline sighed. "Let's get you settled in. Rifanel and I want to see our spouses today, but you will be safe here with our assistants Julia and Star. I will find out whether Federation Security will have an appropriate agent interview you here or on Galactic Central. Our travel date depends on the health of our spouses, which means at least two more turns. Do you need us to send anyone to fetch your things?"

Erith shook her head, her antennae relaxing once more. "Everything I need is here." She patted her bag.

Caroline rose. "Then I will bring the others back inside." She closed the cone of silence. "We will discuss our next steps, before Rifanel and I go to the hospital."

Her stomach felt hollow as she rose.

Memaj is why Albert and Mother left Earth.

Had to be.

And Abe?

Much as she actually liked *this* brother, there was no way in the Universe that she would talk to Abe right now. Not at all. Not until she knew more. Was Abe just a GCSA agent, like he claimed, or—did he play a more complex role in this mess?

Too many uncertainties. Better to remain silent.

"BLACKBURN WILL BE HERE NEXT TURN," Rifanel told Caroline. "While you were talking to Dr. Erith, he sent us a message saying that he is coming to Memaj, with a representative of the Galactic Rodeo. They are taking an express transport." She cocked her head, eying Caroline. "The information is that significant?"

Caroline nodded, swallowing hard. "It's not something I can talk about, but it definitely provides an explanation for what's happened."

Rifanel stomped a hind foot, switching her tail. "Why weren't we told—" she snorted and shook her head. "Money is involved. Much money. And our spouses have paid the price."

"Yes," Caroline said. "Unfortunately."

"THEY ARE STABLE," the medic supervising Jeff and Fenarmin's post-operative status said when Rifanel and Caroline arrived at the secured hospital wing where their spouses were located.

"What does that mean?" Caroline asked, as Rifanel groaned.

The medic—this one reptilian—raised its forelegs, spreading its claws wide. "Honorable Starshine, we can say no more than this. Directives from the Guardians of Memaj, the Galactic Controlled Substances Agency, and the Ethereal Confederation Controlled Substances Agency."

"But they're our *spouses*," Caroline insisted.

"That is all we can say."

Rifanel nudged Caroline. "It is not worth pushing for more information, Caroline. Not with those authorities forbidding it. Let us see how our silly males are doing, with our own eyes."

"All right," Caroline sighed.

Fenarmin's room was closest. Caroline joined Rifanel because she didn't think they should be alone. Even with security present to protect them—not just their own, but a Plasmoid in a blue-shaded bubble and some of the GCSA agents who had arrested Albert yesterday—or at least tried to arrest Albert. None of the GCSA agents would confirm if Albert was actually in custody.

Caroline shuddered as they looked at Fenarmin. Rifanel's only show of emotion was her flicked back ears. The chestnut stallion slumped in slings designed to keep him safely upright, with no weight on his injured legs or on his trauma-tized gut. It didn't look comfortable to Caroline, especially the sling for his head and neck, or the ones around his hind legs. Fenarmin roused a couple times while they were there, flailing until a new dose of sedative kicked in and he slumped against the slings. Rifanel approached, nuzzling his neck briefly before he started thrashing again. Then she retreated.

"Why can't they put him in stasis?" Caroline growled. "That has to be better than this—" She gestured at the slings.

"The trip back to Galactic Central will push the boundaries of safe stasis for horses," Rifanel said slowly. "As it is, I fear he may develop colic. There are means for feeding horses sedated like this but—" she blew heavily and shook her head.

"Oh."

Jeff was no better. His broken leg was cast up to his groin and his broken ribs were bound. At least he lay still on the bed, not thrashing about. He flinched when Caroline touched him, so she stepped away.

"I don't know what to do," she said to Rifanel.

"Their records say they can be transported to Galactic Central in two more turns, so we will make plans for that." Rifanel switched her tail. "That is all we can do—here. Come, Caroline. Let us return to our quarters."

———

While Dr. Erith wouldn't share her knowledge about Memaj's past, she was able to enlighten them about ristenal.

"When the Fizzrts consume rella, they excrete ristenal," she told them.

"My impression from what Whixit said is that all Fizzrts excrete ristenal," Rifanel said.

"Only when they consume rella. It's an addictive substance for the Fizzrts," Dr. Erith admitted. "However, without rella—no ristenal."

Caroline left the questioning of Dr. Erith to Rifanel. Perhaps she would be more forthcoming with the brown mare since Rifanel didn't have connections to Hart Mercantile. Meanwhile, Jeff had given her his sampler for safekeeping after he ran his scans, so she ran her own analysis on his results.

She wasn't the expert that Jeff was when it came to rella, but—there *were* deviations from the gene sequencing between rella on Memaj and rella on Cartain. Enough that even an amateur like Caroline could see the difference. Significant? Perhaps.

Caroline considered sending the results to Darcy to get her opinion—then decided to wait until they were away from Memaj, for security's sake.

THE LAST TURN before they could leave for Galactic Central. Another hospital visit, as frustrating and inconclusive as the previous one, although this time the head medic acknowledged that both Jeff and Fenarmin had progressed sufficiently that Fenarmin could be placed safely in short-term stasis while Jeff could be sedated heavily enough to travel.

That was one small gain.

Blackburn, Richardson, and the Galactic Rodeo representative, a big red bull named Carfen who reminded Caroline of Bloohowt, only more polite and measured in his expressions, arrived shortly after their return to Rifanel's quarters. Blackburn and Richardson spoke privately to Dr. Erith while Carfen questioned Caroline and Rifanel about the sequence of events leading up to Jeff and Fenarmin's duel.

At last, the big bull shook his head, emitting a soft bawl before speaking. "It is clear from what you have said, as well as the information that Logan Easystar has provided us, that a very powerful entity coerced Tophand and Fenarmin into this duel. The Rodeo will not hold them liable for their actions."

"Was that entity Hart Mercantile, operating through Albert McKinnon?" Caroline asked.

A quiet bellow from Carfen, before he spoke. "Alas,

Honorable Starshine, I am not free to say one way or the other."

Rifanel flicked an ear at Caroline. But before she could speak, the cone of silence containing Dr. Erith, Richardson, and Blackburn dropped. Richardson's expression was grim and Blackburn's ears pinned hard against his head.

"Honorables Starshine and Rifanel. We request that you come with us to meet the Guardians of Memaj," Richardson said.

"What's going on?" Rifanel asked.

Blackburn thumped hard against his platform, with both hind paws.

"You will know when we meet," Richardson said.

A NODE LATER, they gathered in the Guardians' private audience chamber. Three bubbled Plasmoids in shades of teal and green, a human, and two of the upright reptilians awaited them. The human looked very nervous. Caroline wasn't certain about the reptilians or the Plasmoids, but she *thought* the reptilians appeared to be concerned. As for the Plasmoids—who knew?

Caroline and Rifanel were backed by a full squad of Federation Security agents. Abe and his GCSA agents surrounded Logan Easystar and Albert. Additional Plasmoids in orange variants followed Whixit—Caroline realized she could recognize Whixit not just by shade but bubble size and shape—they were larger and more ovoid than their smaller, rounder counterparts.

Blackburn thumped hard on his platform with both hind paws. He rose to all fours, ears pinned back hard, tail extended behind him, his ruff fur bristling.

I wouldn't want to confront him. Caroline stifled a shudder. She had never seen the black rabbit so furious until now. And

Richardson's stiff, stern expression appeared to conceal anger as well.

"Honorables Starshine and Rifanel. Logan Easystar and Albert McKinnon. Guardians of Memaj," Richardson said. "Agent Blackburn, Assistant Director of the Federation Security Service, along with Their Grace, Whixit of the Ethereal Confederation Controlled Substance Agency, issues this verdict on the incident involving the Honorables Tophand and Fenarmin. As of this click, Memaj has been placed under temporary Interdiction by both the Federation of Solid Peoples and the Ethereal Confederation. With the exception of the transport necessary to take the Honorables, their staff, and all other Federation and Confederation agents off of Memaj, no transports will be allowed to enter or leave Memaj system space until the Final Ruling is issued."

"You can't do that!" one of the Plasmoids blustered, turning pale pink.

Blackburn thumped again, turning to face that Plasmoid.

"He *can* do that, and he *is* doing that," Richardson said dryly.

The Plasmoid's bubble began to change to a yellow shade.

"One should not take that action," Whixit said. "Attacking Blackburn is not a good idea."

"He is nothing but a meager mammal! He can't even speak his own words!" The yellow deepened in intensity.

Blackburn stomped on his platform with a front paw. Instead of resonating like his hind paw thumps, the touch caused a small laser gun to emerge from the platform. It glowed red as a darker red target formed on the side of that Plasmoid's bubble.

"One should not underestimate the rabbit," Whixit said. "As a species, they may be small, but their size is not reflective of their bravery. Trust one. Blackburn has much more battle experience than you do!"

The Plasmoid's color slowly changed back to pale pink.

"Are we done?" Richardson inquired, a sarcastic tone in her voice. "We leave at Fourth Node tomorrow. Blackburn has spoken!"

The black rabbit's loud thump with both hind paws emphasized her words.

Caroline exhaled a ragged sigh.

Now what?

13

RECKONINGS

THEIR PARTY OF JEFF, Fenarmin, Caroline, Rifanel, Star, and Julia returned to Galactic Central with Blackburn and Richardson on the express transport that Blackburn had commissioned for his trip to Memaj, turning a five-turn trip into two turns. At least Logan Easystar, Albert, and Abe weren't with them. Easystar and Albert were under arrest, and Abe was in charge of bringing them to Galactic Central on an express transport set up to handle prisoners.

Once they were away from Memaj space, Blackburn called them together.

"Dr. Erith, this is a safe venue to share your information —*all* of it," Laura Richardson said. For the first time since Caroline had met her, the elegant brunette appeared weary. Or was it that she could finally let down her guard now that they were all safely enclosed in a private transport, away from Memaj?

Erith glanced at Caroline. "But her connections to Hart Mercantile—"

"Are immaterial," Caroline said. "I renounced them a cycle ago and will do so again, if necessary. I already have my suspicions about the role my family has played in this entire —situation."

"*Well said*," Blackburn mindspoke to her. Even his mind-speech sounded weary, matching Richardson's vocal tone. A letdown after the events on Memaj, or reflecting everything he and Richardson had been involved in since Caroline last saw them on Galactic Central?

Erith swallowed hard and her antennae quivered. "There were three native sentient species on Memaj. One—reptilian —developed naturally, the other two—avian and humanoid —through ancient Plasmoid sentience seeding. The reptilian and humanoid species exterminated the avian species, and nearly drove themselves into extinction as well before Hart Mercantile Services discovered the planet."

"I see," Caroline said. So her worst suspicions were true.

"Hart Mercantile was seeking a location that would serve to fulfill contracts they had created with an Earth-based suballiance in the Federation to deport sentients they considered to be undesirable," Erith continued. "They had also approached the nearest Plasmoid suballiances to perform the same function."

"How long ago was this?" Caroline hadn't seen anything about this type of contract in the Hart Mercantile records she was familiar with. Which—either these transactions were very, very secret or else this had happened many cycles past. Hart hadn't been involved with planetary exploration for a *long* time.

At least as far as she knew.

"Five hundred cycles," Erith said.

Nothing new, then—and the timing matched the initial arrival of colonists on Memaj. She might even be able to find the contracts in old Hart records. At the minimum, she could guide Federation Security authorities to the proper places to look within the Hart archives.

Caroline's spirits lifted slightly. Maybe her future wasn't

quite as dire as she feared. She would definitely be of further use to the Federation.

"What did Hart Mercantile do?" she asked.

"To prepare the planet for their colonists, Hart Mercantile encouraged a nuclear war between the reptilian and humanoid sentient species. Then they sterilized the planet of all evidence that there had ever been a sentient species on Memaj." Erith's antennae danced with greater agitation. "But they forgot one sentient. The planet itself."

Oh. *Oh.* And Erith came from a planet that possessed limited sentience.

That made *five* sentient planets within the loose Federation boundaries—that they knew about. And with the Sentient Planet Alliance stirring as well—*oh.*

"So you asked the planet about its past? How do you do that?" Caroline studied Erith, wondering just how one communicated with a sentient planet. Through weather? Gas emissions? Mold spores? Something tied to Erith's antennae? Dr. Knowledgechaser was the most well-informed Mars University professor about sentient planets—and even he admitted he didn't know very much.

"Planets speak to mild empaths. They send images but you have to be properly grounded in the planet's ecosystem to hear them, away from developed areas. For me, what works best is to find a large communal organism. Since you're from Earth, that would be equivalent to large mushroom bodies or aspen groves. I meditate within one of those organisms, and the images come to me." Erith pointed to her antennae. "Through these."

"Oh. That makes sense." Caroline nodded. Most empaths *did* possess antennae.

"And planets speak very slowly unless they are extremely angry. Those expressions are usually through weather or geologic actions. Unpredictable storms. Unexpected rock slides or avalanches. Flash flooding. Most often, however, an angry sentient planet will develop toxic flora targeted toward the object of their anger."

"How many sentient planets have you studied?" Richardson raised her brows, exchanging glances with Blackburn.

"My home planet—and Memaj. It has taken me many cycles to create a positive bond with Memaj. I came to Memaj fifteen cycles ago. It was a full cycle before I knew that Memaj was sentient. Ten cycles more before it trusted me to record what it had to say, with its permission, of course." Erith took a deep breath. "Translation of its recorded testimony has been challenging. Memaj is deeply injured, and sometimes it reverts to self-protective behaviors when talking about its history, especially when discussing particularly distressing events. I am not always positive about the accuracy of my translations, but I have the original recordings I made for others to analyze."

"And no one else has suspected Memaj's sentience?" Rifanel exhaled hard, her nostrils flaring wide enough to show the red interior.

"It did not exhibit the typical signs of planetary sentience like my home planet does, because Memaj has been so traumatized that it has completely withdrawn from any attempts to communicate with moving beings, except for moments of anger and frustration. Which is why most moving beings avoid isolated areas on Memaj. Unlike many sentient species on Memaj, I am comfortable traveling to undeveloped places in my free time, especially mountains. Because of my empathic abilities, I regularly seek spaces away from other sentients." Erith looked down, then back up. "I kept encountering familiar sensations by a high mountain lake with a communal tree species as well as a communal mushroom species. It reminded me of my home. I started speaking to the planet, talking about how much I missed my home—and it eventually answered me. Memaj's language is very similar to my home planet—all symbols using natural phenomena, transcribable using empathic recording technology. Certain people are qualified to speak the language. I have had training in the fundamentals of using planetary symbols, and it takes me a long time to translate what it says. Memaj's expression is repressed and much more limited than that of my home world."

"Why wasn't this known before now?" Caroline frowned. She didn't know that much about sentient planets, but the signs *should* have been clear.

"The first non-native contact on Memaj came from Earth," Erith said flatly.

"Oh." Of course. Earth humans of five hundred cycles ago wouldn't acknowledge that a planet could possess sentience. Even now—Caroline had heard Alice McKinnon speak disparagingly about the concept. "So no one recognized the possibility, even with later settlement?"

"Why would they?" Erith countered. "The concept is so unfamiliar to the leadership of Memaj—not just the Guardians but upper-level bureaucrats—that I was hired at Memsij University without a fuss. Otherwise, do you think that a xenologist who was also a certified empath, from a sentient planet, would have been allowed to set foot on Memaj? I was surprised they even considered my application. So many planetary authorities won't admit empaths from sentient planets in any sort of long-term professional position. We can—make things more complicated."

"True," Caroline conceded.

A soft smile touched Erith's lips. "The planet has its means of striking back besides dramatic weather, and earth movements."

"How?" She couldn't conceive how that could work. Unless—Erith *had* said that an angry planet could develop toxic flora.

Does that explain ristenal?

"Where do you think the Plasmoids learned about the connection between rella, ristenal, and the removal of sentience? The planet influenced mild empaths amongst Fizzrt researchers to make that discovery." She paused. "I don't know for certain exactly how this happened. I am still translating this communication from Memaj. I suspect the planet intended to use ristenal to strike back at the invaders that have hurt it so severely. However, it lacks the ability to discern between destructive invaders and collaborative friends amongst the moving beings on its surface. I have been trying to teach it that, with slow results."

"Ristenal was developed on Memaj?" Richardson frowned at Blackburn.

"Yes," Erith said.

"This is becoming very, very complicated," Rifanel said. "And it is getting us away from what is important—restoring sentience to Fenarmin and Jeff. Why were they targeted? Why would the planet want to harm them?"

"This information is important because it establishes a motive for Hart Mercantile's recent behavior," Richardson said slowly. She glanced at Blackburn for several clicks as he flicked his ears, twitched his tail, then fluffed his fur, ending with a shake. "What we do not know is if Hart Mercantile is aware that Memaj is sentient," she continued. "And we also do not know if Memaj either knows or is willing to share a possible antidote for ristenal poisoning that is this severe."

Caroline's heart sank. "What do we know about Hart Mercantile's motives for causing harm to Jeff and Fenarmin?"

A pause while Blackburn and Richardson gazed at each other once more. Blackburn flicked his ears, then sat up to groom himself.

"Some of this will be revealed in public testimony," Richardson said. "But between Dr. Erith's information, preliminary questioning of Easystar and Albert McKinnon by Their Grace Whixit and Abraham McKinnon, and other information which has come into our hands, there were two reasons to target Tophand and Fenarmin. First, to discourage further investigation into Memaj. That is apparently Albert McKinnon's primary motivation. We are still investigating if he is the only one from Hart Mercantile involved in this action."

"Given Alice McKinnon's uncharacteristic behavior during her testimony and my suspicion that she was influenced—" Caroline let that sentence hang.

Richardson nodded. "Memaj is clearly a delicate subject for Hart Mercantile."

"And Logan Easystar?" Rifanel switched her tail. "For that matter, the incident that injured Fenarmin?"

"We have not found any links between Fenarmin's injury and any of these conspiracies," Richardson said. "As for Easystar—he is a reluctant co-conspirator. We can't say more right now, but the situation also involves Lara Wordtrust."

"Politics, then," Rifanel said.

"Definitely. And more will be disclosed after we have had the opportunity to meet with Geraint and other Congressional and Federation leaders," Richardson said. "Including Federation Security, the Galactic Controlled Substances Agency, the Bureau of Interstellar Commerce, Space Fleet, the Federation Planetary Ethical Coordinators, and, well—I'm certain you understand the complexities involved in all of these issues."

"Oh, absolutely."

A bureaucratic mess, no doubt about it. And for Wordtrust to be involved as well—while that wasn't surprising, it spoke to a conspiracy much larger than the fate of two minor Planetary Representatives who had been injured in the course of a Congressional investigation. Under normal circumstances, Caroline would find this situation worthy of a case study that would provide the foundation for an advanced degree.

But these weren't normal circumstances. The thought of

using Jeff—or Fenarmin, for that matter—as a subject for study turned her stomach.

"THERE MAY BE *some necessary unpleasantness when we arrive at the Representative reception portal,*" Blackburn mindspoke to Caroline as their transport began the docking process. The smaller size of the express transport and its ability to serve as an emergency medical vehicle allowed it to offload passengers and cargo directly planetside rather than through runabouts.

"*What is that going to be?*" By the Void, not still another issue! Caroline stifled a sigh. Clearly this must be something that only affected her—not Rifanel or Star.

"*Your mother is waiting to confront you.*"

Caroline groaned.

"*We provided this opportunity for her to challenge you so that we can apprehend her in a controllable setting,*" Blackburn hurried to explain. "*Other possibilities such as your quarters have too many variables and are too visible to the media. Here, we can control access much more easily, and make it harder for her to escape, since Alice McKinnon has eluded our past attempts to arrest her. She expects you to be traveling with your brother Albert, under restraint, so that he can ship you back to Earth with her. She will not expect to be arrested since she thinks she is working through clandestine ties to gain access to the Representative reception portal.*"

"*I see. There's not a chance she can actually abduct me, is there?*"

The black rabbit stomped a hind paw, softer than usual. "*Absolutely not! I regret this necessity. Forgive me if it is too traumatic an experience. We may need to get quite realistic. I hope not —and staging it in this setting will hopefully keep her or others acting in the name of Hart Mercantile from capturing you.*"

"It will not be traumatic, especially since I now know the reasoning behind it. Should I tell Star?"

"No. The fewer who know, the better."

"Thank you."

Blackburn bobbed his head at Caroline.

She gripped the arms of her seat as they went through the final docking process.

I can endure this. I will endure this.

Even knowing that her mother was going to be arrested didn't make the prospect of facing Alice McKinnon in a rage any more palatable to Caroline, however.

At least Blackburn warned me.

That allowed her to prepare to counter whatever her mother said, rather than be taken by surprise and not able to respond effectively.

RICHARDSON RESTED a hand on Caroline's forearm as the express transport docked with the portal. "Let them get Fenarmin and Jeff loaded into the hospital transport first to avoid any complications. Blackburn and I will come out with you."

"All right." That helped ease the nervous fluttering in her stomach. "Star, please go with Jeff."

"Why?" Star mindspoke.

"You'll see. Politics. I'll be there as soon as possible."

"All right." Star flicked her ears halfway back to express silent disapproval.

Caroline took a deep breath as they waited. Nearly time for the drama to begin. Was she ready? She had mentally rehearsed several possible responses, depending on how Alice McKinnon presented herself.

Anger flooded toward her from Star. *"Caroline, that evil dam of yours is here!"*

"I know. Go with Jeff! Watch over him for me, please."

"You'll be safe?"

"Blackburn and Richardson are with me. Watch Jeff. Please. I have to do this, much as I want to be with him instead."

"I will." Star sent wordless reassurance. *"She looks awfully mad. Are you sure you'll be all right?"*

"Yes. Go!"

They waited. At last, Richardson nodded to Caroline. "Walk between me and Blackburn."

"All right." Caroline swallowed hard as Blackburn moved his platform to her left, while Richardson was on her right.

"So!" Alice McKinnon snapped as soon as they came into sight. Three Hart Mercantile security staffers flanked her. She glowered at Caroline, legs braced, arms akimbo. "All of your puffed-up notions about *escaping Earth* have come to nothing —wait. Where's Albert?"

"Keep her distracted," Blackburn directed. *"Their Grace Whixit and your other brother are almost in position. They were delayed. She is still too close to the exit!"*

"Understood," Caroline said to Blackburn. *"Let me walk slightly ahead. In this mood she'll try to put hands on me. Slap me. I'll let her do it because then she won't be thinking about anything else happening."*

"Understood. Be careful."

To her surprise, Blackburn sent wordless concern and caution. That was enough to bolster Caroline further as she raised her chin defiantly, glaring at her mother.

"I'm not going back to Earth, *Alice,*" she said.

Her mother flinched. "Oh yes you are, *girl.* You're going to give up this notion of being independent of the family, especially since I've *finally* found the right man for you to marry, not this jumped-up cowboy who is—"

"I'm not going back. Didn't you hear me, *Alice*?" It was *so sweet* to see her mother flinch when Caroline used her first name—Alice McKinnon had *very* strong opinions about children addressing their parents by anything besides *Mother* or *Father*. "My place isn't on that backwards planet I was born on. I'm not your little dynastic afterthought." Caroline took two steps forward. "I am *Caroline Starshine*, not *Agatha McKinnon*. I am the assistant and spouse of a Planetary Representative. I am respected and acknowledged in my own right, not as a broodmare for the Hart family!"

Her mother's scowl deepened, and her face flushed with even more anger.

"Ungrateful chit of a girl! After all these cycles of planning and preparation for our final triumph, *Agatha*, and you have to gum it up by running off with that blackamoor cowboy in that farce of a fake marriage—well, *that's* going to end. As soon as I get you back to Earth, we'll dissolve that travesty of a formal marriage association contract. At least Brent Smith isn't worried about damaged goods."

Brent Smith? That's who she dug up to marry me? That ancient debauched stick?

Caroline burst into shaky, relieved laughter. "Come on, Alice! Marrying me to that feckless playboy? I'd be—what? Wife number seven or something like that? He's older than you are, and you're no young thing!"

"You're fertile and maybe *you'll* be the one who bears him a child, *Agatha*!" Alice squinted at Caroline, clearly hoping to see a reaction to the use of her oldname.

Caroline laughed again, stronger this time, fueled by Alice's angry flush at her mirth. "I don't want children. I got sterilized my first span on Galactic Central. I don't want Brent Smith. I'm not going back to that puritanical, provincial planet that I was born on, Alice. I'm married to Jeff Tophand and that's how it's going to stay. My home is now on Cartain, with my husband and his family, who are much more family to me than my own. Jeff's family sees me as a *person*, not a pawn to be played in corporate power games!"

"*You will listen to me.*" As Caroline had hoped, fury overcame Alice McKinnon. She marched toward Caroline, breathing heavily, and raised her hand. Caroline tensed in preparation for the slap.

I will not cry. I will not react.

It took every ounce of will for Caroline to remain unreactive when Alice slapped her.

"I am not going back to Earth!" she yelled instead.

"Oh yes you are, *Agatha*." Her mother grabbed Caroline's forearm, fingernails digging hard into Caroline's bicep as she tugged at it. Caroline sank her weight into her heels, refusing to give ground—now grateful for her large frame and strength. She was *bigger* than Alice McKinnon, which meant her mother couldn't just drag her off.

"Damn you," Alice growled, half-turning her head toward her staffers. "Come on, are you just going to stand there like the useless lumps you are? I thought you were supposed to be the best of Hart's security! If you don't help me you're going to be fired when we get back to Earth."

"*Let go of her.*" Caroline had never heard such anger in Laura Richardson's voice, accented by one of Blackburn's powerful thumps. That brought Alice's attention back to Caroline—just in time, as agents in GCSA uniform burst through the several hallway doors.

"Let go of her!" Abe repeated from behind Alice, as the GCSA agents disarmed the Hart Mercantile staffers and approached Alice, accompanied by several Plasmoids.

Alice whirled, finally releasing Caroline's arm. "Abraham! What are you doing here?"

"Under the authority granted me by the Galactic Federation, I am placing you under arrest for violation of the Galactic Controlled Substances Acts," Abe said.

"And I am here as a representative of the Ethereal Confederation to further charge you with offenses against the sovereignty of the Confederation, under my authority as Their

Grace Whixit, third in line for the leadership of the Ethereal Confederation," Whixit said.

Wait what? Whixit is part of the Confederation's leadership? Their Grace—a bureaucratic title, but third in line for leadership? Yikes.

"Speaking for Blackburn as Assistant Director of Federation Security, we are here to charge you with offenses against the Galactic Federation of Solid Peoples," Richardson said.

"For what?" Alice thrust her chin out defiantly as the GCSA agents restrained her.

"Amongst other things, conspiring to overthrow the Galactic Congress and replace it with an Empress." Abe's voice was cold as he glared at their mother.

"And doing the same for the Ethereal Confederation," Whixit said.

What? Mother—a traitor to the Federation? Caroline stared at her mother.

She had never *dreamed* that Alice McKinnon would do —*this.* Yes, she knew that her mother held royalist inclinations—but to act on them against the Federation? And the Confederation? Ambitions beyond Earth?

And what did Alice mean by *cycles of planning and preparation for our final triumph? Whose* final triumph?

Combined with what Abe had told her about Hart Mercantile Services and drug smuggling—what was going on? Was Hart Mercantile's wealth just a sham?

It's a good thing I left Earth!

She wondered about her father and her other brothers. How deeply involved were they in this mess? As the family castoffs, she and Abe might turn out to be the lucky ones.

ONCE THE AGENTS had removed Alice from the reception area, Blackburn and Richardson hurried Caroline into an autoskimmer. They escorted her into the hospital, Blackburn projecting his Federation Security badge at anyone who would have kept Caroline from Jeff.

At last they arrived at the highly secured private area where Jeff and Fenarmin were sequestered.

"Is everything all right?" Star turned her head, face tight with worry, as Caroline hurried into Jeff's room.

"Yes." Caroline eyed the reptilian doctor examining Jeff. "Do we have any news yet?"

"I'm afraid it's a loss of sentience," the doctor said, straightening up and frowning. "My researchers are studying the information from Memaj about ristenal, but alas, we do not have enough information yet to determine if it's reversable. It will manifest very much like a senile dementia, except that he will be physically able to move around, unlike an elderly human. You will need to prepare adequate care facilities."

Caroline gulped. She hadn't wanted to admit to herself that this was a possibility, hadn't wanted to think about the likelihood that Jeff's sentience would never return, had hoped that perhaps Galactic Central might provide better options… but now…no life with Jeff, no future except by herself…she burst into tears, leaning on Jeff's bed rail.

She had her freedom from Alice McKinnon's schemes, for good, it looked like, given the charges against her mother.

But was gaining freedom from her mother's plots worth the loss of Jeff in her life?

Caroline bent over to kiss Jeff's forehead, half-hoping that maybe it would make a difference, like it did in the sappy old vids and books. That maybe he would open his eyes and recognize her.

Nothing. At least he didn't flinch away screaming from her touch, like he had on Memaj. That was one tiny piece of progress.

"Caroline?" Rutan stood just inside the doorway.

Caroline exhaled. She had known that Congressional business was not about to stop just because of what had happened to Jeff and Fenarmin. But to be confronted with it now, of all times…. She took a deep breath and turned to face Rutan.

"S-s-s-sorry. Geraint and I—and Ssgaldir—send our regrets. Do you know what happened?"

Caroline pressed her lips tightly together. Where to start?

"How much do you know?" she asked in return. "Because a lot has happened and is still happening. Have you spoken to Their Grace Whixit and to Blackburn? Or Abraham McKinnon?"

"Their Grace Whixit? S-s-s-s." Rutan grew more agitated. "You mus-s-s-t tell me more, Caroline."

"All right, then." Another deep breath, while she thought over what could and could not be disclosed. "Some things I am not at liberty to say. But what happened to Jeff and Fenarmin is about much more than plain old drug smuggling."

AFTER A NODE of explaining everything to Rutan that she felt free to talk about—which did *not* include what had happened with her mother, or Dr. Erith's revelations about Memaj's sentience—Caroline was exhausted. And partway through her explanation, one of Blackburn's minions appeared with a summons to testify in front of the Federation Planetary Ethics Commission—next turn, Sixth Node. Rutan also suggested that she appear in Jeff's stead at the Congressional floor session at Fifth Node, next turn.

"S-s-s. No need to try to attend any of your committees-s for several turns, not with your s-situation. Tyrone and Paula are doing a good job covering for you and Jeff. But bes-s-t you appear for floor votes."

Caroline nodded, fighting back still more sniffles. *Political pragmatism.* This meant she was to be sworn in as Jeff's replacement for the remainder of the Congressional session. The Federalists needed her there. Nearly two cycles more to go before this session would be completed.

Oh Jeff.

She kissed his forehead one last time before leaving to check on Rifanel and Fenarmin.

At least I'm not the only one in this situation.

Rifanel could use her support, especially since Fenarmin's condition might be worse than Jeff's, due to equine biology.

The stallion hung in slings like he had before they left Memaj. It looked as if a feeding tube had been set up, and equine surgeons fussed over the big stallion. Rifanel stood outside of Fenarmin's stall, gazing through the bars, ears half-flicked back, nostrils wide and flaring with distress.

"How is Fenarmin?" Caroline swallowed hard. Her throat felt scratchy and rough from all the crying.

Rifanel huffed softly. "Complete loss of sentience. No more awareness than an ordinary horse, even less than a first-gen cross. They don't know if it can be recovered."

"The same for Jeff," Caroline said softly. "It's like a form of senile dementia."

"Hrwhinir's best scientists are working on ristenal. There *has* to be a solution." Rifanel whickered softly.

Caroline wordlessly patted Rifanel's neck.

Rifanel sighed. "I have been informed that I need to appear at tomorrow's floor session."

"So have I. Floor but no committees."

"They will swear us in to fill our spouses' terms until they recover—" Rifanel faltered and her translator choked, obscuring what else she might have said.

"Or until the end of the Congressional term."

"Yes," Rifanel said. "If—that is what happens."

AT LAST IT WAS TIME—RELUCTANTLY—TO return to quarters, as darkness fell. The quarters she had left so recently to go to Memaj, looking forward to their return when she could finally marry Jeff. And now—

How can I face Tyrone and Paula? Much less figure out what to say to Jeff's mother Darcy? Caroline was not looking forward to that conversation, especially since she would need to reveal her family's role in what happened to Jeff.

Lights blazed from the building as the autoskimmer holding her and Star approached, more than she would expect from just Tyrone and Paula being there.

What is going on? Weariness swamped Caroline. Perhaps some of her friends from intern days had rallied to support her—but much as she would appreciate the thought, she was worn out. Contemplating facing *anyone's* pity was just another burden, another difficult event to endure.

She wanted comfort. Someone who understood her agony. Until now, she hadn't realized just how much she had shared of herself with Jeff. All those cycles of being alone, relying only on herself because family could betray her—and then to suddenly have someone in her life who understood, who cared for her—who was just as suddenly taken away—

Star nuzzled her. *"I am here. You are stronger than you think. I can't even begin to understand how you can face this—this—awfulness without the support of a herd."*

"Thank you, Star. You are my herd—you and Jeff."

"I am honored."

Caroline stopped, burying her head on Star's withers. The dark bay mare delicately wrapped her head and neck around Caroline in a comforting embrace. Caroline sagged against Star. Her friend. Her—*herd.*

Did the massive dose of rella that created the bond between her and Star also leave her open to Jeff? Or had she simply wanted a connection with someone, anyone, so much that she was vulnerable to his affectionate gestures? And now he was gone, possibly forever.

Caroline groaned.

"She's here!" Tyrone called to someone.

Caroline tensed. *Now comes the outpouring of sympathy. The pity. The—*

"Caroline. Honey." Darcy's gentle voice was a welcome relief followed by dread as she walked toward Caroline and Star.

How can I tell her what really happened? About my family's role?

Caroline raised her head. "How did you—?"

"Geraint told us, and brought us here by express transport." Darcy joined Caroline and Star. "Oh, honey. How is he?"

Facing Jeff's mother—seeing the worry and concern on her face—was too much. Caroline burst into tears. Again. She had cried more over the last ten-turn than she had all the cycles of her life.

"Oh, honey." Darcy held her arms open.

Caroline exhaled, trying to wipe away her tears, leaning on Star. "You have to know. My damn family played a role in what happened. My brother Albert McKinnon and my mother Alice McKinnon. Are you sure you want any part of me?" She steeled herself for what had to be the inevitable rejection.

"Geraint told us about them. He also said that you had renounced your ties to your family before coming to Galactic Central, and that you would never willingly return to Earth." Darcy kept her arms extended. "I know what I saw between you and my son. I know what I'm seeing now." Her voice trembled. "Caroline Starshine, my son loved—*loves*—you enough to plan to marry you, above and beyond a formal marriage association. As far as I'm concerned, you're already my daughter-in-law. We will face whatever happens with Jeff *together*. As a *family*. You are one of us now."

Caroline gulped, her sobs coming harder than ever.

Star released Caroline and gently pushed her toward Darcy.

"Go with your human herd. You need them now. I will see you next turn."

"Star, are you all right?"

"I will be with Rifanel and her herd. You need other humans. Jeff's herd will care for you."

Caroline went to Darcy, leaning hard against her. Darcy wrapped her arms around Caroline, crooning softly.

At last Caroline was able to stop crying long enough to raise her head. "Complete loss of sentience. It's as if he rapidly underwent senile dementia. And the doctors don't know if they can restore his awareness." She choked back more tears. "I have to testify next turn, and swear in to replace Jeff as Planetary Representative—" Sobs overtook her again. "That sentient duel was just awful. And not knowing— oh Darcy, I am so, so sorry. I wish I could have stopped him but he wouldn't listen—"

"Shh." Darcy's voice wobbled. "Jeff is a strong man. He will return to us. I have confidence in that. But for now—oh woman, you are clearly exhausted. Come. Darla and I are here. We've made you Third Meal." Her voice grew stronger. "I *will* see you and Jeff truly married, even if I have to march into that hospital and slap some sense into my son."

Somehow, that image made Caroline chuckle.

THE NEXT TURN passed in a numb blur, feeling separated from her body, as if she watched Caroline Starshine go through the actions required through her while her real self was sequestered in a tiny closet, screaming at the horror of it all.

But *that* Caroline Starshine had to be locked away until she was safe back in her quarters. She didn't dare let herself feel any of it. Too much depended on her remaining calm, professional, and above all else credible.

For Jeff and Fenarmin's sake, she kept telling herself when the façade threatened to crumble. *For Jeff and Fenarmin's sake. And the planet. And Dr. Erith.*

And me.

Fifth Node. Appear on the Congressional floor. Proceed through swearing her oath to replace Jeff, along with Rifanel for Fenarmin. Lara Wordtrust glaring at them, while the seats for Logan Easystar and Albert remained empty.

Tyrone and Paula whispering vote recommendations to her.

Nodding and acknowledging sincere and insincere condolences from other Planetary Representatives. Then off with Rifanel to testify before the Federation Planetary Ethics Commission starting at Sixth Node. Realizing from the Commissioners' questioning that Erith had already testified. Identifying archive locations to track down Hart Mercantile records about the original colonization of Memaj. Repeating her renunciation of any connection, including financial, to Hart Mercantile or the McKinnon family.

A second, late, summons during that hearing to appear before the Controlled Substances Committee at Ninth Node, immediately after Second Meal. Accepting Darcy and Star's bullying her into eating something she couldn't taste in her offices during Second Meal. Food was fuel to keep her going. That was all it was to her right now. Fuel.

Ninth Node. Controlled Substances Committee. Introducing Jeff's sensor data about rella on Memaj in *that* committee. Answering questions about her renunciation of all ties to Hart Mercantile. The unexpected support from Blackburn and Whixit, who joined her at the witness table to confirm her testimony.

Eleventh Node. Appearing with Geraint, Blackburn and Richardson, and Whixit at a press conference announcing the Planetary Ethics' verdict of Isolation Status upon Memaj, all Federation colonists required to leave Memaj immediately. Whixit confirming the same for the Confederation.

Finally, *finally*, delaying Third Meal at Twelfth Node so she could see Jeff. Little change, except that Caroline fancied she saw his lips twitch in a smile when she kissed him.

Then back to quarters to collapse under the support of her new family.

Was this going to be her life from now on?

14

SEARCHING FOR SOLUTIONS

To get through the turns, Caroline ended up shifting into automatic coping mode, keeping emotions at arms-length for her own sanity. It was the only way she could handle everything that was happening in the Congress—and what wasn't happening with Jeff.

Everything happening included consequences for the events on Memaj. Caroline's past experience, based on her internship cycle at the Galactic Congress, was that change happened in a deliberate, orchestrated dance. In spite of the immediate action taken within a single turn by the Planetary Ethics Commission to place Memaj on Isolation Status, she expected that the rest of the fallout from Memaj would take the entire eighteen spans remaining in the current two-cycle Congressional session. If not longer. Justice happened slowly at the Galactic level.

Not so this time.

The very next turn saw the arrest of Lara Wordtrust on charges of treason against the Federation, followed by matching charges of sedition brought forth by Whixit for the Ethereal Confederation. *These* charges required the entire Congress to sit through testimony in a trial that, to Caroline's surprise, was resolved within three turns. Alice McKinnon had conspired with unnamed allies—*The Confederation is dealing with our own*, Whixit had said—in order to place Lara Wordtrust in charge of an Empire consisting of *both* the Federation and the Confederation.

With Alice McKinnon as one of Wordtrust's high-level advisors, of course.

In Alice McKinnon's defense, the Hart Mercantile attorneys revealed Caroline's family ties, insinuating that she was part of the conspiracy and had sought to advance herself through connecting with Geraint and then Jeff.

That brought Dr. Knowledgechaser and her other professors at Mars University out in loud and vocal support for Caroline, and further backing from her intern friends, Geraint, constituents from Cartain, and from Darcy Ford.

It all seemed to be happening to someone else. Not her. Not Agatha McKinnon, now Caroline Starshine.

To her surprise, when it came time for the Congress to issue a verdict regarding Lara Wordtrust and Alice McKinnon, the vote was unanimous. Guilty. And the two were exiled permanently to a prison planet—*after* they went through a second trial within the Ethereal Confederation.

Frrinx nal Thogh took over sole leadership of the Statist Party. The Statists quietly changed their focus from Earth boosterism to a more balanced, though still corporate-friendly, stance.

During the Breaks Caroline and Darcy spent most of the three turns with Jeff. The Galactic Center doctors had healed his broken bones, so that he could sit up and move around. Occupational therapists managed to teach him rudiments of self-care such as toileting, bathing, and using utensils to eat. But he still stared at the two of them unknowingly, not responding to their attempts to get him to talk.

"We just don't know if he will be able to speak or even recognize either of you," the head doctor warned. "This is very similar to dementia as recorded from Old Earth. However, those treatments are not working on him."

Fenarmin's broken legs were also healed. The nameless filly that Caroline had met earlier had qualified for Conversion and was undergoing a slow Conversion process. She apparently was interested in studying to become a doctor, and spent time with Fenarmin and the Hrwhinir medical personnel, not just keeping Fenarmin company but learning more about ristenal and potential treatments.

All the same, despite small positive moments as the ten-turns and then the spans passed—Jeff starting to smile at her and Darcy on occasion, his improving physical condition—Caroline did not see any potential for significant change over the unfolding cycles of her life ahead. Oh, there were no more worries about her family. Abe kept her informed about developments in the further investigations of Hart Mercantile Services. It seemed that there had been many, many problems with the company over hundreds of cycles, and that the rest of the family—except for their father, thankfully, who had remained within the well-funded McKinnon tradition of research and study—needed to scramble to ensure that they had an income of some sort.

Albert and Logan Easystar had their own trials, and a sentence to a prison planet.

But otherwise, Caroline could see nothing in her future but her role as a Planetary Representative. Ten-turns upon ten-turns unfolding. Relying on Darcy—Darla had returned to Cartain—for support after yet another sad visit to Jeff. Spending most of her Breaks with Jeff, doing her best to encourage the reawakening of sentience in him. Trudging through the turns, performing her duties, focusing on what worked for Cartain. Working with Star, Tyrone, and Paula to ensure that they did their best for the peoples of Cartain. Arguing in committees and on the Congressional floor. Writing her first bill and getting it passed.

Caroline was so focused on *getting things done* and *not thinking about whether Jeff will ever get better* that she had not consciously realized several spans had gone by until Darcy spoke up one turn after Third Meal.

"Have you considered the prospect of re-election?"

Caroline startled. "We still have almost two cycles to think about that—don't we?"

"Check your calendar."

Caroline did, and gasped.

Five spans had passed by without her really paying attention to the passage of time. Fourteen more spans until the end of this Congressional session. Three more spans until the Long Break that signified the end of the first cycle of this session.

Caroline shook her head. "I'm not going to run if Jeff hasn't recovered."

"Oh honey. Are you sure about that?" Darcy frowned at Caroline. "I've heard so many good things about everything you've been doing for Cartain this session. The girls keep sending me reports on how everyone back home just loves the job you're doing."

"I'm not from Cartain," Caroline said softly. "If it wasn't for Jeff, I wouldn't even be in this position. Darcy—once the session's over, I think the best place for Jeff is to be at home. On Cartain. I—I just can't even consider dumping him off there and coming back to be the Planetary Representative next session. Or bringing him back here, in his condition." She swallowed hard. "Everything I'm doing is based on what Jeff and I talked about doing for Cartain. His ideas, not mine."

"Then what are you going to do?"

"I guess I'll learn to be a rella farmer and practice politics on Cartain. Do what I can to advance some of the programs Jeff wanted to achieve."

Darcy frowned. "Caroline. Are you really going to do this

to yourself? What if Jeff never recovers?"

"I owe him," Caroline said. "Without Jeff, I wouldn't have gotten free from Earth and my family. What happened was in part my family's doing. I—" she shook her head again. "I owe him," she repeated. "And I don't know if I'll ever be able to completely repay him. Or atone for what my family did to him."

"You can't let guilt rule your entire life," Darcy sighed. "Or tie yourself down to a different family. Not that we wouldn't welcome you—far from it! But you deserve the opportunity to have a choice in your life."

"I *am* making a choice. It's not guilt. It's an obligation. A responsibility. There wasn't any ending date on our formal marriage association." Caroline looked down, then back up again. "I suppose I could invoke a disability clause but—I fully intended to go for a reproductive access contract with Jeff. I—I love him, Darcy. Even now. And maybe he'll come back to me. The things I want to accomplish can be done on Cartain." She tried to smile and failed. "Maybe I'll run for Boss of Cartain one of these cycles."

"Well, you darn well better," Darcy said. "Because I will tell you this. I don't believe my son would want you to martyr yourself for his sake. At some point, woman, you have to think about what you want. What you need. And what is best for Caroline Starshine, as well as Jeff Tophand."

"I am," Caroline said. "Believe me, I am. But right now, Jeff's recovery and acting as Planetary Representative in his place has to be my focus."

ANOTHER SPAN PASSED BY. Jeff moved to an outpatient facility. He smiled at Darcy and Caroline regularly now, and was able to go on short walks. However, he had lost a lot of weight and muscle. He made noises but not speech.

Fenarmin, too, had recovered physically, though he showed no more sentience than a non-Converted horse.

The big event this span was the elevation of that brown, nameless filly to full Converted status. Caroline, Star, and Darcy attended that celebration—Caroline and Darcy were the only non-equines in attendance, with special permission to be there.

"Do you wish you had been able to undergo something like this ceremony to acknowledge your Conversion?" Caroline asked Star as they watched Rifanel preside over the final injections.

"It wouldn't fit what happened to us," Star answered. *"I am happy with things the way they are. No need to make the situation more complicated!"*

The filly snorted, then coughed.

"What is your name?" Rifanel asked.

"I take the name of Vinsartel," the filly said, her translator snapping and popping as her speech sped up. White showed around the rim of her eyes, indicating her nervousness. "Vins to honor my dam—" The translator cut out and she coughed.

"I didn't have this many problems with my translator." Star's mindspeech held a slightly critical note. *"On the other hand, she is speaking better sentences than I could at first."*

"Vinsartel," the filly repeated after she blew hard, speaking slower this time. "Vins to honor my dam. Artel to honor my sire."

"And what is your goal as a Converted person?" Rifanel asked.

Vinsartel bobbed her head nervously. "I wish—I wish to study healing. I hope to be able to heal our herd stallion and —and—and—"

"Her translator's stuck." Star snorted. *"I don't know if the problem is her nervousness, or if she has faulty equipment."*

"I wish to help heal Jeff Tophand as well," Vinsartel finally said, her translator finally settling.

And *that* made Caroline sniffle.

LONG BREAK ENDED the first cycle of this session of the Galactic Congress. Darcy and Caroline discussed the prospect of taking Jeff to Cartain—Caroline needed to return in order to meet with the Boss and other political leaders on Cartain.

"I'm just worried he'll lose ground if we take him out of the outpatient facility now," Caroline fretted. "Or that the trip will somehow upset him."

"Or it could bring back memories and associations that might help him recover," Darcy pointed out.

Well. There was that. Perhaps a dose of home, and familiarity might bring Jeff back.

JEFF SEEMED to recognize his suite on the Interstellar Roundup Ranch. He walked around the bedroom, smiling and stroking some of the artwork. And yet, when he turned his head to look at Caroline and Darcy, the same emptiness remained in those gold-flecked brown eyes.

The medics on Cartain concurred with those on Galactic Central.

"Advanced dementia," the Crested Flyer doctor said. "He might recover some parts of himself in a familiar setting, but more than that—" The Flyer shook their head.

Darcy and Caroline allowed short visits from friends carefully at first, concerned that Jeff might become upset. As it turned out, Jeff's visitors were more upset than he was. Bloohowt in particular marched away after trying to talk to Jeff, switching his tail and rumbling deep in his chest. Caroline followed the big bull.

"Bloohowt—"

"It's not right. It's just not right," Bloohowt roared. "Jeff Tophand has always been one of the most thoughtful humans

I've ever encountered. For him to be more mindless than a newborn second-generation-sentient calf is just not right!"

Caroline rested her hand on the big bull's shoulders. "I know, Bloohowt. I keep hoping." She exhaled. "But as every day passes...." her voice trailed off.

"Are you planning to run for his seat?"

"No. I plan to stay here, with Jeff, once this session ends. If he doesn't get better and can run himself, that is." She gulped. "Maybe, just maybe, someday...."

The bull turned his head and nudged her hand, then licked it. "I will try to visit every ten-turn while you are here, Caroline. Perhaps that will help."

"Perhaps. Thank you, Bloohowt. You are a loyal friend."

"Huh. You and Jeff have done much for Cartain. Of course I want him to recover, and will do whatever I can to help!" The bull bellowed and pawed, barely touching the grass, as if Jeff were there to growl at him about *don't mess up my graze.*

That unconscious action brought quick tears to Caroline's eyes, though she held them back until Bloohowt was safely out of sight. The bull meant well. She didn't need to disturb him with her emotions.

JEFF'S HORSE Red was disturbed by Jeff's loss of sentience. At first Red would shove his nose hard against Jeff, trying to get him to respond. Then Red started pinning his ears every time Jeff entered the pasture. One turn, Red tried to charge at Jeff and drive him away when Caroline and Star brought Jeff into the field for a visit. It was only through Star's intervention that Caroline was able to get Jeff safely out of the pasture. After that, she only took Jeff into the field when Red was confined.

The gelding became moody and difficult to handle. At last, Caroline sent him to Darcy's ranch, under Star's guidance. Red followed Star's lead and settled in there without fretting.

"He just doesn't comprehend what happened," Star said on her return. "And he doesn't have the awareness needed to understand when I try to explain what is going on."

Jeff appeared to be aware that Red was gone. He stopped by Red's stall whenever they went to the barn, and made unhappy sounds, staring inside the empty space.

If only—Caroline had hoped that perhaps Red could bring Jeff back.

Apparently not.

DARCY, Caroline, and Jeff's brother Ken met with lawyers on Cartain to draw up a guardianship agreement for Jeff. To Caroline's relief, the Boss accepted their drafting of a reproductive contract at Galactic Central as indicating that she and Jeff had indeed planned a relationship beyond a formal marital association. Not only did Terrianna Abbott sign off on a guardianship split between Darcy, Caroline, and Ken, but she upgraded Caroline and Jeff's marital association contract to conditionally full, until Jeff could sign the contract himself.

"I thank you so much." It was all Caroline could do to keep from crying when the Boss made this announcement. "I —all of you have been so kind."

"This is an absolute horror of a situation," Abbott replied. "And you have demonstrated your commitment not just to Jeff but to Cartain. Are you running for re-election if he doesn't recover?"

Caroline sighed. That question again. By now she could respond without thinking about choosing her words carefully. "I am only following through on Jeff's ideas and Jeff's priorities. Once this session is done, we will return to Cartain and I will care for him here—unless he recovers."

"That would be a waste of talent." Terrianna Abbott fixed Caroline with a stern gaze. "You have done so much for Cartain, Caroline."

"And I wouldn't be in the position to do it if it hadn't been for Jeff," she said.

"I hope he improves," the Boss said.

"So do I."

"Do you have a potential successor in mind?"

Caroline hesitated. She had been considering this possibility for a while. Perhaps it was time to start laying the foundation for it to happen. "Star. The recently Converted mare who has been my assistant. I haven't talked to her about the possibility of her running for office yet, but she has been working hard during the first half of this session. She can do the job."

"Hmm." Abbott tapped her chin thoughtfully. "That would make her the first non-humanoid Representative from Cartain."

"Both the Federalists and Councilists were looking at non-humanoid candidates on Cartain this past session," Caroline reminded the Boss.

"So they were. So they were." Abbott nodded decisively. "Which party does Star favor?"

"The Federalists, of course." Caroline let herself smile briefly. "I plan to bring the possibility up to Geraint when we return to Galactic Central. I just—well, I wanted your opinion first."

That made the Boss beam. "Send her to me, Caroline. Let me talk to her."

"I will," Caroline promised.

As she expected, Star was excited at the possibility of being considered as the Federalist candidate for Planetary Representative. She didn't share details of her conversation with Abbott.

But the Boss's pithy message after the meeting was

sufficient.

–She'll do.

One more detail managed.

ONE TEN-TURN REMAINED in the Long Break before they needed to return to Galactic Central and the second cycle of this Congressional session.

Rifanel sent a message.

–Vinsartel and Dr. Erith want me to bring Fenarmin to Cartain. They claim to have a solution for him and Jeff, and apparently Cartain is the best location to implement it.

Caroline stared at Rifanel's message. Dare she hope?

–Yes, of course, she finally answered. *–We wait for your arrival.*

GALACTIC CENTRAL medical staff along with Hrwhinir scientists descended upon the Interstellar Roundup Ranch along with Vinsartel, Rifanel, Fenarmin, and Dr. Erith. Whixit, Blackburn, and Richardson arrived a half-turn after the others.

"We've been reviewing the scans taken of you and Star after you were exposed to that massive dose of rella, Caroline," Erith explained. "I received permission to return to Memaj and consult with the planet. Thanks to help from other researchers, I was able to refine my communication with Memaj. There may be a solution."

"What does it involve?"

"That is the problem," Rifanel said. "We need to replicate the incident as closely as possible. Jeff on Fenarmin."

"Then one dispenses a massive amount of half-processed

rella on them," Whixit said. Their bubble oscillated between peach and teal shades. "One is not—certain this is a good idea. However, one feels a certain obligation to repair this situation."

"Is there a risk?" Caroline asked.

"Mostly to Jeff and Fenarmin," Vinsartel said. "Neither are in dueling condition. Neither will remember their training. They must be in contact with each other when Whixit dumps the half-processed rella on them. But—before that happens, and immediately afterward, they could cause further injury to themselves."

Caroline swallowed hard, remembering the disorientation she had experienced after that rella exposure. "Is there a way to minimize the possibility of injury?"

"We're bringing in support from the Galactic Rodeo," Richardson said. "They will be here next turn."

"And if this does not work?" Rifanel asked.

"Then it is unlikely that anything will," the head surgeon said.

Caroline and Rifanel gazed at each other.

"Are you all right with taking this drastic an action?" Rifanel asked. "Fenarmin can function as a non-sentient horse without resorting to—this. But can Jeff manage as a non-sentient human?"

They both turned to watch Jeff and Fenarmin wandering in the paddock. Fenarmin at least stopped to graze and acted like a normal horse, although his coat was dull and his ribs showed slightly. Jeff just walked around aimlessly, staring at things. He stayed clear of Fenarmin.

"What do you think, Rifanel?" Caroline couldn't keep the bitter note out of her voice.

Rifanel blew hard. "You have lost more than I have. Fenarmin can still function as a herd stallion. But Jeff—" She shook her head. "It is up to you to decide."

Caroline threw up her hands. "If it's our last chance to get them back, then yes." She gulped. "I just hope we can do this safely."

"We will take every precaution," the head surgeon said.

It took the Rodeo representatives a full turn to set up a safe enclosure and chute.

"It's uncommon to have two non-sentients dueling each other," Joharn, the horse who was the former ranch manager that had trained Jeff, told Caroline. "The difficulty is in persuading the non-sentient rider to mount. Sentient horses and bulls know how to make the situation easier. But with both being non-sentient?" The bay stallion snorted and tossed his head. "We need to proceed with great caution."

"It will be a matter of timing," Vinsartel said.

"We can't risk any sentients in contact with them when Whixit drops the rella on them," Dr. Erith said.

"I didn't lose sentience," Caroline said.

"It's not the sentient humans who are at risk from this attempt," Erith said. "It's the other sentient species involved."

At last everything was ready. Whixit dropped their bubble long enough to dispense a dose of ristenal to both Jeff and Fenarmin—much less than the initial dose they had received. Then they flew into the nearest mature rella field to gather and half-process the drug.

Meanwhile, the Rodeo representatives carefully coaxed Fenarmin into the chute, while Vinsartel and Joharn, Caroline and Star took up positions just outside the enclosure's gate, ready to gallop in once Erith pronounced them safe from the rella exposure. Everyone wore masks, except for Jeff and Fenarmin. Just in case. Star wore a saddle but no bridle, to make it easier for Caroline to hopefully get Jeff off of Fenarmin. They had gone through coaching by the Rodeo representatives the day before about how to safely do it—*not optimal,* one of them said, *but given the circumstances, better it's you two than an experienced pickup rider.*

Jeff stood on the walkway above the chute that restrained Fenarmin, between two Rodeo colleagues. They put Jeff's equipment on Fenarmin, a challenging duty since Fenarmin began to rear and strike at the rails confining him.

"He doesn't have the strength to fight like that," Vinsartel fretted. "I wish I could be there to calm him—"

"Best that you not put yourself at risk." Rifanel's ears remained halfway flicked back as she watched. "You are too valuable to our herd. If it wasn't for the bond between you two...."

Jeff shook his head as he waited. His expression—Caroline wasn't sure, but it almost seemed like he remembered *something.*

"One has harvested the rella," Whixit announced through the comm that Caroline carried. "Processing. Ready to drop as soon as one arrives." A pause. "That will be in three clicks."

"Three clicks!" Caroline called to the Rodeo representatives.

"Got it," one of the reps answered in a relaxed tone.

How can they be so calm?

Fenarmin went into a fit as the representatives started to ease Jeff onto him. They tried to pull Jeff out of the chute but he shook his head, sliding into place, leaning back as he took a firm grip on the halter rope.

Chills trickled through Caroline. *He remembers.* She clutched Star's mane tighter, hope rising.

Whixit drifted toward the enclosure. The chute gate slammed open. Fenarmin exploded out of the chute, bucking high and hard, so much like—

Jeff seemed to struggle to stay on, sliding in the saddle. Caroline moaned. What if he fell off before Whixit—

Fenarmin bellowed as Whixit glided toward him and Jeff. He reared high, striking at the Plasmoid as Whixit descended upon them. Higher, higher—*oh no he's going to go over backward again.*

Then steaming plant matter cascaded upon horse and rider, Whixit hovering just out of Fenarmin's striking reach. Fenarmin dropped to all fours, shaking his head, staggering. Jeff slumped over the pommel of his saddle. Fenarmin swayed back and forth, his steps uneven.

"Wait until the smoke disperses," Erith said.

"They're going to fall!" Caroline itched to send Star in as Fenarmin's balance became more precarious. Jeff's legs flopped against the red stallion's sides and it almost seemed like he was going to fall off, though he still managed to cling to the pommel.

It seemed to be an eternity before the smoke finally dissipated.

"Now!" Erith swung the gate wide.

They galloped to Jeff and Fenarmin. Vinsartel steadied Fenarmin on one side while Star and Caroline pressed hard against his other side. Caroline tugged at Jeff's nearest hand. He shook his head and sat up slowly. Then his hand shakily wrapped around her waist as she reached around his. He let her pull him off of Fenarmin, easing him onto the ground. Jeff's legs wobbled and would have given out except that Caroline held him upright. Joharn slipped in to take their place at Fenarmin's side to move him away from Caroline and Jeff as the stallion swayed.

Caroline clung to Jeff. He buried his head on her thigh. He began to tremble, one arm resting across Star's back, the other on her leg.

"Oh Jeff," she groaned. Was it working? Or had they gone through all this—for nothing?

She brought her other arm over to hold him up. What was taking so long for the others to reach them?

Jeff's hand grabbed hers. Squeezed it tight. Then brought it to his lips to kiss her palm, before the shakes got worse. He collapsed, pulling her down with him.

But he turned his body to keep her from falling hard onto the ground.

And his arms tightened around her for one brief tap, before they sagged loose and he fell back onto the ground, unconscious.

VINSARTEL AND RIFANEL fussed over Fenarmin in the barn while Caroline hovered over Jeff in his bed. Fenarmin was back in slings because he was also unconscious.

Let them sleep it off, was the universal verdict. *We will see what happens when they waken.*

Star added extra reassurance. "I needed slings after our exposure."

Vinsartel and Rifanel stood on either side of Fenarmin, nuzzling the red stallion as he slumped in his slings.

Meanwhile, Jeff lay on his back. Caroline held his hand as she sat by the bed. He hadn't let her hold his hand without fussing since Memaj, not even when he was sleeping. Did that mean something? Possibly.

She wasn't ready to get her hopes up too high just yet.

CAROLINE ENDED up sleeping in Jeff's bed, on top of the covers with a blanket over her. At some point, she half-woke when he turned from his back to his side, curling around her, and tossing his arm over her. She tensed, wondering. An automatic action or—or?

Wait until he wakes up, she told herself. But the contact was enough to soothe her back to sleep.

A SOFT GROAN ROUSED HER.

"Jeff?" Tension tightened her throat. *If this didn't work....*

"Caroline?" he rasped. "My head...."

"Jeff!" she squealed, turning over to look at him. "Jeff. Oh Jeff."

He gazed at her, but *awareness* was in those beloved gold-flecked brown eyes instead of the blankness that had been there before. "Why are we on Cartain instead of Memaj? My head hurts. Bad."

"Oh Jeff." She couldn't say anything more but burst into tears, as Darcy raced into the room.

"Mama?"

"Oh my, oh Jeff," was Darcy's reaction as well. "You're back. You're back."

"Back from what?" Now he sounded grumpy and confused. "How badly did Fenarmin hurt me? Last thing I remember was challenging him to a duel on Memaj. How did I get here?"

"It's been almost a full cycle since that duel," Caroline gasped between sobs. "The two of you were drugged. Both of you lost sentience."

Jeff blinked at her. "What? How? Really?"

She wrapped her arms around him. "You're back. You're back. Oh darling, you're back."

"I'm confused."

"For good reason. Don't worry about it right now. Just— get better, Jeff. Please. *Get better.*"

A raspy chuckle from him. "I don't understand what's going on, but yes. I'll get better."

JEFF AND FENARMIN took longer to recover than Caroline and Star had.

"An effect of the ristenal," was the final conclusion of the medical staff.

Both Jeff and Fenarmin suffered from headaches—to be expected, or so Caroline was told. Jeff tired easily and needed to rest. It wasn't just vertigo and headaches, but a lack of muscle tone, despite all the occupational therapy he had undergone. She spent most of the remaining ten-turn before their return to Congress by Jeff's side, bringing him up to date on Congressional activities.

Two turns before they had to board the transport taking them back to Galactic Central, Caroline married Jeff in a quiet family ceremony at the Interstellar Roundup Ranch, presided over by the Boss of Cartain. Vinsartel and Fenarmin also engaged in Hrwhinir's version of a reproductive rights contract.

"Are you all right with that?" Caroline asked Rifanel after she learned about it.

"They are both part of my herd." Rifanel flicked her ears. "It is a good match. Fenarmin adores Vinsartel, and it will make my work simpler. He listens to her when he would not listen to me."

All the same, Caroline was glad she wasn't sharing Jeff with anyone. Especially after their first, exquisite, lovemaking session.

Another thing that Mother was wrong about.

"YOU NEED to swear the oath of office for the second cycle of this session," Jeff said while they were en route to Galactic Central.

Caroline frowned at him. "Jeff—you're the elected one. I just filled in for you."

"Darling, there's aftereffects." He frowned. "My thoughts aren't as quick as they were before the ristenal. I think it will come back—but Cartain deserves to have a representative who can keep up with fast-paced arguments, and that's not me. Better that I work as your assistant."

"Oh honey. I'm sorry. But the position should be yours."

To her surprise, he chuckled. "Honestly? Caroline, you managed to get more done in the Congress than I could. After everything that's happened over the past cycle—at least what little I can remember of it—I'm ready to settle back in at the Ranch, for multiple reasons." His expression became more solemn. "I'm concerned about Cartain's future. I spent some time talking to Blackburn and Whixit before they left for— wherever they were going. He thinks that there are more persons who think like Alice McKinnon and Lara Wordtrust. Too many of the Federation's planets are—well—undefended. Whixit feels the same way about the Ethereal Confederation. And there are just too many dreams of Empire out there. I'm not convinced that the Congress is capable of handling the problem. Add in the possibility of more unhappy, sentient planets like Memaj—"

Caroline nodded. Jeff *had* talked quite a bit to Blackburn and Whixit—one reason why she had thought he would be willing to resume his role as Planetary Representative. "What do you have in mind?"

"Besides the issues involving sentient planets, the Bit-fives are the next biggest problem when it comes to thoughts of Empire, according to Blackburn. Whixit reports that the Bit-fives are a concern in the Confederation as well. And the whole Memaj debacle also suggests that there may be future problems with rella. Whixit doesn't think that Memaj is the only planet where illegal rella cultivation is happening."

"You're the rella expert."

Jeff raised his brows at her. "You're doing pretty good at it yourself, from everything I'm hearing. I'd sooner be your advisor, and spend this next cycle on Galactic Central talking to people and studying, rather than doing the job of legislating."

"The Boss *has* approved the possibility of Star running instead of me, had you not recovered," Caroline said carefully. "I had been making arrangements—just in case we couldn't restore you to sentience."

Jeff chuckled. "You see? You've been thinking ahead, like a Representative should be doing. I like your plan. If you're the Rep, and I'm your primary assistant, then I can spend this next cycle in the Congress introducing Star to useful people." He paused. "I also want to return to Cartain for—reasons, after talking to Blackburn and Whixit. I fear that Galactic Central itself is at risk. Both Blackburn and Whixit think so. Currents are stirring in the Galaxy that we only partially understand. While both the Federation and Confederation have been stable for a long time—Memaj and its issues are not alone. I'm sure there are other planets with hidden problematic colonization histories and, possibly, even hidden sentience."

"You've been talking to Dr. Erith."

He shrugged. "Not just her. But think about this, Caroline —what happens if enough sentient planets decide to act against moving beings? Fenarmin and I were just pawns in whatever scheme it was that Memaj had been contemplating. What if there are other planets that are more sentient, more skilled at hiding their awareness, and more able to take action?"

Caroline contemplated the possibility, frowning. "I see what you mean."

"I hope to get at least a minor degree in Xenology while you finish out the term," Jeff said. "Dr. Erith will be leading a study group on Galactic Central, and she's been able to transfer credentials to the Federation University, so that it's possible to earn degrees studying with her."

"I could talk to Dr. Knowledgechaser about getting a graduate degree," Caroline said. "We could work together studying sentient planets and their political implications."

"Could be interesting," Jeff said.

"But this sure sounds pretty ambitious. Are we going to be able to get this all done in the next cycle?" Caroline considered the possibilities. "There's an awful lot to be done."

"Oh, we won't need to have it *all* finished by the end of the session," Jeff said. "The Galaxy took a while to get into this state. More than a single ten-cycle or even a hundred-cycle."

"True," Caroline said, thinking of the five hundred cycles it had been since Hart Mercantile meddled in Memaj's affairs.

"But if we can lay the foundation for the Federation and the Confederation to collaborate in keeping the Galaxy peaceful, then we've achieved a lot."

"It's certainly worth a try. Especially given the harm my ancestors have done."

Perhaps she couldn't completely repair the damage done across the Galaxy by Hart Mercantile Services.

But she—no, *they*—could certainly try.

THE END

NEWSLETTER

Like what you've read? Want to follow Joyce either through her monthly newsletter or through an email feed of her irregular blog posts?

Sign up for Joyce's newsletter here:

https://tinyletter.com/JoyceReynolds-Ward

Or follow Joyce's irregular blog posts on her Substack, here:

https://joycereynoldsward.substack.com/

BOOKS AND PUBLICATIONS

The Martiniere Legacy

First Meetings: A Martiniere Legacy Short Story
Inheritance: The Martiniere Legacy Book One
Ascendant: The Martiniere Legacy Book Two
Realization: The Martiniere Legacy Book Three
A Belated Christmas Honeymoon: A Martiniere Legacy Short Story
The Enduring Legacy: The Martiniere Legacy Book Four

People of the Martiniere Legacy

The Heritage of Michael Martiniere: A Martiniere Legacy Novel
Broken Angel: The Lost Years of Gabriel Martiniere: A Martiniere Legacy Novel
Justine Fixes Everything: Reflections on Mortality

The Martiniere Multiverse

A Different Life: What If?
A Different Life: Now. Always. Forever.

Goddess's Honor titles currently available (chronological order):

The Goddess's Choice: A Goddess's Honor Short Story
Beyond Honor: A Goddess's Honor Novella
Exile's Honor: A Goddess's Honor Novelette
Birth of Sorrow: A Goddess's Honor Short Story
Pledges of Honor: Goddess's Honor Book One
Return to Wickmasa: A Goddess's Honor Short Story
Crown Anniversary: A Goddess's Honor Short Story
Challenges of Honor: Goddess's Honor Book Two
Cleaning House: A Goddess's Honor Outtake Story
Unexpected Alliances: A Goddess's Honor Rough Draft Outtake Story
Choices of Honor: Goddess's Honor Book Three
Judgment of Honor: Goddess's Honor Book Four

Netwalk Sequence Author Preferred 2022 Editions
Life in the Shadows: Book One
Netwalk: Book Two
Netwalker Uprising: Book Three
Netwalk's Children: Book Four
Learning in Space: Book Five
Netwalking Space: Book Six

Bright Star Fair Witches
Becoming Solo: A Bright Star Fair Witches Novella

Non-Series Titles currently available:
Alien Savvy: A Western SF Novella
Klone's Stronghold
Beating the Apocalypse
Bearing Witness
Fabulist and Fantastical Worlds: A Short Story Collection
Federation Cowboy

Vella Titles:
Falcon of the Martinieres (part of Justine Fixes Everything)

Bearing Witness

Beating the Apocalypse

A Different Life—What If? An Alternative Martiniere Legacy Novel

Becoming Solo

A Different Life—Linda's Story: An Alternative Martiniere Legacy Novel

Federation Cowboy

Audiobooks Available:

Alien Savvy: A Western SF Novella

Released from other publishers:

"Queen of the Snows," in *Once Upon A Winter: A Folk and Fairy Tale Anthology*, edited by H. L. Macfarlane

"My Man Left Me, My Dog Hates Me, and There Goes My Truck," in *Black-Eyed Peas on New Year's Day: An Anthology of Hope*, edited by Shannon Page

"Lost Loves," in *All Worlds Wayfarer*

"The Wisdom of Robins," in *Whimsical Beasts: A Campcon Anthology*, edited by Joyce Reynolds-Ward

"The Cow at the End of the World," in *Well…It's Your Cow*, edited by Frog Jones

"To Plant or Pull Up Stakes," in *Pulling Up Stakes: A Campcon Anthology*, edited by Joyce Reynolds-Ward

"The Notice," in *Children of a Different Sky*, edited by Alma Alexander

ABOUT THE AUTHOR

Joyce Reynolds-Ward has been called "the best writer I've never heard of" by one reviewer. Her work includes themes of high-stakes family and political conflict, digital sentience, personal agency and control, realistic strong women, and (whenever possible) horses. She is the author of *The Netwalk Sequence* series, the *Goddess's Honor* series, and the recently released *The Martiniere Legacy* series as well as standalones *Klone's Stronghold*, *Alien Savvy*, and *Beating the Apocalypse*. Samples of her Martiniere short stories / novel in progress and her nonfiction can be found on Substack at either Speculations from the Wide Open Spaces (general, writing) or Martiniere Stories (fiction). Joyce is a Self-Published Fantasy BlogOff Semifinalist, a Writers of the Future SemiFinalist, and an Anthology Builder Finalist. She is the Secretary of the Northwest Independent Writers Association, a member of the Science Fiction and Fantasy Writers Association, and a member of Soroptimists International.

facebook.com/authorjoycerw
twitter.com/JoyceReynoldsW1
instagram.com/jreynoldsward